DYING FALL

'A memorable, breathless race against time'
Daily Telegraph

'You will be educated and entertained, as well as being
engrossed in a damn good murder mystery'
Raven Crime Reads

'The characters, as ever, were an absolute delight . . . this
series just keeps getting better and better'
Crimepieces

'Griffiths expertly weaves her story into the brooding
landscape of the Pendle Forest . . . and the windswept
[Lancashire] coast'
Shotsmag

'Griffiths subtly conveys a sense of menace'
Crime Fiction Lover

Elly Griffiths was born in London, and worked in publishing for many years. Her bestselling series of Ruth Galloway novels have three times been shortlisted for the Theakston's Old Peculier Crime Novel of the Year, and twice for the CWA Dagger in the Library. Her new series is based in 1950s Brighton. Elly lives near Brighton with her husband, an archaeologist, their two children and her cat.

Also by Elly Griffiths

THE DR RUTH GALLOWAY MYSTERIES

The Crossing Places
The Janus Stone
The House at Sea's End
A Room Full of Bones
The Outcast Dead
The Ghost Fields
The Woman in Blue

THE STEPHENS AND MEPHISTO MYSTERIES

The Zig Zag Girl
Smoke and Mirrors

and coming soon
The Blood Card

ELLY Griffiths

Dying Fall

A Dr RUTH GALLOWAY MYSTERY

Quercus

First published in Great Britain in 2013 by Quercus
This paperback edition published in 2016 by

Quercus Editions Ltd
Carmelite House
50 Victoria Embankment
London EC4Y 0DZ

An Hachette UK company

A CIP catalogue record for this book is available
from the British Library

PB ISBN 978 1 78648 215 0
EBOOK ISBN 978 0 85738 888 9

10 9

Printed and bound in Great Britain by Clays Ltd, Elcograf S.p.A.

For John Maxted
and for Sarah and Michael Whitehead

'That strain again! It had a dying fall:
O, it came o'er my ear like the sweet sound
That breathes upon a bank of violets
Stealing and giving odour! Enough, no more;
Tis not so sweet now as it was before . . .'

Shakespeare, *Twelfth Night*

Dying Fall

PROLOGUE

At first he isn't even scared. Even though his room is full of smoke, and when he reaches the top of the stairs the heat makes him stagger backwards, eyes stinging. It's only a fire and he knows what to do in a fire, he learnt it at Cubs some thirty years ago. Besides, he's in a tiny two-storey house, not the Towering Inferno (a film that he must have watched at about the same time, come to think of it). He knows the bedroom window doesn't open and the bathroom window's too small but the front door is only a few steps away, just down those stairs. How hard can it be? Still calm, he goes back into the bathroom and soaks a towel, just like Akela told him. He wraps the towel round his face and starts to descend the stairs. It *is* hard, far harder than he thought possible. In the past he has read about people in fires being 'beaten back by the heat' and, deep down, he had always thought, 'Wimps. It's just hot air. Push through it.' But this doesn't seem like air any more, it's solid, and he has to batter against it with his whole body. After three steps he is exhausted and the heat is just getting stronger. He can't see much because of the towel, but he can *hear* the fire – a sort of dull rushing sound filling the whole of the downstairs. He can smell it too; it smells industrial and serious.

But he can hear something else. Sirens. Someone must have called the fire brigade. Hallelujah. He's saved. He falls the last few steps, right onto the front door. The handle is so hot that it sticks to his hand but he holds on and turns with all his might, pushing against the door with his shoulders. The towel slips and suddenly he's choking. The hall is full of dense black smoke and he's gasping for breath. With his last atom of strength he hurls himself against the door. Only then does he realise that it's locked. From the outside.

And now he's scared.

CHAPTER 1

The phone is ringing when Ruth opens the front door. She pauses on the threshold, wondering whether she should just let it ring. Her friends all have her mobile number. The landline can only mean her mother or someone trying to sell her double glazing, and even though the windows of her cottage rattle in the wind she likes it that way, thank you very much. Her mother will only be ringing to torment her ('I saw Janice's daughter the other day, she's a GP, ever so slim and attractive, and she's got three children and they all play the violin. How's the diet going?'). She decides to ignore it but Kate, her eighteen-month-old daughter, runs past her yelling 'Ring! Ring!' Kate picks up the phone and says clearly, 'Piss.' Cursing Cathbad, Kate's Druid godfather, who has taught her the all-purpose salutation, 'Peace', Ruth snatches the phone away.

'Hello?'

'Ruth?' It's a woman and she's laughing. 'Did someone just say "piss"?'

'That was Kate.' Ruth is rifling through her mental list of acquaintances. Who can this be? Someone from the university? A chatty window saleswoman? But she sounds familiar . . .

'Ruth,' says the voice, 'it's Caz. Carol.'

Carol. One of Ruth's best friends from her university days. A fellow archaeology student, ex-flatmate, loyal drinking companion and repository of secrets. With a rush of guilt, Ruth realises that when she transferred her contacts onto her new phone last year she must have forgotten Caz. They haven't spoken for almost three years.

'I tried you on your mobile,' Caz is saying, 'but there was no answer.'

As Ruth's old mobile is currently reposing at the bottom of the sea, or washed up like flotsam on some North Norfolk beach, this is hardly surprising.

'I'm sorry,' says Ruth. 'I've got a new one. I've been a bit crap about updating it.'

'Don't worry about it,' says Caz. 'It's great to hear your voice.'

'Great to hear you too.' Ruth feels a rush of affection for Caz, cool spiky-haired Caz, expert exponent of drinking games, fan of explosive cocktails and dry-stone walls, anarchist and fearless beret-wearer. She's an accountant now.

'I'm really sorry, Ruth,' Caz is saying, and all the laughter has gone from her voice. 'But I'm ringing with bad news.'

'Oh God.' Again Ruth rifles through her list of friends. Is anyone dead, sick? She has just reached the age when her friends start to seem mortal. She watches as Kate staggers into the room carrying Ruth's cat, Flint. 'Ahh! My Flinty.'

'Put him down, Kate.' Flint is giving her martyred looks over Kate's shoulder.

'What?' says Caz.

'Sorry. Just talking to Kate.'

'Oh, I forgot you had a child. How old is she now?'

'Nearly two.' She feels stupid saying eighteen months and thinks that Caz, who has three children of her own, doesn't sound particularly interested.

'Cute,' says Caz briefly. 'The news. It's Dan. Dan Golding.'

'Dan? Dan the Man?'

Dan Golding. Dan the man. The coolest archaeologist ever. The Indiana Jones of UCL. Ruth hasn't heard from him for years but she has always imagined that he's doing impossibly exciting things, finding the Lost Ark of the Covenant, starring in a Hollywood film, marrying Angelina Jolie.

'What's happened to him?' she asks.

'He's dead,' says Caz. 'I read it in the paper. He was working at Pendle University and he died in a fire.'

'Jesus.' In all her imaginings, Ruth never thought of anything like this. Dan Golding the victim of something as simple and devastating as a fire. And Pendle University? It's one of the new ones, like North Norfolk, the university where Ruth works. Nothing wrong with that, just that she'd always imagined Dan working at Cambridge or Harvard. Or diving for pearls off some South Sea Island.

'I didn't know he was working at Pendle,' she says stupidly.

'Nor did I. It's just round the corner from me.' Of course, Caz lives up north.

'It was awful,' Caz is saying, 'I just read it in the local paper. Archaeologist Daniel Golding found dead in his Fleetwood cottage. I didn't even twig at first because I've never thought of him as Daniel.'

'How did the . . . what happened?'

'The article just said that he'd died in a house fire. The place was completely gutted apparently. They think it was caused by faulty electric wiring.'

Faulty electric wiring. Could Dan the Man really be destroyed by a bit of flex, a badly earthed plug, a few pluses and minuses going the wrong way? It just doesn't seem possible.

'Are you sure it was him?' asks Ruth with sudden hope. '*Our* Dan?'

'Yes,' says Caz sadly. 'I rang his sister. You remember his sister Miriam, two years above us?'

Ruth dimly remembers a darkly glamorous presence at some of their parties. Miriam Golding. She had heard rumours that she became a model.

'How did you track her down?'

'It was easy enough. She's on Facebook.'

Ruth has never got to grips with Facebook. It's another aspect of the modern world that seems beyond her. She can't understand why you'd want to update your friends every time you make a cup of tea. In any case, her friends are a small select group. Smaller now.

'The funeral's tomorrow,' Caz is saying.

'So soon?'

'It's the Jewish tradition, Miriam says.'

Ruth had never even realised that Dan was Jewish. They didn't talk much about religion when they were students – the meaning of life, yes, everyday beliefs, no. In any case, Ruth had been in full-scale flight from her parents' evangelism. The G-word would have sent her running for cover.

'I wish I could be there,' she says, meaning it.

'I know. I don't know if it's appropriate to send flowers or not, but if I do I'll send them from both of us.'

'Thanks, Caz.'

'Good to speak to you, Ruth. It's been too long.'

'Yes, it has.'

'Maybe you'll come up to Lytham some time?'

Ruth laughs. 'Maybe.' Secretly she's thinking that, after the events of the past few years, she needs to take Kwells if she goes further afield than the Chinese takeaway.

'Maybe you'll come to Norfolk,' she says.

Now it's Caz's turn to laugh. 'You never know. Take care, Ruth.'

As Ruth makes supper she thinks about the fact that Caz, in the north of England, seems further away than her neighbour, Bob, who's currently in his native Australia. It's more than distance, surely. The truth is that when Caz got married (to Pete, another university friend) and had her children, she began to move away from the single, childless Ruth – just as, some eight thousand years ago, the sea levels rose and Britain was separated from the European landmass, the channel river widening into a sea – so that, now Ruth feels herself almost a different species from her erstwhile friend. True, Ruth now has a child of her own (interesting that Caz had forgotten, but then Ruth herself sometimes still finds it hard to believe) but she still doesn't feel that she is a Mother (capital letters) and certainly she's never been a Wife. She has her work but Caz, along with most of Ruth's other classmates, long ago abandoned archaeology for a more lucrative career.

There is something quixotic, almost eccentric, about carrying on digging and sifting and lecturing on flint hand-axes. Come to think of it, Dan was probably the only other member of the class of '89 still involved in archaeology. Ruth and Dan were the only two students in their year to get firsts but Ruth feels now that she wasn't really passionate about archaeology until she did a post-graduate degree and met the brilliant and charismatic Professor Erik Anderssen, Erik the Viking. Well, Erik is dead now, and though he still haunts her dreams he does so less and less. But Ruth is still plugging away at archaeology. It is just a surprise that Dan was doing similar badly paid, unglamorous work. And now he, too, is dead.

Ruth makes pasta and they eat at a plastic table in the front garden, a sensible precaution given Kate's predilection for smearing food over all surrounding surfaces, but also a real joy on evenings like this. It is still light but there is a soft, diluted feel to the air. Beyond Ruth's fence the long grass is tawny and gold, with the occasional flash of dark blue water as the marsh leads out to the sea. In the distance the sand glimmers like a mirage, and further still the sea comes whispering in to shore, heralded by the seagulls flying high above the waves. Ruth has lived here for thirteen years now and she has never tired of the view, the lonely beauty of the marsh-land, the high-arching wonder of the sky. The situation is isolated in the extreme; just three cottages perched on a road to nowhere. One neighbour, Bob Woonunga, is an Indigenous Australian poet who spends much of the year on the other side of the world. The other cottage is a holiday home owned by a couple who seem to have forgotten its existence, although their son and his univer-sity friends sometimes come down for noisy weekends of surfing and partying. Ruth finds herself quite looking forward to these weekends, although Flint hates the smell of dope and Kate is kept awake all night by N-Dubz remixes.

Bob will be back in July but Ruth knows that this June is probably as good as it will get. By August the sky will be grey and the streets of King's Lynn full of bored school-children looking for distraction. But now, in term-time with exams in full swing, the unfeeling sun shines for day after unbelievable day. Ruth feels sorry for the chil-dren but the good weather has come at the perfect time for her. June is the month of their annual university dig which, this year, is taking place at a Roman site near Swaffham. Ruth teaches forensic archaeology, her students are mainly postgraduates from overseas, and it seems unfair to expose them to Norfolk in the winter or even the spring. So the June dig will be their first practical assignment. For Ruth, too, it's her first dig for a while and one which is close to her heart. The Roman remains, which promise to be part of a sizeable settlement, were first discovered by Max Grey, an archaeologist at Sussex University and Ruth's . . . But, as ever, at the thought of defining her relationship with Max, Ruth's mind skitters away in a panic.

Kate has finished throwing her pasta around and she totters off to look for Flint. Ruth follows, glancing at her watch. Seven o'clock. If she can keep Kate busy for another half hour, she'll sleep well tonight. Ruth feels pretty tired herself. It's been a long time since she's spent the whole day in the open air. She enjoys teaching archaeology but her real love is digging. She loves the mixture of painstaking order and backbreaking work, hauling earth about like a navvy one minute and dusting the sand away from a shard of bone the next. She loves the sight of a neat trench, its sides perfectly straight, the soil below exposed in clear layers. She remembers the moment, here on the Saltmarsh, when she found the body of an Iron Age girl, a bracelet of grass still around one wrist. That was the day when she first met DCI Harry Nelson.

Kate discovers Flint in the back garden and chases him through the blackberry bushes. Ruth sits on the grass and watches them. She thinks of Max and Nelson and Dan. She was never in love with Dan but, right now, their friendship seems sharper and sweeter than any love affair. She can picture Dan's face perfectly whereas she would have difficulty recalling the features of Peter, the man she lived with for almost ten years. Similarly, her university years suddenly seemed bathed in a light much brighter than the dusky twilight glow in the garden. She thinks of Gordon Square, the University of London Union, beer at a pound a pint, the night bus, Bilal's kebab shop, the sound of a radio playing on a still afternoon, Sonia singing 'You'll Never Stop Me Loving You'. Why hadn't she kept in better touch with Dan? She knows that as a working-class girl from South London she had always felt slightly in awe of him, the son of wealthy Islington intellectuals. She remembers that Dan had played the piano to almost concert standard, had been able to tell off-colour jokes in several languages, had spent a year teaching English in Japan. They had been friends and classmates, but in other respects they were worlds apart. When did she last see Dan? She thinks it was at Caz's wedding. She recalls Dan jamming on a piano with a glamorous girl draped around him like a stole. 'Keep in touch', he'd said, scribbling his number on a page ripped from a cheque book. She'd kept the page for years (cheque book! who writes cheques now?) but had never dialled the number.

Kate starts to cry because she has been scratched by a bramble and Ruth takes her upstairs for her bath. Flint follows. Ruth has noticed before that, though the cat spends most of his time running away from Kate, he seems keen to stay in her vicinity. He always comes upstairs for the bath and the story and usually sleeps on the landing outside Kate's bedroom. The strict night-time regime is a fairly recent innovation and Ruth is determined to stick to it. By insisting on bed at half-seven and lights out at eight she has eventually managed to claw some of the evenings back for herself. All day she has been looking forward to sitting downstairs with a glass of wine, limbs pleasantly heavy, watching crap TV and thinking about the dig. Except that now she knows that she will think about Dan – about the time that he dressed up as Margaret Thatcher to heckle a visiting dignitary, about the time he allegedly kidnapped a penguin from the zoo, about his amazing knowledge of Bowie lyrics, about the time when – drunk on cheap Pernod – he had kissed Ruth on the Number 68 bus to Camberwell Green.

Tonight the routine works smoothly. Kate is asleep before Ruth has finished her deliberately boring recital of Dora the Explorer's antics. Ruth tiptoes downstairs. As she is pouring the wine she thinks that she wasted her friendship with Dan, her acquaintance with a truly unusual and anarchic mind. She should have kept in touch with him; they would have had something in common after all. Class differences fade with the years and, besides, she is middle-class now; she listens to Radio 4 and reads the *Guardian*. It has been decades since she has said the word 'pardon'. They could have talked about archaeology, visited each other's universities. Maybe, in some bizarre way, if Ruth had kept in touch with Dan, he wouldn't have died in a house fire, far away from everyone who knew and loved him. She should have been a better friend to Dan but now it's too late. She will never hear from him again.

The next day she receives a letter from him.

CHAPTER 2

The letter has been forwarded from the university:

Hi Ruth. Dan here. Dan Golding. I hope you remember me as otherwise this is going to get embarrassing. How is life treating you? I'm in the inhospitable and frozen north, teaching archaeology at Pendle University. I know you're at North Norfolk. In fact, I've been following your career with interest and admiration. I know that you are one of the country's leading experts on bone preservation.

So that's why I'm writing. (Although, of course, it would be great to catch up. Do you see anything of Caz these days? Or Roly? Or Val?). I've made a discovery, Ruth, and it could be big. It could be huge. But I need your help. I need a second opinion on the bones. Things are a little sensitive here, which is why I'm writing not emailing. Can you ring me on the number below? I think you'll be interested. Have you heard of the Raven King? Well, I think I've found him. Jesus, Ruth, it seems a long time since UCL, doesn't it? We're all older and sadder, if not wiser. This discovery, though, could change everything. But I'm afraid ... and that's just it. I'm afraid. Do ring me as soon as you get this letter. With love from your old friend

Dan

Ruth reads this letter standing by her front door, which is still open. It has been another exhausting day on the dig and her bones ache to be immersed in warm water. But there's Kate and her night-time routine to be got through first. Kate is searching for Flint in the kitchen. Ruth can hear her calling through his cat flap. On a sudden, ridiculous impulse she dials the mobile-phone number at the foot of the letter. Dan's voice, deep, amused, slightly sleepy, comes clearly across the years and the miles, from the land of death itself.

'Hi. This is Dan Golding. I'm not here right now but if you leave your name and number I'll get back to you. Promise.'

That, muses Ruth, as she puts her rucksack on the floor and goes into the kitchen to rescue Flint, is one promise that Dan won't be able to keep. Hearing his voice – in the letter and over the phone – has shaken her badly. The jaunty Dan of the first paragraph she had recognised instantly. Of course, he knew that she would have remembered him. Dan wasn't the sort of man that people forgot. And, despite everything, Ruth had felt a glow at the thought that he had remembered her and even followed her career 'with admiration'. But the Dan of the last paragraph, the Dan who is older and sadder and afraid ...

she doesn't recognise that person at all. What can have happened in the frozen and inhospitable north to have made Dan – *Dan* – so scared that he dared not write an email, so desperate that he needed help from her – Ruth Galloway from Eltham, the girl who was eighteen before she drank champagne and nineteen before she lost her virginity?

She extricates Flint from Kate and feeds them both. It has been another lovely day and from the open front door comes the scent of grass and the sea. Ruth makes herself a cup of tea and tells herself that this is all she fancies but before too long she's tucking into cold pasta. She really must get a grip and stop eating Kate's food. If someone asked her if she'd like a gourmet meal of sucked toast soldiers, congealed egg and soggy carrot sticks, she'd say no, thanks very much, but that's what she eats every time she clears the table. Ruth has never been thin but she has an uneasy feeling that now she's less thin than ever. Still, all that digging will have used up a few calories. Ruth takes another piece of fusilli.

'Mine,' says Kate.

What was Dan's great discovery? It obviously included bones, by the sound of it. What sort of archaeology is there up there anyway? When Kate has finished eating, Ruth forces herself to throw away the remaining pasta then adjourns to the sitting room in search of an atlas. The cottage is tiny, just two rooms plus loo downstairs, with the front door opening straight into the sitting room. This room is full of books, overflowing on the shelves that reach up to the low ceiling and piled in heaps on the wooden floor, the sofa and the table. Ruth loves reading and is eclectic in her tastes: scholarly archaeological tomes jostle for space next to romances, thrillers and even children's pony books. She's sure there's an atlas in there somewhere. She starts pulling books from the shelves and, enthralled, Kate joins her. 'Me too.'

Here it is. *The Reader's Digest Atlas of Great Britain.* Ruth takes the book to the table by the window. Where was Dan living? Fleetwood, Caz said. Near Lytham. Bloody hell – Ruth smoothes down the page – it's right next door to Blackpool, the much-loved and much-missed home town of DCI Harry Nelson. She had no idea that Dan had strayed into Nelson's territory. Fleetwood is right on the coast – there could be Viking remains, maybe even a Roman garrison town. But what could be so earth-shattering that Dan was scared to write about it in an email?

The Raven King, he had said. Abandoning the printed word, Ruth switches on her laptop. Kate is sitting on the floor, apparently absorbed in Ruth's tattered edition of *The Women's Room.* Excellent choice, Kate.

Ruth googles 'raven king' and, seconds later, her screen is full of heavy metal lyrics, on-line gaming tips and images of swarthy men in feathered cloaks. The Raven King is obviously a potent symbol but, trawling through the sites, Ruth can only find a few solid references. One is to a Celtic God and hero called Bran, or Raven. The other is to a fifteenth-century Hungarian king famous for his library. Neither of these seems to fit Dan's great discovery.

Interestingly, though, the Raven King myth is often especially linked to the north of England. Ruth thinks of Erik's descriptions of the Norse God Odin, who sits with his ravens, Huginn and Muninn, on each shoulder. Huginn and Muninn; thought and memory. Odin, Erik used to say, saw all and knew all. Rather like Erik himself, or so Ruth thought once.

Ruth is reading about the ravens in the Tower of London when the phone rings. For a second, she has the ridiculous idea that Dan is ringing back, calling from the realms of the lost. Her hands are shaking when she picks up the phone.

'Hello?'

'Hi, Ruth, it's Caz.'

'Oh, hi, Caz.' Ruth watches as Kate abandons Marilyn French for the TV remote. Oh well, perhaps eighteen months old is too young to be a fully fledged feminist. Soon the soothing strains of *Emmerdale* fill the room. Kate snuggles on to the sofa and Flint sits beside her, though not too close.

'I said I'd ring to tell you about the funeral.'

'Oh, yes, it was today, wasn't it?'

So Dan was buried on the day that she received his letter. Ruth shivers.

'It was grim, Ruth. Only a few people. His parents, Miriam, his ex-wife.'

'Ex-wife?'

'Yes, apparently they were divorced a few years ago.

She seemed very upset though, cried all the way through the service.'

'Did they have children?'

'No. Miriam said that was partly why they split up, she wanted children, he didn't.'

'Is Miriam married?'

'No. She's as stunning as ever, though.'

Ruth thinks of her friend Shona, who is also often called 'stunning'. To stun someone – it's quite a violent image. What must it be like to be so beautiful that looking at you is like a blow on the head? Ruth can't imagine.

'It was so sad, Ruth,' Caz is saying. 'All that promise, all that brilliance, ending in a bleak little synagogue in Blackpool. Only a handful of people to mourn him.'

'Was anyone else from UCL there?'

'No. I don't know if he was in touch with anyone.'

Thinking about the letter, with its enquiries after Caz, Roly and Val, Ruth doesn't think so. The north, it seems, was inhospitable in more ways than one.

'I got a letter from him,' she says. 'Weird, isn't it?'

'What do you mean, you got a letter from him?'

'Just that. It was forwarded from the university. He'd made a discovery and he wanted my opinion.' Ruth can't quite keep a note of pride from creeping into her voice.

'Jesus. What an awful coincidence.'

'Yes. It really shook me up. It sounded just like him, the letter I mean.' She doesn't tell Caz about the voice-mail.

'What was it, the discovery?'

'He didn't say.'

'Maybe you'll have to come up to Pendle, do some research?'

'Maybe,' says Ruth, without much conviction.

Things are a little sensitive here, Dan had said. Ruth somehow doesn't think that she'll be getting an invitation from Pendle to look at Dan's discovery, whatever it is. But Dan was afraid. And Dan is dead.

Ruth knows that when Kate has gone to bed she will ring Nelson.

Detective Inspector Harry Nelson is having a bad day. It's not the pressure of fighting crime in King's Lynn (though that's tougher than you'd think). Work is fine, though his best sergeant, Judy Johnson, is away on maternity leave and his other sergeant, Dave Clough, seems to be enjoying a second childhood. The team broke a drug-smuggling ring last year and are still dealing with the clean-up. Clough, who played rather a heroic role in the operation, has compensated by acting ever since as though he's auditioning for a role in *Starsky and Hutch*. He has even taken to wearing woolly jumpers. He has just split up with his girlfriend Trace and is currently, if the rumours are to be believed, dating every nubile girl in the Norfolk region. 'I'm young, free and single, boss,' he keeps telling Nelson, who knows better than to reply. He thinks the break-up with Trace has hit Clough hard.

No, it's not policing that's doing his head in. It's the

insistence of his wife, Michelle, and his boss, Gerry Whitcliffe, that he go on holiday. Nelson always ends up with leave owing at the end of the year, and this time Michelle wants him to take a holiday in August, 'when normal people go away, Harry.' Whitcliffe keeps reminding him that he was seriously ill at the end of last year and implying that he's still not quite up to scratch. 'You need a break, a complete rest, recharge your batteries.' Recharge your batteries. What the hell does that mean? Nelson prides himself on not needing batteries. He's an old-fashioned, wind-up model.

Michelle has told him that she'll be home early but she's going out again with some girlfriends at eight. That's partly why Nelson is still at the station at half-seven. He loves his wife, but now that his two children have left home they just have too much time together. Enough time, certainly, for Michelle, who's good at getting her own way, to persuade him into some God-awful summer holiday. Memories of Lanzarote a year ago rise up in horrific Technicolor, sitting in some Tex-Mex-themed bar chatting to the most boring couple in the world about computer programming. Never again. He'd rather go to the North Pole and eat whale blubber.

So Nelson is still in his office when Ruth rings.

'How's Katie?' is the first thing he says.

'*Kate's* fine.'

'Good,' says Nelson. Then, after a pause. 'And you?'

'I'm OK. A bit knackered, we've being doing a dig all week. Look, Nelson, I wondered if you could help me. A friend of mine died a few days ago in a house fire in Fleetwood.'

'I'm sorry to hear that,' says Nelson. Then, 'Fleetwood, Lancashire?'

'Yes. I know that's your ... where you come from ... and I wondered if you still had any contacts in the police force up there.'

'My old mate Sandy Macleod's the DCI at Blackpool CID.'

'Well, I just wondered if you could find out if there were any ... you know, suspicious circumstances.'

'What makes you think there might be?' asks Nelson.

'I had a letter from my friend, written just before he died. He mentioned that he was afraid. I wondered if someone might have been intimidating him.'

'I see,' says Nelson. 'Well, I'll give Sandy a call. There's probably nothing in it, mind. Just a nasty coincidence.'

'Coincidence,' says Ruth in an odd voice. 'Maybe. But I'd be very grateful if you could ask around a bit.'

'Be glad to,' says Nelson. 'I haven't spoken to Sandy for years.'

Nelson drives home thoughtfully. Normally he man-oeuvres his car as if he is being pursued by mafia hit-men but, today, lost in the past, he stops meekly at traffic lights and even allows a bus to pull out in front of him. Sandy Macleod. Just one mention of that name and it all came back. Harry and Sandy, new recruits to the Blackpool police force, patrolling the pleasure beach, interrogating tax-evading landladies in guest houses filled with plastic models of Elvis, eating chips in the squad car, the windows so steamy that every villain in Lancashire could have gone past unnoticed. Suddenly Nelson can smell the Golden Mile – chips and doughnut fat and the heady tang of the sea.

It's not the first time recently that he has been hit by a wave of nostalgia. When, in May, Blackpool was promoted to the Premier League he had surprised himself by being close to tears as he watched the final match against Cardiff at Wembley. He had wanted to be there, in that joyous tangerine crowd. He wanted to be part of the victory parade in Blackpool, saluting the heroes who would – incredibly enough – soon be facing Manchester United and Chelsea. He has been a Seasiders fan all his life and has a tattoo (and a chip) on his shoulder to prove it. But as his wife and daughters do not share this enthusiasm he has got out of the way of going to matches, has become, in fact, a typical Southern softy armchair fan. Now, more than anything, he wants to be in Blackpool for the new season, he wants to go to Bloomfield Road and watch his team play. He turns into his drive, dreaming of Ian Holloway lifting the Premier League trophy.

Michelle is out but she has left his supper in the microwave and a tasteful array of holiday brochures on the breakfast bar. Italy, France, Portugal, the Seychelles. Nelson pushes them to one side and gets a beer from the fridge. When Michelle comes home, he is at the computer, taking a virtual ride on the Big Dipper, three empty cans at his side.

'I know, love,' he says. 'Let's go to Blackpool.'

CHAPTER 3

'There's a man in a purple cloak looking for you.'

Ruth isn't unduly surprised by this news. She looks up at the student peering over the edge of the trench, a nervous-looking American woman called Velma who is always asking questions about health and safety. Velma has already had to be driven to A & E twice, once after scratching herself on a flint (although students have up-to-date tetanus jabs) and once after an allergic reaction to ice cream.

'Where is he?' asks Ruth, straightening up.

'Over by trench number one.'

'OK. Do you want to take over here?' Ruth has had enough of her trench, which has yielded only three rusty nails and a few flakes of animal bone.

Velma climbs carefully into the hole, holding aloft a hand which is still wrapped in a bandage.

'I think I saw a snake over there in the grass,' she says.

'Grass snake,' says Ruth breezily. 'Harmless.' She knows nothing about snakes. She'll have to ask Cathbad who, last year, narrowly escaped death from a poisonous adder.

Cathbad, the figure in the purple cloak, is kneeling down to examine a tray full of pottery fragments found earlier in the week. From a distance, he looks like he's at prayer, an impression heightened by the cloak and the bowed head. Cathbad's long hair is loose around his shoulders, and as he raises his head at Ruth's approach he looks somehow ageless, a figure turned to stone. Then his mobile rings.

He gets to his feet. 'Yes,' he says. 'Yes. Thanks for telling me.' As Ruth gets closer, she gets the feeling that Cathbad is somehow shrinking and growing older before her eyes.

'Hi Cathbad,' she says. 'What brings you here?'

Cathbad looks at her, and for a second she thinks that she can see tears in his eyes.

'Judy's had her baby,' he says.

'Oh,' says Ruth. 'Good.' She doesn't know quite what to say as she's not sure if Cathbad is the father of Judy's baby and she suspects that Judy herself doesn't know. What is clear is that Judy's relationship with Cathbad is over and she intends to bring up the baby with her husband, Darren.

'Who told you?' asks Ruth.

'I've got a friend at the hospital.' That figures. Cathbad has friends everywhere.

'But I knew anyway,' he says. 'My sixth sense told me.' Ruth is glad to hear Cathbad sounding more like his old self even though she's distinctly ambivalent about his sixth sense.

'Of course it did,' she says. 'Is it a boy or a girl?'

'A boy. Seven pounds, two ounces.'

'Oh,' says Ruth again. She knows that Cathbad has a daughter from a previous relationship. She knows that he will be wondering whether he now has a son.

'Of course, children don't belong to us,' he says, as he and Ruth walk towards the outer edge of the dig. 'They belong to the universe.'

Ruth says nothing. She never knows what to reply to pseudo-religious utterances, a fact that probably goes back to her upbringing by devout Born Again Christians. But thinking of Judy and her baby makes her remember the day that she had Kate, with Cathbad as her unexpected birth partner. She squeezes his arm.

'It's all part of the great web.' This is one of Cathbad's favourite expressions.

He smiles at her. 'Yes it is. The great web ordained before time began.'

'Mustn't mess with the great web.'

'We must not.' But he is still smiling.

They stop at the brow of the hill. From here you can just see the sea, a fact that always led Max to believe that this was a *vicus*, part of a Roman garrison town, on the way to the port at Borough Castle.

'What happened to the Janus Stone?' asks Cathbad.

The stone head depicting the two-faced Roman God was found on this site almost two years ago. Thinking of it reminds Ruth of Max, and of someone else who was obsessed with the old, bloodthirsty gods. Obsessed to the point of murder.

'It's in the museum,' she says. 'I'm sure you don't approve.'

Ruth and Cathbad first met when Ruth was part of a team excavating a Bronze Age henge on a North Norfolk beach. Cathbad and his fellow druids had protested when the henge's timbers were removed to a museum. They should be left where they were, they said, part of the landscape, open to the sky and sea. Erik had been in sympathy with them but the henge had been dismantled nonetheless.

'Oh well,' he says. 'It can still work its magic in the museum.'

'You're mellowing,' says Ruth.

'It happens to us all.'

Cathbad turns to look at Ruth, his dark eyes uncomfortably shrewd.

'How are you, Ruth? You look a bit shaken.'

Cursing Cathbad's sixth sense or plain nosiness (not for the first time), Ruth says, 'A friend died a few days ago. An old friend from university. I hadn't seen him for years but, yes, it has shaken me.'

'Maybe his soul is calling to you,' says Cathbad.

Ruth gives Cathbad a dark look. She feels sorry for him but she's not going to let him talk like that.

'I just feel sad,' she says. 'That's all.'

'That's enough,' agrees Cathbad.

They stay looking at the gentle hills as they lead to the

sea. High above them a skylark is calling. It's nearly Midsummer's Day, a major event in Cathbad's calendar.

'I wonder if Nelson knows,' says Ruth, 'about Judy.'

'Ask him,' says Cathbad.

And Ruth knows, without looking round, that Nelson is behind them.

Nelson doesn't know quite why he has come up to the dig. He could easily have spoken to Ruth on the phone. Besides they're busy at the station, what with no Judy and Clough tearing round the backstreets in a (metaphorical) red sports car. All he knows is that as soon as he had finished speaking to Sandy he was reaching for his car keys and telling Leah, his PA, that he'll be out for an hour or two.

'I think Superintendent Whitcliffe wanted to catch up with you,' she'd said.

Then want, thought Nelson, taking the stairs two at a time, must be his master. Jesus. Where had that come from? It was something his mother used to say.

And now, striding over the grass towards Ruth and Cathbad, he is glad he came. It is good to be in the open air after days in the station, completing paperwork and assuring Whitcliffe that his team didn't cut any corners in the drug smuggling case (they did, but Nelson hopes he's covered up adequately). And it's good to see Ruth. Over the last few months he has battled to shape his relationship with Ruth into one of benevolent friendship. He is the father of her child. Michelle, after a nightmarish year, has accepted this. All three adults can now work on doing what's best for Katie. Sounds simple but, as Ruth turns and smiles at him, Nelson reflects ruefully that nothing's ever that simple. Not where women are concerned.

And trust Cathbad to be there. Nelson is now used to Cathbad popping up all over the place, usually where there's trouble. Cathbad had once told Nelson about a saint who could be in two places at once and Nelson concluded instantly that the druid must share this gift. Not that he's a saint. Far from it. Cathbad, under his original name of Michael Malone, is well known to the police. Which makes it all the more surprising that Nelson considers him a friend. After all, Nelson once saved Cathbad's life and Cathbad claims to have visited a dream world between life and death in Nelson's company. It beats Sunday morning football for bonding.

'Nelson,' Ruth greets him. 'What are you doing here?'

'Well, you know how interested I am in archaeology.'

'This is the man who can't tell the difference between the Stone Age and the Iron Age.'

'They're both old, that's all I know.'

'All ages are as one,' offers Cathbad.

'I might have known you'd have something bloody silly to add.'

Ruth and Cathbad are exchanging glances. Nelson wonders what they were talking about when he arrived. Then Ruth says, 'Have you heard about Judy?'

'No. Has she had it?'

'A boy. Seven pounds something.'

'A boy, eh?' Nelson is genuinely pleased. He approves of babies and he likes Judy. It would never have occurred to him that Judy could have had an affair with Cathbad or that Cathbad could be the baby's father. Judy is married to Darren, her first love, and now they're starting a family. That's the way things should be. After all, it's what he did.

'How did you hear?'

'Cathbad heard on the druid grapevine.'

Nelson grunts. He finds it all too believable that such a thing exists.

'I'll get Leah to send some flowers,' says Nelson. 'Dave Clough will be sure she'll name the kid after him.'

Cathbad has veered off to talk to Phil, Ruth's head of department. Nelson lowers his voice. 'Got some news for you.'

'About Dan?'

'About your friend, yes. I spoke to my old mate Sandy in Blackpool.' One word from Sandy and the years had fallen away. That suspicious Northern growl, softening to comedy Lancastrian when he heard who it was. Nelson had felt his own voice becoming more and more Blackpool as they spoke. Sandy Macleod. They don't make coppers like that down here.

'Well, looks like you may be right. There were suspicious circumstances.'

'There were?'

'Yes. Seemed like a straightforward house fire at first. but when the SOCO team got there they found that the door had been locked from the outside.'

'Jesus.' Ruth's voice is almost a whisper. 'They locked him in?'

'And there were things missing. Things that ought to have been there.'

'Like what?'

'Like his mobile phone and his laptop. Sandy's launching a murder enquiry.'

CHAPTER 4

Ruth seems to be stuck in a never-ending traffic jam on her way to collect Kate from her childminder. Usually she frets and steams at this point. She hates being late for Kate although Sandra is always extremely understanding. 'I know what it's like for you working mums.' All her life Ruth has been a punctual person. Like Nelson (it is almost the only thing they have in common), she is highly organised and likes lists and schedules. But since becoming a mother she has discovered the nightmare of always running late. Kate does not seem to share her mother's liking for schedules and often manages to make Ruth late for work. Then Phil insists on holding staff meetings at five p.m., which means that she is then late at Sandra's. These days Ruth seems to spend her whole time in traffic, drumming her fingers on the steering wheel and counting to a hundred under her breath.

But today she is almost grateful for the time spent staring at red lights. Her mind is still struggling to comprehend Nelson's words. *Sandy's launching a murder enquiry.*

Could Dan really have been murdered? It doesn't seem possible. But then Ruth recalls the letter and its strange note of fear, almost of panic. *I'm afraid . . . and that's just it. I'm afraid. Do ring me as soon as you get this letter.* Well, Ruth had rung Dan but who had received her call? Nelson said that Dan's mobile was missing. Is it even now in the hands of his murderer? Who would want to kill an archaeologist working at an obscure university? Could it possibly be linked to Dan's discovery? It could be big, Dan had said. It could change everything. And now Dan is dead and everything has changed.

Seeing Nelson always disturbs Ruth anyway. When she saw him today, dark-suited and sombre, walking through the chattering students, she was struck – as she was the first time they met – at how *grown-up* Nelson looked. It wasn't just the clothes (he had been to an inquest in the morning, hence the black tie), there was something in his face, in his whole demeanour, that set him apart. Ruth's students might be post-graduates but they still looked like teenagers, with long hair and keen expressions. Nelson, striding over the grass, frowning, not looking right or left, looked grim and uncompromising, even slightly dangerous. Ruth wishes, more than anything in the world, that she wasn't still attracted to him.

As she turns into the King's Lynn road she vows, as she has done many times before, to put Nelson behind her. They have a child together, they will always be linked, but Nelson is happily married and Ruth is in a relationship with Max. But what is that relationship? 'I can't really call him your boyfriend, can I?' said her mother, archly, when she first found out about the affair (not through any fault of Ruth's; her brother had snitched). Someone at work referred to him the other day as 'your partner', which seemed far too official.

Max lives in Brighton, Ruth sees him perhaps twice a month and they do coupleish things together; they take Kate to the park, they go to the cinema, they eat take-aways in front of *Doctor Who*. And they sleep together. If it wasn't for the sex, Ruth would say they were just good friends. And they *are* friends. They get on really well, they're both archaeologists, they share a similar sense of humour and have both been through rather a lot, one way or another. They never argue and are always consid-erate of each other's feelings. And that's just it. Nelson is hardly ever considerate and he and Ruth argue all the time, but the two nights they spent together are etched on Ruth's soul and she can't erase them, however hard she tries. Much as she disapproves of Nelson, fiercely as she sometimes hates him, there is something slightly wrong with any man who isn't him.

Sandra greets her with a smile, cutting off Ruth's apologies with a tolerant 'Doesn't matter, love'. And Kate doesn't seem worried; she has been playing in the paddling pool with Sandra's other two charges, but by the time Ruth arrives Kate is dry and dressed and eating an irreproachably healthy snack of raisins and apple chunks. Sandra is an excellent childminder; Ruth is lucky to have her. And if she sometimes wishes that Sandra wasn't so bloody good at all the kid stuff, that just shows how unreasonable she has become. She needs a holiday.

Ruth sings all the way home. She needs to keep Kate awake so that she'll go to sleep at bedtime. Ruth keeps looking in the mirror and, as soon as Kate's head droops, she launches into another manic chorus of 'The wheels on the bus'. Meanwhile her thoughts, like the bus's wheels, go round and round. Was Dan murdered? Why? Is Cathbad the father of Judy's baby? Is he still in love with her? Why did Nelson come to the dig when he could easily have telephoned? Who is the Raven King and how is he linked to Dan's death?

At home she checks her answerphone and is relieved there are no messages. No one else is dead then. She switches on her laptop and finds the usual stream of mail from the department, and from Amazon hoping to interest her in any book with 'stone' in the title. She is in the middle of deleting when a new sender catches her eye. University Pals, it's called. Thinking of Dan and of Caz, she clicks on the message. 'Hi Ruth,' runs the cheery salutation, 'want to catch up with your old mates from uni? Join our website and hear about your old chums from **University College London, Archaeology 89**. One click and the years will roll away.'

Ruth has been thinking so much about UCL recently that she almost clicks on the link. Then she hesitates. More than most people, she knows the dangerous lure of the past. When, two years ago, her old boyfriend Peter had got back in touch, he had wanted to dive straight back into their relationship, regardless of the fact that ten years had passed and that he himself was now married with a child. And it had taken all Ruth's strength to refuse him. She knows that you can't go backwards, only forwards. Every archaeologist knows that. Time is a matter of layers, of strata, each firmly fixed in its own context. You can dig down through the layers but you can't change the fact that time has passed and new strata have been laid on top. But, says a reproachful voice in her head, if she had joined a website like this earlier, she might have kept in touch with Dan. She would have known all about his work at Pendle University, they could have sent each other photos, updated each other on their lives. She wouldn't now be left with this terrible feeling of waste.

As she is still deliberating, the landline rings. In the background, she hears Kate saying interrogatively, 'Piss?' Bloody Cathbad.

'Hello?' Ruth snatches the phone away.

'Hello. Dr Ruth Galloway?'

'Yes.'

'Oh super.' The voice becomes expansive. 'This is Clayton Henry from Pendle University.'

What an odd name, thinks Ruth irrelevantly, it sounds as if it's the wrong way round. Then – *Pendle University*.

'I hope you don't mind me ringing you at home. I got your number from Phil Trent.'

Ruth does mind and thinks that Phil should have more respect for her privacy. But, then again, she is dying to know why Clayton Henry is calling.

'It's OK,' she says.

'Well, Ruth, I'm in rather a fix.' Clayton Henry's voice is a strange mix of posh and Yorkshire. He sounds a bit like Alan Bennett. Ruth doesn't like the confiding note that has crept in and she hates people she doesn't know calling her by her first name.

'Yes?' she says, unhelpfully.

'One of our archaeologists – delightful chap – died tragically last week. Dan Golding. Don't know if you'd heard of him.'

'We were at university together.'

'Oh.' Clayton Henry stretches out the syllable. 'Then I'm so sorry to be the bearer of bad news.'

'It's OK. I already knew.'

'Oh.' A slightly different note this time. 'Well, I don't know if you knew that Dan had recently made what he considered to be a significant find.'

Ruth waits. A trick she has learnt from Nelson.

'Bones,' says Henry. 'At a Roman site near Ribchester. The burial led Dan to think that the remains might be . . . important.'

'Important?'

'A significant figure historically.'

Ruth knows that burial can be an indicator of status. An elaborate tomb, grave goods, weapons and treasure – all signs that a rich or powerful person lies within.

'I've asked around,' Henry is saying, the unctuous note back in his voice. 'And you are one of our foremost experts on bones.'

This description always makes Ruth think of a dog. Nevertheless, recognition is always welcome. She remembers how pleased she had been that Dan had followed her career.

'I wondered if you might possibly consider coming up and having a look at our bones.'

Our bones. Ruth feels a prickle of resentment. The bones belonged to Dan. But she would like to see Dan's discovery very much indeed.

'I know it's a long way,' comes the Alan Bennett voice, 'but we could put you up. A colleague's got a lovely holiday cottage out Lytham way. You could make a real break of it. Bring the family.'

For a moment Ruth wishes she had a real family – a husband, four children and a dog – all of them longing for a proper seaside holiday with buckets and spades and Blackpool rock. Still, Kate would like the donkeys.

'I'll think about it,' she says.

'Please do,' says Clayton Henry. 'I really think it might be worth the journey.'

Tonight, everything conspires against the peaceful bedtime routine. Flint is sick, regurgitating dead mouse on the kitchen floor, Kate doesn't like her supper and cries bitterly into her scrambled egg, and Ruth's phone rings constantly. First it's her mother asking if she fancies going to a Christian camp in the summer. 'There are special meetings for single parents. It's all very friendly.' As this invitation comes every year, Ruth has no difficulty in refusing. Thanks very much, she says breezily, but she has other plans. 'With Max?' asks her mother hopefully. She has never met Max and probably suspects that he and Ruth are living in sin, but with a daughter over forty you can't afford to be choosy. 'Not sure,' says Ruth, truthfully. 'Where are you going?' asks her mother. 'Blackpool,' says Ruth, on impulse. '*Blackpool*?' repeats her mother. 'Why ever would you want to go there?' 'There's some interesting archaeology in the area,' says Ruth, knowing that this answer will silence her mother, at least temporarily. Neither of her parents shares her passion for the past and her mother is often heard loudly lamenting that Ruth (such a clever girl at school) couldn't have studied something more useful, like nursing or accountancy or fulltime religious mania.

The next caller is Max. He is interested to know about the Swaffham dig. He was the first archaeologist to excavate the site and is full of theories and suggestions. He thinks that Ruth's animal bones might point to the existence of a butcher's shop or even a tannery. Ruth is happy to chat about bones and slaughter. She is aware of an odd reluctance to tell Max about Dan's death. She wants to keep the conversation on a workaday note, a pleasant chat about cattle skulls and animal skins. But, eventually, she tells him that a college friend of hers has died. He says all the right things – how awful, he was so young, makes you think, doesn't it, is Ruth OK? 'I'm fine,' she says. 'Sad but fine.' She doesn't want to tell him about the invitation to Lancashire and she's not sure why. Maybe it's just because she doesn't want Max, the Roman expert, offering advice on the possible find. At the moment that's her secret. Hers and Dan's. After a few more minutes' chat they ring off, promising to see each other in a week's time.

By now, Ruth is carrying a tired and irritable Kate up for her bath. She almost doesn't answer her mobile when it rings again. She has left it downstairs on the sofa and can't be bothered to retrace her steps. But it could be Nelson, or Sandra ringing to say that she can't have Kate tomorrow. So Ruth comes slowly back downstairs, holding her sleepy daughter against her shoulder.

'Hi, Ruth.'

'Hi, Shona.'

Ruth supposes that Shona is her best friend in Norfolk. But it's not like her relationship with Caz, which had been a friendship of equals, unmarked by jealousy or resentment. Ruth is both in awe of Shona's beauty and slightly wary of her. A few years ago, she had found out something about Shona that had shaken their friendship to the core. Now the rift has healed but Ruth feels she will never be able to trust Shona again. It doesn't help that Shona is living with Ruth's boss Phil, whom she doesn't trust either.

'How are you?' she says now. 'How's Louis?'

In February, Shona had given birth to a son, her first child and Phil's third. Shona, with her willowy grace and Pre-Raphaelite hair, is so essentially feminine that Ruth had been sure her baby would be a girl. But Louis is, not to put too fine a point on it, a bruiser. A delightful boy with a shock of ginger hair and the build of a prize-fighter. At birth he weighed over ten pounds and now, at five months old, is in clothes meant for one-year-olds. In fact, he's not that much smaller than Kate, who is a slight child, causing Ruth to panic every time she looks at her growth chart at the doctor's.

'He's great. Huge. Eating all the time.'

Shona has thrown herself into the role of earth mother, vowing to breastfeed Louis 'until he goes to university'. Ruth, who found the whole business difficult and uncomfortable, tries not to feel envious.

'What about Kate?'

'She's fine. A bit tired at the moment, I was just putting her to bed.'

'Oh, I won't keep you. I just wondered if you could pop in tomorrow. It seems like ages since I've seen another adult.'

'What about Phil?'

'He's a man. He doesn't count.'

'It's a bit difficult. We're digging all week.'

'I know,' says Shona fretfully. 'It's all I hear about from Phil. Samian ware this, bath house walls that.'

Ruth can see that life with Phil as your only link to the outside world could feel rather stultifying. 'I'll try to pop in on my way home,' she says.

Kate is almost asleep so Ruth skips the bath and puts her straight into bed. A few lines from Dora and Kate is fast asleep. As Ruth tiptoes out of the room, her mobile phone bleeps. Jesus. Who is it this time?

It's a text message. Sender unknown.

Don't come to Pendle if you know what's good for you.

CHAPTER 5

Shona lives in King's Lynn, near Sandra the childminder, so Ruth drops in on her way home. Kate loves children younger than herself and has developed a convincingly patronising attitude towards them. 'Baby,' she says as soon as she sees Louis. 'Little baby.'

'Yes,' says Shona admiringly. 'But you're a big girl, aren't you?'

Kate looks pleased at this description but Ruth, who is also sometimes called a 'big girl', is rather more ambivalent.

But Louis really isn't that little. In fact, he seems to have grown since Ruth saw him a few days ago. He dominates Shona's stylish sitting room, surveying the world from his bouncy chair like his namesake, the Sun King himself. Toys and baby clothes cover every surface, nursery rhymes play on a manic loop in the background. Ruth is reminded of the time when Shona looked after Kate, then only a few months old. Kate had screamed the entire time, and in minutes Shona's beautiful sanded wood floors had become covered in toys, books, tapes, bottles of milk – evidence of abortive attempts to placate her – and when Ruth had arrived, all she had to do was take her baby in her arms and the crying had stopped immediately. Ruth remembers that day well. It was the first time she had really felt like a mother.

Shona still doesn't look like a mother. She is too slim for one thing, having miraculously regained her pre-pregnancy figure. 'It's the breast-feeding,' she says smugly, floating away to put the kettle on. She is also too well dressed. Ruth spent her entire maternity leave in track-suit bottoms; Shona is wearing a short flowery dress, and high-heeled sandals tied with ribbon. She has even done her hair, though, as usual, it looks artfully dishevelled. It is only when Ruth sees her close up that she notices the shadows under the mascara'd eyes.

'How are you?' asks Ruth, when Shona reappears with tea, and juice for Kate.

'OK. Knackered.'

'They are tiring, the first months,' says Ruth. 'I remember it well.'

Louis starts to bang his rattle on the table in front of him.

'Noisy baby,' says Kate, primly sipping her juice.

'When are you going back to work?' asks Ruth. Shona teaches English at the university, which is how they first met.

Shona pulls a face as she reaches down to pick up Louis' dropped rattle.

'I'm not sure I want to go back.'

Ruth stares at her friend. She remembers the emotional intensity of those months alone with your baby. She remembers the feeling that work was another world, one that you are no longer equipped to enter. But not to go back at all?

'I remember feeling like that,' she says. 'But, when I went back, it felt great. I felt like I was a person again.'

She had almost cried with happiness when she saw her office again, but she's not going to tell Shona that.

'I don't know,' says Shona. 'I just love being with Louis. I'm so enjoying him.'

Maybe it's different if you have another adult at home, thinks Ruth. Mind you, that other adult is Phil.

'What does Phil think?' she says.

'Oh,' says Shona dismissively. 'He thinks I should go back. He says we need the money. He says we should get a childminder. He's always going on about how well you cope.'

'He is?'

Part of Ruth is gratified to hear this. She has tried hard not to let her motherhood intrude on her work or to burden her colleagues with excuses about illness or child-minding problems. But on the other hand – *cope*? How many men are complimented on how well they 'cope' with fatherhood?

'Well, you've got a while to decide,' says Ruth. 'You can take a year now if you want.'

'But you only get paid maternity leave for six months,'

says Shona. 'Honestly, I never knew Phil was such an old woman about money.'

But Shona didn't know Phil that well at all, thinks Ruth, until she moved in with him. They had been lovers for some time but, as we all know, lovers are more attractive than husbands or boyfriends. Phil probably made efforts to disguise his chronic stinginess (a standing joke in the department) when he was only seeing Shona twice a week, stolen hours in a country pub or in the office after dark. Even so, Ruth bets that he kept the receipts.

'Louis is gorgeous, though,' says Ruth, retreating to a safer topic. 'I can see why you don't want to leave him.'

Shona puts her son on a rug on the floor, propped up by cushions. Kate sits next to him and solemnly shows him how to work his shape sorter. Louis doesn't seem that interested in shape-sorting himself. He just sits and smiles goofily at Kate.

'Isn't it sweet?' says Shona. 'Maybe they'll get married.'

'Maybe,' says Ruth drily. 'Maybe they'll achieve something neither of their mothers managed.'

Shona looks sideways at Ruth. She knows about Nelson but is usually very good about ignoring Kate's parentage. Like most of Ruth's friends, she acts as if Kate sprang fully formed from the maternal egg.

'How's Max?' she asks.

'OK,' says Ruth. 'He's down next weekend.'

'We should get babysitters and go out, the four of us,' says Shona.

'We should,' says Ruth. She has no desire to see more of Phil than she has to but maybe it would be good for them to socialise with another couple. It might make her relationship with Max seem more like a relationship.

'We might be going on holiday,' says Ruth.

'You and Max?'

'No.' Ruth realises that this isn't what she meant. 'Me and Kate.'

'Oh.' The sideways glance again. 'Where?'

'Blackpool. Well, Lytham.'

She tells Shona about Dan and about the invitation from Pendle University. She doesn't tell her about the text message or about the possibility that the fire might not have been an accident. Shona listens, entranced. She always loves a story. Her subject is English literature, after all.

'Oh you must go,' she says. 'Kate would love Blackpool. She could ride on the donkeys, go on the rides at the Pleasure Beach.'

'Most of the Pleasure Beach rides look terrifying.' Ruth had looked on the website last night.

'Well, there must be a carousel or something,' says Shona. 'You ought to go. Dan might have discovered something big after all. It would be good for your career.'

Her career. In recent years Ruth has wondered whether her career hasn't, in fact, become a job. She still loves archaeology but she has never written a book or made her name in any way. She did discover the Iron Age girl and has certainly helped the police a few times, but students in years to come are hardly going to talk about the Ruth Galloway Theory or the Ruth Galloway Method. She is a jobbing forensic archaeologist, that's all.

'I might go,' says Ruth. 'Funny, I've travelled all over Europe but I've hardly ever been further north than the Midlands.'

'Oh, it's all different up north,' says Shona. 'I've got an aunt in Hartlepool, so I know.'

Nelson, too, is on mother and baby duty. He had been surprised when Leah informed him that Judy was already back at home. 'They only keep them in one night these days.' Then, as he and Clough had driven back from investigating a reported shooting near Castle Rising (turned out to be an airgun being fired at pigeons), Clough remarked casually, 'Judy lives near here, boss. Shall we pop in?' So they had stopped at a petrol station and bought flowers and chocolates and were now, rather self-consciously, examining the tiny object wrapped tightly in a yellow blanket.

'Can I hold him?' asks Clough. Nelson looks at him curiously. He'd heard rumours that Clough and Trace had been talking about starting a family, but now the relationship is over and Clough has custody of the couple's dog, a rather demented labradoodle. Certainly Clough seems better with babies than is usual for an unmarried (straight) man.

'Say hello to your Uncle Dave,' says Clough, but the baby's eyes remain resolutely shut. He is very dark with soft down over his forehead.

'How are you?' Nelson asks Judy. She looks exhausted, he thinks, her hair dark with grease and her eyes bloodshot.

Darren, on the other hand, who is now preparing tea in the kitchen, seems manic with happiness.

'Bit tired,' says Judy. 'It's hard work, having a baby.'

'So Michelle tells me.'

'He's beautiful,' says Clough. 'Have you got a name yet? What about David after his favourite uncle?'

'Michael,' says Darren, coming in with the tray. 'We've decided on Michael.'

'Why Michael?' asks Clough. 'After Michael Owen?'

'No. I'm a Chelsea supporter. My granddad was called Michael and we just liked the name, didn't we, love?'

Judy nods. To Nelson's expert eye (he has three daughters, after all), she looks close to tears. He wishes they hadn't come. It's far too soon for visitors. Clough, slurping tea and scoffing cake, is oblivious to everything. Darren has now taken charge of the baby and is looking with wonder at the wizened little face.

'He's very dark,' observes Clough. 'You must be glad he isn't ginger like you.'

Nelson raises his eyes heavenward. Just when Clough is almost behaving like a civilised human being, he comes out with something like that. But Darren, who is undoubtedly red-haired, just laughs. Today, nothing can offend him.

'Oh, he's got Judy's looks. And Judy's brains too, I hope.'

'He's a grand little chap,' says Nelson.

'Do you want a hold?' asks Darren.

'You're all right,' Nelson begins, but the proud father has placed his son in Nelson's arms. On cue, Michael's eyelids flutter and he looks at Nelson out of big, dark eyes that are somehow oddly familiar.

As Ruth and Kate approach their house, they see a dilapidated car parked in front of it.

'Cathbad!' shouts Kate in delight.

She can hardly wait until Ruth has undone her car seat before she throws herself in her godfather's arms. Ruth's eyes prickle, and not just from the salt wind blowing in from the sea. She is glad that Kate has Cathbad in her life, a solid male figure (albeit one in a purple cloak) who will continue to be there for her whatever happens to Ruth and Max – or Ruth and Nelson.

'Hi, Ruth.' Cathbad comes towards her carrying Kate. 'I've brought that book I was telling you about.'

Yesterday, Ruth had mentioned Dan's letter and the reference to the Raven King. Cathbad had thought that he had a book about the mythology of birds and, sure enough, here he is, holding it out as if it is his alibi. But Cathbad doesn't need a reason to visit. He knows that he is always welcome.

It is such a lovely evening that they walk down to the beach, swinging Kate over the little streams and ditches. The tide is coming in but there is still a stretch of sand, wide and clear. Ruth takes off Kate's shoes and the little girl runs delightedly towards the sea, stopping occasionally to look at starfish and clam shells.

'A water baby,' says Cathbad. 'Typical Scorpio.'

Nelson is also Scorpio, thinks Ruth. She's never thought to ask if he likes water. He is certainly no fan of the Saltmarsh.

Ruth and Cathbad also take off their shoes and walk in the shallows. The water feels heavenly against Ruth's tired feet.

'Have you seen Judy?' asks Cathbad.

'No,' says Ruth. 'I sent a card but I thought they ... she ... might like some time alone.'

'You're probably right,' says Cathbad. He looks out to sea for a moment, his cloak blowing back in the wind. Ruth is reminded of the first time she saw him, standing on the beach trying to defend the henge, looking as if he could stop the tide itself. Then he turns and he is Cathbad again, a middle-aged man in a cloak, looking slightly sad. 'When you see Judy,' he says, 'will you give her my love?'

'Of course I will.'

'I cast the baby's horoscope, you know, and he's going to have a full and happy life.'

'That's good.'

'Yes. Yes it is.'

Cathbad looks as if he is about to say more but Kate runs up to them, her little feet soundless on the sand. Cathbad lifts her high above the waves, sadness vanishing momentarily.

'This is a magical place,' he says.

'I know,' says Ruth. Then, thinking of her prospective holiday, she asks, 'Is the sand at Blackpool like this?'

'I don't know,' says Cathbad. 'I've never been there.'

Ruth explains about the invitation from Clayton Henry.

'My friend Pendragon lives in Lancashire,' says Cathbad. 'In the Forest of Pendle. It's an interesting place, by all accounts.'

In bed that night, Ruth opens Cathbad's book and turns to the chapter on ravens. There is a rather horrible illustration of a black bird perching on a skull. She hopes it won't give her nightmares. As a precaution, she puts on her headphones and tunes in to Bruce Springsteen. The Boss will protect her.

Because of its black plumage, croaking call and diet of carrion, she reads, the raven has long been considered a bird of ill omen. Great, thinks Ruth, I don't think I'll buy one as a pet. But, she reads on, the raven is a significant and benevolent figure in many cultures. For some indigenous American tribes Raven is a deity and is known as He Whose Voice Must be Obeyed. In many legends, Raven is a creator figure, sometimes the creator of the world. In Norse mythology (Ruth turns up the sound on her iPod so as not to hear Erik's voice), the ravens Huginn and Muninn sit on Odin's shoulders and bring him all the world's news. The Old English word for raven was *hraefn*, which also means a premonition of bloodshed. 'The raven himself is hoarse that croaks the fatal entrance of Duncan under my battlements,' says Lady Macbeth. And, of course, that visit went spectacularly well.

But the raven is also a trickster god. In the culture of the Pacific Tlingit people, there is a Creator Raven, known as the Owner of Daylight, but there is also a childish Raven, forever performing nasty tricks such as stealing the sun.

According to Livy, the Roman general Marcus Valerius Corvus had a raven settle on his helmet during combat with a gigantic Gaul. The raven flew into his enemy's face and allowed Marcus to win the fight. Henceforward, the general always had a raven on his flag. The Vikings too often went into battle under the device of the raven. Ragnar Lodbrok had a raven banner called *Reafan*. It was said that if the banner fluttered, Lodbrok would carry the day. King Harald Hardrada had a raven banner known as *Landeythan*, the land-waster.

The Norse names are making Ruth's eyelids droop. She scans the next few pages quickly – Tower of London, Edgar Allen Poe, *corvus corax* ... Then her eyes light on two familiar words.

'It is sometimes thought (she reads) that King Arthur's spirit left his body in the form of a raven. For this reason, Arthur is sometimes known as the Raven King.'

King Arthur.

Could Dan possibly have found the body of King Arthur?

Her phone bleeps, alerting her to a text message. She has a bad feeling about this, a premonition, you might say.

Keep away from Pendle. You have been warned.

Tramps like us, sings Bruce Springsteen, baby we were born to run.

CHAPTER 6

'A summer holiday in Lancashire,' says Judy. 'You must be mad.'

'I haven't definitely decided to go,' says Ruth, rather defensively. 'But I've been asked to look at some bones at Pendle University.'

'Sounds wild,' says Judy. 'I went to Southport once. Never again.'

Ruth sighs. She is finding Judy rather hard going. She has popped in on her way home from the dig to see mother and baby. Actually, it was rather a trek from Swaffham and Ruth is feeling that Judy ought to be, well, not grateful exactly, but at least pleased to see her. So far, Judy has not even offered her a cup of tea. It's another lovely evening but they are sitting in a stuffy sitting room with the windows closed. The air smells of nappy bags. Judy, wearing stained jeans and a man's shirt, is obviously conforming to the Ruth style of post-birth wardrobe rather than the Shona yummy-mummy look. Ruth doesn't blame her for this in the least but she does feel that Judy could make some effort. She didn't even laugh at the latest Clough story. (Last week Clough burst into an illegal gambling den with such force that he fell down two flights of stairs; the den turned out to be the local bridge club.)

'Has he got a new girlfriend yet?' asks Judy, with something like a sneer.

'Nelson says he's going out with a lap dancer.'

Judy snorts. 'Wishful thinking. Bet that's just what Nelson would like to do himself.'

'I don't think so,' says Ruth, appalled at the idea. 'Nelson's quite prudish really.'

'If you say so.'

There is a slight pause. Ruth looks down at the baby, asleep in his Moses basket. His hands are clasped on the crocheted blanket as if he's praying.

'Have you thought of a name yet?' she asks.

'Yes,' says Judy.

'Well, what is it?' asks Ruth. 'Are you going to make me play twenty questions?'

Judy looks away. 'Michael,' she says, towards the window.

Ruth wonders if she's heard right. 'Michael?'

Judy looks back at her, chin raised. 'Yes, Michael.'

Ruth looks back at the sleeping baby, her mind racing. Why has Judy named her child after Cathbad? Does this mean that Cathbad is the father? Does Judy think that Ruth doesn't know Cathbad's real name? Does she suspect that Ruth suspects about Cathbad?

'It's a lovely name,' she says at last. 'Strong.'

Judy shrugs. 'He's got strong lungs at any rate.'

On cue, Michael wakes up and starts crying. Ruth takes the opportunity to escape.

'I'd better be going,' she says. 'Max is coming down tonight.'

'Romantic evening in, eh?' says Judy. Her tone is distinctly unfriendly. She picks Michael up and jiggles him against her shoulder. The yelling increases.

'No,' says Ruth, gathering up her bag. 'We're going out for a meal with Shona and Phil.'

Judy knows how Ruth feels about Phil but she elects to take this as evidence of Ruth's glamorous baby-free lifestyle. 'It's all right for some.'

Ruth has had enough. 'Bye, Judy,' she says. 'Take care of yourself.'

Judy says, in a more conciliatory tone, 'Do you think you *will* go to Lancashire?'

'I'm not sure. I quite fancy the idea of a holiday but it's a bit of a long drive.' Judy looks at her over Michael's fluffy dark head. 'The boss is going to Blackpool for the summer. Did you know?'

Ruth shakes her head.

'You might all meet up on the beach,' says Judy. 'That would be fun.'

Ruth drives to King's Lynn to collect Kate and then heads off home. She's tired from the day's digging and can't, offhand, think of anything she'd like less than squeezing herself into smart clothes and going out for a meal with her boss and his gorgeous partner. But when she'd told

Max he had been surprisingly keen. He'd even offered to come down early on the Friday night. Ruth looks at the clock on the dashboard. Six o'clock. Max might even be there now. He has probably bumped into Cathbad on the doorstep. Cathbad is babysitting tonight.

She feels strangely disturbed by her visit to Judy. It's not that she expected Judy to be enveloped in a happy cloud of baby love. She can remember the strange, disorientating days of early motherhood too well. But Judy seems odd, almost angry. Is she angry with Cathbad? Herself? With Ruth for being Cathbad's friend and for having a child with a conveniently invisible father?

And those text messages. At first Ruth had almost been able to convince herself that it was a joke, that some student had got wind of her possible visit and was trying to wind her up. But last night's message, coming just after all those creepy stories about ravens, had chilled her to the core. *You have been warned.* Who is warning her and why? And Nelson's policeman friend thinks that Dan might have been murdered. Should she tell Nelson about the texts? She probably should but she shrinks from it somehow. One way and another, she's needed Nelson's help rather a lot over the last few years. She doesn't want to play the damsel in distress again. It's not a flattering look for a twelve-stone woman. She takes the turn onto the Saltmarsh road, over-steering slightly and coming dangerously close to the ditch. Get a grip, Ruth. Being rescued by the AA would be only one step up on being rescued by Nelson.

As she approaches her cottage, she sees Cathbad's ancient Morris parked by the long grass. Max hasn't arrived yet. A wave of what she doesn't want to acknowledge as relief sweeps over her. It's just because I'm tired, she thinks.

Kate wakes up as soon as she sees Cathbad.

'Piss,' she shouts ecstatically.

'Peace, Hecate,' says Cathbad, leaning in to release her from her car seat. 'I'm going to look after you tonight.'

'Please don't teach her any more words,' says Ruth.

'Words are power,' says Cathbad.

'I think I can do without the power of piss,' says Ruth, opening the door.

Ruth makes tea while Kate and Cathbad play on the floor with stickle bricks. Flint watches from a safe distance. It's all so cosy that Ruth finds herself wishing that she wasn't going out that evening. That she and Cathbad could get a takeaway and watch *Have I Got News For You* after Kate has gone to sleep.

'When's the demon lover arriving?' asks Cathbad.

'Any minute,' says Ruth, not bothering to rise. She sits on the sofa, fiddling with her phone. It's a smart model, new last year and she still hasn't plumbed the depths of its powers. Cathbad watches her from across the room.

'What's up?'

It's no good; Cathbad's extrasensory powers have been awakened.

'I saw Judy today.'

Cathbad doesn't react, just carefully balances a red brick on top of a blue brick. Kate undoes them again.

'How was she?' he asks.

'Fine. The baby's lovely. He's ...' She pauses, clicking random buttons on the phone.

'What? Ruth, what is it?'

Ruth looks up. 'He's called Michael.'

Cathbad's expression of pure joy is painful to see. Ruth almost wishes she hadn't told him but how could she not?

'After me?' he whispers.

'I don't know,' says Ruth, but deep down she thinks that Judy did name her baby after Cathbad. Why else would she be so defensive about it? What does it mean? That Judy is acknowledging Cathbad as Michael's father or that she's giving the baby his first name because he'll never have his last?

'Do you think she wants to see me?' asks Cathbad.

'I don't know,' says Ruth. 'After Kate was born I really wanted to see Nelson. It seemed all wrong that he wasn't there. But it's different for Judy. She has a husband.'

'But who does she love?' asks Cathbad.

'Don't ask me,' says Ruth. 'I don't even know who I love.'

And, as if inspired by druidical sixth sense, Max walks into the room.

The evening isn't too bad. They go to a nice Italian restaurant and Phil doesn't complain too much about the prices.

Shona looks stunning in a pink velvet mini dress but Ruth, in black trousers and a vaguely sparkly top, doesn't feel too frumpy in comparison. Max and Phil talk easily about the Swaffham dig, about surveying and total stations and the impossibility of gaining English Heritage funding. After a while, Ruth gets fed up with being relegated to baby talk with Shona.

'I might be involved in an interesting dig soon,' she says.

'Really,' says Phil, his money-making antennae on alert. 'Anything to do with that guy at Pendle? I was the one who gave him your number.'

What do you want, thinks Ruth, a medal? She hasn't forgiven Phil for this intrusion on her privacy.

'Yes. He wants me to give my expert opinion on some bones.'

She stresses the word 'expert'. God, she must be drunk.

'Were these the ones found at Ribchester?' says Phil. 'He mentioned something about them to me.'

'Ribchester?' says Max. 'That's a really important Roman site. There have been excavations there since the eighteenth century. It's a cavalry fort. Very interesting. I've dug there myself.'

Ruth doesn't like the way that Phil turns to Max as if relishing the chance to hear from a real expert. She was the one requested by Dan, she is 'one of the country's leading experts on bone preservation'. At that moment, she resolves to go to Pendle.

'I'm looking forward to seeing it,' she says, sprinkling parmesan on her pasta.

'When are you going?' asks Max. He smiles at her across the table, making Ruth feel ashamed of her annoyance.

'At the end of July,' she says, smiling back. 'When term ends.'

'Perhaps I could come too,' says Max. 'For some of it at least.'

'That would be great,' says Ruth, wondering why she doesn't feel more enthusiastic about the idea. 'I'm not quite sure when I'm going yet.'

'Will you take Kate?' asks Shona. She is leaning against Phil's shoulder, hair tousled and eyes sparkling. How can she fancy him?

'I don't know,' says Ruth. 'Depends how long I'll be there. If it's only for a few days, I might ask my parents to look after her. They'd love it.'

This is true. There is nothing Ruth's parents would like better than to get their hands on Kate while she is still young enough to brainwash.

'You should go,' says Phil, pouring himself more wine without offering it round. 'It's been a while since you've done any original research, hasn't it?'

Ruth feels rather embarrassed, coming home with Max to find Cathbad on the sofa watching Graham Norton. It's as if she and Max are carrying a huge banner saying 'We're just about to have sex'. Max is rather tactful, though. He goes into the kitchen to make tea, leaving Ruth and Cathbad to talk.

'How was Kate?' asks Ruth. She has sobered up at bit but is still finding it an effort not to slur her words.

'Fine. Not a peep out of her.'

'It was very kind of you to babysit.'

'Not at all. I enjoyed it.' He gets up and reaches for his jacket. Ruth feels rather sad that he isn't wearing his cloak.

'Bye, Cathbad,' says Max from the kitchen. 'See you soon.'

At the doorway, Cathbad turns and says, with elaborate casualness. 'Oh, Ruth. If you are going to Lancashire, I'd love to go with you.'

CHAPTER 7

As they turn onto the motorway, a huge sign above them points the way unambiguously to The North. Ruth, rather stressed from following Cathbad's directions ('I think it's this way— Oh, look at that bird! Is it a buzzard?'), views it with relief. At least this must mean that they're going the right way. All the same there is something, to her, slightly chilling about the wording. She remembers Dan's letter with its reference to the 'frozen and inhospitable north'. She is going into alien territory, and for a moment she thinks she understands how the Roman legions must have felt, leaving the sunny comfort of Italy and travelling northwards to the barbarous lands of the Anglo-Saxons.

It is July 29th and, as Ruth had predicted, the good weather has broken and rain is forecast. Ruth, Cathbad and Kate are on their way to Lytham. When they stopped for petrol outside King's Lynn, Ruth thought how much they must look like a normal, nuclear family. Cathbad, in jeans with his greying hair in a ponytail (no cloak –

thank God), could be any hippyish dad, siphoning unleaded into the battered family car. Ruth, coping with a fretful Kate and buying sweets for the journey, was aware that she looked every inch the frazzled mum. This must also have been the vision in Max's head when he had said, 'Everyone will think you're a couple, you and Cathbad.' It had been an odd thing for Max to say. For one thing, he prides himself on not caring what people think. For another, he knows that Ruth and Cathbad are just friends, he even knows about Judy. And, for another ... well, he hasn't any right to comment, has he?

For the last few weeks, Ruth has been thinking a lot about her relationship with Max. In July, after term had finished, Max came down for a week and they hired a boat on the Broads. Having nearly been murdered on a boat once, Ruth is not that keen on sailing as a pastime, but despite being involved in the same incident Max is a keen waterman. And it had been lovely, drifting through the flat Norfolk fields with the sky high and blue above them, Max at the helm, Kate shouting out with pleasure whenever she saw a swan, or a cormorant, or another boat – or anything really. That had been the only problem; Kate had been so excited that Ruth had had to keep hold of her all the time. She had been fitted with her own cute baby life-jacket, but even so Ruth wasn't taking any chances. By evening, as they moored under willow trees or in shallow backwaters, Ruth was exhausted, far too tired (and conscious of Kate only a few feet away) to make love in the narrow double bed.

On their last evening, as they drifted along the Wherryman's Way, Max had said, 'Kate's had a great time, hasn't she?'

'She's loved it,' said Ruth. Max had bought Kate a miniature captain's cap and she was sitting on his lap with her hands firmly on the helm. It would make a great picture, if only Ruth could remember where she'd put her phone or camera.

Max turned to Ruth, who was sitting on the bench seat behind him.

'Do you worry about her being an only child?'

Ruth had been surprised. She had been so shocked to have a baby at all that she had never considered Kate's single-child status. Of course, in theory she had two half-sisters, but in reality it was just the two of them – Ruth and Kate. Was there something wrong with that?

'No,' she said. 'It's not as if I have much choice.'

'But you do,' Max had said, turning back to Kate. 'We could have a baby.'

Now, filtering into the motorway with all the other families, hot and fractious at the beginning of the summer holidays, Ruth thinks about Max's incredible statement. She has honestly never thought about having another baby. Getting pregnant with Kate had seemed like a miracle and, like all miracles, it was a one-off, inconvenient as well as wonderful. She has always thought that Kate was her one chance at motherhood – a chance she once thought she would never have. But she is only forty-two, it's not impossible that she should have another child (though she ought to get a move on if she's considering it). She thinks back to her fantasy family on the beach at Blackpool. Is it possible to imagine a baby next to a toddler Kate? A baby with Max's curly hair? Would Max be in the fantasy too? He didn't mention marriage or even living together. In fact, after dropping his bombshell, he had never mentioned the subject again, had not even waited for Ruth's reply (just as well as she had no intention of giving one). They had parted on easy, affectionate terms, Max saying that he would try to come up to Lytham for the second week of Ruth's holiday. Now she wonders if she had imagined the whole thing. Does Max really want her to have his baby? He doesn't have children, maybe he is just desperate to be a father. But, if so, why not pick on some fertile twenty-something graduate student? Max is an attractive man, it shouldn't be too difficult. Why bother with her – overweight, introverted, an expert on old bones?

'Kate's asleep,' says Cathbad, looking over his shoulder.

'Good,' says Ruth. Kate had been grizzling quietly for about half an hour. They made an early start but traffic has been bad. It's now midday and they are only just past Doncaster.

'I'll take over driving when we stop for lunch,' says Cathbad.

Ruth says nothing. She is not sure that she trusts Kate's life – or her own – to Cathbad's driving.

She is not sure, even now, why she decided to embark on this long and potentially tedious journey. Partly it was

Phil's breezily dismissive attitude to the Ribchester bones. And she still remembers his crack about 'original research'. If Dan really had made a momentous discovery, then she could be the one to bring it to light, thus fulfilling her debt to her friend and making her reputation in the process. Phil's comment had underlined the feeling that her career is going nowhere; she has published nothing in the last few years, not even an article or a review. She really needs something big, and if Dan had found the grave of King Arthur, that could be the biggest archaeological find of the decade.

There is, of course, the mysterious person who wants to stop her coming to Pendle. Ruth had thought hard about the fact that she could be placing herself, and, more importantly, Kate, in danger. But, deep down, she can't imagine that Dan really was murdered because of his discovery. Things like that just don't happen to archaeologists. Besides, she'll never let Kate near the university. Cathbad has said that he'll look after her while Ruth does her investigations. He can take her to the beach, for rides on donkeys and carousels. It'll all be perfectly safe.

When they stop at the Welcome Break in Preston, Kate is awake and in tearing spirits. She eats most of a McDonald's Happy Meal and wants endless goes on a Thomas the Tank Engine ride. Cathbad and Ruth watch her, listening to the maddeningly repetitive theme tune and drinking giant frothy cups of coffee. Ruth looks at her watch. She has told Clayton Henry's colleague, a woman called Andrea Vickers, that they will be at the cottage some time after three. Even with Cathbad's eccentric driving, they will be at Lytham before two. What can they do while they wait?

Unsurprisingly, Cathbad has an idea. 'Why don't we pop in to see Pendragon? It's not far from here, just along the A59.'

Ruth quite likes the idea. She could do with some fresh air and doesn't feel like turning up on Andrea Vickers' doorstep on the dot of three. If she's anything like Ruth, she'll still be changing the sheets.

'Can we ring him first?' she asks. 'I don't want to turn up out of the blue.'

'He doesn't have a phone.'

Of course he doesn't.

As they turn off the A59 the world changes. They pass through a stunningly pretty village with a stream running down the middle. The pub is called The Swan With Two Necks. Ruth, looking round, sees a goat standing in the middle of the road – there's not a single other living soul to be seen. The road snakes slowly upwards, past crumbling dry-stone walls and the occasional ruined farm building. In the distance is a vast hill, its summit wreathed in cloud. It's a curious shape, like a long flat table. Ruth thinks of the Stone Table in the Narnia books. As far as she remembers, something very nasty happened on that table.

'Is that Pendle Hill?' she asks.

'Yes,' says Cathbad. 'There are lots of legends about it. George Fox had a vision of God's love on top of Pendle Hill. That's where Quakerism started.'

Ruth quite likes Quakers – compared to other religions anyway – but the high bare hill doesn't suggest divine love to her. Quite the opposite. It's a sinister, lowering presence, black against the sky. The clouds leave shadows on the grass and in the distance Ruth sees a gleam of dark water. The foreground, too, is full of white cloud-like shapes.

'Sheep!' shouts Kate. 'Sheep! Sheep!'

'Yes, sheep,' says Ruth. 'And nothing else. Why's it called a forest? There aren't many trees here.'

'I'm not sure,' says Cathbad, shifting down through the gears. Ruth's aged Renault is finding the gradient a challenge. 'I think in ancient times a forest just meant a place where the king used to hunt.'

'It's beautiful,' says Ruth, 'but it's a bit spooky.'

'There's old magic here,' says Cathbad. 'Have you heard of the Pendle Witches?'

'I don't think so.'

'They were a group of women at the beginning of the seventeenth century. There were lots of rumours about them – that they had familiars, that they made clay images and cursed people, made animals die and killed people's children. Anyway, they were accused of witchcraft and ten of them were executed. They all lived around here, in the hills and in the forest. Pendragon actually lives in a cottage that was owned by one of the witches.'

Ruth can see why this would appeal to a druid but she doesn't think that the subject matter is very suitable for Kate. Still, with any luck she won't have understood. Ruth looks round at her daughter, who is humming quietly to herself.

'OK, Kate?'

'Sheep,' says Kate.

There are more and more sheep in their way and Cathbad is constantly stopping to let them pass. The sheep don't hurry either, gazing at them balefully out of their onyx eyes and meandering slowly in front of the car, woolly nether-regions matted with mud (or worse).

'Dirty sheeps,' says Kate.

'Sheep,' corrects Ruth.

'But why?' says Cathbad maddeningly. 'Why isn't it sheeps? I'm going to say sheeps from now on.'

The road has narrowed considerably, and although they are still climbing they're now surrounded by high grass banks. For Ruth it's the worst of both worlds: she feels claustrophobic and agoraphobic at the same time. She wonders why she, who loves the lonely marshes, should feel so threatened by these lowering hills. Perhaps it's the absence of the sea. When you've got used to being able to see as far as you can, it feels strange to be hemmed in on all sides by grassland and trees – and wall-eyed sheep.

They stop at a crossroads while Cathbad consults the map. Ruth reads the place names out loud: 'Fence, Stump Hall Road, Crow Trees Brow. Weird names.'

'The magistrate who tried the Pendle Witches came from Fence,' says Cathbad. 'It must have been quite an important place once. I think it's this way.'

He takes the smallest and least prepossessing of the roads. The car crawls between dark hedgerows. The rain, which has been threatening all day, begins to fall. Kate starts to cry.

'Look, Kate,' says Ruth desperately. 'Sheeps!'

But there are suddenly no sheep. When they turn the corner they are in the cleft of a sharply sloping valley and there are no animals of any kind to be seen.

'Look,' says Cathbad, pointing.

Halfway up the hill is a small, white house. A flickering light shows in one of the windows.

'Dame Alice's Cottage,' he says.

'What?' says Ruth.

'Dame Alice's Cottage. That's what Pendragon's house is called. Dame Alice must have been one of the witches.'

It isn't the cosiest house name that Ruth had ever heard, but right now she'd do anything to get out of the car, give Kate a cuddle, go to the loo and have a cup of tea. She looks up at the isolated little cottage.

'Does the road go that far?' she says.

'We can park by the gate. We'll have to walk across the field.'

Ruth lifts Kate out of her car seat and, as she is still inclined to be whiny, carries her across the uneven grass. The rain is heavier now and Ruth hasn't unpacked her cagoule. Cathbad strides beside them, looking around with every appearance of pleasure.

'Wonderful place. Wonderful energies.'

As far as Ruth is concerned, it can keep its energies to itself. She'll never be horrible about Norfolk again.

'Cheer up, Kate,' she says. 'We're going to see a nice man and have a cup of tea.'

'Stop!' shouts a voice. 'Or I'll shoot.'

Ruth looks up and sees a white-bearded figure brandishing a rifle. As they stop and stare at him, a pit-bull terrier runs towards them, barking hysterically.

CHAPTER 8

The dog makes straight for them, teeth bared. Ruth presses Kate against her shoulder and tries to think of everything she's ever heard about pit bulls. They go for the throat, when they bite you they never let you go, if you run they chase you ... She turns, shielding Kate with her body, trying not to think about that woman in France who had her face bitten off. Then she is aware that Cathbad is lying on the grass next to her. Oh God, the devil dog is savaging Cathbad. What should she do? She can't put Kate down and, anyway, how can she fight off a trained killer, maddened by the smell of blood? Then she realises that Cathbad is, in fact, embracing the devil dog, pulling its ears, even kissing it between its wide-apart eyes.

'Hello, Thing. How are you, boy? There's a good dog.'

'Dog,' comes Kate's muffled voice.

'Yes,' says Ruth, 'dog.'

The man with the gun is now running towards them though he has, mercifully, lowered his weapon.

'Cathbad? Is that you?'

Cathbad gets to his feet. 'Call this a welcome, Pendragon, you miserable sod.'

Pendragon puts the gun on the grass and, with almost a sob, rushes forward to embrace Cathbad. The two men stand, entwined, as the dog frolics around them. Cathbad is tall but Pendragon is even taller, a huge Father Christmas of a man, dressed in a dirty army pullover and jeans. His beard reaches to his waist and snow-white hair cascades down his back. The dog is also white, with a pinkish snout and merry, dark eyes. He comes over now to investigate Ruth.

'Want dog,' says Kate, but Ruth doesn't put her down. She still can't forget stories about these dogs savaging children and, besides, there is a lethal weapon a few feet away.

Pendragon finally releases Cathbad and wipes his eyes on his jumper.

'Pen,' says Cathbad, 'I'd like you to meet some friends of mine, Ruth and Kate.'

To Ruth's surprise, she too gets a hug, Pendragon wrapping his arms with ease around both her and Kate. He smells of wood smoke.

'Welcome,' he says. 'Welcome to my hearth.'

Cathbad makes an odd little bow in return. 'What's with the firearms?' he asks.

Pendragon strides over to the gun and picks it up. 'Airgun,' he says, 'not loaded.'

'Natives not friendly then?'

'It's a long story,' says Pendragon. 'Come inside. I'll make some herbal tea.'

The cottage is low-ceilinged with bumpy, plaster walls. Pendragon has to stoop to cross the threshold, which makes him look like an adult in a child's playhouse. The door opens onto the main room, which smells of herbs and smoke. There is a huge fireplace with little iron seats on either side, a wooden settle and what Ruth instantly recognises as a version of Cathbad's wizard's chair. When she makes her urgent trip to the loo, she notices shells hanging from the roof like one of Cathbad's dream-catchers. Druid interior decorating.

When she returns, Kate is playing happily with a pile of little wooden dolls. As Ruth enters the room, she hears Cathbad saying, '. . . not my child, not biologically anyhow.' Clearly druids are not immune to nosiness. The white dog is sitting next to Kate, tail wagging noisily on the wooden floor. Pendragon sees Ruth's glance.

'Bull terriers are actually very good with children,' he says. 'They used to be known as nanny dogs.'

That's not what the headlines say, thinks Ruth, but the dog does seem amiable enough. He had a jolly, piratical look with a black patch over one eye. She pats him and he leans against her, panting.

Pendragon makes herbal tea that tastes of wood shavings. He also offers home-made bread and butter. Despite having eaten a burger for lunch, Ruth tucks in. She thinks she could get to like it in Dame Alice's Cottage. It's certainly very cosy in the main room with the oil lamps lit and the rain outside. The fire is smouldering gently and the dog is now sleeping in front of it, paws twitching.

'What's his name?' asks Ruth, indicating the dog. She heard Cathbad refer to it as Thing, which is typical. It's rare for Cathbad to call any creature by their given name. He usually refers to Kate as Hecate and has been known to call Ruth 'Ruthie', an appellation which only Erik was allowed to use.

But Pendragon's answer surprises her. 'He's called Thing,' he says with a grin. 'Shall I tell you why?'

Cathbad smiles as if he knows the answer and Pendragon assumes his storyteller's pose, leaning back in the wizard's chair, eyes half shut.

'Four hundred years ago,' he says, 'this house was owned by a wise woman. Her name was Alice Barley, Dame Alice. She was the person you went to if you needed a spell to make your sick child well or to help your wife conceive. She was full of ancient wisdom and lore. For many years she helped the people in these hills.' He looks at the three faces turned towards him, even Kate is listening intently. 'But as time went on, people turned against her. There was some dispute about land. One family in particular had a grudge against Alice. They went to the magistrate and claimed that Alice had put a spell on their child, who subsequently died. They said that Alice boasted that she had a familiar – a Thing – who did her bidding. They said that Alice did not take Communion at the church; she saved the holy bread for her Thing. It was said that the Thing could take the form of a dog or a human man. It was said that Alice lay with the Thing and that she suckled it – its teeth, it was claimed, had left a mark on her belly. The Devil's mark. Alice was accused of witchcraft. She refused to defend herself, saying only that the Great Mother would protect her. Those words probably signed her death warrant. She was hanged the next day.'

There is a silence. The dog – Thing – moans in his sleep.

'So you called your dog after Dame Alice's familiar?' says Ruth.

'Yes.' Pendragon leans over to pat the animal's head. 'He's my familiar, my companion.'

'Do you see Dame Alice?' asks Cathbad in a matter-of-fact voice, just as if he's asking if he sees the postman.

'No,' says Pendragon, rather regretfully. 'I don't see her but I feel her presence. Sometimes I leave gifts for her – hops, apples, corn dollies. The offerings are always gone in the morning. Sometimes I smell her herbal infusions. Once, when I was troubled with headaches, I went and lay in what had been her herb garden. I slept the night there, and when I woke the headache had gone, never to return.'

And you had rheumatism instead, thinks Ruth. As for the apples and corn dollies, she suspects the local fox. There's a fox in her garden in Norfolk that steals her wellingtons if she leaves them out on the back step.

'Thing sees her, I think,' says Pendragon. 'Sometimes he'll look up, staring straight past me, tail wagging in recognition.'

Despite herself, Ruth shivers. She looks at the sleeping dog who, thankfully, does not look up, ears pricked, to greet his ghostly mistress.

'So, why the gun?' asks Cathbad, helping himself to another hunk of bread. 'You seemed pretty scared when we arrived.'

'It's a long story,' Pendragon says again. But, unlike the Dame Alice story, this does not seem to be a tale he is inclined to tell. Instead he drops down on his knees next to Kate. 'Do you like those dolls, Kate?' He looks up at Ruth. 'I found them in the house, under one of the floorboards. I think they belonged to Dame Alice. One of the stories told against her was that she made wooden effigies of her enemies and then burnt them.'

Ruth looks at her daughter playing happily on the floor with the voodoo dolls. Next to her, the devil dog sleeps on.

'Harry Nelson!'

The large man behind the desk gets up, arms outstretched. The two men don't actually embrace – the desk is in the way for one thing – but they exchange a hearty handshake.

'Sandy Macleod! How long has it been?'

'Too long. But you don't look a day older.'

'I feel a hundred years older,' says Nelson, sinking into a chair. It feels wrong to be this side of the desk but it's great to be with Blackpool CID again. Bonny Street Station hasn't changed a bit: there's still the blue light outside the door, still the rather grim Victorian brickwork, still what looks like the same graffiti outside, 'Pigs Go Home'. Sandy himself, though balder and fatter, looks much the same. He has a lugubrious, rubbery face, like an old-style music-hall comedian. Nelson remembers that it was always hard to know whether Sandy was joking or not.

'How's the countryside treating you?' he says now, sending a WPC out to make tea with an admirable lack of political correctness. ('Make us a cuppa, there's a good lass'.)

'I've had a tough couple of years,' says Nelson, thinking that this is an understatement. Child abduction, murder, a serial killer, not to mention the mess of his personal life. But Sandy looks quite admiring as he says, 'You've had a few high-profile cases.'

'God save me from high-profile cases. My boss loves press conferences. Just hearing the word *Crimewatch* gives him a hard-on.'

Sandy laughs. 'We've got a few like that here. Same everywhere, old-style coppers are dying out. They've all got degrees now.'

'You're not wrong there.'

The WPC comes back with tea in proper cups and even a couple of Kit Kats. Nelson thanks her, thinking of the response he'd get if he sent Judy or Tanya out for refreshments. The word Kit Kat reminds him of Katie.

'How's the lovely Michelle?' asks Sandy. He had been a guest at their wedding, twenty-odd years ago.

'Champion. She manages a hairdressing business. Nice little set-up.'

'And the girls?'

'Both at uni.'

Sandy groans. 'My boys too. Don't know why the hell they have to go. Costing me an arm and a leg and all they do is get pissed in Thailand.'

'How old are your sons?' Nelson remembers them as little boys in identical Blackpool strips. He can't remember their names.

'Tom's nineteen. He's at Sheffield reading engineering. Ben's just finished at Birmingham. God knows what he wants to do. Advanced piss-artistry perhaps. He's living back at home, driving Bev and me mad.'

'It's tough, isn't it,' says Nelson. 'Just when you thought they were off your hands.'

It'll be another eighteen years before Katie is off his hands, he thinks. That is, if Ruth continues to let him be part of her life.

'So, Harry,' says Sandy. 'What brings you to these parts?'

Nelson is so surprised to be referred to by his first name that he almost doesn't answer. Somehow, in Norfolk, everyone calls him Nelson, except Michelle, that is. Ruth had even called him Nelson in bed.

'I'm on holiday,' he says, at last.

Sandy laughs again, the folds of his face turning upwards. 'A holiday in Blackpool! Things must be bad.'

'I wanted to spend some time with Mum,' Nelson says, not entirely truthfully. 'She's getting on a bit.'

'We all are, cocker,' says Sandy. 'I'm going to put in for early retirement in a few years.'

'You're joking.' Nelson doesn't know what shocks him more: that a contemporary of his might soon be eligible for early retirement or that Sandy Macleod, whom he has always considered the ultimate coppers' copper, would ever want to quit the job.

'I've had enough,' says Sandy. 'Too many bloody graduates, too much paperwork. Do you remember the old days? Drinking after hours in the Red Lion? Sid the Greek? Fat Bernie?'

'I remember,' says Nelson, though Sid the Greek and Fat Bernie are just names to him now. He's sure that every police station has their equivalent. Suddenly he feels rather sad.

Sandy, though, seems to pull himself together. He sits up straighter, brushing chocolate crumbs off his paunch.

'That case you mentioned, the fire. Professional interest, was it?'

'Not really,' says Nelson carefully. 'Woman I work with, forensic archaeologist, victim was a friend of hers.'

Sandy groans. 'Don't talk to me about forensics. Every Tom, Dick and Harry's a forensics expert these days. Put on a paper suit and you think you're God.'

'This woman's OK,' says Nelson. 'Bit of a pain sometimes but OK.'

'Well, we're definitely treating her mate's death as suspicious,' says Sandy, pulling a sheaf of papers towards him. Nelson tries not to wince at the state of his friend's in-tray. Though he'd never admit it to Sandy, Nelson quite likes paperwork and his desk at King's Lynn is always immaculate.

'Emergency services called at one a.m.,' says Sandy, reading from a sheet. 'Alerted by a neighbour. Arrived at one-twenty. Front door was locked, victim was just inside the door, looked as if he'd been clawing at it, traces of wood under his fingernails. Cause of death, smoke inhalation.'

'Door locked from the outside?'

'Yes. The key was still in the lock. No attempt to hide it. Seat of the fire was in the hallway. We found pieces of material just inside the front door, doused with petrol. Looks as if they'd been pushed through the letterbox.'

'Jesus.' Nelson is silent for a moment, thinking of Ruth's friend – Dan Whatshisname – trapped in a burning house, clawing at a locked door. What a way to go.

'Did you find anything else?'

'No,' says Sandy. 'We had the bloody forensics buggers in there, sealed the place off, went over everything with a fine tooth comb. There were a few things that seemed out of place. For one, we didn't find a mobile or a computer. You'd expect a university professor to have a computer. Probably one of the latest iPricks.'

Sandy speaks with contempt, and certainly his own computer, which looms over the desk, is not of the cutting-edge variety. It has 'Property of Blackpool CID' stamped on the back.

'Maybe it was at the university,' suggests Nelson.

'No, we checked. He shared an office with another chap. Lots of books but no computer.'

'Why would someone take his computer?' asks Nelson.

'Search me,' says Sandy.

'But you're thinking murder?'

'I don't think it was an accident, put it that way. I think someone wanted Dan Golding dead.'

'But why? I mean, he was a university professor.'

Despite his association with Ruth – and with Erik – Nelson still imagines a university professor sitting in a book-lined room, writing with a quill.

Sandy looks at him consideringly for a moment, as if wondering how much to tell him. Then he seems to make a decision, reaching for another file which is lying (Nelson can hardly believe this) on the floor.

'Dan Golding taught at Pendle University,' he says. 'It's one of the new ones, on the outskirts of Preston. Thing is, we've had a few funny incidents at Pendle recently.'

'What sorts of incidents?' asks Nelson. He's expecting some loony lefty behaviour, animal rights activism perhaps (he's had experience of that himself recently). So he is amazed when Sandy says, his comedian's face deadly serious, 'White supremacists.'

'White supremacists? You mean, like the Ku Klux Klan?'

Now Sandy does smile, a brief, gummy grin which is soon replaced by the sad clown expression. 'Lancashire's version,' he says. 'No burning crosses but offensive notes sent to black members of staff, an attempted fire-bombing of a gay pride event, statue of Nelson Mandela defaced. Obviously an organised group, though we haven't made much headway in identifying the ringleaders. The feeling on campus is very twitchy.'

Nelson remembers Ruth's description of Dan feeling 'intimidated'.

'But why would they target Dan Golding?' he asks.

Sandy shrugs. 'He was Jewish, apparently. That might be cause enough for these bozos. But if this was them – arson with clear attempt to kill – it's a step up from sending anonymous notes with pictures of monkeys on them.'

'Is that what they do?'

'Yes. Crude little leaflets about the superiority of white Aryan men. Last one was so badly spelt that my sergeant – a university boy – said that if this was Aryan supremacy he was glad to be black.'

This fits with Nelson's own experience of the far-right – most of the Neo-Nazis he has met have been so stupid that walking and talking at the same time was an effort. Didn't stop them being violent, though. He remembers policing a demonstration in Salford that got very nasty.

'Have you got any suspects?' he asks.

'A few names,' says Sandy. 'Nothing definite.' He doesn't seem inclined to share these names with Nelson and Nelson doesn't blame him.

'So Dan Golding might have been killed by Nazi arsonists?'

Sandy smiles sardonically. 'Welcome to my world,' he says.

CHAPTER 9

Nelson thinks about Sandy's last statement as he drives across Blackpool to his mother's house, the house where he grew up. *Welcome to my world.* Does Sandy think that Nelson's world does not include racists, arsonists and other unpleasant forms of humanity? Does he think that Norfolk is all about sheep-stealing? But Sandy mentioned Nelson's recent cases, he must know that his old friend has been to some very dark places. He was probably just trying to wind him up. That *would* be like the old Sandy. One thing is clear though: the death of Ruth's old friend Dan is starting to look very suspicious. He will have to ring her and let her know. He wonders what she and Katie are doing at this moment. He knows that Ruth and her archaeologist boyfriend have been on a boating holiday and (grinding gears) he doesn't mind this in the least. Nevertheless, when he thinks of Ruth and Katie he always thinks of them on their own, walking on the beach or sitting in Ruth's untidy cottage playing with educational toys given by Ruth's trendy lefty friends. He smiles, vowing silently to buy Katie a toy gun for her next birthday.

Welcome to my world ... The trouble is, Nelson is not sure which is his world any more. Being back in Blackpool is having a disorientating effect. On the one hand, as he said to Sandy, he feels about a hundred years old. The strain of the last couple of years – several murder cases, including two involving children, tensions at home and at work, a serious illness – sometimes he thinks it's a miracle that he's still functioning at all. On the other hand, as he passes through the familiar streets – the signs for the waxworks and the tower and the South Shore, the guest houses, their multi-coloured facades and cheerfully corny names (Funky Towers, Youanme, Gracelands) belying the desperation of their appearance – the continual delusional associations with New York (he passes three Broadway Diners in five minutes), the stalls selling barm cakes and chips with curry sauce ... he can't believe that a day has passed since he left the place. It's as if on every street corner he might bump into his young self. Harry Nelson the gawky schoolboy in his hated grammar-school blazer, the swaggering youth with gelled-back hair, the young policeman fresh from his encounters with Fat Bernie and Sid the Greek. The sight, sound and smell of the town is in his DNA; how can he have stayed away so long?

Since he has been in Blackpool he has been plagued by this Jekyll and Hyde sensation. The place feels like home, everyone is friendlier here and motherly old ladies in shops call him 'love'. Yet, at the same time, everything has changed. People look poor. They were poor in the old days, he supposed, but they seemed to be having more fun. He remembers Scotland Week, when the factories up north were closed and their inmates streamed down to Blackpool for their annual holiday. Those factory workers must have been poor but, by God, they used to enjoy themselves. Now there is a general sense of depression, even among the star-spangled posters for the Pleasure Beach and lookalike acts at the Grand Theatre. A few years ago there was great talk of regeneration, of building a super casino, Blackpool as the new Las Vegas but, as far as Nelson can see, this has come to nothing. About a third of the shops on the High Street are boarded up, and when he and Michelle wanted to eat out last night their choice was either chips or an American-themed pizza restaurant. He hates to think that he's become the kind of effete southerner who can't cope without his daily sushi fix but, all the same, a person can get tired of a carbohydrate-only diet. Jesus, he must be getting old.

On impulse he drives past his turn-off and follows the signs to Bloomfield Road. Since he last attended a football match the place seems to have become one vast car park, a concrete wasteland bordered by rows of terraced houses, all in the primary colours he remembers from childhood (when he first watched *Balamory* with his daughters he thought of Blackpool). He spots the 'Donkeys Crossing' sign that always makes him smile and a new Travelodge that seems to have sprung up next to the stadium. He is looking for the statue of Jimmy Armfield, his father's hero, which was unveiled a few months ago.

He finds it at the corner between the South Stand, the Jimmy Armfield Stand, and the hotel. Jimmy, nine foot tall and raised on a plinth, smiles into the distance, bronze foot on bronze football. Nelson parks by the kerb, gets out and touches the football boot for luck. A proper boot it is too, not one of these flimsy day-glo affairs (or, worse, white) favoured by modern players. You got out at the right time, Nelson tells the statue. You never got to see players paid half a million a week but still miss sitters from the ten-yard box. Your wife was probably just a wife, not a WAG in seven-inch stilettos. You never tweeted or blogged or appeared on *I'm a Celebrity Get Me Out of Here*. God bless you, Jimmy.

The bronze figure smiles kindly down on him. Nelson gets back into his car and drives back to his mum's house.

Lytham is a pleasant surprise. When Ruth drives along the promenade, the rain has stopped and the sun is sparkling in the puddles. They pass hotels, a lighthouse, a charming town square complete with floral clock, winding streets full of picturesque cottages. 'Pretty,' says Kate, who has just woken up. 'Suburbia by the sea,' says Cathbad, but he smiles to show that this is a joke.

Number One Beach Row turns out to be the end house in a terrace, white-painted with black eaves. It's a fisherman's cottage, situated just behind the coast road, with a tiny garden full of hollyhocks and giant daisies.

Andrea Vickers, a smiling woman with wispy grey hair, greets them at the door.

'Welcome to Lytham,' she says.

'Thanks,' says Ruth, straightening her aching back and breathing in the salty air. 'It's lovely to be here.'

It's just as charming inside. In fact, it reminds Ruth of a house in a fairy tale. Everything is pretty and faded and slightly the wrong size. The sitting room has a rocking chair and a high-backed sofa covered in roses. In the kitchen, there are even three chairs at the round kitchen table.

Cathbad puts on a deep, growling voice. 'Who's been sitting in my chair?'

Andrea turns to Kate, who is staring, wide-eyed. 'You'll have to ask your daddy to read you that story.'

'He's not . . .' begins Ruth but she's not sure how to go on. It seems unnecessarily intimate to be explaining Kate's parentage to a woman she has only just met. Across the room Cathbad grins at her. Ruth scowls back.

Upstairs it's worse. Andrea throws open the door to a charming double with white-painted bed and matching wardrobe. 'That's for you two. Kate's next door. It's a lovely room for a little girl.'

Ruth smiles tightly but says nothing. The room next door has a pink bed and ballerina wallpaper. She hopes that Cathbad will be very happy there.

Back downstairs, Andrea explains the heating system and extols the attractions of Lytham. 'There's the park and the windmill and the lifeboat museum. And if you want adventure, Blackpool's just up the road.'

Ruth doesn't want adventure, she is quite certain of

that. Lytham suits her – the average age of the inhabitants, as they stroll along the promenade later that evening, seems to be about eighty. The seafront itself feels old-fashioned, almost Victorian, a wide green verge with stuccoed hotels on one side and the sea on the other. Dominating the view is the huge black-and-white windmill. They walk towards it, enjoying the exercise after a day spent cooped up in the car. Kate runs along the grass, chasing the seagulls and Cathbad and Ruth follow at a more leisurely pace, Cathbad occasionally commenting on good energies and the psychic qualities of people who live within sight of the sea.

The windmill is shut, although a sign on the wooden steps announces proudly that it is open for an hour every afternoon. Kate is inclined to have a tantrum about this but Ruth bribes her with an ice cream. They walk back along the beach which is actually more of a marsh, with little streams making their way through waterlogged grass down to the sea. It reminds Ruth of the Saltmarsh. Fishing boats are moored above the tide line and seabirds peck their way across the mud. Across the estuary, they see houses, hills and, in the far distance, mountains.

'What's over there?' asks Ruth.

'Southport, I think,' says Cathbad. 'You can see as far as Wales apparently. That must be where those mountains are.'

Hadn't Judy said something about Southport? thinks Ruth. She decides not to mention it.

'I'd expected it to be more built up,' she says. 'You know, amusement arcades and piers.'

'I think that's what Blackpool's for,' Cathbad says. 'This is nice, though. Peaceful.'

'Yes,' says Ruth. 'That's just what I want. A really peaceful holiday.'

CHAPTER 10

Lytham is a surprise; Pendle University is a shock. After the beauty of Pendle Forest Ruth was expecting something rather picturesque, but as she follows Clayton Henry's directions through the back streets of Preston, her confidence starts to falter. She passes grim terraced houses, boarded-up shops, deserted mills and factories. Surely the university can't be here? Even her own university, often described as the poor relation to the University of East Anglia, has landscaped grounds and an ornamental lake. She drives between Indian supermarkets and Polish bakeries. Preston may be multicultural but none of the cultures seems to be having a very good time. The brilliant saris of the women in the streets contrast with their glum expressions. It's a cold summer's day and many of them are wearing anoraks over their saris, heavy boots visible under the bright silk hems. It's like a metaphor for the dampening effect of British life – or British weather.

How had Dan – urban, sophisticated Dan – fitted in here? Perhaps Fleetwood, where he lived, is a bijou artists' quarter, full of antique shops and espresso bars. But he must still have driven in to Preston every day, past these depressed estates and cheerless parades. Dan, whose parents lived in an elegant town house, each floor crammed with books (Ruth went to a party there once when Dan's parents were away). Dan, who sometimes wore a dinner jacket over jeans and knew the right way to eat asparagus. How had he coped with a place where the only cafe offers chips with prawn cocktail sauce? Well, maybe his colleagues were brilliant, witty sophisticates. And of course it was here, in the 'frozen and inhospitable north' that Dan had made his great find. That would have made up for anything.

The directions seem clear enough but Ruth gets lost several times, driving into deserted industrial estates and dead-end streets. She stops once to ask the way but she picks a man who doesn't understand her and clearly thinks she's rather frightening. At any rate, he backs away before she can finish her sentence. Ruth turns the map upside down, performs a thirty-point turn and retraces her steps. Surely a university would be hard to miss? She drives down another side road and sees a grim industrial building with the words 'Sickers Tobacco' painted in vast white letters on one of the walls. This can't be it, can it? It is. A small sign welcomes visitors to 'Pendle University: A new way of learning'. Ruth learns later that the students' nickname for the place is 'The Fag Factory'.

Inside, the reception desk sits uncomfortably in a cavernous space, three storeys high. It looks like a prison, thinks Ruth; it even has those inner balconies running round the central atrium, linked by flights of wrought-iron stairs. All it needs is a suicide net. Ruth asks for Clayton Henry, thinking again how odd the name sounds. The receptionist, too, seems to find it strange.

'Who?' she asks, manoeuvring her chewing gum to the other side of her mouth.

'Clayton Henry.'

'What department?'

'Archaeology.'

'We haven't got an archaeology department.'

Ruth stares at her. For one moment she thinks she has imagined the whole thing – Dan dying, Clayton's invitation, the Raven King, the lot. But Andrea Vickers had seemed to know Clayton Henry quite well ('He's quite a character') and Ruth has an email from him, with directions, printed out in her pocket.

This last provides the clue. At the bottom of the email are the words 'History Department'. The receptionist reluctantly concedes that such a department exists and puts through a call. 'Mr Henry? Visitor for you.' She then puts down the phone and goes back to her gum, ignoring Ruth altogether.

There is nothing Ruth can do but wait, hoping the message got through to someone. She walks around the atrium which is decorated – if that is the word – by posters advertising the work of the engineering and chemistry departments. Underground piping, laboratories, men in hard hats, women in white coats. There is no sign that anything as effete as history – much less archaeology – is even taught here.

'Ruth!' A figure is scurrying down one of the iron staircases. Ruth looks up to see a smallish, plumpish man coming towards her, both hands outstretched.

'Mr Henry?' she says.

'Clayton. Please.' He takes her hand in both of his. For one horrible moment she thinks he might be about to kiss her. 'So good of you to come.'

'That's OK.' Ruth extricates her hand.

'How do you like Andrea's cottage?'

'It's lovely,' says Ruth. 'Lytham's very pretty.'

'Lytham? I've seen Stone Age burial mounds that are livelier than Lytham.' He laughs heartily. Ruth smiles. She is surprised to hear him use the term 'Stone Age'. An archaeologist would usually distinguish between Palaeolithic (old Stone Age), Mesolithic (middle) and Neolithic (new). She begins to suspect that Clayton Henry is not an archaeologist.

And once they are sitting in his cramped fourth-floor office she finds that her suspicions are correct. Clayton Henry is a historian, and head of a department that includes archaeology and anthropology as well as sociology and classical studies. Dan Golding, described by Henry as 'one of our archaeologists', was, in fact, their only archaeologist. 'It's only a module, you see,' said Clayton Henry apologetically. 'Not many people opt for it because it's very demanding. Funnily enough, we're thinking of changing the name to "forensic archaeology".

Kids go for anything with "forensic" in the title these days. Especially the girls.'

Ruth, a forensic archaeologist to her fingertips, looks disapproving. Forensic archaeology is a discipline in itself, not just a phrase to appeal to teenage girls who enjoy watching *Silent Witness*.

This explains, of course, why Henry was so keen to get Ruth up to Lancashire. It's not so much a question of her being better than anyone in-house – there *is* no one else in-house. Ruth feels self-satisfaction seeping out of her. And Dan – not only was he an archaeologist in an obscure university, he was the *only* archaeologist in an obscure university. What had happened to her brilliant friend?

Clayton Henry puts on a concerned face to talk about Dan. 'Such a tragedy. A lovely man. We're all devastated. Did you know the family well?'

'Dan and I were at university together,' says Ruth. She feels uncomfortable discussing Dan with this stranger whose sad voice does not match his curious eyes. Besides, the Dan she knew was not Dan Golding, lone archaeologist at a university that used to be a cigarette factory, but Dan the Man, the piano-playing, Pernod-drinking student.

'I never really knew his family,' she says. 'They must be in shock. It was such a terrible way to die.'

'Yes, indeed,' Henry allows his voice to fade away respectfully before launching, with evident relief, into the next topic.

'Did Dan tell you anything about his discovery?' he asks.

'No,' says Ruth. For reasons she has not explored, even with herself, she doesn't want to discuss the letter, or its disturbing echoes, with Clayton Henry.

'Well . . .' Is it her imagination or does the head of department relax a little? 'As I'm sure you know, there was a significant Roman settlement at Ribchester, not far from here.'

'I've read about it,' says Ruth guardedly.

'Well, Dan's excavations centred on a location a little way outside Ribchester,' says Henry, settling cosily in his chair. 'He was convinced that he had found the site of a temple dedicated to a god who was at once Celtic and Roman. That's not uncommon, you know.'

'I know,' says Ruth.

'Well, the really exciting find was under the temple altar.' He pauses, enjoying the moment. 'A stone sarcophagus containing human remains. The remains, Dan was sure, of a very important military man.'

'What made him think that?' asks Ruth, although she can guess.

'The body was buried with ceremony, within the temple itself, and with funerary goods,' says Henry. 'But the really significant thing was the inscription on the tomb. *Rex Arthurus. Britannorum Rex.*'

He looks expectantly at Ruth, who is frantically working out the Latin. She wishes Max were here to translate it.

'King Arthur,' she says at last. 'King of Britain.'

'King of the Britons,' corrects Henry.

There is a silence. In the distance, Ruth can hear somebody hoovering. Of course, it's the holidays; there will be no students, only cleaners.

'Did Dan really think it was King Arthur?' asks Ruth. '*The* King Arthur?'

'What do we mean by *the* King Arthur?' asks Henry, sounding like a typical historian. 'There are so many legends, very few historical facts. Documentary evidence for the post-Roman period is scarce. Arthur's not even mentioned in *The Anglo-Saxon Chronicle*, for instance. Geoffrey of Monmouth writes about him in his *Historia Regum Britanniae* but that's a very dodgy historical source, full of mythology and sheer imagination. There's also a ninth-century Latin source, the *Historia Brittonum*. That depicts Arthur as a Romano-British king who unites the warring British tribes after the departure of the Romans. The Welsh Annals link Arthur to the Battle of Badon in about 516 AD. The dating of the temple would tie in with this. One interesting thing, though, neither the *Historia* nor the Annals uses the word "Rex" to describe Arthur. That would make our inscription unique.'

His Alan Bennett voice is as light as ever but Ruth thinks she can hear the excitement underneath. The tomb of King Arthur – or even the tomb of a man who might be King Arthur – would be the biggest thing ever to happen to Pendle University, and to Clayton Henry. In fact, Ruth is surprised that Henry has not already alerted the press. She is sure that if Phil found even a hint of a legendary British king, he'd be on *Newsnight* in two seconds flat. She asks the question.

For the first time, Clayton Henry looks really uncomfortable. He fiddles with his letter-opener – a rather ornate silver knife – and avoids meeting Ruth's eyes.

'It's a bit sensitive,' he says at last. 'I wanted to make sure. Our department . . . well, our department isn't that popular in the university.'

'Why's that?'

Clayton laughs though he still looks rather shifty. 'Oh, probably just because I'm Yorkshire and this is Lancashire. The old Wars of the Roses stuff, you know.' Ruth looks at him incredulously and Clayton must feel the inadequacy of this explanation because he says, still not meeting her eyes, 'History doesn't bring in much money. There are always people who'd like to see us replaced with something sensible like metallurgy.'

'But if you made a really big discovery . . .' says Ruth.

'Exactly.' Clayton Henry looks up with almost painful eagerness. 'If this did turn out to be the real thing, we'd be made. Press, TV, conferences. It'd put Pendle on the map all right. But if I went public with it and the bones turned out to be a hoax, I'd be a laughing stock. That's why I wanted you to look at them.' Now he does look at Ruth. His eyes are a very clear blue, almost childlike,

'I'd be happy to look at them,' says Ruth. In fact, she can hardly wait. This could be the biggest find of the decade and she is right there, the first archaeologist on the spot. After Dan, of course.

'I can take you to the site now, if you like,' says Henry.

'The bones aren't still there. We've moved them somewhere safer.'

Ruth wants to ask if the bones have been excavated with due care but realises that this would sound insulting. All the same, she wishes that she had been able to supervise. One false move, one mistake in recording and an entire excavation can be ruined. She would have taken days over this – cataloguing, examining the context, just looking. As Erik always said, 'First, you look. Look as long as you like. You won't get that first sight again.'

'Did Dan send any samples for analysis?' asks Ruth.

'Yes, he sent samples off for carbon 14, isotopic testing and DNA. We haven't had the results yet.'

Again, Ruth feels a thrill of excitement. Who knows what the results might show? And she will be the first to see them.

'The temple,' she says. 'Who was it dedicated to?'

'A strange deity,' says Henry. 'A version of the Celtic god Bran, which means . . .'

But Ruth knows what it means. Bran means Raven.

The Raven King.

CHAPTER 11

Nelson, though he doesn't know it, is only a few miles away from his youngest daughter. His mother has insisted on taking him and Michelle to Rook Hall, a nearby stately home. Nelson's sister, Maeve, has accompanied them, along with her granddaughter, Charlie.

'Charlie?' Nelson had said, peering at the blonde moppet in a fairy dress. 'I thought she was a girl.'

'Of course she's a girl, Harry,' said Maeve, hoisting a nappy bag on her shoulder. 'Don't be stupid.'

'Is it short for Charlotte?' asked Michelle, crouching down to say hello to the baby.

Maeve had shrugged. 'Not as far as I know.'

Nelson can never get used to these new androgynous names. He has a colleague with daughters called Georgie and Sidney. At least Judy had chosen a traditional name for her baby. Michael. But why does that name choice make him feel uneasy?

He also can't get used to his sister being a grandmother. But since Maeve, at fifty-three, is ten years older than him, she's not especially young to have grandchildren. Her daughter, Danielle, had married at twenty-three and had Charlie at twenty-five. All very respectable. It's just that it makes Nelson feel old. He's a great-uncle now. Jesus wept.

Maeve seems to do most of the childcare while Danielle is out at work. Nelson's mother helps too, still fit at seventy-five. She now looks critically at Charlie's uncovered head.

'She needs a sun hat on her, Maeve.'

Maureen Nelson's voice is still unashamedly Irish after five decades in England. Her daughter, on the other hand, is broad Lancashire. The first thing Maeve had said to Nelson was, 'You've lost your accent.'

'I haven't!' said Nelson, outraged. His colleagues in Norfolk think that he talks like a combination of Peter Kaye and Wallace from *Wallace and Gromit*. He's heard them imitating him.

'You have a bit, Harry,' said Michelle. 'So have I.'

And that's always the pattern of visits to Blackpool. Michelle is continually shocked at the abuse directed at Harry by his ever-loving mother and sisters. She throws herself into the breach as a peacemaker, not realising that all four of them actually enjoy these exchanges.

Now Maeve snaps at her mother. 'She's fine, Mum. The sun's not out anyway.'

'It's not the sun that gives you heatstroke,' says Maureen unanswerably. Maeve rolls her eyes and wheels Charlie off in the direction of the gift shop.

Rook Hall is a perfect Georgian house, almost scarily symmetrical, set in beautiful landscaped grounds. Nelson doesn't mind trudging round over-decorated rooms and oohing and aahing over dovecotes and lily ponds but he does wonder why, in her seventies, his mother has suddenly got into culture. When he was growing up, Maureen would have been actively suspicious of anyone whose idea of a good time was visiting National Trust properties. He still remembers what she said about their neighbour who listened to classical music. But now Maureen is actually a member of the National Trust as well as a friend of the local theatre and a frequent opera-goer. Do you just get more interested in these things as you get older? Nelson, remembering a God-awful modern play Michelle made him see two years ago, doesn't feel that the process has started with him.

In one aspect, though, Maureen hasn't changed at all. She is determined to get her money's worth and to see every inch of the house, even though she has visited many times before. Maeve soon gives up and takes Charlie out into the grounds but Nelson and Michelle follow Maureen's indomitable figure through dining rooms laid for some invisible banquet, up and down ornate stair-cases (marvelling at the rococo ceilings), through kitchens complete with plastic meat that reminds Nelson of an autopsy, and into myriad rooms whose only function seems to be to display collections of eighteenth-century thimbles.

Nelson is soon tired of ancestral portraits and moulded

cornices. His mind starts to wander, reliving his conversation with Sandy yesterday. Was Dan Golding murdered and, if so, what does Ruth expect him to do about it? Where is Ruth anyway? He rang her at home last night and there was no answer. He'll have to try her mobile. He still has to be careful where Ruth is concerned. Michelle might have forgiven him for the affair (if two nights counts as an affair, which Michelle assures him it does) but the subject is still very raw. Michelle understands that he wants to see Katie (and few wives would understand as much, he knows) but any sign that he is interested in the mother rather than the baby would jeopardise the whole, fragile consensus.

He thinks they've finished but, at the last moment, Maureen leads them up another staircase into a green and white room that reminds Nelson of a Wedgewood vase he once impounded as stolen goods. Bored, he looks out of the window, wondering if he can catch sight of Grandma Maeve and Charlie.

As he scans the paths criss-crossing the lawn at the front of the house, his eye is immediately drawn to a figure with a pushchair. But it's not Maeve. It's a man in a flapping cloak-like jacket with long grey hair in a ponytail. Nelson rubs his eyes. He must be going mad because, for a moment, he thought that the man with the baby was Cathbad.

Ribchester is a picturesque town nestling in a bend in the river. Ruth is beginning to realise that Nelson was speaking the truth when he once told her that there were pretty places near Blackpool. Preston isn't one of them but Lytham is certainly an attractive town and the Pendle Forest – well, if she had nightmares last night about Dame Alice and her familiar, that's not the fault of the countryside, which was undeniably beautiful. Ribchester is cosier – grey stone houses looking as if they've grown there rather than been built, a church, pubs, the winding river – it's all very English and tranquil.

Clayton Henry parks his car, a sporty red number, behind the church.

'The church was actually built slap-bang on top of the Roman fort,' he says, 'You can see the remains of a granary in the graveyard. The baths are behind one of the pubs. The White Bull.'

As they walk around the town, Ruth begins to realise that the Romans are living side-by-side with modern-day Ribchester. The White Bull has ornate pillars at the front, said to be taken from the Roman fort. Terraced houses have Roman walls in their gardens and the church shares its graveyard with medieval tombs and more recent excavations showing floors and hypocausts.

'The museum's next door,' says Henry, stepping carefully over a gravestone. 'There are lots of wonderful things there.'

'The Ribchester helmet?' asks Ruth, remembering something she once read.

'A replica,' says Henry. 'The original's in the British Museum.'

He leads the way through a low gate and along a lane overhung with brambles and cow parsley. 'Dan's excavations centred on a spot further down the river,' he says. 'You don't mind a short walk, do you?'

Ruth wonders how short a short walk is. She likes walking only in moderation. Something Max and Nelson have in common is that they are always striding off without looking back to see if she is following. One day she won't be.

She is also worried about getting back to Kate. She rang Cathbad from the university, saying she was going to be longer than she'd thought and he'd been unconcerned. 'I'll take Kate out for a bit, explore Lytham,' he'd said. 'Take your time.' Cathbad really is the king of the walkers, covering miles in a day, sometime walking all night, across dark fields and through shuttered towns. He used to be a postman, he explained once, and that taught him the value of exploring places on foot. 'You see more,' he says, 'At eye level.' Ruth hopes he won't take Kate too far.

But Clayton Henry does not look like much of a rambler. He looks essentially urban, dressed in a pink shirt and freshly ironed chinos with distinctly unhikerish shoes, pointed and highly polished. Ruth doesn't imagine that he will drag her miles over fields and stiles. In fact, he seems out of breath by the time they reach the river.

'Not far now,' he pants.

The river is obviously on its last lap before the sea, looping extravagantly across the fields, dotted with little islands and crescent-shaped pools. Sheep graze on the

flat ground between the loops and, in the distance, Ruth
can see a black shape, half lost in the clouds.

'Is that Pendle Hill?' she asks, thinking that she knows
the answer.

'Yes,' says Henry. 'Have you been up there? There's a
grand view, but it's a bit spooky, to my mind.'

'I went there yesterday. I've got a friend who lives near
Fence.' She hesitates, aware that 'friend' doesn't really
cover her tenuous connection with Pendragon.

'Sooner him than me,' says Henry. Ruth thinks it's interesting that he assumes the friend must be male.

Birds swoop low over the water, reminding Ruth once
again of the Saltmarsh. She wonders what this area was
like in Roman times. The river would still have been here,
though its course may well have changed; it would have
been a valuable link in the supply chain, carrying goods
inland, and back out to sea towards other parts of the
great Empire. When the Roman troops left, the ships
would no longer have come into port, laden with wine,
olive oil and pottery – that distinctive orangey-red Samian
ware found on the site at Swaffham. Was this where
Arthur made his last stand, abandoned by Rome, beset
on all sides by invading Picts and Celts?

'Here we are,' says Henry.

They are on slightly higher ground, a field just outside
the wall of the church. The excavation, which is about
ten feet across, includes walls and some tesserae, which
could have formed part of a mosaic. In one corner a
tarpaulin covers what is obviously a deeper hole. Ruth

wonders how long ago it was that Dan dug here. The excavation has a lonely look, outside the city walls. Sheep are cropping the grass near the exposed stones.

'The Roman Road was near here,' says Henry. 'Funny how place names survive. There's a village nearby called Street and the road across the bridge is still called the Roman Road.'

Ruth knows that the word 'street' comes from the Latin 'strata', meaning layer, and refers to the many layers that went into constructing a Roman road, one of the wonders of that empire.

'So the temple would have been on the road to the port?' she says.

'It looks like that, yes,' says Henry. 'There's another temple at Ribchester with altars dedicated to Apollo and Victory. Just what you'd expect. But Dan thought this was later. Mid to late 400s, he reckoned.'

Ruth looks down at the ancient walls, exposed to the wind and the air. It is generally thought that the Romans left Britain between 383 and 410 AD, which would mean that this temple was built after the withdrawal, in the mysterious world of warring tribes, the battle for the soul of Britain, the beginning of the Dark Ages. It would also fit that, whoever lay in this tomb, he was buried rather than cremated. By the first century AD, cremation was already a thing of the past. Her heart beats faster. A temple, built in the Roman style, dedicated to an unknown god – even without King Arthur, this is a thrilling discovery.

'The sarcophagus was here,' says Henry, lifting a corner of the tarpaulin. 'Buried about six feet down, under the central altar. The lid was broken, but the piece with the inscription remained almost intact.'

'Where is it now?' asks Ruth, peering into the trench. She can see the shape of a burial cut into the surrounding soil, a deep rectangular void, and some pieces of heavy stone. Nothing else.

'At the university,' says Henry. 'We have a strong-room there. We would have used it for the bones but we felt they needed ... well, special treatment.' Ruth turns to look at him. She wonders why he is being so shifty about the excavation. Did something go wrong?

'There were a few other significant finds,' he says, rather hurriedly. 'A carving of a raven with the words Bran and Corvus below it, and a great deal of skeletal matter.'

'Human skeletal matter?'

'No, avian. It looks as if a number of birds were sacrificed here.'

Offerings to the Raven King, thinks Ruth. She looks around her, at the marshy plain with the wide sky high above. Seagulls are hanging in the air, black against the clouds. If you had to invent a spot for a temple dedicated to a strange pagan bird-deity, this would be the place for it.

Clayton Henry is still looking slightly embarrassed. He stoops down to brush the mud off his cream trousers. Ruth wonders if he is going to change the subject, but even so she is surprised when what he actually says is,

'Would you like to come to a barbeque at my house on Saturday?'

'Thanks,' stammers Ruth. 'But I've got my daughter with me and . . . and a friend.'

'Bring her too,' says Clayton breezily, leaving Ruth to ponder, once again, on his choice of pronoun.

Nelson rings just when Ruth is getting into her car. Clayton had driven her back to the university and she is keen to get back to Kate. In fact she almost doesn't answer the phone.

Nelson, typically, goes straight onto the attack.

'Where have you been?' he says. 'I've been ringing your home number for days.'

'I'm on holiday. Just for a week or so.'

Thank God he doesn't ask where, instead he says, 'With Katie?'

'Of course with Kate.' What does he think she's done, thinks Ruth, left Kate at home with a week's supply of nappies? Asked Bob Woonunga to look after her as well as Flint, putting food for them both through the cat flap? And why can't he ever bloody well get her name right? But she does feel slightly uncomfortable as she's not sure why she hasn't told Nelson that she's in Lancashire. He has a right to know where Kate is, after all. Is it because she thinks it will seem as if she's stalking him? *Is* she stalking him?

'I talked to Sandy about your friend Dan Golding.'

'What did he say?'

'The fire was definitely arson. Someone pushed petrol-soaked rags through the letterbox.'

'Oh my God. Why would anyone do that?'

'Well, Sandy says there are some funny things going on at Pendle University.'

'What sort of things?'

'Racist groups. Neo-Nazis. White supremacists. They've had trouble on campus before.'

'But why would white supremacists want to kill Dan?'

'I don't know. Sandy thought maybe because he was Jewish.'

Ruth thinks of her easy-going friend Dan. Can he really have been killed for this most horrible of reasons? She's not a stranger to racism, she was brought up in Eltham, a south London borough that has its share of such problems. She had already left home by 1993 when a black student called Stephen Lawrence was killed by a gang of white thugs, but she remembers many smaller incidents, taunts in the playground, graffiti on walls, a general sense of anger, bitterness and frustration. She's seen racism in Norfolk too, mainly directed towards Eastern European incomers, but somehow she never thought it would happen at Pendle and certainly never to Dan.

'Anyway,' Nelson is saying, 'Sandy's going to do some investigating. I'll let you know how he gets on.'

'Thanks,' says Ruth. 'How's your holiday?'

Nelson grunts. 'OK. My mum and sisters are driving me mad.'

'Happy families.'

He gives a short laugh, then says. 'Funny thing, Ruth. I was at Lytham today and I thought I saw Cathbad.'

'Cathbad?' echoes Ruth rather wildly.

'Yeah. Cathbad pushing a pushchair. Crazy, eh?'

Clayton Henry turns out to live in a converted windmill just outside Kirkham, another picturesque town on the Roman road to Ribchester. Ruth, expecting a few charred sausages washed down with warm wine, is amazed to see a marquee, a bouncy castle and what looks like liveried staff carrying trays of champagne glasses.

'Bloody hell,' says Cathbad, as they park behind two Porsches and an Alfa Romeo. 'Is it a wedding?'

'He said barbeque,' says Ruth, getting Kate out of her car seat. Kate looks up at the pink castle swelling out of the side of the windmill.

'Balloon,' she says, in wonder.

Ruth feels rather embarrassed, turning up with Kate and Cathbad in tow. She doesn't know quite why she accepted Clayton's invitation in the first place. For years, her instinct has been to start inventing excuses at the first mention of the word 'party'. What an earth has made her become sociable in her old age? Partly it's curiosity. She wants to meet Dan's colleagues. Up until now she has been unable to imagine her glamorous friend in the grim surroundings of the cigarette factory or even digging outside the city walls in Ribchester. Maybe the party will shed some light on Dan's decision to abandon the dreaming spires for a shabby ex-polytechnic. And Cathbad had been keen to come. Unlike Ruth, he enjoys a party and she feels that he deserves some fun. He has been sweet to her over the last few days, looking after Kate, cooking for them all, asking interested questions about the finds at Ribchester. But it makes her sad to see him so muted and domesticated. He has even stopped wearing his cloak. Maybe a party will awaken the old, eccentric, libation-loving Cathbad.

All the same, as they walk towards the windmill, she wishes they didn't look so much like a *couple*. But Kate insists on holding one of Ruth's hands and one of Cathbad's so that they approach the house as a unit – man, woman and child. It's like an advertisement for a company strong on family values but weak on style. And that's another thing; she's wearing the wrong clothes. Cotton trousers and loose top are OK for a family get-together but all wrong for a party with waiters. As they walk through a rose-strewn archway into the garden all Ruth can see are women in flowery dresses. Although it's a cool summer's day, there seems to be an abundance of flesh on show – spaghetti straps, Lycra minis, strapless midi dresses. She sees men in striped blazers, women in hats. No one else is wearing beige cotton trousers.

'Ruth!' Clayton Henry comes towards them, resplendent in a Hawaiian shirt and white trousers.

'Hi.' Ruth has brought a bottle, which seems wrong now. She pushes it into Henry's hands nonetheless.

'How kind.' He looks around for somewhere to put it.

'This is Cathbad,' says Ruth, 'my friend. And Kate, my daughter.'

'Pleased to meet you.' Cathbad and Henry exchange a hearty handshake though Ruth thinks there is something watchful about both men, as if they're summing each other up.

'Cathbad, did you say?'

'Yes,' says Cathbad modestly. 'It's a druidical name.'

'How fascinating,' says Henry and looks as if he's going to say more, but at that moment a glamorous woman with long blonde hair floats out of the house.

'Darling, have you seen the . . .' She stops.

'Pippa,' says Henry, with apparent delight. 'Do come and meet Ruth and Cathbad and their little girl. This is Pippa, my wife.'

If Clayton Henry is making assumptions about Ruth, Ruth realises that she has been guilty of the same crime. Without thinking much about it she had assumed that Henry, with his soft voice and pointed shoes, must be gay. She could just about imagine him married to some plump Bohemian type but not this willowy beauty with model-girl hair and the kind of shoes that make Ruth nervous. Apart from anything else, Pippa Henry is at least four inches taller than her husband.

She seems very friendly though, kissing Ruth on the cheek and bending down to talk to Kate.

'Would you like to go on the bouncy castle, sweetheart?'

Kate, perhaps, like her mother, intimidated by glamour, hides behind Ruth. A white fluffy dog appears from nowhere and starts barking furiously. Pippa Henry scoops it into her arms.

'What a lovely poodle,' says Ruth, drawing Kate away.

'Actually it's a bichon frisé.'

Of course it is.

In the end Ruth takes Kate onto the bouncy castle. This is the great thing about having a child, she thinks, grabbing a glass en route. You can escape to play with them and no one thinks you're unsociable, they just think you're a great mother. Ruth watches Kate bouncing on the Barbie castle, sips champagne and thinks that she wouldn't mind if she spent the entire afternoon like this. Across the lawn, she can see Cathbad chatting animatedly with Pippa. He has always been susceptible to pretty women. She hopes Pippa will take his mind off Judy for a bit. Still, she'd better corner him before long and establish who's driving home. God, they really are getting like a married couple.

'Ruth?' says a voice in her ear.

She swings round to see a pleasant-faced man of about her own age, with thinning sandy hair and a hesitant smile.

'I hope you don't mind me introducing myself but Professor Henry said that you were a friend of Dan's.'

'Yes, I was,' says Ruth, thinking that the past tense is both sad and appropriate. She was a friend of Dan's in the past, when they were both young.

'I'm Sam,' says the man, extending a hand. 'Sam Elliot. I was a friend of his too. I just can't believe that he's gone.'

'Nor can I,' says Ruth. 'I hadn't seen him for ages but even so . . .' Her voice dies away. Suddenly, surprisingly, she feels close to tears and has to cover up by checking on Kate, who is sitting on the very edge of the pink castle, rocking to and fro while the other children caper around her.

When she turns back, Sam Elliot is also looking sombre but he smiles when he sees her looking at him. His face isn't made for sadness, all the lines go upwards. Ruth can easily imagine him being friends with Dan.

'This is quite a party,' she says.

'Yes,' says Sam. 'It's a yearly event, Clayton's barbeque. He always has a big do at Christmas as well.'

Ruth tries to imagine Dan at one of Clayton Henry's parties, playing the piano, drinking champagne, flirting with the prettiest women. She remembers him as something of a party animal and says as much to Sam.

'Funny,' he says. 'I think of Dan as rather quiet. Always friendly but a bit aloof until you got to know him. Were you at university with him?'

'Yes, at UCL.'

'I was at Leeds,' says Sam. 'It seems a hundred years ago now. Mind you, a hundred years is nothing to an archaeologist, is it?'

'Are you an archaeologist?'

Sam shakes his head. 'I teach modern history. I was one of Dan's colleagues. As Clayton may have told you, we cover everything from Boadicea to Adolf Hitler.'

'I'm a teacher too,' says Ruth. 'I teach forensic archaeology at North Norfolk.'

'I know,' says Sam. 'Clayton said you'd come to look at Dan's discovery.'

'Oh, do you know about that?' asks Ruth, surprised. From Clayton's manner, she had assumed that the whole thing was a deadly secret although, come to think of it, Dan could never have managed an excavation that size without some help.

Sam's reply confirms this. 'I was on the first dig with Dan,' he says. 'We were all volunteers then. Later he got a grant and was able to get the professionals in. It was really exciting though, when we first realised that there was something important buried there.'

Ruth knows this excitement well. She remembers when they had first discovered the wooden henge on the beach in Norfolk. The incredible feeling of something rising from the ground, something that had been hidden from sight for thousands of years, the sense of looking at the world through ancient eyes. All the same, she wonders exactly how much Sam knows.

'Did he tell you about the bones?' she asks.

'Bones?' says Sam. 'Oh, they found a tomb, didn't they? That was later. When I was digging Dan was just happy to have found the temple. The Temple of the Raven God. He was going to write a book about it.'

So Sam didn't know about King Arthur. For reasons of his own, Dan had kept that quiet. But he had still been excited enough to think about writing a book. Did he start the book and, if so, where is it now? On the missing laptop, she supposes.

'The Temple of the Raven God?' says a mocking voice. 'What nonsense are you talking now, Sammy?'

A man and a woman are walking towards them. They look like something out of *Brideshead Revisited*, the man in white trousers and shirt, the woman in a short, rose-patterned dress that makes Ruth feel about a hundred stone.

'Hi, Elaine,' says Sam without enthusiasm. 'Hello, Guy.'

'Aren't you going to introduce us?' says Elaine. Close up, she isn't so gorgeous. Her hair is dyed blonde and her eyes are too close together.

'This is Ruth Galloway from the University of North Norfolk.'

'Oh,' says Elaine, eyes widening. 'The famous archaeology expert.'

Ruth registers the mockery but elects to take this at face value.

'That's right,' she says.

'You've come to look at the bones,' says Guy. His voice is an elaborate upper-class drawl, with traces of Lancashire still clinging to the vowels. Ruth wonders if he was really christened Guy.

'I didn't know there were any bones,' says Sam.

'Sammy doesn't know anything about real history,' says Elaine to Ruth, 'he only knows about the Second World War and the rise of communism in China. Stuff like that.'

Sam laughs but Ruth thinks he looks rather hurt.

'It's a really important discovery,' says Guy. Something in his tone makes Clayton Henry, who is a few feet away, look over towards them. Ruth thinks that he is going to intervene, but at that moment Kate causes a distraction by falling off the bouncy castle and bursting into noisy tears.

Elaine and Guy are post-graduate students. Clayton explains this as they eat lunch in the marquee. There are tables inside too but Ruth elected for the outdoors in case Kate starts one of her food-throwing fits. At the moment, though, she is being angelic, eating potato salad and actually using her spoon. She looks like Little Miss Muffet.

'We don't get many graduate students these days, I'm afraid,' says Clayton, throwing a piece of chicken skin to the drooling bichon frisé. 'Young people just aren't interested in history because there's no money in it. But Guy is very able. He's ex-Oxbridge actually. Could have had his pick of post-grad places but he chose us. Never really knew why.' He laughs heartily.

'What about Elaine?'

Clayton must have detected something in her tone because he looks up, the shrewdness of his expression not completely undermined by the blob of coronation chicken on his chin.

'You mustn't take Elaine the wrong way. She's got an odd manner but she's a dear girl underneath, a real sweetie.'

Ruth thinks she will reserve judgement on this but nothing in the prancing figure she can see laughing uproariously in the garden, surrounded by admiring men, makes her think 'sweetie' exactly.

'They were talking about Dan's dig,' she says. 'The Temple of the Raven God.'

'Guy was very involved with the investigations. They both were.'

'What about Sam?'

'Sam Elliot? No, he's a modern history man. He was great friends with Dan though. Devastated at his death. Well, we all were.'

Anything less devastated than the laughing, champagne-swilling crowd in the marquee would be hard to imagine. Still, Ruth supposes that they were upset at the time.

She takes another mouthful of salmon. The food is really delicious, though this hasn't stopped Kate picking all the spring onions out of the salad and putting them on Ruth's plate. Now Kate is feeding cocktail sausages to the dog.

'Don't,' says Ruth. 'It might make him sick.'

'It won't,' says Clayton. 'He eats what he likes. Spoilt little beggar.'

'What's his name?'

'Willoughby. Don't blame me. It was Pippa's idea.'

'It's a great name,' says Ruth. 'We met a dog called Thing the other day.'

'Thing,' repeats Kate, patting Willoughby on his curly top-knot.

'How old is she?' asks Clayton.

'Nearly two,' says Ruth. 'Do you have children?'

'Sadly not,' says Clayton, looking anything but sad. 'I've got a stepdaughter, though, Chloe. She's away at uni at the moment but I'm a doting dad, I promise you.'

So Pippa was married before. Ruth tries, and fails, to imagine the path that led her to Clayton Henry. She also wonders what happened to Chloe's father if Clayton can refer to himself as 'Dad'. Maybe he died and Clayton provided a shoulder to cry on. It's hard to imagine any other circumstances in which the affable, but distinctly rotund, Clayton would end up with the beautiful Pippa. Still, there's no doubt that they look happy together and the house is fantastic (she's had the tour). Cathbad had been delighted to discover that it was built on the site of an old plague pit. He's probably off somewhere now, communing with the unquiet spirits. She hasn't seen him for ages.

'Must be hard,' says Clayton. 'Combining motherhood with work. How do you and Cathbad manage?'

She really must get this straight. 'We're not together,' she says. 'We're just friends. Cathbad isn't Kate's father.'

'Oh ...' Clayton looks intrigued, his eyes bright, but Ruth has no intention of saying any more.

'I'm looking forward to seeing the bones on Monday,' she says.

Clayton shudders. 'You forensics girls are always so bloodthirsty.'

Ruth is annoyed at being called a girl. 'I hardly think there'll be any blood,' she says coldly.

'No. Just a pile of dry bones,' says Clayton. 'But you can tell everything from bones these days, can't you?'

'I wouldn't say that,' says Ruth cautiously. 'Accuracy of tests vary. Carbon 14 tests can be out by as much as hundreds of years. They can be affected by sun spots, solar flares, nuclear testing – things like that. Isotopic analysis should be able to tell us where the individual was born, judging by the chemicals present in the bones.'

'And how accurate is that?'

'Usually pretty accurate. Analysis of calcified tissue gives a good indication of the palaeodiet.'

'Paleo what?'

'What the individual ate,' explains Ruth, adding a cheese roulade to her palaeodiet. 'By using oxygen isotope analysis we can get information on diet which can then point to the region where this man or woman originated and perhaps where they spent their last years.'

'Why do you say "or woman"? Dan was pretty sure it was a man.'

'I'm sure he was,' says Ruth. 'It's just . . . I was caught out that way myself once.'

Clayton laughs. 'Be a great thing if King Arthur turned out to be a woman. It'd make the papers all over the world. The feminists would love us. I'd be rich.' He corrects himself. 'The university would be rich.'

Ruth thinks that he sounds rather bitter. She remembers what he said about the department being unpopular, about not being able to attract students. She says, rather diffidently, 'You said the department wasn't very profitable.'

'My dear girl,' says Clayton. 'We're in desperate straits. Absolutely stony broke. But a big find could change everything. The publicity would mean everything to us. And I'm not going to keep this quiet, whatever anyone says.'

He looks quite steely as he says this and, for the first time, Ruth sees the head of department as someone to be reckoned with.

'Who wants it kept quiet?' she asks.

'Oh, no one important.' The breezy host is back. Clayton leans back in his chair and gestures to a waiter, who immediately fills his glass before turning to Ruth. 'No thanks,' she says hastily. As Cathbad has disappeared, she assumes that she's doing the driving. Clayton raises his brimming glass to her.

'We're counting on you, Ruth,' he says, jovially. 'If you confirm that the bones are ... who we hope they are ... then I'm saved. We're all saved. You really do hold the future of the department in your hands.'

After lunch, Clayton makes a little speech, full of in-jokes and many references to the Dean (Gail Shires) who isn't present. Ruth gathers that Ms Shires is not a fan of the history department, also that the feeling is reciprocated. She is starting to feel tired and wishes they could go home. She has switched to orange juice as the last time she saw Cathbad he was in the conservatory with Pippa and several other gilt-edged women, holding forth on exorcism, glass brimming. Despite herself, she feels rather resentful. She wanted Cathbad to enjoy himself but not to become a fully fledged member of Clayton's beautiful people. He might really be her husband, the way he's taking her for granted.

Grumpily she takes Kate back to the bouncy castle and watches her falling about. The motion of the giant pink mushroom is starting to make Ruth feel slightly sick.

'Look, Mum!'

'I am looking.'

'Hello. Ruth, isn't it?'

Ruth swings round and finds herself facing the Brideshead man, Guy Whatsit. Like Elaine, he isn't as glamorous close up. Although the day isn't exactly torrid, he is sweating heavily and his white shirt is sticking to his back.

'We didn't get a chance to chat earlier,' he says, smiling charmingly. Only because your girlfriend seemed hell-bent on insulting me, thinks Ruth. She doesn't smile back.

'I was a great friend of Dan's,' says Guy, wiping his brow with one of Clayton's linen napkins.

Another one, thinks Ruth. She must remember to ask Caz if any of these so-called friends were at his funeral.

'I worked very closely with Dan on the Ribchester dig,' says Guy. 'It was really a joint project.'

The hell it was, thinks Ruth. She remembers Dan's words in his letter. *I've made a discovery*. No mention of anyone else. Ruth is as sure as if she had been present at the excavation that this find was Dan's alone, his personal discovery.

'So,' Guy is saying, 'if you find anything, anything interesting, and want to discuss it with someone . . .'

I'll ring Max, Ruth vows silently. Aloud, she says, 'Clayton tells me you're a graduate student.'

'Yes,' Guy stiffens slightly, recognising the challenge in her words. 'But Dan treated me as an equal, we were always bouncing ideas off each other.'

Before Ruth can answer, Kate does her own bouncing, falling heavily on her face. She bursts into tears. Ruth gathers her up. 'She's tired,' she says, over Kate's head. 'I'd better take her home. Have you seen Cathbad anywhere? My . . . er . . . friend?'

'He must be inside,' says Guy. 'I'll come with you.'

This is the last thing Ruth wants but she can hardly protest. Carrying a still sobbing Kate, she allows Guy to shepherd her through the French windows.

In the conservatory, she finds Cathbad attempting to find ley lines using a barbeque fork as a dowsing stick and Elaine in floods of tears, weeping on the shoulder of a very embarrassed Sam Elliot.

*

Cathbad and Kate sleep all the way home. Ruth winds her way through the unfamiliar roads accompanied only by gentle snoring. That's the last time she's going to a party with Cathbad.

The barbeque had not been without its compensations though. She has, at least, met some friends of Dan's. But were they really his friends? She can imagine Dan getting on with Sam but is not so sure about Guy, with his cricket flannels and claims of joint projects. But then again, how well did she really know Dan? She hadn't seen him for twenty years. People can change a lot in that time; she knows she has. Maybe Dan was best friends with Guy and spent many a happy evening bouncing ideas around with him. She just knows that if the bones yield any great surprises Guy won't be the first person she rings. And what about Elaine (such a sweetie), where does she fit in? And why was she crying at the end of the party? Is she Guy's girlfriend or Sam's? Oh well, the tangled love lives in the history department are nothing to do with her, thank God.

And why are the bones being held at a private forensics laboratory? Clayton gave her the address as she left. Why weren't the bones kept at Pendle? Clayton mentioned a strong-room, and surely with all those science departments there must be a few laboratories going spare? She knows that the police are using private forensics firms more and more but surely this isn't a police case? These bones are hundreds of years old, there's no need for an inquest. She wonders again who it was that wanted the investigation kept quiet.

Back at Lytham, Cathbad goes straight to bed. Kate, though, is awake and inclined to be grouchy. Ruth decides to take her for a walk to the windmill. It's seven o'clock but a mild evening and at this rate Kate won't be asleep for hours.

Their progress, without the pushchair, is painfully slow, but when they reach the promenade, Kate cheers up and runs towards the windmill. It looks very different from Clayton Henry's carefully restored home, thinks Ruth, following more slowly. This windmill, although obviously scenic, is still workmanlike, standing sturdily on its patch of grass, looking out to sea, its black sails intact. Clayton's home had been a wonder of glass and exposed wood, old and new artfully combined, with a minstrel's gallery and an observatory at the top, where the sails had been. How could a professor in a failing department afford a home like that? Ruth wishes there was someone she could ask. Not for the first time, she imagines chatting to Dan about his colleagues, forgetting that if Dan were here she wouldn't be.

Her phone bleeps. Probably Cathbad, wondering where they are. Kate runs up to her and Ruth hoists her onto her hip, clicking on Messages with her free hand.

But it's not Cathbad. It's her mystery friend again.

'If u know what's good for you,' runs the text, 'stay away from the bones.'

Ruth stands still for so long that Kate becomes bored and scrambles down. Is this message from someone who was at the party? Someone who, only a few hours ago, she was chatting to by the bouncy castle? How many people know that she's going to see the bones on Monday? What *is* the mystery about Dan's discovery? Something or someone is responsible for Dan's fears, Clayton's bluster, maybe even Elaine's tears. But what or who? She knows she should ring Nelson. Someone is threatening her and, by implication, Kate. But she shrinks from Nelson knowing that she has followed him to Lancashire. The texter is probably just a nutcase. None of the preening figures at the barbeque struck her as dangerous exactly. Nevertheless, she shivers in the mild evening air and, gathering up her daughter, walks home without looking back.

CHAPTER 13

Sunday in Lytham has a beguiling, Fifties feel to it. Cathbad, Ruth and Kate stroll in the park, eating ice creams and watching the world go by. Pensioners are playing bowls and children are shrieking from the swings. They walk past brilliantly clashing flowerbeds and a curious metal fountain in the shape of a man holding what looks like a rake.

'Funny, isn't it,' Cathbad says. 'Sunday has a different atmosphere from other days, even if you don't go to church.'

'I know what you mean,' says Ruth. She has noticed this herself, even in her house where the only sign of the Lord's Day is the omnibus edition of *The Archers*. She thinks of her parents, who will often spend all of Sunday in church. It seemed a joyless thing to her when she was growing up, but lately, she has been thinking more charitably about her parents' faith. It keeps them off the streets at any rate.

'Did you go to church as a child?' she asks Cathbad as they stop at a cafe overlooking the bowling green. Cathbad orders tea for himself and Ruth. He still looks slightly delicate after yesterday. Ruth wipes Kate's face and hands. She even has ice cream on her neck.

'Of course I did,' he says. 'I was brought up in Ireland and we all went to Mass every Sunday.'

'I'd forgotten you were Irish,' says Ruth. The tea comes in a proper pot with thick china cups.

'I'm Celtic through and through,' says Cathbad. After a pause he says, 'She was a great character, my mammy. I wish you could have met her. I thought of her when Pendragon was telling us about Dame Alice.'

'Why?' asks Ruth, surprised. Kate, who loves the word, repeats 'Pendragon' in a whisper.

Cathbad grins. 'In olden days Mam would have been called a witch. Oh, she was a good Catholic but she thought you could mix praying to the Virgin with making spells and no harm done. Everyone knew if you had a problem Bridget Malone was the person you went to.'

'Is she still alive?' asks Ruth. It's funny but she has never thought of asking Cathbad about his family. She has never really thought of him as having a family.

'No.' Cathbad looks away, towards the white-coated figures on the green. 'She died when I was sixteen.'

'What about your dad?'

'I never knew him. Mam never talked about him. Of course, that was a real scandal in our village, Bridget Malone having a baby with no man in sight. But she toughed it out, never said a word about it, just went about her business as usual. My gran was a big support to her, I know. She was another amazing woman. I lived with her after Mam died – before I went away to college.'

No wonder you like the company of women, thinks Ruth. She knew that Cathbad did a chemistry degree (presumably in Ireland) and then went on to study archaeology at Manchester under Erik. At some point he acquired a daughter. Beyond that, he is a blank. Almost as if he is the semi-mystical figure he pretends to be.

'All kinds of families work, don't they?' she says now, very much wanting to believe it. 'Not just the traditional kind.'

'They sure do,' says Cathbad. 'Look at us. Mother, child and passing warlock, having a whale of a time. Why don't we go into Blackpool this afternoon?'

Nelson's mother, like Cathbad's before her, is at Mass. She always enjoys sung Mass on a Sunday although her enjoyment is usually expressed in running criticism of the choir, the flowers and, most of all, the priest. Father David, a nervous and sincere young man, is a convert and so, to Maureen, deeply suspect. 'Not a cradle Catholic,' she told Michelle in a piercing whisper before the service started. 'Not really one of us.' In Maureen's mind Father David compares very badly to his predecessor Father Damian, of whom Maureen always talks as if he's gone to his blessed reward. He is, in fact, drying out in a clinic in Ireland.

Today, though, Maureen's enjoyment is marred, not only by Father David's suspiciously Protestant sermon, but by the fact that she doesn't have her son at her side. It's a rare treat for her, showing off her son and his decorative wife to her fellow worshippers. But today Nelson has refused to play ball. He has a complicated relationship with his baptismal faith. On one hand he has an almost fearful dread that it's all true, on the other he loathes the whole flower-arranging, Cafod-collecting apparatus of his mother's church. His refusal to attend had quickly escalated into a row, ending with Maureen storming off with Michelle in tow, warning Nelson that he would soon burn in hell. 'I'll see you there,' Nelson had growled.

Harry has been strange this holiday, thinks Maureen as she bows her head piously at the elevation of the Host. Every homecoming is always marked by a series of pyrotechnic rows. Maureen quite looks forward to them, to be honest. Harry has always been short-tempered but his mother and sisters are more than a match for him. This time, though, he seems different. Quieter, sadder. A couple of times Maureen has caught him on his own, staring out of the window. Even as a child Harry was never one for sitting and staring; he always liked to be doing things, playing football, going out on his bike with his friends, driving his mother demented. Of course he has been sick. Maureen remembers that awful journey to Norfolk last November, how she had prayed all the way for Harry to survive that terrifying mystery illness, the bargains she had made with God, cheerfully offering to die in his place. She had meant it too. In fact, when Harry had miraculously pulled through, she had half expected to be taken up to heaven on the spot. And does he seem grateful for this devotion? No. He skulks around with a face like thunder, disappearing off to see his old police friends, refusing to accompany his mother to Holy Mass. He doesn't deserve to have such a mother and such a wife. He really doesn't.

Now Maureen prays angrily for her favourite child. Please, God, let him see the error of his arrogant ways. Keep him safe, Lord, and let him realise his many blessings. At the sign of peace she holds Michelle's hand tightly. Though she doesn't know why, she suddenly feels very protective towards her daughter-in-law.

'Peace be with you, my darling,' she says huskily.

'Thank you,' says Michelle, who can never remember what she's meant to say in return.

The beach is beautiful. The tide is out and the sand stretches for miles beyond the piers, the sea only a blue haze in the distance. Kate falls in love with the donkeys and clamours to go on one. This is a relief as, when they parked the car, she had seen a poster with Dora the Explorer on it and has been demanding Dora every since. The poster is advertising the Pleasure Beach, where there is apparently something called 'Nickelodeon World' starring giant cartoon characters, as well as a selection of truly terrifying rides. The biggest of these, a roller-coaster called the Big One, dominates the Blackpool skyline. It is higher than the seagulls, a nightmare railway track in the sky, swooping downwards in an almost vertical death plunge. Never, Ruth vows, never will I go on that thing. Cathbad thinks it looks great.

But the donkeys are lovely. Kate's is called Jolly Roger. Ruth pats him, marvelling at his soft coat – more like fur than hair. Roger flicks his ears to and fro and looks irritated. He is black with a grey muzzle and his harness is yellow. Other children are lifted onto Roger's companions and the cavalcade prepares to set off.

'Hold on, love,' says the Donkey Man and Kate holds on, looking delighted and not at all scared. For the hundredth time, Ruth wishes that she had remembered her camera. She should take a picture with her phone. She fumbles in her bag.

'Ruth,' says Cathbad.

'What?' Damn, why can she never find anything in her organiser handbag?

'Isn't that Nelson coming towards us?'

Ruth looks up and, sure enough, advancing over the sand is an all-too-familiar figure. Nelson in jeans and a blue shirt, accompanied by Michelle, two other women and a baby in a pushchair.

Ruth is paralysed. Should she call out to him? Hope that he won't see her? Oh why didn't she tell him that she was coming to Blackpool?

Cathbad, though, has no such qualms.

'Nelson!' he shouts. 'Over here!'

Nelson looks across, says something to Michelle and takes a few steps towards them. But Cathbad has already bounded over and is shaking Nelson's hand enthusiastically. There is nothing for Ruth to do but follow, keeping an anxious eye on Kate and her donkey.

'Cathbad,' Nelson is saying. 'What the bloody hell are you doing in Blackpool?'

'Language, Harry,' says one of the women, a formidable matron in blue who looks vaguely familiar.

'Harry,' says Michelle. 'It's Ruth.'

'Hi, Nelson,' says Ruth. 'Hi, Michelle.'

Nelson just stares at her, a muscle is working in his cheek and he looks furious.

'Where's Kate?' asks Michelle.

'On a donkey.'

'Oh, the kiddies love the donkeys,' says the woman in blue. Then, as no one else seems about to do it, she introduces herself. 'I'm Maureen, Harry's mother, and this is Maeve, my oldest, and her granddaughter Charlie, though why she's got a boy's name I'll never know. She's such a pretty little thing.'

Nelson's sister. Ruth can see the resemblance. Maeve is tall with black wavy hair liberally streaked with grey. She has Nelson's heavy eyebrows and his fierce expression. And she's a grandmother! Ruth never imagined that Nelson's sisters would be so much older than he.

'Charlie can be a girl's name now,' she is saying, rather impatiently. 'Pleased to meet you, Ruth.'

'I've seen you before, haven't I?' says Maureen. 'At the hospital.'

That's why she looks familiar. Ruth briefly met Nelson's mother on the morning after the night when they thought that Nelson was dying. Ruth glances at Michelle and is sure that she is remembering the same thing.

'Ruth works with me,' Nelson says shortly. 'She's an archaeologist.'

'That must be interesting work,' says Maureen. 'I never miss *Time Team*, do I, Maeve?'

'They did a programme near here,' says Ruth. 'At Ribchester.'

'I saw it,' says Maureen, sounding delighted. 'Is that why you're here?'

'Sort of,' says Ruth, feeling uncomfortable. The donkeys have reached the pier and are turning back. In a few minutes, though she won't know it, Maureen will be face to face with another grandchild.

'Is this because of Dan Golding?' Nelson asks Ruth. He still looks angry. Ruth sees Michelle touching his arm as if to placate him.

'Yes,' says Ruth. 'Pendle University asked me to look at a discovery he made before he died.'

'Why didn't you tell me?'

'I don't know.'

Maeve looks curiously from one to the other. Luckily Maureen is chatting to Cathbad. 'Kilfinane!' Ruth hears Maureen exclaiming, 'but that's next door to me, so it is.'

The donkeys approach. Despite everything, Ruth's heart contracts with love when she sees Kate's radiant face, beaming from ear to ear as she wobbles on Roger's back. The Donkey Man puts up a hand to steady her. Ruth waves; she knows that Nelson is looking too.

'Mum!' shouts Kate. 'Mum! Mum!'

'Oh bless her heart,' says Maureen. 'Is that your little girl?'

'Yes,' whispers Ruth.

But Kate has seen Nelson. 'Dada!' she yells in delight. 'Dada!'

'Do you think she suspected?' asks Ruth.

'No,' says Cathbad reassuringly. 'Kate calls everyone Dada. She said it to the Donkey Man, didn't she?'

They are on their way back to Lytham. Ruth is driving; Kate is in the back, humming a tune from Dora, lost in a dream of donkeys. They pass the Pleasure Beach, the Big One looming above them, posters advertising the many different ways in which humans can be flung into the air, rotated or just plain terrified. One of the rides is in the form of a vast raven, its black wings outstretched: a slide spews out from its open beak into a continual, churning waterfall. Its name is spelt out in lights, 'Raven Falls'. Ruth thinks of the Raven King, of the two deities that seem to rule in Lancashire. The Raven King in his lonely grave on the way to the sea and the Demon King of pantomime that presides over Blackpool. Glittering lights, garish costumes, bread and circuses.

Ruth stops at the lights next to a gypsy caravan offering 'Genuine Romany Fortune Telling'. Perhaps she should make an appointment. 'But Nelson's face,' she says. 'I would have suspected if I'd been Maureen.'

This is a new departure for Ruth and Cathbad. Although Ruth knows that Cathbad knows about Kate's parentage, this is the first time that they have discussed it openly. Ruth usually tries to ignore the whole fatherhood issue but she is so shaken by the afternoon's encounter that she just has to talk to someone.

'Maureen was too busy chatting to me,' grins Cathbad. And it is true that he and Maureen had hit it off immediately. It is largely Cathbad's fault that Maureen has invited them to tea in three days' time, 'so we can talk some more about the old country.' Ruth, remembering Nelson's face as his mother issued the invitation, wonders if she'll live that long.

They hadn't stayed too long on the beach. Maeve was meeting Danielle at the south pier and didn't want to be late. The two parties had separated with shouts of 'See you on Wednesday' (Cathbad and Maureen), embarrassed waves (Ruth and Michelle), yells of 'Dada' (Kate) and complete silence (Nelson).

'She won't guess,' says Cathbad, twisting round to smile at Kate. 'She won't guess because it's so unlikely.'

Is it unlikely, wonders Ruth. She supposes it is. Unlikely that a man who is married to Michelle would ever look at an overweight, forty-something academic like her. Unlikely that the man who looked at her with outright hostility could ever have ... But she won't think about that. She'll file it away along with Max and the baby question. Things she will deal with when she feels strong enough. For now she concentrates on driving. They pass fairy lights, trams, a giant glitter ball.

'Nelson looked furious, though, didn't he?' says Cathbad.

Ruth doesn't answer. She stops at a red light and a horse-drawn carriage draws alongside. There are hundreds of the things, bowling up and down the Golden Mile, skinny horses pulling fat tourists. This one is pink and glittery, shaped like a pumpkin.

'Cinderella,' breathes Kate.

Nelson, Michelle and Maureen are also on their way home. Maeve has gone back to Danielle's house. Although the beach is within walking distance Maureen has decreed that they bring the car. Nelson agreed, partly to make up for refusing to go to Mass that morning. Now, as his mother embarks on a voluble critique of his driving, he's beginning to regret this peace-making gesture. His patience with Maureen is wearing very thin. Thank God they're going to Michelle's mum's place next week.

In fact, Nelson, for him, is driving rather tamely. In Norfolk, he scorches round corners on two wheels and acts, in general, as if he is involved in a Seventies TV police series car chase. Now he contents himself with revving up furiously at the lights and stopping at the last possible minute. Maureen is exaggerating the effects of this, throwing out a hand as if to save herself, other hand clutching her throat.

'For pity's sake, Harry,' she says, 'take some care.'

'It's the idiot in front,' says Nelson.

'You were too close,' says Maureen who, despite not having a licence, considers herself an expert on driving. 'Does he always drive like this, Michelle? You should make him take a refresher course.'

Michelle, wisely, says nothing. She knows, from the angle of his neck, that Harry is in a real rage. She tries not to think exactly why this is.

'Well, she was a nice girl, wasn't she,' says Maureen, turning round to Michelle. 'That Ruth whatshername. Quite a pretty face. Shame she's a bit on the plump side.' Maureen, who hasn't seen her feet for decades, disapproves of women 'letting themselves go'.

'She is nice,' says Michelle tonelessly. Nelson grinds the gears furiously.

'And a lovely babby. Kate. Now that's a proper girl's name. Not like Charlie. And I did like her boyfriend. What's was his name? Cuthbert?'

'Cathbad,' says Michelle.

'And he's from Limerick, did you hear? Kilfinane. That's in the Ballyhoura mountains. Where I was brought up.'

Nelson, who has never thought of Cathbad as being from anywhere, says nothing. Why the hell is Ruth in Lancashire? And why didn't she tell him when he spoke to her yesterday? It must have been Cathbad he saw in Lytham that day. Cathbad, pushing *his* daughter in her pushchair. Cathbad, posing as Ruth's boyfriend. Maybe he *is* Ruth's boyfriend now? But what happened to that Max bloke? He knows that Ruth still sees him. Maybe she has half a dozen boyfriends in tow. What sort of environment is that for Katie? He takes a corner too fast and narrowly misses a bollard.

Maureen shrieks. 'Are you trying to kill us?'

Nelson slows down at they reach Maureen's house. Nelson's family home. The house where he grew up. A three-bedroomed terrace painted a rather violent pink. For the first time he wonders what his dad – not a man in touch with his feminine side – thought about the pink. It's possible that he just wasn't consulted. The house has been pink as long as Nelson remembers. His dad died twenty-eight years ago, when Nelson was fifteen. Sometimes he finds it quite hard to recall his face, though he can still hear his voice, quiet Lancastrian, far gentler than Maureen's.

Nelson searches for a parking space in the crowded street. When he lived at home hardly anyone had a car, now they seem to have two or three each. Most of the houses have satellite dishes too. He remembers how thrilling it was when they got their first colour set, just in time for Princess Anne's wedding.

Somehow Nelson squeezes the Mercedes into a space vacated by a Fiat Panda. Maureen helpfully tells him which way to turn the wheel.

'It'll be nice having Ruth and Cuthbert to tea, won't

it,' she says, as they approach the house. Michelle agrees that it will.

'You can play with the baby, Harry,' says Maureen. 'You're good with children.'

'I might be out that day,' says Nelson.

CHAPTER 14

The forensics laboratory is in an industrial estate near Blackpool airport. It's a curiously desolate place, a dead end in more ways than one. Ruth drives round and round, trying to find CNN Forensics; all the buildings look the same, square and featureless, and there are very few signposts. Such signs as there are bristle with unfriendly acronyms: DDR Office Furniture, AJM Industrial Fencing, RRB Surgical Appliances. The roads loop round and back again, going nowhere, like a child's railway track. Eventually, more by luck than judgement, Ruth spots Clayton Henry's sports car parked outside a long, low building that looks as if it is made out of corrugated iron. CNN Forensics reads the tiny metal sign, pale grey on white. Clearly they are not expecting passing trade.

Clayton Henry gets out of his car and comes to meet her. Gone is the genial host in his Hawaiian shirt. Today he is soberly dressed in a dark suit and looks distinctly uncomfortable, glancing around the empty car-park as if he is expecting to be tracked by the FBI. Ruth thanks him for the party and he acknowledges this with a weak smile.

'This place is a bit out of the way,' she says, as they approach the (locked) doors.

'Yes but they're very good. The police use them a lot for forensic science services.'

'But why did Dan use them? I mean, this isn't a police case, is it?'

'No.' Clayton fiddles nervously with his phone. 'But we wanted to make sure the bones were safe.'

Safe from what? thinks Ruth. But she doesn't say any more. They press a bell and are admitted.

Inside, the place is spotless; sterile blue and gleaming white. The receptionist, also in antiseptic white, asks them to check in their bags and change into protective clothing.

Clayton is holding what Nelson would probably describe as a handbag, a discreet document case in mulberry leather. He hands it over reluctantly with a quip about it containing explosives. The receptionist smiles coldly. Ruth passes her organiser handbag without comment. If any terrorist finds what he's looking for in under half an hour, he's doing better than she ever does.

'Thank you,' says the receptionist. She hands them two sets of disposable coveralls. 'You can change in there.' She points to a discreet room marked 'Changing'.

'Is it unisex?' asks Clayton.

'Yes.'

Ruth hates coveralls. She thinks they make her look like a barrage balloon. Add a hairnet and you've got instant Ena Sharples. They are given two pairs of gloves each, one long and blue, which pull up over the coat cuffs, the other short and flesh-coloured.

'It's a bit excessive, isn't it?' says Ruth.

Clayton shrugs. In his paper suit he looks oddly like an ageing toddler. 'I suppose they've got a lot of sensitive stuff here. One spot of DNA in the wrong place ...'

'I suppose so.' Ruth doesn't like the idea of all Lancashire's unsolved murders being pinned on her. She pulls the gloves higher and puts on her face mask. Thus attired, they waddle out into the reception area.

A man is waiting for them. He pulls down his mask to say, 'I'm Terry Durkin, forensic analyst. You're from the university?'

'Yes.' Clayton introduces himself and Ruth.

'This way please.'

Afterwards, Ruth's main memory is of swing doors. Door after door, swishing silently as they pass. What was that Bowie song about memory being a swinging door? Dan would have known. The corridors seem endless, blue light and grey carpets. Eventually they reach a row of lifts.

'It's on the third floor.'

Ruth hates lifts. This one judders painfully between floors, making her worry that she and Clayton together have exceeded the weight limit. What a way to go. Too fat for a lift. When they reach the third floor, she practically jumps out onto the landing, leaving Clayton and Terry Durkin to fend for themselves.

Durkin ushers them into a small room where a numbered container sits on a metal table.

'The bones are in there.'

'Who logged them in?'

'I did,' says Durkin. 'I was on duty that day.'

'Who brought them in?'

'It was Guy. Guy Delaware.'

Interesting, thinks Ruth. Does this support Guy's claim to be closely involved on the project or was he just running Dan's errands? 'Do you know what happened to the samples that were taken away for testing?' she asks.

'When were they taken?'

Ruth looks at Clayton. 'At the dig,' he confirms.

'I only know what happens in this building,' intones Durkin. 'Nothing enters or leaves this building without us knowing.'

'We'd better not leave anything behind then,' laughs Clayton.

'Oh, you'll leave something behind,' says Durkin, unsmiling. 'A hair, a trace of sweat, some fibres. We'll have your DNA somewhere, you can be sure of that.'

Once again, it strikes Ruth that this is a very high-tech place to store archaeological finds. She asks Clayton if there was any suggestion that the bones were, in fact, modern.

'No,' says Clayton. 'None at all. After all, they were buried inside a sarcophagus. We could date the tomb fairly accurately.'

'Then why not keep them at the university?'

Clayton looks uncomfortable. He doesn't meet Ruth's eye as he says, 'As I mentioned, there was some bad feeling about the dig.'

'Why?'

'Oh . . .' Clayton seems suddenly completely preoccupied in adjusting his plastic gloves. 'Waste of resources. That sort of thing.'

'Bad feeling towards Dan?' Ruth persists.

Clayton looks up, his plump face shocked. 'No! Dan didn't have an enemy in the world.'

That's not what the police think, though. Ruth remembers her conversation with Nelson. The police think that someone killed Dan. That that someone may well be at Pendle University and may well be the same someone who is sending Ruth texts, warning her to stay away from these very bones. Well – she squares her shoulders as she takes the box from Durkin – she can't be scared that easily. Well she can, but that's not the point. The point is that she's here despite being scared. She starts to lay the bones out on the examination table.

She starts to arrange the skeleton in correct anatomical order, looking for any distinguishing marks – disease, malnutrition, trauma – anything that would help her create a picture of the person who died so many years ago. At first sight the bones look to be those of an adult male, which is a relief, whatever Clayton says. They also look old, which may not mean anything. Recent skeletons are usually fairly obvious but it's often not easy to distinguish between a body that died fifty years ago and one that has lain in the earth for hundreds of years. So many factors can affect the preservation of bones.

Clayton Henry watches her closely but does not attempt to help. After all, this isn't his area of expertise. Durkin also stands respectfully in the background. The room is cold; it is obviously kept at a mortuary-like temperature.

Ruth starts by examining the skull, observing the pronounced nuchal crest which confirms that the skeleton is male. Then she looks at the teeth. Teeth are a forensic archaeologist's best friend. They show signs of age, nutrition and diet. Horizontal ridges can indicate periods of arrested development such as illness or malnutrition. Teeth also carry an indelible record of the time and place when the adult teeth first erupted. Bones renew themselves; teeth do not.

Ruth looks at the upper jaw for a long time, then she picks up the lower jaw, which has become detached. This she examines for so long that Clayton Henry starts to shift from foot to foot.

'Found anything interesting, Ruth?'

Ruth beckons him over. 'See the teeth in the upper jaw? They're really ground down.'

Clayton peers over. 'Yes. Shows our bloke must have been a good age. Or else he was just a worrier.' He laughs heartily.

'But look at the lower jaw.'

'What?'

'The teeth aren't ground down nearly as much.'

'How can that be? Wouldn't they grind against each other?'

'Exactly,' says Ruth.

'What do you mean?'

Ruth puts the two halves of the jaw side by side on the table. 'They don't fit,' she says. 'These are from two different heads.'

'I don't understand,' says Clayton Henry for the umpteenth time. They are sitting in a cafe next to a derelict funfair. It's the nearest place they could find. You couldn't imagine anyone actually choosing the cafe for anything other than convenience. The owner looks as if she lost all hope in about 1953 and the air is fuggy with chip oil and steam. Clayton, in his dark suit, looks as out of place as a food inspector. He looks sadly into his tea, which is grey with a sort of beige scum on top.

Ruth sips her coffee, which oddly also tastes of chips. 'There are two explanations,' she says. 'Either there were parts of two skeletons in the sarcophagus, laid out so as to look like one body, or some of Dan's bones were switched, either at the dig or at the lab.'

Clayton shakes his head. 'Dan would have noticed if there were parts of two different skeletons,' he says. 'I mean, he wasn't a bones expert but he would have noticed the teeth. He looked at the skull for a long time, trying to age the bones. He would have noticed.'

'Yes,' says Ruth. 'He would have.' She thinks of Dan, the star of the UCL archaeology department, and feels suddenly very angry that anyone could have considered playing such an obvious trick on him.

'Let's think about it,' she says. She scrabbles in her organiser handbag for notebook and pencil. Ruth likes lists; it is something she has in common with DCI Harry Nelson. 'Who was at the dig on the day that the bones were excavated? I assume it was done over one day?'

'Yes. Dan was very particular about that. Every bone had to be recorded.'

'Where are those records now?'

Clayton shrugs helplessly. 'I don't know.'

On Dan's laptop, Ruth supposes, along with his notes and the novel. But there may be hard copies somewhere in the department. She resolves to look.

'You're sure he took the samples for testing at the dig?' she asks.

'Yes, I saw him take soil samples and he also put aside some teeth and small bones to be sent off for analysis. He bagged them up and put them in his car, I think.'

So the test samples will actually have be taken from the original skeleton, thinks Ruth.

'What about photographs?' she asks. 'He would have photographed the skeleton when it was fully exposed, before excavation.'

'There were official photos,' says Clayton. 'Taken by the county archaeologist, I think. And Dan took pictures on his phone.'

Bloody Dan, thinks Ruth. Why did he have to be so high tech? She takes photographs on digs with a digital camera but she also always does a sketch in her note-book and takes copious notes. And notebooks, unlike mobile phones, tend not to go missing. She says as much to Clayton.

'Oh, I love technology,' he says unexpectedly. 'I'm a real gadget boy, just got the new iPhone 4.'

Ruth stops him before he can get into one of those iPhone conversations that their owners think are so fascinating. 'So,' she says, getting out her (low tech) notebook. 'Who was there that day?'

Clayton crumples up his face in thought, looking more like a peevish baby than ever. 'Some people from the local archaeology society,' he says. 'I could get their names for you. Susan Chow, the county archaeologist. I was there, and a couple of other people from the department.'

'Who?'

Clayton takes a sip of tea, grimaces and pushes the cup away. 'Guy was there, I think. Yes, Elaine and Guy. They were very interested in the excavation.'

'Did you actually see Dan box up the bones?'

'Yes. We were going to take them to the university but Guy thought . . .'

He stops.

'What?' asks Ruth. 'What did Guy think?'

'He thought they would be safer at the lab so he drove them there himself.'

When Ruth gets back to Lytham, Beach Row is deserted apart from a blonde woman walking her dog. Cathbad is out with Kate. He has left a message saying that they wanted to see the lifeboat museum, for all the world as if Kate has expressed a keen interest in marine rescue. Still, Ruth is grateful that Cathbad is prepared do so much babysitting. What's more, he seems to enjoy it. All in all, living with Cathbad is not as difficult as she feared. Ruth hasn't lived with anyone since Peter. Max's weekends don't really count, though by Sunday Ruth often catches herself looking forward to being on her own again, free to have Flint in bed with her or to watch TV in her pyjamas. But Cathbad is different. He's not a boyfriend so she doesn't really care how he sees her. Also, for someone who claims to be outside the normal rules of human behaviour, he's surprisingly domesticated. He gets up early, goes for a dawn walk and then is back in time to make Ruth a cup of tea and watch breakfast TV with Kate. For the first time since Kate's birth, Ruth is actually able to have a lie-in. And, if instead of dozing peacefully, she lies in bed worrying about Nelson, Max, Dan and mysterious text messages, then that's her own fault, isn't it?

Now Ruth puts some shopping down on the round kitchen table. It's one o'clock and she wonders whether Cathbad and Kate will already have had their lunch. Should she make a salad, just in case? Put on some potatoes to bake? She is trying to take her turn with the cooking but Cathbad is so much better at it than she is. Last night he made a wonderful vegetarian lasagne and, when she opens the fridge, she sees that another delicious dish is already in there, neatly covered in cling-film. Really, Cathbad would make someone a wonderful husband.

As the house is quiet, she decides to do a bit of work. She opens her laptop and clicks on her inbox. She has sent messages to a few labs that she knows, hoping that Dan might have used them for his isotopic analysis. Maybe one of them will have answered. But there are only two new emails: one from Max enclosing a jokey picture of his dog, Claudia, in a hard hat and one from a company called University Pals. Where has she seen that name before? She clicks onto the message. 'Hi Ruth! Your friends from **University College London, Archaeology 89** miss you. Why not get back in touch? Just click on the link below.'

Ruth looks at the email with its cheery message of emotional blackmail. Why does it give her a slightly uneasy feeling? Because she first heard from this company the day after she heard of Dan's death? Because it brings back memories, not only of Dan, but of Caz, Val and Roly, the friends who were once central to her life but have now, somehow, become lost to her? She is going to see Caz tomorrow. Maybe that will help put things in perspective. They can talk about Dan, maybe find a way in which they can resurrect their old friendship or, better still, forge a new one. Ruth bets that Caz would never join a site calling itself 'University Pals'.

She is so deep in the past that when her phone rings she assumes it must be Caz. But it's Max.

'Hi, Ruth. How's it going?'

'Hi, Max.' She starts to relax. Max sounds so cheerful and normal that she's suddenly incredibly grateful to him for not being a shadowy figure from her past or a sinister one from her present. Besides, she wants to tell him about Dan's discovery.

Max is fascinated, as she knew he would be.

'I've never seen a temple dedicated to a raven god but the Romans were good at this, taking a local religious cult and making it their own. It's one of the ways they assimilated. Sometimes they even combined a Roman and a native God, Minerva and Sulis, for example, in Bath. How old is your temple?'

'Dan thought mid to late fifth century.'

'Interesting.' Ruth can hear a genuine note of excitement in his voice. 'The Romans banned ancient religions in 391 AD and Christianity became the established religion. But, of course, by 410 AD they'd left. There must have been plenty of belief in the old religions left. And, of course, the further north you go, the less Roman people were. Up there, you're near the very outposts of the empire. They might have had Roman roads and Roman engineering but they were still natives at heart.'

'What about the inscription? Could it really be King Arthur?'

'Depends who King Arthur was,' says Max, echoing Clayton Henry. 'But certainly some historians think he was a Romano-British figure. Also the raven link could fit. There's a tradition of Britishness about ravens; think of the legend that if the ravens leave the Tower of London, Britain will fall. Your Roman chap could be using the raven as a symbol of British unity against the Picts, the Celts and the Saxons.'

Rex Arthurus, thinks Ruth. *Britannorum Rex*. King Arthur. King of the Britons. Aloud, she says, 'There's a legend that Arthur's spirit left his body in the form of a raven.'

'There you are then. It all fits. Have you seen the bones?'

Ruth explains about the two sets of bones. 'My guess is that the original skeleton is missing and these other bones were put in its place.'

Max whistles. 'But why?' he says. 'Why would anyone want to do that?'

'I don't know,' says Ruth. 'But I do know that someone wants to stop me looking at the bones, Arthur's bones. I don't know why or even who's behind it. There's lots of weird stuff going on at the university.'

'It sounds a bit serious,' says Max. 'Look, I can come up next week if you want. I could take a look at the bones, maybe scare off the bad guys.'

Ruth is silent for a moment, watching two seagulls fight over the crumbs Cathbad put out in the garden that morning. Why doesn't she want Max to come to Lytham? Is it because she still doesn't want to surrender Dan's discovery to his expertise? Is it because he used the words 'bad guys' as if the whole thing is some silly children's game? Or is it just because she doesn't want to see him? Not enough, anyway.

'Let's talk about it nearer the time,' she says at last. 'I'd better go now. I think I can hear Kate and Cathbad coming back.'

CHAPTER 15

Caz lives in St Anne's, the posh part of Lytham where the houses all look as if they are made out of Lego. It's quite a long walk, but since Cathbad has taken the car to visit Pendragon Ruth has no choice but to stride out with Kate in her pushchair. When Cathbad first asked if he could have the car, Ruth had quite fancied the idea of a long, bracing walk, but when Tuesday morning dawned it was a grey blustery day with the promise of rain in the clouds.

'Are you sure you don't mind walking?' asked Cathbad at breakfast. 'What if it rains?'

'It'll be OK,' said Ruth heartily. 'Kate won't shrink, will she?'

She didn't want Cathbad to change his plans. She knew he was worried about Pendragon and, besides, she didn't want to be the sort of pathetic woman who can't walk for half an hour in the rain. Her own mother has never learnt to drive but Ruth remembers, as a child, accompanying her all over London, on buses and trains sometimes, but usually on foot. 'Come on, Ruth,' she'd say.

'Best foot forward.' Ruth used to wonder which was the favoured foot, as her mother never specified, but, it has to be said, in those days both feet worked pretty well.

Now, she checks that the rain cover is on the pushchair and sets out, intrepid in her yellow cagoule. It's not quite the sophisticated image that she wanted to present to Caz but you can't have everything. Cathbad has already driven off in the Renault. 'I'll be back this evening,' he said. 'I'm sure Pendragon is OK really. It's just that he seemed worried, all that business with the gun . . .'

'He's got Thing to protect him,' Ruth pointed out.

'That dog's as soft as they come,' said Cathbad. 'Still, I'm glad Pen's got some company. He's a funny bloke, a bit prone to black moods.'

He's a druid, Ruth wanted to say, of course he's odd. He wears white robes and leaves gifts out for a witch who died four hundred years ago. But she didn't say any of this because, despite being a druid, Cathbad had unblocked the sink that morning. As she trudges along the coast road she thinks about the phrase 'black moods'. Isn't there another phrase, about having a black dog on your shoulder? A black dog sounds a bit like a witch's familiar. She remembers Max once telling her that the Romans sacrificed black animals, particularly dogs, to Hecate, the goddess of witchcraft. Black birds too, she remembers, thinking of the Raven God and the birds' bones found in the temple at Ribchester. Animals and birds are everywhere in language and mythology, something that probably started as soon as the first primitive man and dog decided to team up together. Cats too. As far back as the Egyptians, cats have been found buried with honour. Ruth thinks of her own familiar, her beloved Flint, now being looked after by Bob Woonunga, a man who believes that the world was created by a sacred rainbow snake. Maybe humans need animals to help them understand the world. Certainly it's hard to see what else cats do for humans, aside from looking cute and killing the odd mouse. But then, thinks Ruth, pushing her untidy hair back inside her cagoule hood, looking cute has always had too high a value in society.

As soon as she sees Caz, Ruth realises that she needn't have worried about looking good. She's clearly out of her league. Caz's whole lifestyle oozes sophistication and laid-back style, from the rambling Victorian house to her beautifully cut jeans and crisp white shirt, to the photo-genic offspring seen scattered in photo frames around the house.

'How old are your children?' asks Ruth, hanging her wet cagoule on a curly coat stand (it started raining roughly five minutes into her walk).

'Fifteen, twelve and eight,' says Caz. 'Pete's taken them sailing but they'll be back after lunch. Pete's dying to catch up with you.'

Ruth and Kate follow Caz into a dauntingly perfect kitchen, all islands and French windows and retro chrome. There is even a sofa and a piano, displaying a Grade 5 scales book. Ruth feels sunk into inadequacy. Not only has Caz got a fifteen-year-old child (something chrono-logically possible but, to Ruth, almost miraculous) but she's got children who play Grade 5 piano and go sailing. Sailing! Who on earth does that on a Tuesday morning?

'How is Pete?' she asks. Pete was also at UCL; he studied maths and played rugby. But, even so, he wasn't a bad bloke.

'Fine,' says Caz. 'Going bald, longing for retirement. Aren't we all?'

Ruth doesn't know how to answer that one. She never thinks about retirement, except as a far-off dream involving a lake in Norway. She's only forty-two, and at this rate she'll have to carry on working into her seventies to pay for Kate to go to university. Are there really people who retire in their forties?

Caz gets out a basket of toys for Kate and she plays happily on the floor. Caz crouches down next to her, helping her assemble a wooden rail track. The trains are battered and chipped, obviously much-loved family heirlooms.

'Oh, you are lucky, Ruth,' says Caz. 'Having one this age. I'd give anything to go back.'

Ruth takes this with a pinch of salt, looking round Caz's perfect kitchen. If she had a baby, the house and Caz herself would probably look a bit different. Ruth reckons that those jeans are a size eight.

Caz makes coffee in a professional-looking machine that takes up half her working surface. She gets out carrot cake and animal-shaped biscuits for Kate.

'So, Ruth,' she says, perching on a chrome stool that looks like something from *Happy Days*. 'What are you doing these days? It seems like ages since I saw you.'

Ruth feels uncomfortable. She's always acutely aware of how dull her life sounds to others. 'Oh, not much,' she says, watching Kate enact a high-speed rail crash. 'Still working at the university. The head of department's a bit of a pain but the students are lovely and I get to do a few digs.'

'How do you manage with Kate?' asks Caz. 'Have you got a nanny?'

A nanny? She's speaking a different language again. 'No,' says Ruth, 'but I've got a child-minder. She's very good. Very flexible.'

'What about Kate's father?'' asks Caz. 'Are you still with him?'

'No,' says Ruth. 'We were never really together but he does see Kate.'

'Who was that I spoke to on the phone?' asks Caz. 'He sounded nice.' When Caz rang up to arrange this meeting she had, of course, got Cathbad, who had talked at length about the magical powers of sea air.

'Cathbad. He's just a friend.'

Caz looks at her curiously, head on one side, the sun catching the expensive highlights in her short hair. Is my life as alien to her as hers is to me, wonders Ruth. All the same, it's lovely to see Caz again. Within minutes they are off down memory lane, reminiscing about Dan and university and the day that Roly dressed up as a nun for rag week.

'Dear Roly,' says Caz. 'I haven't seen him for ages, have you?'

'No, just cards at Christmas,' says Ruth. 'He's living in Edinburgh now.'

'Still with Christian?'

'I think so,' says Ruth. 'Do you think Roly knows about Dan?'

'I don't suppose so. Why?'

'Oh, just that Dan mentioned him in the letter he wrote to me. He asked about you, Roly and Val.'

'Well, that was our group at uni, wasn't it? The four of us.'

Ruth thinks about the four of them – sardonic Caz, sweet Roly, easy-going Val, earnest Ruth – how is it possible that they have lost touch like this? But Roly is in Scotland and Caz and Val lost to the land of marriage and motherhood. And Dan, Dan who was always too cool for their group, is lost forever.

'It's so strange that he wrote to you,' says Caz. 'Just before he died.'

'I know,' says Ruth. She doesn't mention her recurring nightmare that Dan is calling for her help, trapped in some nightmare hyperspace between life and death. She thinks of his answerphone message: *I'll get back to you. Promise.* She tries to rid herself of the notion that Dan will, in some way, get back to her.

'It's been odd,' she says. 'Meeting his colleagues. Looking at his archaeology. I keep thinking that I'll be able to discuss it all with him.'

'What was the great discovery?' asks Caz, who is now putting together a gourmet lunch with what looks like superhuman ease. On the floor, Kate slams her trains into each other. She's as bad a driver as her father.

Ruth hesitates. She has told Caz only that the university wanted her to look at a discovery Dan had made. She considers telling Caz the whole story, about King Arthur, the Raven God, the awful suspicion that Dan was murdered. But then she thinks of the text messages, the fear in Clayton Henry's face. It's better for Caz if she doesn't know.

'It was a temple,' she says. 'On the outskirts of Ribchester.'

'There's lots of Roman stuff there,' says Caz. 'I took the kids to the museum once.'

'Yes, it's a well-known site,' says Ruth, 'but this temple's interesting for a few reasons. It's in the Roman style but Dan thought it was built after the Romans withdrew from Britain. And it's dedicated to a god in the form of a raven.'

'An unkindness of ravens,' says Caz.

'What?'

'That's the collective noun for ravens,' says Caz, drizzling oil and shredding basil. 'Like a murder of crows.'

'Jesus,' says Ruth. 'What is it about these birds?'

'I don't like birds,' says Caz. 'I think I saw that Hitchcock film at an impressionable age. I don't like the way they gather on the telegraph lines. It's as if they're waiting for something.'

'I live near a bird sanctuary,' says Ruth. 'They're very

beautiful sometimes.' She thinks about her ex-neighbour, David, who was the warden of the sanctuary. He loved the birds; it was just humans who were the problem.

'How are you getting on with Dan's colleagues?' asks Caz. 'Are they being helpful?'

Ruth thinks about Guy and Elaine at the barbeque, Elaine's antipathy and Guy's bid for ownership. She thinks about Clayton Henry drinking champagne in the rosy hue of the marquee and staring glumly at his tea in the backstreet cafe.

'They're an odd bunch,' she says. 'The head of department only really cares about making money out of Dan's find. One of his colleagues was really nice and genuinely devastated about his death. The others seemed a bit ... I don't know ... I wondered how much they really cared about Dan. I was going to ask – were any of them at his funeral?'

Caz pauses, pine nuts in hand. 'I think so. There was a man and a blonde woman. She seemed very upset. I remember wondering if she was a girlfriend. She didn't come back to the hotel with the rest of us. I wondered if she didn't want to meet Dan's ex-wife.'

Guy and Elaine, thinks Ruth. Or Sam and Elaine. Was Elaine Dan's girlfriend? It's possible, she is glamorous enough in a hard-faced way. That might explain her attitude towards Ruth and her rather brittle behaviour at the party. At any rate, she at least had been sad at the funeral. And what about Guy? Where does he fit in? He seemed very close to Elaine, rushing over to comfort her when she was crying. Is he her boyfriend or just a devoted follower?

'What about the man? What was he like?'

'Medium height. Sandy hair. He seemed nice.'

Sam Elliot. So neither Guy nor Clayton Henry had been at Dan's funeral. So much for the whole department being heartbroken. And despite Clayton's claim that Dan 'didn't have an enemy in the world', the police think that someone murdered him. She decides not to say any of this to Caz.

'That's looks delicious,' she says. 'Can I do anything to help?'

Sandy Macleod and Harry Nelson are together again. They are Starsky and Hutch, Bodie and Doyle, the Sweeney, the good-looking ones from *The Bill*. Or rather, they are two middle-aged men driving too fast in a Ford Mondeo. When Sandy asked Nelson if he'd like to go with him to interview Professor Henry from the university, Nelson had jumped at the chance. He wanted to find out what happened to Ruth's friend and he liked the thought of spending some time with Sandy, but more than anything, he was desperate to get away from Maureen.

'Asking you to work in your holiday,' said Maureen. 'What a cheek.'

'All part of the job,' said Nelson, waiting by the door so that he could be away as soon as Sandy drew up outside. The last thing he wanted was for Maureen to lure him in for a cup of tea.

'You'll miss our trip to the Trough of Bowland.'

'I know. I'm that disappointed.'

Michelle looked sceptically at her husband. She had heard him on the phone to Sandy and the word 'disappointed' hadn't come up once.

Now Sandy and Nelson are bowling along the A583 to Kirkham. Nelson approves of Sandy's driving style. So many young PCs these days have done advanced driving courses and drive like old ladies in hats but Sandy has a fine disregard for speed limits. 'There's not a traffic cop in the area would dare pull me in,' he boasts. Nelson would like to say the same but he's afraid that the uniforms (like the WPCs) are not as amenable in Norfolk. He is starting to wish that he'd stayed in Blackpool and become a fully fledged rule-breaking chauvinist. The move south has emasculated him.

'Who's this bloke we're going to see?' he asks as they bounce merrily over a mini roundabout.

'Head of the history department at the university,' says Sandy. 'He was Dan Golding's boss. He ought to know if there was any funny business going on. Mind you, most of these academic types are on a bloody different planet half the time.'

Nelson thinks of Ruth Galloway, who is definitely an 'academic type'. Is she on a different planet? It's true that sometimes their priorities don't coincide – Ruth has, for example, signed Katie up with a library but hasn't yet even thought about schools – but, for the most part, Ruth is definitely of this world. What's more annoying, she's currently in *his* part of the world. What the hell is she doing in Lytham? She knows that Dan's death is being treated as suspicious, how dare she bring Katie anywhere near a murder enquiry? He fumes silently, watching the countryside fly past.

The windmill takes them both by surprise.

'Bloody hell,' says Sandy, as they screech to a halt on the gravelled drive. 'Does he actually live in this thing?'

'It's like something from a crazy golf course,' says Nelson, who played this particular game yesterday with his older sister Grainne and her family.

'Must be worth a pretty packet,' says Sandy. 'How much do these lecturers earn?'

'Not much,' says Nelson, thinking of Ruth and her poky cottage on the edge of nowhere. 'He must be a closet pop star or something.'

But Clayton Henry, who comes bustling bare-footed across the paved courtyard to greet them, doesn't look like a pop star. True, he is wearing a top which instantly makes Nelson categorise him as 'eccentric, possibly gay', but he is also overweight and slightly anxious, rubbing his hands together and laughing loudly at Sandy's windmill jokes.

Sandy introduces Nelson and Henry says, with a nervous attempt at banter, 'Two DCIs. I'm honoured.'

'It's a special offer,' says Sandy, deadpan. 'Buy one, get one free.'

Professor Henry ushers them into the windmill and up what seem to be hundreds of twisty metal steps.

Eventually, they reach a room at the very top of the house which Henry describes as his study. To Nelson it looks like something from one of those poncy design programmes that Michelle likes so much. The walls are glass, the floor shiny wood and there is nothing as utilitarian as a desk or an office chair anywhere. Sandy and Nelson sit on low sofas and Henry (to Nelson's amazement) on what looks like a giant beach ball. 'It's for my back,' he explains, bouncing gently. 'Ergonomically sound.'

'I'll take your word for it,' says Sandy. 'Now, Professor Henry, as I said on the phone, I'd like to ask you a few questions about the late Daniel Golding.'

Nelson admires Sandy's complete lack of what Judy would call 'empathetic echoing'. He simply gets out a notebook and barks questions. How long had Professor Henry known Daniel Golding? Five years, ever since he came to work at Pendle. Was he a good archaeologist? Yes, excellent. He could probably have taken a more prestigious job elsewhere but his wife had got a job at Preston University and wanted to move north. (Nelson sympathises with this; it was at Michelle's insistence that they moved to Norfolk and, deep down, he's never forgiven her.) Was Golding still married? No, they divorced about three years ago, it was very sad. Girlfriends? Don't know, but he was a good-looking chap, so it's possible.

'Was Daniel Golding popular in the department?'

For the first time, Clayton Henry falters. The ball stops bouncing and seems to deflate slightly.

'Yes,' he says. 'He was a lovely man. Everyone liked him.'

'Could you give me the names of his closest friends?'

'Look,' says Henry. 'What's all this about? Daniel's death was a tragedy. There was nothing sinister about it, was there?'

Interesting choice of word, thinks Nelson. Also, by his reckoning, Henry should have asked this question about ten minutes earlier.

Sandy hardly looks up from his notebook. 'We're treating his death as suspected murder, Professor Henry.'

'What?' For a second, Henry seems to lose his balance and rocks wildly on the ball. His feet scrabble on the floorboards. Nelson looks at him with distaste – in his book bare feet are for women or children.

'The fire in his house was started deliberately,' says Sandy.

'Oh my God.'

'So we're interested to know if anyone had a grudge against Golding, either professionally or personally.'

All the bounce has gone out of both Henry and the ball. He stands up and walks quickly round the circular room. Sandy and Nelson both watch him impassively.

Eventually, Henry comes to a halt between the two policemen. He sits heavily on the sofa next to Nelson.

'I can't think of anyone who would do this,' he says. 'Daniel was very popular, a little reserved perhaps, but a charming, personable man.'

'Professor Henry,' says Sandy. 'In the past Pendle University has had trouble with the extreme right. Is there any chance that Daniel could have been involved with one of these groups?'

Henry laughs. For the first time, he sounds almost natural. 'Daniel? Never! He was a real *Guardian*-reading liberal. Like the rest of us in the history department.'

Nelson thinks of Ruth, who also reads the *Guardian*. He can't really see the point of newspapers himself, he prefers to get his news from the TV, but Michelle rather likes the *Daily Mail*.

'Could these right-wingers have had something against Golding?' asks Sandy.

'Why?'

'Maybe because he was Jewish?'

Henry is silent for a moment, then he says, 'I don't know. You can't put anything past these idiots. But most people didn't even know Daniel was Jewish. He wasn't a religious Jew. Didn't make a song and dance of it.'

'He didn't refuse to work on the Sabbath?' asks Sandy. Nelson doesn't know if he's joking or not but Henry takes the question seriously.

'No. On the contrary. He did most of his digging – archaeology, you know – at the weekends.'

'Professor Henry,' says Nelson. 'Is it true that Daniel Golding had recently made a significant archaeological find?'

Sandy looks at his friend in amazement but Henry answers eagerly.

'Yes. How did you ...'

'I have my sources,' says Nelson grandly. 'Was there any controversy linked to this discovery?'

Now Henry really does look worried. He glances from one policeman to the other and then down at his feet. Nelson waits. He knows the power of silence, of leaving a space for the suspect to convict themselves, and is, therefore, rather irritated when Sandy butts in.

'Answer the question please, Professor Henry. Was there any controversy attached to this archaeological discovery?'

Henry rubs his face with his hand. Eventually he says, in almost a whisper, 'The right-wing group on campus, they're racists, idiots, not a brain cell between them. But there's a sub-group, a kind of secret society. They call themselves the White Hand. They're obsessed with history, particularly with King Arthur.'

'King Arthur?' echoes Sandy.

'Yes. That's what Dan thought he had discovered. The tomb of King Arthur.'

Sandy and Nelson look at each other. Sandy says, 'Isn't he meant to be buried in Cornwall somewhere?'

'There are all sorts of legends,' says Henry. 'And some link Arthur to this area, to the northern borders. The thing is, this group, they've got a special thing about Arthur.'

'What do you mean, a special thing?' asks Sandy, sounding impatient. Nelson would have been impatient himself once but his association with Ruth has made him more tolerant.

'For them he's the big English hero,' says Henry, still

sounding scared. 'They call him the White King, the High King. They wouldn't want him associated with the Romans. They see the Romans as foreigners, invaders. And that's where Dan uncovered the tomb. At Ribchester, a famous Roman site.'

'And was Golding aware of any intimidation from the group, the White Hand?' asks Sandy.

'I don't know,' says Henry miserably. Nelson wonders if he's telling the truth.

'Do you know the names of anyone involved with this group?'

'No,' says Henry. 'It's all deadly secret. They wear masks when they appear in public, on demos and the like.'

'Would they have known about Daniel Golding's find?'

Clayton Henry attempts a jocular tone. 'You know what universities are like. Nothing stays secret for long.'

'No, I don't know what universities are like,' says Sandy. 'Barely managed CSEs in art and metalwork. So you think that someone in this secret society may have found out that Daniel Golding had discovered the lost tomb of King Arthur?'

'It's possible,' says Clayton Henry miserably.

'Is it possible that one of these White Hand people killed Daniel Golding?'

'No,' says Clayton Henry. 'I can't believe that anyone would do that.'

'You'd better believe it,' says Sandy brutally. 'Daniel Golding died of smoke inhalation. The door of his house was locked from the outside.'

Clayton Henry puts a hand over his face. 'Don't.'

'Ever see anyone dead after a fire?' asks Sandy. 'Pretty nasty way to die.'

Henry's shoulders shake. Nelson wonders if he's going to break down altogether. Sandy, obviously thinking the same thing, moves in for the kill.

'Professor Henry, do you know anything about Dan Golding's death?'

Henry says nothing but another voice cuts through the air.

'What the hell do you think you're doing?'

The two policemen turn as a tall woman stalks into the room, followed by a small fluffy dog. The woman hurries to Clayton Henry's side and puts her arm round him.

'It's all right, Clay. It's all right.'

The dog, sensing tension, starts barking wildly. Nelson sees Sandy's foot itching to kick it.

'What's going on?' The woman looks up. Despite being casually dressed in sports clothes, she is extremely attractive, with the sort of classic good looks that need no adornment. Nelson guesses that she's in her early forties. Is she Henry's personal assistant? His therapist?

'I'm Pippa Henry,' says the vision. 'Clayton's wife. Can you please tell me what's happening here?'

Nelson and Sandy exchange glances. Clearly there's more to the bare-footed, ball-bouncing Henry than meets the eye. Not only does he live in a *Grand Designs* show home, he also has a show wife. A show wife who is looking distinctly angry. She scoops up the dog and glares at Sandy.

'Well?'

'We're police officers,' says Sandy woodenly. 'Investigating the death of Daniel Golding.' He shows his warrant card.

'What's that got to do with Clay? He was devastated by Dan's death.'

'We're following several lines of enquiry,' says Sandy.

'Well, you'll have to come back another day,' says Pippa Henry. 'Unless you want to arrest him, that is. Can't you see how upset he is? He's been under a lot of strain lately.'

For a second they glare at each other, the lugubrious policeman and the whippet-slim woman. The dog lets out a single shrill bark. Clayton sobs silently in the background.

'We'll come back another day,' says Sandy.

CHAPTER 16

By the afternoon it is raining heavily. So when Ruth says, for the second time, that she really must be going, Caz offers to drive her. Ruth, who is feeling tired and full of food, accepts gratefully. It has been a good day, though. Pete arrived after lunch with the children: Ashley, Becky and Jack. Ruth, after she'd got over the shock of Ashley being about six feet tall, had to admit that they were nice kids and very good with Kate. Perhaps this is what Kate has wanted all along, three older children to pander to her every need. 'It's good for them,' said Caz. 'They don't know any babies.' Caz has a breezy, authoritative way with her children that Ruth much admires. Within two seconds of coming into the house, they have changed their sailing gear for indoor clothes and are playing trains with Kate on the sitting-room carpet. 'You're in charge, Ash,' Caz had said. 'We grown-ups want some time together.'

Caz, Pete and Ruth sat in the kitchen, drinking white wine and talking about life, children, jobs and whether everything has gone downhill since the Eighties.

'The music,' said Pete. 'They have all this manufactured pop these days. The X Factor and all that.'

'We had Kylie and Jason though,' said Ruth. 'It wasn't all plain sailing.'

'But we had Adam Ant and Boy George as well,' said Caz. 'Be fair.'

'Do you remember,' said Pete, 'when Dan had that party and everyone thought that Boy George was coming?'

'He was a friend of Dan's sister,' said Caz. 'She knew lots of famous people.'

That was the way it had been all afternoon. Dan was mentioned often and with affection but they didn't allow themselves to be caught up in nostalgia. Dan was the reason that Ruth was sitting there, in that state-of-the-art kitchen in the frozen north, but none of them mentioned this. They all said how good it was to see each other again, but they didn't dwell on the fact that if they had wanted to be reunited they could have done it any time over the last twenty-odd years. Fire and death have brought Ruth to Lancashire but no one says these words either.

But as Ruth and Caz set out in Caz's gleaming 4x4, a sleepy Kate in the back, Ruth knows that there is something she has to ask.

'How far is it to Fleetwood?'

Caz glances at her. 'About twenty minutes. Do you want to see where it . . . do you want to see Dan's house?'

'Yes please.'

They don't speak much on the drive along the coast road, past Blackpool and the giant glitter ball and the roller-coaster reaching up to the sky. Despite the rain, families trail along the Golden Mile carrying candy floss and virulent cuddly toys won in arcades. Once past the north pier, the landscape changes again, with long stretches of windswept grass and grey sea. At Fleetwood the sea stretches out into an estuary, with boats beached high on the sand. They pass shuttered Victorian hotels, derelict dockyards, red-brick houses.

Ruth knows from reading up about Ribchester that the town used to be a thriving port. In fact, the Roman Road might well have led from Ribchester to Fleetwood. But now, in the afternoon rain, the town doesn't look as if it is on the road to anywhere. It looks tired, as tired as Kate, who is fast asleep in Jack's old car seat.

Caz turns down a side street and stops suddenly in front of a row of pebbledash houses. Nothing in Ruth's imagination has prepared her for the horror of it. The middle house in the terrace has been reduced to a blackened stump, windows smashed, door boarded up. The walls are streaked with soot, half the roof is missing. Ruth thinks of Dan, trapped inside, choking with acrid smoke, breathing his last . . .

'Are you OK?' says Caz.

'Yes,' says Ruth, wiping her eyes. 'It's just . . . thinking about it.'

'I know,' says Caz. 'I drove past the day I found out about it. You hear the words "house fire", but you just can't imagine the damage a fire can do.'

'Why didn't he jump out of the window?' asks Ruth. 'It's such a tiny house.'

'At the funeral his father told me that the bedroom window didn't open,' said Caz. 'They all wondered why he didn't get out though. He was found right by the door. I guess the heat was just too intense.'

Ruth remembers Nelson telling her that the door had been locked from the outside. She imagines Dan pounding away at the door, slowly losing consciousness. Someone had pushed petrol-soaked rags through the letter box. The hall must have been the white-hot heart of the blaze. Did Dan know, as he tried desperately to escape, did he know that he was going to die? Did he know that someone had killed him?

'Shall we go?' says Caz gently.

Ruth nods. As Caz performs a U-turn, with difficulty as the car is about the size of a Blackpool tram, Ruth looks back at the house. And she sees two people, a man and a woman, letting themselves in next door. They are youngish, dressed in jeans and windcheaters, and, for some reason, she thinks that she might know them. It is only when they are halfway back to Lytham that she realises who they were. Elaine and Guy. The Brideshead couple, who turn out to live in a run-down backstreet, next to a burned-out house.

'Well,' says Sandy, overtaking with a perfunctory blare of the horn. The rain has reduced visibility to almost nil but this has not affected Sandy's driving. 'What did you think of Professor Henry?'

'He's hiding something,' says Nelson.

'He's got an alibi for the night of the fire, though.' This last had been ascertained from Pippa Henry in an icy exchange on the door step. 'He was with his wife all evening, apparently.'

'She's quite something, the wife,' says Nelson.

'You can say that again. How did a little pipsqueak like him ever end up with a woman like that?'

'Sometimes beautiful women like ugly men,' says Nelson. 'Look at Michelle and me.'

'You might be ugly but you're not a pipsqueak in a pink jumper.'

'Thanks.'

'Clayton Henry's afraid of something,' says Sandy. 'It might be his wife, it might be these White Hand bozos, it might be something else entirely.'

'How much do you know about these White Hand people?'

'Never heard of them,' admits Sandy. 'Tim, my sergeant, might know. He's the one who's put in all the work on these extreme right-wing groups. In general the people he's investigating are pretty much what you'd expect, low income, not very well educated, wound up over immigration and lack of jobs. There are some very deprived areas round here, you know.'

Nelson looks out of the window. They have reached the outskirts of Blackpool now. He has never thought of the area as being deprived exactly but there's no denying that the rows of glum terraces are not looking their brightest in the driving rain.

'But the recent trouble at the university is something else,' Sandy is saying, putting his windscreen wipers on full speed. 'There have been some very nasty threats made, a real undercurrent of violence.'

'What about all that King Arthur stuff? Have you come across anything like that before?'

'No, that's a new one on me, I must admit, but nothing would surprise me about these idiots. They have all sorts of heroes – Hitler, Enoch Powell, Boadicea, Asterix the Gaul.'

'Asterix? Isn't he French?'

'He stood up to the Romans, didn't he? I tell you, these people would hero-worship anyone, even the French.'

The image of that horrible blackened house remains in Ruth's head all evening. When she gets back, Cathbad is still out and the rain is still falling. Kate wakes up as soon as they enter the cottage and, deprived of her teenage minions, she is grumpy and determined not to be placated. Ruth makes toast for them both (she is too tired to attempt any Cathbad-style gourmet cooking and, besides, she's still full up from lunch) and prepares to start the night-time routine. Kate cheers up slightly in the bath (whether it's to do with being a Scorpio or not, she does love the water), but as soon they go into the bedroom, she starts to look mutinous. Ruth tucks her into the double bed, gives her a bottle and reads interminable multi-lingual adventures featuring Dora the Explorer. Kate endures this for a while, watching Ruth out of her big dark eyes, so like her father's. But as soon as Ruth closes the book and prepares to leave the room, Kate starts to cry. Eventually Ruth lies down on the bed next to her daughter. The rain batters against the windows and the little house seems almost to shake under the onslaught. For once Ruth is happy to have near neighbours. Through the curtains she can see the orange glow of streetlights, hear cars going past. If this was the Saltmarsh she'd have only the wind and the rain for company. And Flint, of course. She wonders how he is. Perhaps she should text Bob.

She looks down at Kate. The bottle has fallen out of her hands and she seems to be breathing heavily. Slowly, trying to make herself weightless, Ruth sits up and swings her feet to the floor. Kate murmurs but doesn't wake. Leaving the bedside light on, Ruth tiptoes out and goes in search of her mobile phone. Where can she have left it?

The cute little house seems different at night, furniture seems to loom at her or appear in odd places. Surely that bookcase wasn't there before, thinks Ruth, rubbing her shins. She thinks of Dame Alice's cottage, the little white house in the hollow of the hills. Has Cathbad decided to stay the night with Pendragon? If so, he'd have told her surely. Yes, he's probably left a message on her bloody phone. Where is the damn thing? She goes into the kitchen, which still smells of toast. She eats a soggy crust, rejected by Kate. Stop eating, she tells herself sternly. If you don't eat for a year maybe you'll be as slim as Caz. But being thin has never seemed worth being hungry, which is one reason why Ruth weighs nearly thirteen stone.

She stops. A floorboard creaks upstairs. Could it possibly be Kate? There's no stair-gate at the cottage and Ruth is in constant fear that Kate will get up in the night and fall down the stairs. Ruth goes upstairs and looks into the master bedroom. Kate is sleeping deeply, arms flung out. The milk bottle is dripping on the floor and Ruth picks it up. Then she goes into Cathbad's room. She is not sure what she is expecting to see, but the bed, with its pink flowery duvet, is neatly made and the ballerinas gaze down demurely from the wallpaper. There are no clothes anywhere; Cathbad must have packed everything into the little wardrobe under the eaves. Unlike Ruth, who still has half her stuff in her suitcase. There is a book next to the bed. Ruth picks it up. *Wicked Enchantments*, it's called, *A History of the Pendle Witches and Their Magic*. The cover shows a cauldron and a black cat. Ruth puts the book down hastily but, as she does so, a photo falls out. Ruth picks it up, trying not to look but, of course, she has seen who is in the picture. Judy, standing on the beach, her hair loose, looking entirely unlike a policewoman. Ruth tucks the photo back into the book and goes downstairs. Where is Cathbad? Has he got lost in the winding paths through the Pendle Forest? Has he strayed into a local coven? If so, he's definitely likely to stay the night.

Ruth goes back downstairs and – hooray! – finds her phone in her cagoule pocket. She clicks on to Messages. Just one.

Ladybird, ladybird, fly away home. Your house is on fire. Your children are gone.

Ruth stands in the hall, frozen in terror. She sees the ruined house with its blank, staring windows. She thinks of Dan in his own hallway, trying desperately to open the locked door. Then she turns and runs back upstairs. Kate is still asleep. Ruth turns off the bedside lamp because lamps can overheat, houses can burn down. Instantly her phone clicks into life.

A new message.

Don't turn out the light.

Ruth has had enough; she rings Nelson.

CHAPTER 17

Cathbad and Nelson arrive at the same time. They exchange a few words on the doorstep and then Nelson barges in and takes charge. First he runs upstairs to check on Kate, then he holds out his hand for Ruth's mobile.

'Can you trace the messages?' she asks.

'Yes,' he says. 'Mobile phones have a unique number that they send out when they make a call. If I have the number I can trace the call to its local base. That'll give us a geographical location.'

'Can you find out who owns the phone?'

'We can force mobile phone providers to give us that information under the Regulation of Investigatory Powers Act. Of course, that only works if they've got a contract. If this person's got any sense they'll be using pay-as-you-go.'

Ruth sincerely hopes that the texter doesn't have any sense. 'They must be close,' she says. 'That bit about turning out the light ... I'd ... I'd just turned out Kate's light.'

'I'll get Sandy to send some boys round,' says Nelson, trying to sound reassuring though his brows are lowered ominously.

He gets out his own phone and makes a brief call. Ruth hears the words 'trace ... uniforms ... protection'. She turns to Cathbad and tries to smile.

'Welcome back.'

'What's going on?'

'I've been getting these texts ...' She explains about the mystery texts. In the background, Nelson is grinding his teeth.

'You mean you've been getting these calls for weeks and you didn't say anything?'

'I thought they were just trying to scare me.'

'Well, they should have scared you. Someone was threatening you, for Christ's sake. What about Katie? Didn't you consider her safety?'

'Of course I did!' Ruth flares up. 'I'm with her all the time, unlike you. She's my first priority. My *only* priority.'

Nelson spreads out his hands in a gesture of surrender. 'OK, OK. Sandy's sending a couple of uniforms round to check up on things. In the meantime, let's all calm down a bit. Have a cup of tea.'

Ruth glares at him but she makes the tea. She resents Nelson jackbooting around but she has to admit that she feels safer when he's in the house. The furniture seems to have retreated to its usual places and even the rain has stopped. An uneasy calm descends as they sit in the chintzy little sitting room drinking tea while Ruth tells the whole story of the switched bones, Clayton's nervousness and the texter who didn't want her to come to Pendle in the first place.

'There's a lot of funny business going on at that university,' says Nelson. 'Sandy and I went to see Clayton Henry today. He told us there's this group on campus, a sort of secret society called the White Hand. Apparently they've got a fixation with King Arthur.'

Cathbad makes a sound and Nelson turns on him

'Do you know them?' asks Nelson, half-joking.

'Not this group in particular,' says Cathbad, looking slightly discomforted. 'But there are some druids, Neo-pagans they call themselves, who have these extremist views. They adore King Arthur. They worship the Norse Gods. But it's more than that. They believe that the Norse people, the white Aryan people, are superior.'

'They're racists then,' says Nelson.

'Yes, they're racists,' says Cathbad impatiently. 'But it's more complicated than that. They've mixed it all up, the pagan stuff, the Norse stuff, and they've made it a really potent brew. Anyone who disagrees with them is cursed. There's a lot of secrecy, a lot of fear.'

'Are you involved with them?' asks Nelson.

'No,' says Cathbad, 'but I know of them. Anyone on the druid circuit . . .' (Ruth sees Nelson stifle a smile.) 'Anyone on the druid circuit knows them. They don't like me because I'm Irish, I'm a Celt. Besides I have friends of every colour. I'm very involved with the Indigenous Australian people, for example. It's the spirit that matters with me, not the colour of someone's skin.'

'All very noble,' says Nelson, 'but you know more than you're letting on.'

Cathbad sighs. 'Pendragon . . . since he's been up north, they've been in touch.'

'What do you mean "in touch"?'

'There's a Neo-pagan group at Pendle. I expect it's these White Hand people. I think Pendragon was mixed up with them a bit at first. He's no racist but he loves the Norse stuff. Also . . .' He looks at Ruth. 'He's mad about King Arthur. Well, you can tell that by the name he's taken.'

'Uther Pendragon,' says Ruth.

'Who's he when he's at home?' says Nelson.

'Some sources think he was King Arthur's father,' says Ruth, who has been reading up on this. 'Uther was a fifth-century warlord. He's meant to have defeated Hengest, the Saxon leader, to become King of Britain. They were all fighting at that time, Picts, Celts and Saxons.'

'Pendragon used to live in Ireland,' says Cathbad, 'he's used to Celts. Some of the others, though, they're all for the pure-blood English thing. Load of nonsense, of course. There's no such thing as pure-blood English.'

Nelson, whose own ancestry includes Irish and (so his mother claims) Spanish blood, says, 'Did whatshisname . . . Pendragon, say anything about a campaign against Dan Golding?'

Cathbad hesitates. 'No,' he says. 'But when I went over there today, it was like when we first went there, Ruth.

Pendragon appeared at the door with a gun. He seemed terrified.'

'Did he say what he was frightened of?' asks Nelson.

'No,' says Cathbad. 'My guess is that he was involved with this group at first but then backed out, perhaps when they suggested violence or began with the race-hate stuff. Pendragon's a gentle soul. He wouldn't hurt a fly. I think he's afraid that they'll come for him, try to punish him for leaving. When I got there today he was burning herbs, making sacrifices, trying to draw a circle of protection around the house.'

'Did he ever think it might be more helpful to call the police?' asks Nelson.

Cathbad smiles. 'He's not too keen on the police. That's something else druids have in common.'

Nelson frowns, perhaps thinking of the circumstances of his first meeting with Cathbad. Then he says, 'Did Pendragon give you a name, anything useful like that?'

'No, but he did mention someone called the Arch Wizard. He seems to be the one in charge.'

'He doesn't have any idea who this Arch Wizard is, I suppose?'

'No. Pendragon's seen him but he's always been masked.'

'Typical,' says Nelson. 'Well I suppose I'd better go and see this Pentangle for myself.'

'Pendragon,' corrects Cathbad mildly.

'Whatever.'

'I'll go with you,' offers Cathbad. 'It might be safer. Pendragon knows some ancient magic.'

Nelson's reply, which begins with 'Bollocks', is lost because, at that moment, back-up arrives in the form of two young police officers. Their accents are so broad that Ruth can hardly understand them. She notices that Nelson's own voice changes when he speaks to them. He tells them to check around the house, looking for signs that anyone has been loitering in the area. Ruth notices that even though Nelson can't have any official status in Blackpool both men immediately do what he asks, affording him the same kind of awed respect he receives from his team in Norfolk.

'Right,' says Nelson. 'I'll just check on Katie then I'll be off.'

'What did you tell Michelle?' asks Ruth.

'Just that it was police business,' says Nelson. 'She's used to that. My mum started on at me, though. Apparently it's a capital crime to leave the house in the middle of *Holby City*.'

Ruth lets Nelson have a few minutes alone with Kate and then follows him upstairs. He is standing in her room, looking down at his sleeping daughter. When he turns, there are tears in his eyes.

'She's growing up.'

'Yes,' says Ruth, not wanting to look at him. 'She's nearly two.'

'It goes so fast,' says Nelson. 'Take care of her, Ruth.'

'I will.'

'Where does Cathbad sleep?' he asks, on the landing.

Resisting the temptation to tell him to mind his own

business, Ruth shows him Cathbad's room. For some reason, the sight seems to lift Nelson's spirits considerably. He laughs out loud at the ballerinas.

'Cathbad, lad,' he says as they shake hands in the hallway. 'You've got a room fit for a princess.'

'I like ballet,' says Cathbad. 'It's very soothing to the soul.'

CHAPTER 18

'So you've got a friend who's a wizard?'

Nelson sighs. He's finding it very hard to explain his relationship with Cathbad to Sandy. In fact, he finds it hard to explain it to himself.

'He's not a wizard,' he says. 'He's more a sort of druid.'

'Druid!' Sandy laughs heartily. 'Looks like you've been in Norfolk too long, cocker.'

Sandy's sergeant, a quiet young man called Tim, leans forward and says, 'It's very useful to have someone on the inside of the group.'

Nelson is grateful for Tim's intervention but feels he ought to protect Cathbad's reputation. 'He's not exactly on the inside. It's not his kind of thing at all. He's heard of them, that's all.'

'But this friend of his, Pendragon . . . Jesus, why can't they have bloody normal names? This Pendragon, he was involved in the group?'

'Cathbad thinks so. He says that Pendragon seems terrified that these White Hand people are going to have some sort of revenge on him for leaving.'

'Any idea what Pendragon's real name is?'

Nelson gets out a piece of paper. 'Norman Smith,' he says, with a straight face.

Sandy roars with laughter. He seems in a particularly jolly mood today. Tim, though, nods solemnly. He's probably been on all those PC courses that teach you not to laugh at people's names.

'Do a search on him, Tim, will you? And what about Cathcart, whatever he calls himself. What's his real name?'

'Michael Malone,' says Nelson, wondering why saying this name aloud gives him a slight twinge of unease. 'He's known to the police but no convictions.'

'Known to the police,' says Sandy. 'Is he an informer then?'

Not unless you count information on auras, zodiac signs and lunatic Pagan rituals, thinks Nelson. Aloud he says, 'No, but he has been helpful on a couple of cases.' By his count he has saved Cathbad's life once and Cathbad claims to have saved his in return – though, as Nelson was unconscious at the time, he can't exactly vouch for this. Still, there's no doubt that Cathbad has helped the police. Once he led Nelson across treacherous marshland in the dark, another time he accompanied him on a nightmare river journey in the wake of a madman with a gun. Cathbad, despite appearances, is good in a crisis. Nelson doesn't feel able to explain all this to Sandy, though.

Thankfully Sandy seems to accept his answer. 'Well,' he says, folding his hands over his paunch, 'I suppose I'd better go and see Norman Smith, alias Pendragon.'

Nelson shifts uncomfortably. He knows he has to be tactful and the concept always feels somewhat alien to him. 'I wondered if it might be better if Cathbad and I went on our own,' he says. 'We might get more out of him.'

Sandy looks at him sharply and Nelson gets a glimpse of the tough copper underneath the matey bonhomie. Then he says, 'OK, but you're not officially on the case, mind. You go and see him, prepare the way, then Tim and I can go afterwards.'

'Good idea,' says Nelson.

'OK.' Sandy seems to relax again. 'Tim, have you got that list of names? Tim's been doing some research into Neo-Nazi activity at the university,' he explains. 'He's done a good job considering he can hardly go under-cover.' He laughs uproariously. Tim, who is black, smiles politely. Does he really not mind the joke, wonders Nelson, or has he just learnt that you need a thick skin to get on in this business? Tim's also a graduate, some-thing else that may prejudice Sandy against him, though, as far as Nelson can see, they seem to have a good working relationship.

Now Tim gets out a typed list and puts it on the table. 'Here are the names of anyone linked to the university who has ever been involved with any far-right group.'

'Including the Masons?' asks Nelson. Tim doesn't smile.

Maybe he's a member, like Nelson's own sergeant, Dave Clough.

'This includes people who've stood for the National Front,' says Tim, 'been cautioned at demonstrations, sent letters to us or to the press, or who've been convicted of any crimes of a racist nature.'

Nelson looks at the list. 'This bloke's got a foreign name,' he says. 'What's he doing in the National Front?'

'Like I say,' says Tim, 'they're not very bright.'

'Doesn't stop 'em being dangerous, though,' says Sandy. 'Anybody here linked to Dan Golding?'

'There's one person who studied in the history department,' says Tim, pointing. 'She graduated seven years ago.'

'She? Are there woman fascists too?' asks Sandy.

'It would appear so,' says Tim. 'This woman's called Philippa Moore.'

'What did she do?' asks Nelson.

'She was arrested at a gay rights march. Cautioned for using offensive language.'

'So she doesn't like gays. Think Golding could have been gay?' Sandy turns to Nelson again.

'Henry didn't think so and Ruth ... my friend ... she certainly didn't think so.'

'Another of Harry's mysterious friends,' says Sandy. 'She's the girl who's been getting the threatening texts, right?'

Sandy has put a trace on the number given to him by Nelson. The calls have been made locally but they are no closer to finding the phone's owner. One thing does bother Nelson, though; the last call was made in Lytham, very close to Ruth's rented house. Nelson has also asked for some protection for Ruth and Sandy (though sceptical) has agreed to send a patrol car round every night.

'Very supportive of this girl, aren't you?'

'She's a single mum, on her own,' said Nelson. 'You'd feel the same.'

Now, he says, 'She's a forensic archaeologist and an old friend of Golding's. Henry asked her to come up here and look at the bones he'd found.'

'But they were fakes. Isn't that what you told me?' says Sandy.

Nelson explains again about the bones being from two different skeletons.

'Is she sure?' asks Tim.

'If she says so, it's pretty certain,' says Nelson. 'She knows her stuff.'

'Why would anyone switch the bones?' asks Tim. 'They must have been worried about what she'd discover. What could it be?'

'Archaeologists can get all sorts of stuff from bones,' says Nelson. 'You'd be surprised. They can tell you how old someone was, what they had for dinner, where they lived.'

'So,' says Tim thoughtfully. 'There's something significant about these bones. Something someone doesn't want us to know.'

'Has your friend got any idea what happened to the original bones?' asks Sandy.

'No,' says Nelson. 'Apparently Clayton Henry doesn't know either. They took the bones straight to the police lab because they were already aware that the find was controversial. One thing though, Golding took some of the original bones and teeth for sampling. Ruth's on the track of these. If she finds the results, they might give us some clues.'

'Most of his papers went up in smoke,' says Tim. 'They were in a desk in the sitting room and the whole downstairs was gutted. I went through his office at the university too. There was nothing about the dig there. My guess is that everything was on his laptop.'

'Could the computer have escaped the fire?' asked Nelson.

'It's possible,' says Tim. 'The rooms upstairs weren't badly damaged, but we didn't find anything when we searched the house.'

'If we find the laptop,' says Sandy, 'there's a chance we find the killer. Whoever took it must have known that there was something significant about the bones. Might be worth searching the houses of his colleagues, Tim.'

'Yes, boss.'

'And we'll make a trip to the police lab. They might know something about the disappearing bones.' He turns to Nelson with a smile that's half invitation, half warning. 'Want to come with us, Harry? Strictly as an observer, of course.'

'You're all right,' says Nelson. 'I'd better get home. My mother's invited some people for tea.'

*

When Nelson gets back to the little pink house he sees Ruth's car parked outside. She's done well to get a space. She's not a bad parker, for a woman. Nelson wastes time trying to back into a space the size of a pushbike, then gives up and tries the next street. He's aware that he's putting off the moment when he has to enter the crowded little sitting room and see Ruth and Cathbad and *his* baby, chatting politely with *his* mother, who will be completely unaware that she is entertaining her own granddaughter. An emotion so rare as to be almost frightening sweeps over Nelson: he feels protective towards his mother. It's not fair that she should be in this position. A new grandchild should be a source of joy for her, not a guilty secret to be hidden. He feels obscurely angry with Ruth for coming to Lancashire in the first place, for creating this whole situation. But, then, to be fair, Maureen had invited Ruth, she hadn't wanted to come. Nelson recalls her face when the invitation was issued and almost smiles at the remembered look of horror. If anything, it's Cathbad's fault for getting on so well with Maureen and for coming from bloody Ballywhatsit. He rings the doorbell.

Michelle lets him in. As usual, she's perfectly groomed in white trousers and a tight black top. Nelson feels a wave of affection for his beautiful wife. After all, this afternoon is probably worse for her. He kisses her cheek.

'You look grand, love.'

Michelle steps out of his reach. 'Ruth's in there,' she says, in a voice carefully devoid of any expression. Nelson looks towards the sitting-room door. He can hear Maureen and Cathbad, their voices raised in delighted recognition.

'Paddy O'Brien! He kept the corner shop, so he did.'

How the bloody hell has Cathbad got so Irish all of a sudden? He looks at Michelle, who raises her eyebrows and almost smiles. Encouraged, Nelson pushes open the door.

As Nelson enters, they all turn and look at him. 'Dada!' says Kate, who is on the floor playing with a train set that Nelson remembers from his own childhood.

'She says that to everyone,' says Ruth, too quickly.

'She's as bright as a button,' says Maureen admiringly. 'You couldn't speak at all until you were two, Harry.'

'It must have been embarrassing for you, having such a stupid child,' says Nelson, sitting on the uncomfortable chair at his mother's side. Cathbad and Ruth are side by side on the sofa. The remains of an elaborate tea lie on the coffee table. Maureen has even got the cake forks out.

'Oh, you weren't stupid, Harry,' says Maureen kindly. 'You just didn't try at school.'

'I was the same,' says Cathbad. 'I just wasn't interested in the things they taught at school. I think real learning only begins after you stop being educated.'

This is from the man who has two degrees and works at a university, thinks Nelson. He takes a piece of chocolate cake. Maureen hands him a plate without looking round.

'You wouldn't believe the interesting things that Cathbad's been telling me about Samhain and the Festival of the Dead,' she says. Not for the first time

Nelson wonders at the way that Maureen, not a woman famed for her religious tolerance, can stomach any amount of New Age philosophy, especially when it's about contacting the dead.

'I often see the ghost of Uncle Declan, don't I, Harry?' she says now.

'Frequently.'

'You must have strong psychic powers,' says Cathbad.

Maureen is delighted. 'Well, I do think I've been blessed that way,' she says modestly. 'I have such powerful instincts about people, you wouldn't believe. That's why I knew immediately that you and I would get on, Cathbad. And Michelle ...' She looks up as her daughter-in-law comes into the room. 'I knew as soon as I saw her that she was the girl for Harry.'

'I don't think my instincts can be very good,' says Ruth. 'I'm always being wrong about people.' Does she mean him, thinks Nelson. Does she think that she was, in some way, deceived by him? But he's always been straight with her, never promised her anything. Or perhaps she means Erik, her old professor. She was certainly wrong about him, as they all were.

Michelle sits on the sofa and leans over to look at Kate.

'She's grown so much,' she says.

This simple remark effectively silences Ruth, Cathbad and Nelson. But Maureen is in full flow.

'You wouldn't believe Michelle has grown-up daughters, would you? She looks so young. The three of them look like sisters.' She reaches out for a photograph of

Michelle, Laura and Rebecca, taken when they visited Blackpool last Christmas.

Ruth takes the picture but still seems unable to speak. Cathbad says gallantly, 'Three beautiful women.'

'They are, to be sure,' says Maureen. 'And the girls are clever too. Both of them at university. What are they studying, Harry?'

'Laura's reading Marine Biology at Plymouth,' says Nelson. 'Rebecca's doing Media Studies at Brighton.' These subjects mean absolutely nothing to him. Neither he nor Michelle had any further education; they just pay the bills.

'Clayton Henry was telling me that anything with "forensic" in the title is popular these days,' says Ruth. 'It's because of all those TV programmes about forensic science. Maybe soon they'll be offering courses in forensic media studies.'

'Oh don't talk to me about those programmes,' says Maureen, who never misses an episode of *Silent Witness*. 'It's not right, what they do to those poor bodies.'

CHAPTER 19

After a few minutes in the Pendle Forest, Nelson is
thinking longingly of Blackpool. It's another rainy day
and the clouds are low over the fields. The grass is black,
the streams grey and troubled. Nelson drives slowly
through the twisting lanes, cursing when he has to stop
for sheep or cattle grids. Next to him, Cathbad hums
serenely, looking at the lowering landscape with every
appearance of pleasure. When they stop at a crossroads,
a raven, huge and jet-black, regards them from the top
of the signpost.

'That,' says Cathbad, 'is a very bad omen.'

'Do me a favour,' says Nelson. 'Don't tell me why.'
Cathbad had, earlier, offered to tell Nelson the story of
the Pendle Witches and was rudely rebuffed. 'I don't want
to hear any bloody silly fairy stories, thanks very much.'
Cathbad hadn't been offended although now the bird's
appearance seems to have jolted him.

'Ravens are meant to speak with the voices of the dead,'
he says.

'Save it for my mum,' says Nelson. He hasn't forgiven Cathbad for the tea party, which lasted until nearly seven o'clock. Maureen had told Cathbad all her psychic experiences and he had suggested that she might be a reincarnation of an Egyptian prophetess.

'Your mother's a wonderful woman,' says Cathbad.

'I'll take your word for it.'

Maureen keeps saying that they must have Cathbad and Ruth for dinner one night. She persists in thinking of them as a couple ('the babby's the image of her daddy') and wonders why they haven't got married. It's driving Nelson mad. Today Ruth has gone to see Susan Chow, the county archaeologist. She's taken Kate with her so it'll be a short trip.

'Which way now?' Nelson asks.

'Left. Towards Fence.'

'Jesus. What sort of a person lives in a godforsaken place like this?'

'The same sort of person who lives on the Saltmarsh,' says Cathbad, with a sly sideways glance.

Nelson doesn't reply. He might not approve of Ruth's choice of location (it's no place to bring up a child) but he doesn't like anyone else to criticise her. Besides, Ruth's nothing like this Pendragon nutcase.

They reach the steep valley with the white house in the middle, like the epiglottis in a giant throat. Nelson parks the car by the gate and they approach the cottage on foot. As they walk, the wind suddenly picks up and the stunted trees on the hill lash to and fro. A flock of birds flies overhead, low and sinister.

'Why the hell hasn't he got a proper drive?' asks Nelson. He could walk all day on pavements but something about the countryside makes him uneasy.

'He hasn't got a car,' says Cathbad.

'Typical.'

This time Pendragon does not come out to meet them, gun in hand. Perhaps some sixth sense has told him that this isn't a good idea with a policeman around. They reach the front door undisturbed.

'Pen!' shouts Cathbad. 'It's me. Cathbad.'

His voice echoes dramatically around the valley. Pen, pen, pen, pen. Bad, bad, bad, bad ...

'I knew he'd be out,' says Nelson.' That's what you get for not being on the phone. He's probably gone to some wizard's tea party.'

Cathbad tries the handle. The door opens. The next moment a solid wedge of fur and muscle flies at him.

'Jesus.' Nelson takes a step back.

'It's OK,' says Cathbad, from a sitting position on the hearthrug. 'He's friendly.'

'I can see that,' says Nelson, rather ashamed of his reaction. He likes dogs and once owned a German Shepherd called (funnily enough) Max.

'Hello, boy,' says Cathbad, getting to his feet. 'Where's your master?'

'Away with the fairies,' says Nelson, looking round the low-ceilinged room with its twinkling dream-catchers. It's like stepping back in time, he thinks. No TV, no telephone. Not even, unless he's much mistaken, any electric light. His worst fears are realised when Cathbad lights an oil lamp to search the rest of the house. Thing, apparently undisturbed, lies down in front of the fire.

Nelson squats down and examines the embers. Still smouldering. Wherever he is, Pendragon can't have gone far.

Susan Chow is a small, neat woman who makes Ruth feel like she's more than usually enormous. She and Kate seem to fill Susan's little office above the county library. First the pushchair gets stuck in the doorway, then Ruth can't manoeuvre herself around the wheels to sit at the desk opposite Susan. Eventually she manages, knocking over a pile of books and a papier-mâché model of a Neolithic causewayed enclosure. She leaves Kate in the pushchair, hoping that her picture book will keep her entertained. It's a present from Cathbad, a rather New-Agey publication called *Sun, Moon, Stars*. Kate loves it and refuses to be parted from it. Now she sucks a page ruminatively.

'Thanks for seeing me,' says Ruth, setting the enclosure back on the desk.

'My pleasure,' says Susan. 'I was so sorry to hear about Dan.'

'Me too,' says Ruth. She doesn't know what to say when people seem to offer her condolences about Dan. She isn't qualified to accept them; she hasn't seen him for nearly twenty years. All she can do is say that she's sorry too.

'I wanted to ask you,' says Ruth, 'about the day when Dan excavated the skeleton at Ribchester. You were there, weren't you?'

'Yes,' says Susan, frowning slightly. 'It was a very exciting find.'

'I know,' says Ruth. She hasn't yet told Susan about the switched bones, though she knows she will have to. Now she says, 'The bones were taken straight to the forensics lab, weren't they?'

'Yes,' says Susan, sounding rather defensive. 'I was satisfied that there was no need for an autopsy. The bones were sealed inside the tomb and we could date that pretty accurately. Mid to late fifth century.'

'But was it standard for the bones to go to a specialist laboratory? Why not the university?'

Susan straightens the pens on her desk. 'Clayton Henry felt they'd be safer at the laboratory. I don't know if you know, Doctor Galloway, but there has been some unrest at Pendle recently. Far-right groups who might feel a particular interest in this find.'

'Because of the possible connection with King Arthur?'

Susan inclines her head. 'That's correct.'

'How would they have known?'

'Word gets out. You know what universities are like.'

Ruth does know. When she got pregnant, her students knew before her parents did.

'Did you see the bones when Dan was excavating?' asks Ruth.

Susan looks surprised. 'Yes. He did the actual excavation but we were all observing.'

'All?'

'Me, Professor Henry, his wife, some students, a few volunteers. Why do you ask?'

Ruth doesn't answer straight away. Instead she asks, 'Was Dan satisfied that there was just one skeleton in the tomb?'

Now Susan looks definitely intrigued. 'Yes. We all saw it. The body was laid out in a supine position, arms across the chest, palms in pronation.'

'Anything else?'

'Dan thought the skeleton was definitely male, full grown, adult teeth erupted. Cause of death unclear, no obvious signs of trauma or disease. He guessed the age at about fifty, perhaps older. Of course we won't know until the test results come back. '

'Did you see Dan take any samples of tooth and bone for testing?'

'Yes. He did it at the site.'

'Where did he take them?'

'Back to the university, I presume. Doctor Galloway, what is all this about?'

As briefly as possible, Ruth explains her discovery at CNN Forensics. Susan Chow looks completely stunned.

'Are you sure?'

'I'm sure there were at least two different bodies. I've sent samples for C14 testing and isotope analysis. Then I'll know whether they're from the same period or not.'

'I can't believe it.'

'Professor Chow,' says Ruth, rocking the pushchair with her foot. Kate has started to make ominous growling noises. 'Who drove the bones to the lab?'

Susan frowns. 'I think it was one of the students.'

'Guy Delaware?'

'Yes, I think so.'

'Do you know Guy at all?'

'Only by sight. He was one of Dan's students.'

'Guy says that he was fully involved in the excavation. "A joint project," he said.'

Susan smiles, rather sadly, as if she is remembering something.

'Guy might have been involved but it was Dan's project through and through. He was obsessed with it. As soon as he suspected who might be buried in the tomb, he was a man possessed.'

Despite herself, Ruth feels rather glad. She ought to be pleased that Guy wants to carry on Dan's work but she finds herself feeling oddly possessive about the project – and about Dan.

She leans forward, addressing Susan over Kate's angrily bobbing head. 'Do you know if Dan saw the bones again after Guy delivered them to the lab?'

'I can't tell you that, I'm afraid. We were all waiting for the results to come back before going any further.'

'Do you know which lab Dan used for the analysis?'

'I'm afraid I don't. I left all that to Dan. He was very experienced.' But he's also dead, thinks Ruth, and all his work has vanished. Along with the bones that might belong to King Arthur himself.

'Did anyone take photographs of the excavation?' she asks.

'Dan took some on his phone. And I took some for the county records.'

'Could I see them?'

'Yes. I'll get copies made.' Susan Chow still sounds troubled. 'I've heard that the police are investigating Dan's death. Do you think that this could be connected?'

'I don't know,' says Ruth, 'but I've learnt to be a bit wary of coincidences.'

Susan is about to answer when Kate, with a roar of rage, hurls *Sun, Moon, Stars* from the pushchair, knocking the causewayed enclosure to the floor once again.

As Kate destroys Susan Chow's office, Sandy and Tim are actually at CNN Forensics. They are talking to Terry Durkin about the switched bones. It's a slightly delicate situation. The police use the company a lot but Sandy disapproves of outsourcing anything and views all scientific experts with extreme suspicion. To make matters worse, Peter Greengrass, the CEO of CNN Forensics, was once a senior police forensics officer and an old enemy of Sandy's. Now, he is offending Terry Durkin by treating him as one of his own subordinates. Tim, in between taking notes, tries to stop his boss addressing Terry as 'Durkin' or, worse, 'Constable'.

'So Constable,' says Sandy, 'who assigned you to this case?'

'Mr Greengrass,' says Terry.

'Pete eh,' says Sandy grimly. 'How's old Grassy Arse these days?'

'He's very well,' says Terry. 'He's just received the Queen's Commendation for his forensic work.'

'Did he?' says Sandy, who feels his own OBE is distinctly overdue. 'Nice work if you can get it. So you were asked to look after these bones. Did you log them in?'

'Yes,' says Terry, handing over a plastic wallet. 'The paperwork's all here.'

Sandy doesn't even glance down but Tim takes the wallet and looks through the papers inside. Everything seems correct. The bones were logged in by one Guy Delaware of Pendle University.

'Who has visited the bones since they've been here?' asks Sandy.

'I don't know,' says Terry. 'I'd have to check. A few people from the university have been. And Doctor Galloway the other day.'

Tim reads out from one of the photocopied sheets: 'Bones were logged in on May 10th. Dan Golding visited several times. Guy Delaware visited on May 11th, Elaine Morgan on May 13th, Clayton Henry on May 16th.'

'Guy Delaware,' says Sandy. 'He was the next-door neighbour, right? The one who called the fire brigade.'

Not for the first time, Tim makes a mental note not to underestimate his boss. Sandy has almost certainly lost the record of the 999 call but there's nothing wrong with his memory. Guy Delaware had indeed made that call.

'Yes,' says Tim. 'Elaine Morgan lived next door as well.'

'All very cosy,' says Sandy. He turns to Terry. 'Why would these characters be dropping in? What were they doing?'

Terry shrugs. 'Doing tests, taking samples for analysis, just looking. I don't know. These bones were long dead. It's not as if there was a police investigation.' He looks meaningfully at Sandy.

'Were any of these people alone with the bones?' asks Tim.

'Yes,' says Terry, sounding defensive now. 'I left them to it. Like I say, the site wasn't sealed.'

Sandy, who has had his own experiences with sealed sites, says, 'Could any of these people have taken some of the bones away and substituted others?'

Terry looks amazed, his sandy eyebrows disappearing into his hair. 'Why would anyone want to do that?'

'Just answer the question, Constable.'

Terry looks about to object, but after a martyred glance at Tim, says, 'It's not possible. Bags are checked on entry and departure.'

'Who checks them?'

'The officer on the door. Or me, if no-one else is available.'

'So they couldn't have switched the bones brought in on 10th May and replaced them with the bones of some other poor sod?'

'Is that what you think happened?'

'I'm not at liberty to say,' says Sandy, getting up. 'This is a police matter now.'

The dream-catchers go into a frenzy as Nelson and Cathbad rampage around the house looking for Pendragon. His bed upstairs is neatly made, the ubiquitous collection of shells and feathers hanging overhead as well as (more surprisingly) a large crucifix. The other rooms upstairs seem to be full of junk. Downstairs there's a bathroom and a kitchen, both high on period charm and low on appliances. There is food for Thing in the kitchen as well as a covered saucepan containing what look like herbs in water.

'Funny sort of stew,' says Nelson.

'It's an infusion,' says Cathbad. 'I don't know what for.'

They go outside into the walled garden. Nelson is about to trample over Dame Alice's herbs when Cathbad calls him back. Besides, there's no need to search, they can see the whole garden from the back step. It's a tangle of long grass and cow parsley. The only plants that Pendragon has cultivated are the herbs. Lemon-balm and rosemary stand in neatly turned earth and there is an old beer barrel full of mint. Otherwise the weeds and the brambles run unchecked. At the back of the garden there are apple trees, already heavy with fruit, and in the centre there's a sundial. Beyond the wall, the hill climbs steeply up to the sky, dark purple with gorse. From one of the trees, a blackbird watches them.

Nelson turns to go back into the house and almost falls over a bowl of cherries on the step.

'What the hell's that doing there?'

'I think it's an offering,' says Cathbad. 'The house used to be owned by Dame Alice Barley, one of the Pendle Witches, and Pendragon told me that he leaves gifts for her.'

Nelson stares at him. 'Are you serious?'

'Yes. Pendragon says that the libations have always vanished by morning.'

Nelson picks up the bowl. The fruit looks sticky and rotten; a worm is poking out of one of the cherries.

'Well, Dame Alice isn't playing today.'

They go back into the house, which seems darker and more oppressive than ever. Thing drinks noisily out of a bowl in the kitchen.

'Pendragon's not here,' says Nelson. 'We'd better go back.'

'I'd like to stay for a bit,' says Cathbad.

Nelson turns to stare at him. 'Why?'

'Well, someone's got to look after Thing.'

'Thing?'

'The dog.'

'He'll be fine. He's got enough food for a week.'

'All the same,' says Cathbad. 'I want to stay. Something's wrong. I can feel it.'

Nelson is about to tell him not to talk rubbish but even he feels something odd about the little house. So odd, in fact, that Nelson suddenly feels desperate to get back to Blackpool, the Golden Mile, traffic, Michelle.

'I can't leave you here with no car.'

'I'll be fine. It's only a few miles to Fence. And I've got a phone.' He brandishes an ancient-looking mobile.

'Well, ring if you're in any trouble. I'd better get back to the family.'

When he's back in the car he thinks that there must be something very sinister indeed about Dame Alice's cottage. He's even looking forward to seeing Maureen.

CHAPTER 20

Ruth is bumping the pushchair down the staircase. Kate is still complaining loudly, pushing against the straps and yelling 'Out, out, out' like some miniature activist. Susan Chow had offered to help with the stairs but Ruth just wanted to get away as quickly as possible. Besides it'd take Susan a while to get her room back in order. So Ruth ignores Kate's shouts and heads for the front door of the library. In a few minutes, she'll be out in the open air and maybe they can go to a park or something.

'Can I help you?'

A man appears at the foot of the stairs. Ruth says no thank you, she's fine and is about to hurry past when the man says, 'It's Ruth, isn't it?'

Ruth looks round in surprise. She doesn't expect to know anyone in Blackpool (apart from Maureen, that is, and she wouldn't put it past her to have mastered the art of shape-changing).

'It's Sam,' says the man. 'Sam Elliot. We met at Clayton's party.'

Oh yes. Sam, Dan's friend. He seems friendly enough but Kate is still yelling and Ruth is terrified that the people in the library will hear her.

'I'm sorry,' she says. 'I've got to go. We'll get chucked out in a minute.'

'I'll help you,' says Sam, opening the main doors.

Outside they are on a busy Blackpool street and Kate is quiet immediately. 'Sun,' she says, 'Moon, stars.' None of these things are visible at the moment – it's eleven-thirty on a grey August morning – but Ruth is just relieved that she has stopped shouting.

'Thanks,' she says to Sam. 'I don't think Kate's a big fan of quiet libraries.'

'Libraries aren't quiet these days,' says Sam. 'It's all multimedia and outreach and gift shops.'

Blackpool Central Library is a grand old Victorian building, but inside it is indeed a brave new world of plate glass and electronic displays. Ruth rather misses the dusty bookshelves of her student days.

Sam says, 'I shouldn't complain about outreach. I'm here to give a talk on Blackpool in the war. The library is really hot on local history.'

'Sounds interesting,' says Ruth. 'I was visiting the county archaeologist.'

'Susan Chow?' says Sam. 'Is this about Dan's discovery?'

'Yes,' says Ruth, not sure how much she should tell him. Sam says he was Dan's friend but how can she be sure? And, as Susan said, news travels fast amongst academics.

'Look,' says Sam. 'I've got half an hour before my lecture. Would you like to get a cup of coffee?'

Kate is silent, watching the buses go past, so Ruth says yes.

After a while, Cathbad decides that he'd better tackle Dame Alice head on. It's no good hiding from the fact – Pendragon has disappeared and Dame Alice must know where he is. She didn't seem to like the cherries much so Cathbad searches for something better. In the larder he finds four cans of beer, and some rather crumbly oatcakes. No wine, unfortunately, but Dame Alice was probably a tough countrywoman who liked a good pint of stout. This is Guinness, which, Cathbad reckons, should be good enough for anyone. Pen must have got the taste for it when he lived in Ireland. Cathbad fills a glass with the beautiful black liquid and finishes the can himself. He has a feeling that he might need it before the day is over.

He goes outside into the garden because that's where he felt her presence the strongest. The clouds are still dark overhead and the bird still watches from the tree. Even when Thing runs out of the house, barking wildly, the bird does not fly away.

Cathbad places the Guinness and the oatcake on the sundial. He raises his hands to the sky: 'Dame Alice, accept my offering and help me find my friend.'

Thing stops his mad circling and comes to sit at Cathbad's feet. For a few moments everything is completely still and then, from the apple tree, the bird caws once.

Cathbad reckons that's all the answer he's going to get.

They go to an Italian cafe where Kate is treated like a queen. She gets a special chair, a frothy milk drink and a selection of tiny cakes glistening with glazed fruit. Sam and Ruth get more prosaic cappuccinos, though these too are excellent. The proprietor obviously thinks Kate is their (joint) child and is fulsome with compliments. Ruth is getting used to people making assumptions about Kate's parentage but Sam is obviously uncomfortable.

'She's not . . .' he says when Signor Tino tells him to savour each fleeting moment of Kate's babyhood. 'Oh, never mind.'

'Do you have children?' asks Ruth.

'No,' says Sam. 'Too late now, I suppose.' His voice is cheerful but his eyes look rather sad. He has a weather-beaten face with light blue eyes that look very directly at you. He has a boyish outdoorsy look, like a grown-up scout, though his hair is starting to recede.

'You've got plenty of time,' says Ruth. 'How old are you?'

'Forty-two.'

'Same as me.' Same as Dan, she thinks.

'Anyway,' she says. 'There's no rush for a man. No biological clock, I mean.'

'No,' says Sam, putting sugar in his coffee. 'But I had kind of expected to be married with kids by now.'

He looks like a dad, thinks Ruth. The sort of father who would take his children swimming and cycling. Camping in summer with a small excitable dog in the back of the Volvo. It turns out that she was right about the dog. Sam tells her that he has a Jack Russell called Griffin. Ruth volunteers that she has a cat.

'I always thought I'd end up a single woman alone with her cat,' she says. 'I never expected to be married or have children. Well, I'm not married but I do have Kate.'

'Cake,' says Kate loudly. Signor Tino is instantly at her side with new supplies.

'You're lucky.'

'I know.'

There is a short silence and then Sam says, 'So why were you seeing Susan?'

Ruth is expecting this question but is still not sure how to answer it. She doesn't want to tell Sam about the switched bones but, on the other hand, he might be able to give her some useful information.

'I was asking about the excavation,' she says. 'Were you there?'

'I was at the early digs,' he says. 'But I'm a modern historian, not an archaeologist. Guy's the man you should ask.'

'Was Guy a friend of Dan's?'

'Yes,' says Sam, wincing slightly as Kate drops a cream cake on the floor. 'They were good friends even after . . .'

Ruth picks up the cake. She has to resist a temptation to eat it. 'Even after what?'

'Well, Elaine is Guy's best friend. I don't think there's anything sexual there. They're more like brother and sister. So when Elaine started seeing Dan . . .'

'Elaine went out with Dan?' This would tie in with Elaine's appearance at Dan's funeral (in Sam's company) but Ruth still can't quite see the two together.

'Yes. They had quite a romance. It was all very intense. But then they broke up and Elaine went back to living with Guy. But, all the time, Dan and Guy – and Elaine too – were working on the dig together. It must have been very difficult sometimes.'

'Why did they break up?'

'I don't know. I think, from something Dan said that he just didn't want to get involved in a serious relationship. After all, he hadn't been divorced long.'

'So Dan was the one who finished it?'

'I think so. Yes.'

Then Elaine moved back next door. It sounded like some French farce with the same people going in and out of the same doors, but Ruth is sure that it didn't seem funny at the time. Suddenly, as clear as day, she remembers the 68 bus and Dan's lips pressed to hers. She wonders whether Elaine was in love with him.

'Did Dan tell you much about the dig?' she asks.

'At the beginning. He told me about the Raven God and all that. It was exciting because Britain was meant to be Christian at the time, but here was this pagan temple. But the bones . . . no. He didn't tell me about them.'

I wonder why not, thinks Ruth. 'Have you ever heard

anything about any Neo-Nazi groups on campus?' she asks. 'Anyone who might have had an interest in the dig?'

Sam, like Clayton before him, looks uncomfortable. 'We all know about the far right, but they're a load of nutters. No one takes them seriously.'

'Have you heard of a group called the White Hand? A sort of splinter group.'

Sam shakes his head. 'The White Hand? No, I don't think so.'

But Dan was afraid of something, thinks Ruth. And so, apparently, was Guy. After all, he was the one who insisted on taking the bones to the police lab.

'I've got to go,' says Sam, looking at his watch. 'Nice to meet you again. Do get in touch with Guy, he knows everything about the excavation. After all, he's the one writing the book now.'

'What?'

'Yes. After Dan died, Guy thought that he should write a book about the discovery. As a kind of tribute to Dan. Bye, Ruth. Bye, Kate.'

He pats Kate on the head and she puts a jammy hand on his back. Ruth hopes he won't notice.

'Bye bye, Daddy,' says Signor Tino tenderly.

As the afternoon draws on, Thing starts to get more and more nervous. He whimpers, he stares at the door, he walks round and round the main room, always coming back to sit at Cathbad's feet and stare at him fixedly. Cathbad, after eating some bread and cheese from the larder and drinking another can of Guinness, has decided that the best thing to do is to sit and wait. So he sits in the wizard's chair by the fire and tries to connect with the energies of the house. After a while he is so successful that he falls asleep. He wakes to find the room much colder and Thing with a paw on his knee, looking up entreatingly.

'OK,' says Cathbad, 'you win.'

He gets up, rubbing his arms to bring the circulation back. He's wearing a jacket and a jumper but he's still cold. He wishes he'd brought his cloak, which – as he's always telling Nelson – is warm and practical as well as being a symbol of his druidical power. To be honest, he could do with a little of that power right now.

Thing leads him to the foot of the stairs and Cathbad decides to go up and have another look around. There could be an attic somewhere that they had overlooked the first time. The thought of what they might find in such a room sends the first real shivers of fear down his spine.

Cathbad lights another oil lamp. The house is much darker now, the corners have almost disappeared into the shadows, and it'll be even darker upstairs, where the windows are small. He decides to search thoroughly, looking for clues. What he's looking for he doesn't quite know but he knows something is wrong in the little house; just as Thing knows, his nose pressed to Cathbad's leg, tail between legs; just as Dame Alice knows, although she's keeping her own counsel.

Cathbad makes a methodical tour of Pendragon's

bedroom, a long, low room with a double bed under the vaulted eaves. Pendragon would have had trouble standing up in here, thinks Cathbad. The bed is neatly made with a patchwork quilt, the bedside table empty apart from a teacup containing mouldy leaves and a book of old ballads. Cathbad opens the oak chest at the foot of the bed. It is full of bed linen, carefully folded with lavender. The wardrobe, jammed under one of the beams, contains a collection of robes as well as some more utilitarian garments, mostly jeans and work shirts. There is nothing else in the room, no bookcase, no photographs, nothing of a personal nature at all. Cathbad glances up at the wooden crucifix on the wall and offers up a quick prayer to Saint Anthony, patron saint of finding things. Help me find Pendragon before it's too late.

The other two rooms are full of personal stuff. Tea chests full of books, an old bicycle, sundry items of broken furniture, a huge Victorian bird cage, several gloomy old paintings, even a chipped cistern and sink. Pendragon obviously just shuts the door on these rooms and lives in minimalist splendour in the master bedroom. Cathbad is about to go back downstairs when something flashes across his brain, like a subliminal advertising message. There was another door. It was in Pendragon's bedroom, just by the wardrobe. A low door, half hidden by a curtain. Cathbad turns back, trying to find a calming mantra to slow his heart down.

The door is locked but Cathbad, who has an excellent visual memory, remembers a bunch of keys hanging by the larder in the kitchen. He runs back downstairs, Thing clattering at his side. He spends a few frustrating minutes trying different keys but eventually one – an unobtrusive Yale – fits.

He switches on the light and sees a tiny room, barely six feet wide, containing a desk, office chair and laptop. Cathbad pauses. Something shocking has just happened. What was it? He switched on the light ... In a house lit by oil-fired lamps, he has switched on a light. And in front of him is a perfect slice of twenty-first-century life. Desk, laptop, mobile phone, even an iPod in its dock. Shelves hold lever-arch files and a wireless modem twinkles with green lights. It is as if he has gone forward in time, stepped into the wardrobe and discovered a high-tech Narnia. But even as he sits at the desk, he knows that this hidden room can't mean anything good. Pendragon must have his reasons for hiding his links with the outside world but Cathbad can't think of any that make him see his old friend in a warm and twinkly light.

He opens the laptop. It asks him for a password and – exercising his psychic powers – he guesses 'Thing'. The computer flashes into life. The first file he sees is titled White Hand. Cathbad's heart sinks. He doesn't want to find out any more. He is about to close the case when something catches his eye, a silver pimple at the side of the screen. A memory stick. He clicks onto the C drive and reads the words 'Dan's Computer'.

Ruth is on the beach when she gets Cathbad's message. She felt that Kate deserved some time running about after the library and the cafe. So after a healthy lunch of chips on the pier, they headed down to the sands. As soon as they got there it started to rain and even the donkeys had sought shelter. But Ruth and Kate play on, jumping over puddles and writing in the sand. Kate is wearing a raincoat but Ruth has forgotten to bring hers and soon her hair is hanging in wet ribbons and her feet are soaking in their thin shoes. She takes them off and runs barefoot, enjoying the feeling of the cool sand between her toes. 'Me too,' yells Kate, so Ruth takes her shoes off too and they both run, laughing, in and out of the freezing water. For those few moments, Ruth feels that she is completely happy.

The tide comes in incredibly quickly, faster even than on the Saltmarsh. Now, it's as if the sea is erasing all the frivolities of Blackpool life – the donkeys' hoof-prints, the writing on the sand (Ruth has read at least two 'Marry Me's), the chip wrappers and the half-eaten ice creams. Ruth thinks of an Etchasketch that was given to Kate last Christmas. It was too old for her but Ruth spent many happy hours writing or drawing and then watching as the inexorable line moved across the screen, restoring everything to smooth blankness. *The moving finger writes and, having writ, moves on.* Eventually, Ruth and Kate are standing on the steps, looking out at an expanse of water. The beach has completely vanished.

Ruth's phone recalls her to life. She isn't surprised when she sees that it's from Cathbad but the words make her stand stock still as the cold North Sea breaks over the step and soaks her feet.

Have found Dan's laptop. Tell Nelson.

As night falls Thing becomes more and more frantic. He keeps going to the front door and barking at the rain. Cathbad lights more oil lamps and tries to start a fire. It is something he's good at (Nelson once called him a closet arsonist) but today his skills desert him. He kneels by the hearth, crumpled paper in hand, defeated. Thing whines softly in the background.

'It's OK, boy,' says Cathbad. 'Do you want food? There's food in the kitchen.'

As he says this he hears Nelson's voice, those familiar flat northern vowels.

He's got enough food for a week.

There are several food bowls in the kitchen. Pendragon has left his dog enough food for a week. His friend – the druid who keeps a high-tech office hidden in his bedroom – obviously isn't expecting to return for some time. But why leave the door unlocked, especially when he has all that expensive equipment upstairs? Cathbad stands still, listening to the house. The ancient beams creak, upstairs something – probably a mouse – is scurrying from room to room. Outside, the rain hammers on the windows as it did the day he came here with Ruth. Did Pendragon know then that Ruth was Dan Golding's friend? Was that why he seemed so scared when they arrived? A sudden movement makes Cathbad jump but it's only Thing scratching at the door. The crazy animal evidently wants to go outside. Well, Cathbad believes in following instincts, his own and those of other creatures. Holding the lamp high, he opens the heavy oak door.

Thing runs down the hill. Cathbad follows, more carefully. It's dark now and the ground is steep. Also it's raining heavily, turning the earth to mud. Cathbad stumbles. He doesn't want to break his leg and lie undiscovered for weeks. Also, he doesn't want to lose the dog.

'Thing!' he calls. 'Thing! Come back!'

He sees a white shape at the bottom of the path and heads towards it. Thing is standing by a small group of trees. Hidden in the trees is a building, taller than it is wide, an outhouse of some kind. Cathbad approaches, driven on now by a sick certainty of disaster. By all the gods in the pantheon, he knows that nothing good lies within.

Cathbad pushes open the door. The lamp has gone out but the moon rides out from behind the clouds, illuminating brick walls, a pile of half-chopped logs and Pendragon's body hanging from a beam.

Thing starts to howl.

CHAPTER 21

Cathbad backs away. For a second, he just wants to shut the door and pretend that he hasn't seen the grotesque figure swinging to and fro. It is only the sound of Thing's desolate howling that brings him to his senses.

'It's OK, boy,' he says, ridiculously, to the dog. Because, if anything is clear, it's that things are very much not OK.

He approaches the swinging body. Logs lie scattered on the floor. Presumably Pendragon stood on this pile before kicking it away. There seems to be nothing else to stand on. Cathbad takes out his phone and calls for an ambulance while, at the same time, searching for a ladder, a chair, anything. Eventually, he finds an old water butt and pulls it into the shed. The wood is rotten but he manages to balance on the reinforced rim. He takes a sharp knife from his pocket (the possession of which, as Nelson could inform him, renders him liable to a lengthy jail sentence) and cuts through the rope suspending Pendragon from the ceiling. He had intended to catch the body but Pendragon is a big man and his weight, combined with the perilous perch, is enough to send Cathbad crashing to the floor. Cathbad actually falls onto his friend's body, but even as he scrambles to his feet and starts cutting the rope around Pendragon's neck, he knows it's too late. The wizard is dead: Cathbad knew that as soon as he opened the door.

When the paramedics arrive, they find Cathbad kneeling by his friend's body, the dog at his side. They are very kind and professional, actually covering Cathbad with one of those foil blankets favoured by marathon runners. Pendragon is lifted onto a stretcher and carried into the ambulance which is parked by the gate, its headlights illuminating the rain. They ask if Cathbad wants to accompany them but he thinks that he ought to stay with Thing. 'We'll have to inform the police,' they say, almost sympathetically. Cathbad nods and says that he understands. He has already called the only policeman who matters.

Nelson arrives to find Cathbad sitting by the fireplace with Thing on his lap. There is no fire in the grate and the room is freezing. Dream-catchers swing crazily in the draft from the open front door.

'Is he dead?' he asks.

'Yes. The ambulance took him away.'

'And you found him hanging in a shed at the end of the drive?'

'Yes. He must have been there all day.'

Nelson rubs his eyes, digesting this. Then he asks, 'Have you any idea why he did it?'

Cathbad smiles sadly. 'I've got lots of ideas, none of them very edifying. I found a room upstairs with a computer in it.'

'A computer? I thought this place was still in the Dark Ages.'

'I think that's what Pendragon wanted us to think. Anyway, there's lots on the computer about the White Hand.'

'Think they had something to do with this?'

'I don't know. I only know that he was scared of something and now he's dead.'

'It's enough to be going on with,' agrees Nelson. 'I'd better tell Sandy and he can come and pick it up. He'd never forgive me if the local boys got their hands on it. Where is this hidden room?'

Cathbad shows him but he doesn't show him the memory stick, which is in his pocket next to the illegal knife. He doesn't know why he is keeping quiet about the find. After all, he told Ruth to tell Nelson about the computer. It's just that he has a very strong feeling that Ruth ought to see the contents first. And, after all, his instincts have already been proved right once that day.

Nelson looks all round the secret room but is careful not to touch anything. Then he announces that he is going to drive Cathbad back to Lytham. Cathbad doesn't demur and Nelson, in his turn, says nothing about Thing, who climbs happily into the back seat and breathes down Nelson's neck all the way home.

Ruth is asleep on the sofa when Cathbad gets in. He meant to wake her gently but Thing bounds over and licks her face briskly.

'What?' Ruth sits up immediately, rubbing her cheek.

'Sorry,' says Cathbad. 'I brought Thing back with me.'

'So I see. Why?'

Cathbad explains about Pendragon and about the hidden room and the computer. By now, dawn is breaking and a pink light filters through the curtains. Cathbad makes tea and they sit on the sofa with the dog between them.

'So you say Dan's files are all on this memory stick,' says Ruth.

'I think so.'

'Where is it? Did you give it to the police?'

In answer, Cathbad holds out his hand. On his palm is a little silver object shaped like a bullet.

'Shall I have a look?' says Ruth, almost in a whisper.

'I think that's what he would have wanted,' says Cathbad seriously.

Ruth puts the memory stick into her laptop and immediately two files pop up. One is called archaeology and this Ruth resolves to explore in depth. The other is titled, simply, 'Days'. Ruth clicks onto it:

9 May 2010

I've found him. I know it's him. As soon as we moved that last stone and I saw his face, still with the gold circlet around his head, I knew. Guy said, 'Is there anything inside?' and I said, 'It's Him.' Stupid, I know, and, afterwards Elaine teased me about it, saying that I was 'more Martha than Arthur'. Her latest thing is implying that I'm gay, which doesn't bother me at all. Let her think I am gay if that makes it easier for her.

It was getting dark by the time we had recorded the sarcophagus and skeleton and Clayton suggested that we secure the site and leave the actual excavation until tomorrow. He was right but I hated to leave Arthur there. It was a mild night and we put an awning over him but even so . . . It didn't seem right to treat a king that way. God, Elaine is right. I am getting weird. None of us mentioned the White Hand but Clayton suggested, casually, that we took turns to guard the bones. He volunteered to watch until midnight, then I am going to relieve him. Sounds crazy, I know, but I am looking forward to going back and paying my homage to the Raven King.

'It's a diary,' Ruth says.

CHAPTER 22

Both are expecting a summons from Sandy and it comes at nine o'clock in the form of a marked police car at their front door.

'The neighbours will love this,' says Ruth, but for once the street is deserted. It's Friday morning, maybe everyone has gone away for a long weekend. A polite policeman passes on a message from DCI Macleod requesting their presence at the police station.

'What about my daughter?' says Ruth. Kate is hiding behind her, staring open-mouthed at the uniformed figures.

'Bring her too. DCI Macleod said he'd lay on breakfast.'

'And the dog?' asks Cathbad.

The policeman looks dubiously at Thing, who puts his head on one side and tries to look sweet.

'Can't you leave him here?'

'It's a rented house. I don't like to.'

'Oh, all right. Bring him too.'

Kate enjoys the drive into Blackpool, making siren

noises and waving excitedly at other motorists. Ruth and Cathbad sit in silence. Ruth suddenly feels very tired, not able to cope with Nelson and the famous Sandy Macleod, who is probably Nelson cubed. She wants to sit quietly and read Dan's diaries. The description of finding King Arthur's body had moved her. She remembers that thrill of discovery so well. Dan had sounded so happy but there had been ominous overtones too, the mention of the White Hand, of Elaine's hostility. Less than a month after writing that diary entry, Dan was dead.

At first sight, Sandy Macleod lives up to Ruth's mental image of 'Nelson cubed'. He is a large man, not as tall as Nelson but much heavier. His shirt strains across his stomach and the chair creaks when he sits down. His face is pouchy and almost comically mournful, with turned-down eyes and mouth, like one of those cartoons of a smiley face turned upside down. There is something cartoonish about him altogether, from the broad Lancashire accent to the bustling walk with splayed-out feet. But something in his eyes warns Ruth not to underestimate him. He gives her a sharp look too.

'Ah, the famous Doctor Galloway.'

Ruth wonders why she is famous to him, and while she normally likes people to use her title, on Sandy's lips it has the effect of making her sound like a made-up character. Doctor Foster, Doctor Jekyll, Doctor Dolittle.

But Sandy is nice to Kate, bending down to her level and offering to buy her chocolate from the vending machine. Ruth almost protests but doesn't want to sound like a neurotic middle-class mother. She can always eat it herself to save Kate's teeth.

Sandy is accompanied by another man who introduces himself as Detective Sergeant Tim Heathfield. Ruth takes to him immediately. He is respectful without being creepy, formal without being officious. He ushers them into a meeting room which contains a large breakfast – and Nelson.

'What are you doing here?' says Ruth, without thinking.

'Cathbad called me from Pendragon's house last night,' says Nelson.

'DCI Nelson informed me that there was important evidence at the scene,' says Sandy, sounding as if he is making a statement in court. 'I proceeded to the house and took possession of a laptop.' He points at the computer on the table.

Ruth looks at Cathbad and then at Sandy, who is now tucking into a bacon roll.

'There's something you should know . . .' She gets out the memory stick.

'What's that?' asks Sandy.

'It's a memory stick,' says Ruth. 'For a computer.'

'I know that, love,' says Sandy with menacing sweetness. 'But what's it doing here?'

'I found it in Pendragon's house,' says Cathbad. 'I thought Ruth ought to see it.'

'It's got Dan's files on it,' says Ruth.

'You shouldn't have touched it,' says Nelson angrily. 'It's police property now.'

'I know,' says Cathbad, 'but I thought Ruth should see it first.'

Tim leans forward. 'Have you opened any files, Doctor Galloway?'

'I glanced at one or two,' says Ruth defensively.

Tim looks at Sandy.

'What?' asks Ruth.

'It's possible,' says Tim, 'that there was a virus inserted into the files. As soon as you opened the files, the virus could have sent an email to ... to whoever took the computer in the first place.'

'So they'd know I'd found it?' says Ruth, suddenly afraid. She thinks of the text messages, the sense that someone is watching her. Now they're watching her even when she's on-line. She's got a cyber stalker as well as the old-fashioned kind.

Tim seems to know what she's thinking. 'Doctor Galloway, I know you've had some threatening texts. Have you received anything else unusual, either as a text message or via email?'

'What do you mean, "unusual"?' asks Ruth.

'Somebody wanting your bank account details, personal information, anything like that.'

'Nigerian businessman needs a loan,' says Nelson. 'You know the kind of thing.'

'I'm hardly going to fall for ...' begins Ruth. Then she stops.

'What is it?' asks Nelson.

Ruth is thinking of her cottage on the Saltmarsh. Of

opening her computer and reading that first cheery message from University Pals. *Hi Ruth! Want to catch up with your old mates from uni?*

She describes the email to Tim. He exchanges a glance with Sandy.

'Sounds like a classic phishing exercise,' he says.

'Fishing?'

He spells out the word. 'It's an internet scam designed to elicit personal information.'

'But they didn't ask for bank details,' says Ruth, feeling defensive.

'No. It sounds to me more like someone wanted to assume your identity.'

'Why?' says Sandy, as if this was the last identity *he'd* choose.

'They must have known that Doctor Galloway was going to investigate Dan Golding's discovery. They may have wanted to make enquiries in her name.'

'What sort of enquiries?' says Sandy.

'Test results,' says Ruth. 'Dan sent samples to forensic labs for testing. I'm trying to track them down.'

'Is there anything about the tests on the computer?' asks Tim.

Ruth has had a quick look through the archaeology file. She noticed immediately that Dan had used a laboratory in the US for the DNA and isotopic tests. Why had he done that? There are plenty of excellent labs in the UK. Why bother to send samples all the way to the States?

'I've found the lab he used,' she says. 'They're in New York so I can call them this afternoon.'

'Anything about the White Hand in the diary?' asks Sandy.

'Bits and pieces,' says Ruth. 'I haven't read it all yet.' She feels disinclined to share Dan's secret thoughts with these people who didn't know him and didn't care about his work.

'There's quite a lot on Pendragon's computer,' says Tim. 'A kind of manifesto. Lots of stuff about the Arthurian legends, Arthur being the great White King who'll come again to purge England of all undesirable aliens.' He speaks lightly but Ruth wonders how it feels for him to read such nakedly racist sentiments. She herself has enormous trouble relating them to Pendragon, that kindly Father Christmas figure.

'Any names and addresses?' asks Sandy. 'Anything helpful?'

'We can take it to the forensic recovery people,' says Tim. 'If there's anything there, they'll find it. I'll give them the memory stick too.'

Sandy grunts, probably at the use of the 'f' word. Ruth says, 'Can I take a copy of the diaries? I'd like to read them all. See if I can find ... if I can find any clues.'

'You might as well,' says Sandy. 'Harm's done now. Tim can make copies of everything for you.'

'Thank you.'

'Mind you tell us if you find anything that strikes you as worth investigating,' says Sandy.

Ruth says she will. Sandy takes another roll and turns to Cathbad. 'Think that's why your mate topped himself, because he was mixed up with this Nazi group?'

Even Nelson winces but Cathbad just says quietly, 'I don't know why he did it.'

'Didn't even have the decency to leave a note,' says Sandy. 'Get us some more coffee, Tim, there's a good lad.'

The police car deposits Ruth and Cathbad back in Lytham, to the delighted interest of their neighbours. Neither of them feels like lunch after the huge police breakfast but Ruth makes sandwiches for Kate and Cathbad eats the crusts abstractedly.

'I'll take Kate to the park this afternoon,' says Ruth. 'Give you some time to rest. You must be exhausted.' Cathbad doesn't look tired; in fact he seems almost unnaturally calm and self-controlled. Ruth feels quite in awe of him.

'I'll come with you,' he says. 'Thing could do with a walk.'

Under the table, Thing wags his tail noisily. Ruth doesn't know if animals are allowed in the cottage but what else could they do with him? Cathbad says he'll take him to a dog rescue place but Ruth thinks otherwise. She suspects that Cathbad and Thing are stuck with each other for life.

At two o'clock, Ruth rings New York to be told that the person she needs is in a meeting. *He'll call her back*, says the lilting American voice. *Have a nice day now.*

It's a new experience, going for a walk with a bull terrier. People cross to the other side of the street to avoid Thing, and in the park mothers clutch their children nervously, even though Cathbad doesn't let the dog off the lead.

'Now I know why Pen lived in the country,' says Cathbad, smiling encouragingly at a terrified toddler. It is almost the first time that he has said his friend's name since he told Ruth how he died.

Now he says, almost chattily, 'You know, Ruth. That's something I just don't understand. How Pen could leave Thing like that?'

'Maybe he knew you'd come for him,' says Ruth. She is in the play area pushing Kate on a swing and has to talk to Cathbad across the fence. Thing wags his tail at all the children and crinkles his nose engagingly. 'Look at that dog snarling,' says one grandmother. 'Shouldn't be allowed.'

'I can't stop thinking,' says Cathbad. 'When did he do it? The paramedics thought he hadn't been dead long. Maybe he'd just done it when Nelson and I arrived. Maybe if I'd found him sooner, I could have saved him.'

Maybe he didn't want to be saved, thinks Ruth. Aloud, she asks, 'Did Pendragon have any family?'

'A sister,' says Cathbad. 'They weren't close. I gave her name to the police. I ought to speak to her as well, I suppose.'

A sister, but no children, thinks Ruth. Just like Dan. Are their deaths linked as well? In the sunshine of the park it's hard to believe in shadowy fascist conspiracies. But there is someone out there, someone who wants to scare her too. *Ladybird, ladybird.* Ruth shivers, looking round at the children on the slide, at the parents sitting on benches, at the elderly bowlers on the green. Is he here, the texter? Is he watching her now?

'Don't stop,' orders Kate.

Ruth pushes the swing, enjoying the sight of her daughter, her dark hair and red T-shirt silhouetted against the sky.

'Higher, higher,' shouts Kate.

Cathbad too is watching Kate, leaning on the fence with the devil dog at his side. 'What a wonderful thing it is to be a child,' he says. Ruth thinks he sounds very sad.

When they get home, Ruth has a message to ring Todd Holland at the American lab. She does so and they spend a few minutes establishing her identity, the identity that is, apparently, coveted by someone else.

'I've got the DNA and isotope results here,' says Todd. 'They're very interesting, especially when you think where the bones were found. Of course, the Roman Empire stretched into all sorts of places, but even so.'

'Yes?' says Ruth, encouragingly. Her mouth is suddenly dry.

'Well, oxygen isotope analysis points to the subject originating from the north of England.'

Big news, thinks Ruth. She has known all along that

they are dealing with a northerner, a sort of Ancient Roman version of Nelson – or Sandy. But Todd isn't finished. 'The interesting thing is the DNA result . . .'

'Don't tell me it's a woman.'

'No,' says Todd, sounding surprised. 'Subject is male and at least one of his parents was from North Africa.'

When Ruth puts the phone down, Cathbad is looking enquiringly at her.

'King Arthur was black,' she says.

CHAPTER 23

'What do you mean?' asks Cathbad.

'The tests show that the skeleton found in the tomb had North African DNA.'

'How can that be?'

Ruth paces the room. It's as if some of the excitement described in Dan's diaries has communicated itself to her. Some of the fear too. This could be huge, she tells herself. She sees the headlines in the papers, 'Legendary English King was Black says Archaeology Expert'. Then she remembers that someone burnt Dan alive to protect this secret.

'There was a black Roman emperor,' she says. 'Septimus Severus, I think. The Romans were in North Africa and it stands to reason that some of the population would have become Roman citizens.'

'Didn't you have to be Roman to be a Roman citizen?'

'No. They were quite progressive that way. St Paul was a Roman citizen, remember. I wonder if there were any other black Romans in Britain. I'm going to ring Max.'

Max answers on the second ring. He sounds delighted to hear from her. Guiltily, Ruth remembers that she never really gave him an answer about coming up to Lytham.

'I wanted some information,' she says.

'Oh.' Max's voice changes. 'Of course.'

She explains about the isotope results. Excitement of a different kind begins to creep into Max's voice.

'There were some skeletons excavated in a Romano-British cemetery outside York. I don't think they did DNA tests but the limb proportions and skeletal facial features appeared to point to the men being black African. Also there was a North African legion stationed at Hadrian's Wall. They were from Morocco, I think. They found African DNA in the local populations around Hadrian's Wall which suggests that the soldiers intermarried with the local people. It was actually Septimus Severus who made it legal for serving legionnaires to get married.'

'So our man could maybe have been the son of one of those soldiers?'

'It's possible, yes.' She can almost hear Max's mind working. 'Maybe his father went back to Rome with the legions. Our man could have been trained by his father in Roman cavalry arts and gone on to become a war leader, defending his people against the Picts. Those communities must have felt very vulnerable after the Romans withdrew.'

'So King Arthur could have been black or mixed race?'

'Why not? That could be the reason for all the mythology around him, the suggestion that he was different, somehow "other". It could even account for the Raven King legend.'

'Because ravens are black?'

'Exactly.'

'I wish we still had the bones,' says Ruth. 'Then we'd know for sure.'

'How are the investigations going?'

'Slowly.' She doesn't tell him about Pendragon or about the increasingly threatening text messages. In turn, Max doesn't offer to come up to Lytham. After a few further archaeological exchanges they say goodbye.

Ruth turns to find both Cathbad and Thing staring at her.

'Max says there were African Romans in the north of Britain,' she says. 'There was even an African legion at Hadrian's Wall. King Arthur could have been the son of one of those legionnaires.'

'How are things with Max?' asks Cathbad.

Much later, after Cathbad and Kate are both in bed, Ruth goes back to Dan's diaries.

10 May 2010

Excavation day. I went to the site early to watch the sun go up. So beautiful over the river with the birds flying in from the sea. Made me wish I could paint or sing or something. The others turned up at nine and I started excavating the bones. I still felt bad removing them from their grave but I felt that I had made my peace with King Arthur last night. I felt that he understood.

Clayton determined to do it all by the book. Lots of people watching – Guy, Elaine, Sue Chow, some old dears from LAS. It was a bit of a shock to see Pippa there. Why did she come? It's not as if she has any interest in archaeology. We didn't speak but once or twice I saw Elaine looking over as if she suspected something. Clayton was oblivious, though. All he cared about was whether the local press had got wind of it. For some reason, he wants it all kept quiet until we know for sure. It'll make a bigger splash then, I suppose.

Oh my God, my first sight of the fully exposed skeleton! He looked so kingly and peaceful, lying on his back, hands crossed over his chest. I heard Guy mutter 'Jesus' and even Sue seemed moved. I lifted out the head – the skull is complete, lovely nuchal crest, large mastoid bones, heavy brow ridges. He was a fine, strong man. Beautiful eye orbits, almost rectangular, wide nasal cavity, adult teeth all erupted. I looked at it for so long that Clayton started to get impatient, reminding me that it was imperative to get the excavation completed by the end of the day.

When it was all done – all the bones numbered and bagged, recording sheets complete, bone and teeth samples taken for analysis – I wanted to take him back to Pendle. Actually, what I really wanted was to take him home but (wisely) I didn't say this. Then Guy said that the bones should go to the CNN lab in Blackpool. He has contacts there, apparently. I thought Guy was becoming too obsessed with the White Hand and said so. We shouldn't let ourselves

be dictated to by a bunch of fascist lunatics. But Clayton
agreed with him so Guy drove the Raven King to the lab.
I hated to see him go.

Ruth looks up from her laptop. It's dark outside; the
house is silent. She can recognise so many things in the
diaries – the thrill of discovery, the moving and exacting
task of disinterring a human skeleton – but there are
also many elements that surprise her. She is amazed at
Dan's quasi-mystical identification with King Arthur. All
this talk of paying homage to the Raven King, of making
his peace with him. She just can't relate this to her
memory of Dan – that cheerful, cynical student. The old
Dan would never have gone to watch the sun come up,
she is sure of it. As a matter of fact, once they watched
the sun rise together, after an all-night party in Denmark
Hill. She remembers standing on a balcony drinking
Bloody Marys and watching the first dossers of the day
arriving in Ruskin Gardens. Dan did not declare a
burning desire to paint then: he had expressed a wish
for a McDonald's breakfast and had set out in search of
one. Somewhere along the line Dan had become a fully-
fledged New-Age thinker. She wonders if he was ever
taught by Erik.

And there are other surprises too. The references to
Elaine tie in with what Sam told her but what's all this
about Pippa Henry? Elaine looked over 'as if she suspected
something' but Clayton was 'oblivious'. Was Dan having
an affair with Clayton Henry's wife? It certainly looks

that way, though Ruth can't make out if the affair was over by the time of the dig. She thinks of the elegant Mrs Henry in her scary shoes. She can't imagine Dan being involved with her but, as is becoming clear, she doesn't really know Dan at all. Or rather, the Dan she knew existed twenty-odd years ago. She doesn't know this Dan, the New-Age Don Juan of Pendle University, at all. Dan was always good-looking, women were attracted to him, but she would never have thought that he would be the sort of man to have an affair with another man's wife. But, then again, who would have thought that she'd become the sort of woman to have an affair with a married policeman? Love does funny things to us all.

Was Dan in love with Pippa Henry? Was he ever in love with Elaine? If so, it certainly doesn't come across in the diaries. There is only one loved object here – King Arthur. Dan airily dismisses Clayton as 'oblivious', but what if he wasn't? What if he suspected that the wife (whom he so clearly adores) was sleeping with a member of his department? Wouldn't that constitute a motive of some kind? Ruth resolves to mention this to Tim (she can't face Sandy, even over the phone).

The description of the skull is interesting too. There is no doubt that this isn't the skull that Ruth examined at the lab. It's complete, for one thing. And, with hindsight, it's interesting that he mentions the eye orbits and the nasal cavity. African skulls tend to have rectangular eye orbits and wider nasal apertures. Did Dan suspect, even then? He says that he took a long time examining the head. Did he guess the amazing truth? That the Raven King was, like the bird itself, black? If so, he didn't record it in his diary.

At her feet Thing sighs and twitches in his sleep. He has stuck close to her all evening. Is he missing his master? Pendragon has been an unspoken presence in the house all day. Ruth can't imagine what it was like for Cathbad, finding his friend's dead body in that way. Cathbad doesn't seem to want to talk about it and Ruth respects that. They both took refuge in talking about the dog, about his trauma and possible distress. Ruth leans down to pat him now while she scans the screen. She is, of course, looking for references to herself.

Under 20 May she finds one:

I've been thinking I need a second opinion and suddenly I thought – Ruth! She's made quite a name for herself in forensic archaeology (was involved in a big murder case in Norfolk a few years back) and I know I could trust her. Funny, I haven't thought of her for years, but I can picture her quite clearly. Dark, ungainly, with lovely eyes. Clever, intense, but funny too. I kissed her once and remember thinking that she'd probably be terrific in bed. I looked for her on Friends Reunited but she wasn't there. I didn't think she would be somehow. I got a new invitation from an outfit called University Pals. I sent off my info but I'm pretty sure she won't have joined them either. She's probably married with ten kids by now. Like everyone else from those days. Anyway I can find her easily enough through her university. There can't be many forensic archaeologists in Norfolk. I'll wait until I get the results and then I'll contact her. Until then, I won't tell anyone except

And there, maddeningly, the entry ended. Ruth sits, staring at the words, feeling slightly dizzy. She has often wondered what other people think of her. Well, now she knows. Ungainly, that's about right. But – lovely eyes, terrific in bed? Ruth loves sex but has never wondered whether she's good at it. That's something new to think about it. She recognises the bitterness of thinking that everyone else your age is married with children. How often, over the last twenty years, has she felt the same thing? First it was the wedding invitations, then the birth announcements. When, in her forties, they eventually stopped coming, she had felt relieved. Now, at last, they would leave her alone. And then she had her own miracle baby. Dan couldn't have expected that. No one did, least of all Ruth herself.

Thinking about babies makes Ruth want to check on Kate. She is stretched out sideways in the double bed, sleeping deeply, mouth open. She has caught a slight cold, probably from paddling yesterday. The joys of a summer holiday in England. Not that this is a holiday exactly, what with a sinister fascist group spying on her, death around every corner and the shadow of the Raven King looming over them all. And Dan had been contacted by University Pals, the outfit Tim suspects of being an internet scam designed to steal your identity. It's a frightening thought, put like that.

Cathbad's door is shut and Ruth does not go in.

Downstairs she pours herself a glass of wine and goes back to the diaries. Thing settles heavily on her feet. Like Kate, he's a noisy breather.

22 May 2010

Threatening letter received today. Know it's from the WH as it has all their stylistic signatures. The references to pure-blood, England (not Britain) and the so-called Gods of Yore. The salutation 'Dear Jew' was a nice touch, I felt. What worried me more was they obviously know something about the Raven King. There was a line 'Curst be he who touches the bones of King Arthur'. That mock-archaic sentence structure is also typical. How did they know about the possible Arthurian link? Maybe someone from LAS has been gossiping. News travels fast around here.

I told Clayton about the letter and he panicked as usual. I said I thought that we should involve the police but he said no, the uni had had enough bad publicity lately. Be worse publicity if someone's killed, I said (joking). Clayton went white and said 'Oh, dear boy, it won't come to that'. I wonder if he has been threatened himself.

When I got home there was a dead bird on my doorstep. Neighbouring cat or death threat? It's hard to tell. Elaine looked over the wall when I was burying the bird and asked what I was doing. 'Gardening,' I replied. She flounced off inside, obviously thinking that I was taking the piss. After all, as Howard Jacobson says, who's ever heard of a Jew gardening?

Later
Just occurred to me that if someone did leave the bird
as a message, they must know about the bird skeletons we
found on the site. Uncomfortable thought.

Ruth wonders what LAS stands for. She googles and comes
up with the Lancashire Archaeological Society. She remembers Clayton telling her that some members of the society
were present at the dig, 'old dears', Dan calls them. Even
so, it might be worth the police checking the names of
the old dears. She adds that to her list for Tim tomorrow.

Dan had sounded slightly shaken in the diary entry,
she thinks, but not scared. He was blasé enough to joke
about someone being killed. In fact, he sounds every inch
the contemptuous academic – take the references to
'mock-archaic sentence structure' and 'stylistic signatures'. Even the anti-Semitism is treated lightly, though
Ruth is surprised how much Dan obviously thought of
himself as Jewish. *Who's ever heard of a Jew gardening?* She
is sure that in all the years she knew him he never once
referred to himself as a Jew.

The tone of Dan's letter to her had been very different.
Then he had seemed genuinely frightened. *I'm afraid . . .*
and that's just it. I'm afraid. What happened to make him
change his mind?

25 May 2010
Elaine called me today. That's unusual in itself. And she
suggested meeting at the Mount Hotel, which seemed a

strange choice of venue. I was teaching all day and couldn't get there until six. I knew when I arrived that she'd already had a lot to drink. She started off by railing against Guy, saying that I shouldn't trust him etc. etc. I'd heard all this before but said (quietly) that Guy was one of my best friends and that I'd trust him with my life. She laughed rather wildly and asked me what I thought my life was worth. I said I didn't want to have this sort of discussion with her and got up to leave. She grabbed me then and started crying. She said she still loved me but she was afraid. 'What are you afraid of?' I asked. 'Not what, who,' she said. She was in a really terrible state. I did try to get her to drink water or coffee but she swore at me and ordered another bottle of wine. I half hoped they wouldn't serve her but they did. I escaped to the loo and rang Guy. He came immediately, thank God. By this time she was so drunk that she was hardly able to stand, but she went with Guy quite calmly. He is so good to her. I don't know how he puts up with her behaviour. I don't know if they are lovers or not (Sam says not) and I don't want to know. All I know is that he has been a wonderful friend to her. And to me.

27 May 2010

Horrible day. I heard two of my students talking about the Neo-Nazis. They were saying that there were going to be 'reprisals'. I reported this to Clayton and he admitted that he'd had a letter saying that the department was going to be destroyed by fire and ice. I laughed out loud. What utter Wagnerian nonsense! Clayton was rather hurt and said

that I would be scared, in his shoes. Looking at them, I
think it's safe to say that I'll never be in his shoes.

When I got home though something happened that made
me feel a little different. I had a letter – the usual rubbish
about Jewish upstarts 'dishonouring the memory of the
White King' – but at the end there were the names and
addresses of Miriam and Mum and Dad. Just that. Ms M.
Golding. Dr and Mrs I. Golding. But the threat was plain.
They didn't need to spell it out. I rang Clayton and once
again said that we should call the police. He refused. He's
shielding someone. But whom?

That is the last entry.

Ruth sits in the dark room and thinks about her friend
Dan. In some ways it feels wrong to read his diary, which
was obviously only ever meant for himself, but in other
ways it means that Dan is more real to her than he has
ever been. Her remembered Dan has almost vanished, to
be replaced with a real person – passionate, witty (she
loves the comment about Clayton's shoes) and just a little
pompous. She now knows Dan as she never really knew
him when he was a cool undergraduate and she was a
shy working-class girl from Eltham. To think if she'd played
her cards right she might even have slept with him . . .

Do the diaries shed any light on who killed Dan? The
references to the White Hand are frustrating because,
like Clayton and Sam, Dan seems to treat the group with
casual contempt. He writes as if they are an unfortunate

but inevitable part of university life, like drug-taking in the union bar or cheating in assignments. But these people knew where he lived – they wrote him letters and put dead birds on his doorstep. They knew where his parents lived. Why didn't anyone do anything about it? Dan thought that Clayton was shielding someone but didn't know who it was. Or whom. Ruth loves it that even in his private diary, Dan remembered to write 'whom'.

The tangled love lives in the history department are interesting too. Elaine still loves Dan but doesn't trust Guy. Dan, on the other hand, both trusts and admires Guy. Dan obviously has some sort of past with Elaine and probably Pippa Henry too. Sam thinks that Guy and Elaine aren't lovers, but how would Sam know? Ruth remembers Elaine's behaviour towards Sam at the barbeque, how she'd been first antagonistic, then almost loving, sobbing in his arms. What is the nature of *their* relationship?

Dan's attitude to Clayton seems to be one of affectionate contempt, which, considering he is (or was) sleeping with his wife, seems a little rich. Clayton 'panicked as usual', Clayton fusses about getting the excavation done on time, he 'admits' that he's heard from the White Hand but doesn't do anything about it. Ruth thinks of her experiences of the head of department – the genial host with the beautiful wife, the historian, the enthusiast striding over the fields in his pointed shoes, the scared man in the paper overalls. Did he know all along that the bones had been switched? Who did move the bones and why? Realistically it must have been one of the main players – Clayton, Guy or Elaine.

Or maybe even Dan himself. Tim told her that Dan had been to see the bones several times. Was his identification with the Raven King so strong that he wanted his remains close at hand? After all, didn't he say that what he really wanted was to take the bones home with him?

There are voices outside and Thing gets up, hackles rising. He keeps doing this; it's very disconcerting. Ruth remembers that Flint does the same trick, looking past her as if he can see someone who isn't there. Or someone only he can see. Ruth remembers Pendragon saying that Thing could see the ghost of Dame Alice. Is he now seeing his dead master? Of course not, he's just jumpy because he's in a strange house. Ruth goes to the window but the street is deserted apart from the woman with her little dog. No sign of the patrol car that Nelson has promised. Ruth pats her temporary dog.

'It's OK. It's just someone going past. We're not used to houses with people nearby, are we?'

Thing looks up at her, his eyes liquid with trust. He's really a very sweet dog. Is it too late to ring Bob and ask how Flint is doing? She misses her cat. Hard to believe that she's only been away from him for a week. It seems much longer. She gets out her phone.

There are two text messages in her in-box. One says, simply: *We know where you live*. The other, also caller unknown, reads: *Hi Ruth. It's Guy Delaware here. Got your number from Clayton. I was wondering if we could meet up tomorrow. There's something I'd like to discuss*.

Ruth doesn't know which message worries her most.

CHAPTER 24

Guy suggests meeting on the Central Pier in Blackpool. It seems an inappropriately cheery choice of venue, heightened by the fact that it is the first really sunny day since Ruth arrived in Lancashire. The beach is filling up and on the pier the big wheel is already going round. Ruth and Guy sit outside the ice-cream parlour with mugs of tea and watch the children playing on the sand below, which, this morning, stretches far beyond the end of the pier. In fact, if Ruth strains her eyes, she can just see Cathbad and Kate building what looks like a sand henge. Kate is in her pink sun-suit with Hello Kitty hat and Cathbad has his trousers rolled up like a proper holiday-maker. For some reason, looking at them makes her want to cry. You wouldn't think that Kate is estranged from her father or Cathbad from his child. You wouldn't think that, less than forty-eight hours ago, Cathbad found his friend's body swinging from a beam. They just look like a father and daughter playing in the sun.

Guy asks if Ruth would like something to eat. He is polite, almost too polite, holding doors open and flattening himself against walls to let her past. In the sunlight, the Brideshead features look rather careworn but he's still a good-looking man with thick blond hair and a square-jawed face like a character from a Fifties comic strip. The voice matches the face; surely vowel sounds like this have not been heard in this cafe since Tommy Trinder starred in the end-of-the-pier show. Yet Guy tells Ruth that he is Lancashire born and bred.

'You don't sound like it,' says Ruth.

Guy smiles, showing lots of white teeth. 'I went to a rather posh school, then I did my first degree at Oxford and stayed there for a number of years. The accent stuck, but I can still do broad Lancashire if you want.'

'And now you're back in Blackpool.'

He takes a sip of tea and grimaces, whether at the question or the beverage it's hard to tell. 'I never expected to come back but I met Elaine and ...'

Ruth waits. Guy looks up at the cloudless sky for a moment. Are you meant to look to the left or right if you're lying? Ruth can never remember. Then he says, 'It's hard to explain but I think I'm going to have to. You see, I have a really strong connection with Elaine but we're not lovers, never have been. It's more like we're twin souls. As if we were brother and sister in another life. Does that make any sense?'

Ruth could just imagine Nelson's response to this. She too feels rather sceptical but then she thinks of Cathbad, playing on the beach with her daughter. She and Cathbad live together quite happily yet there's no hint of sexual attraction between them. Maybe they too were brother and sister in a former life.

'Yes it does,' she says.

'Elaine was doing post-graduate research,' says Guy. 'She did her first degree at Preston. She's had a very hard life. Deprived childhood, abusive parents. And she's had her own problems . . .'

Ruth waits, sure that Guy will tell her what these problems were. Sure enough, after a while, 'Mental health issues,' he says. 'She's very sensitive. Fearsomely bright. But, sometimes, the slightest little thing . . .'

Like being dumped by her next-door neighbour, thinks Ruth. She wonders if she dares ask about the affair with Dan. Luckily Guy seems to assume that she already knows.

'That business with Dan didn't help, of course. I don't blame him. I'm sure he never promised anything. Dan hadn't really got over the break-up with his wife. Elaine, though, I think she was really in love with him.'

Ruth really wants to ask about Pippa Henry, but if Guy doesn't know she doesn't want to be the one to tell him. Instead she settles for saying, vaguely, 'I suppose Dan had lots of girlfriends?'

To her surprise, Guy bristles slightly. 'Well, not that many. There was that business with Susan Chow, of course, and I'd heard rumours about a married woman but, that's all it was, rumours. Dan wasn't a lothario, if that's what you mean.'

Lothario, thinks Ruth. It's an odd, old-fashioned choice of word. Guy's vocabulary, like his face, seems to hark back to another era. But the idea that Dan had an affair with Susan Chow, the county archaeologist, is a completely new one. Ruth thinks of the neat little woman in her book-lined office. She doesn't seem a very likely girlfriend for Dan but then neither do Elaine or Pippa. Come to think of it, though, didn't Dan refer to Susan as 'Sue' in his diary? In Ruth's experience, it's always a sign of something when people start using diminutives, or full names for that matter. She remembers her shock when Shona first referred to Phil as 'Philip'.

'What did Elaine think about the other women?' asks Ruth.

'It was a bit awkward,' admits Guy, 'living next door and everything. Elaine became a bit obsessed with watching all Dan's comings and goings. But I'll tell you one thing, Ruth, my friendship with Dan never wavered. I really loved that man.'

Ruth looks up and is surprised to see tears in Guy's eyes. Whatever the truth of Guy's statement, he is certainly in the grip of some strong emotion.

'I was fond of him too,' she says. 'We were at university together.'

'I know,' says Guy. 'I bet he was a wild student.'

'He was super cool,' says Ruth. 'Dan the Man, we called him.'

Guy laughs again, a more natural sound this time. 'Dan the Man. I love it.'

Ruth takes a gulp of tea. It is so strong that it makes her eyes water. 'You said you had something you wanted to discuss?'

'Yes.' Guy looks straight at her, his face serious. Sometimes he looks like a teenager, sometimes a much older man. She guesses he is in his thirties.

'I've heard a rumour that Dan's laptop has been found.'

Ruth stares at Guy, with his dependable Fifties face. Is it possible that Guy stole into the burning house, took Dan's computer and infected it with a virus so he would be able to trace its whereabouts? It doesn't seem possible – but how else would he know that it has been found?

She tries to keep her face blank. 'Who told you that?'

For the first time, Guy looks slightly shifty. 'I'm sorry, Ruth. I can't tell you.'

'Well, you'd better,' says Ruth. 'If you want me to tell you anything.'

Guy looks out over the beach and the jolly, holiday-making crowds. When he turns back, his face looks older again.

'I heard about Pendragon. His sister told me. Your wizard friend was in his house. I was sure he must have found the computer.'

This raises a whole lot of new questions. Guy knew Pendragon, well enough to be on telephoning terms with his sister. Pendragon had links with the White Hand. What other secrets could Guy be hiding behind that *Boy's Own* grin?

'What makes you think the computer was at Pendragon's house?'

'Someone told me.'

'Who?'

'I'm sorry, Ruth.' Guy looks away again. 'I can't tell you. The thing is, there are other people involved here. I can't break their confidence. But if the laptop's been found there must be all sorts of valuable archaeological information on it. I really need that information, Ruth. I want to carry on Dan's work. As a tribute to him.'

And to help your career, thinks Ruth. She resents the implication that Guy – a mere graduate student – is the only person who could make sense of Dan's findings. She is the one Dan asked for help and, right now, that information is going nowhere.

'I'm sorry,' says Ruth. 'The laptop's with the police.' This is, of course, true, but she doesn't add that Tim has given her a brand-new memory stick containing copies of Dan's files.

Guy groans and slumps back in his chair. 'That's it, then. That DCI Macleod is an ignorant bastard. He's got no interest in furthering human knowledge.'

Ruth thinks this is probably true but, on the other hand, she wouldn't call Sandy Macleod ignorant. He seemed uncomfortably sharp to her.

'Don't you have any records of your own?' she asks. 'After all, you were at the excavation.' Too late, she wonders if she should admit to knowing this.

'I've got a few notes,' says Guy. 'Nothing substantial.

Did Dan say anything to you about the discovery? About King Arthur?'

'I'm sorry,' says Ruth. 'I hadn't seen Dan in over twenty years.'

Tim is going through paperwork which, in effect, means checking computer records. He realised, after a few days working for Sandy, that this was the way to make himself indispensible. Sandy loathes paperwork but he knows it has to be done. Tim saw immediately that his best chance of ingratiating himself with the infamous 'Beast of Blackpool' Macleod was to become an expert on forms, procedure and the Freedom of Information Act. It's not what he dreamt of when studying (physics at York) or when he signed up for the graduate fast-track programme, but Tim is a pragmatist, and if his future holds no obstacles greater than a dinosaur DCI who can't work a computer, he will be doing pretty well.

Despite everything Tim doesn't dislike Sandy. He's rude, chauvinistic, and he thinks that Jim Davidson's a fine comedian, but he's also a good copper and, according to his lights, fair. That is to say, he's rude to everyone. Sandy doesn't hold back from a borderline racist joke because Tim's in the room and, in a way, Tim's quite grateful for this. At least this way he knows what's going on. And since they have been trying to infiltrate the White Hand Sandy has appreciated Tim's ironical take on the problems of a black man who wants to join a white supremacist group. 'At least you've got a sense of humour about it, lad,' is his considered opinion.

And now Sandy's old mate has turned up. Harry Nelson, as much of a legend in the department as Sandy himself. So many of Sandy's stories begin 'When Harry and I were young coppers . . .' and end 'that was policing, that was. None of this hand-holding you buggers get, none of this PC nonsense either'. Tim was expecting a Sandy clone, another jovial relic of the good old days. Instead, DCI Nelson turned out to be a good-looking man in his forties, rather quiet and slightly sad. Tim, who prides himself on reading verbal and non-verbal clues (he has done a course on neuro-linguistic programming, not something he'd admit to Sandy), thinks there is more in Nelson's relationship with both Cathbad and Ruth than meets the eye. Either he's having an affair with one or both of them. Tim's straight (something that would surprise some of his colleagues) but he's not against keeping your options open.

Now Tim trawls through the names of participants cautioned at a recent EDL rally. He is cross-checking with a list of recent Pendle graduates so a name that's not on the second list initially passes him by. It's only a mental double take that sends him scrolling backwards until he finds it again. He pauses, thinking hard, and then makes a call on the internal phone.

'Would you like another cup of tea?' asks Guy.

Ruth hesitates. She would like another cup of tea, and

a large slice of cake, come to that, but she should be getting back to Cathbad and Kate. On the other hand, she senses that there is more that she can learn from Guy. He was Dan's trusted friend and he knows Clayton and Elaine too. He might know who took the laptop in the first place.

'Just a quick one,' she says.

Guy stands up. A couple who are hovering, waiting for a table, step back in disappointment when they realise that Ruth is staying put. The pier is getting crowded now; Ruth can no longer see Kate and Cathbad on the beach. Families trail past carrying large stuffed meerkats won on stalls. One of the shops is selling Simon Cowell masks and it's rather disturbing to see the grinning features of the X-Factor Mephistopheles attached to a two-foot child or waving from the helter-skelter. Ruth sits, waiting for Guy, feeling the unusual sensation of the sun on her face. If it wasn't for the fact that she is scared to death half the time, she would be quite enjoying this holiday.

When Guy returns, she says, 'Clayton Henry seemed to think that Dan's discovery might be a lifesaver for the department.'

'Yes.'

Ruth is interested to see that Guy has bought a beer for himself. It's nearly midday so not an outlandish time to be drinking but, even so, he must be more uptight than he seems. She remembers how much he was sweating at the barbeque. He seems over-heated now too, taking a deep draught from his glass and mopping his brow.

'Clayton's in trouble financially,' he says. 'You've seen his house. He likes a grand lifestyle, good food, good wine, nice holidays. My guess is that he's been dipping into department funds for years. Well, when Dan made his discovery, that was Clayton's chance. If the bones really were the remains of King Arthur, well, that would change everything. There would be books, TV programmes, personal appearances. Clayton could make a packet and pay back everything he'd borrowed. But if anything went wrong ...'

Like the bones going missing, thinks Ruth. She wonders if Guy has got wind of this.

'What about the White Hand?' she asks. 'Is Clayton scared that they'll make trouble?'

'Oh, no one takes them seriously,' says Guy. 'They're just a bunch of idiots who think that God was a white Englishman. Complete losers, all of them.'

Except you did take them seriously, remembers Ruth. You insisted that the bones be taken to the forensics lab. What had Dan written? *I thought Guy was becoming too obsessed with the White Hand.* And a few days after writing those words Dan was dead. She wonders again exactly why Guy wants Dan's computer so much.

'What if the White Hand were responsible for Dan's death?' she asks.

'Is that what the police think?' counters Guy.

Ruth curses herself for saying too much. 'They're investigating the fire,' she says.

Guy shivers, looking out over the sea of holidaymakers.

'Don't talk about the fire. I still have nightmares about it. Elaine and I were just coming back from the pub and we saw the flames. Couldn't believe it was Dan's house at first. It was an inferno.'

'Did you try to save him?' asks Ruth, trying not to sound judgemental.

'We couldn't get near,' says Guy. 'The heat was just too intense. I called the fire brigade,' he adds, as if in mitigation.

'When did you know that Dan was dead?'

'We saw them bring his body out,' says Guy, shivering now, despite the sun. Whatever his motivation about the laptop, there is no denying his genuine distress. 'They were giving him mouth-to-mouth, there on the path. But I knew it was too late.'

'Must have been upsetting for Elaine too.'

Guy looks at her, his eyes anguished. 'What do you think? She saw his body blackened from the fire. She was screaming. I don't think she'll ever be the same again. I don't think either of us will,' he adds, almost as an after-thought.

'Terry Durkin,' says Sandy. 'Well, well, well. That's one in the eye for old Grassy Arse.'

'Doesn't mean he's necessarily involved,' says Tim.

'Rubbish. He's a racist, isn't he?'

'Well, he's a supporter of the English Defence League.'

'Same thing. He'll be hand in glove with these white supremacists, you mark my words. As soon as he gets word that their precious King Arthur might be one of your lot ...' Ruth had rung Tim with the news that morning. Sandy had laughed for ten solid minutes.

'Actually, my ancestry is Caribbean, not North African,' says Tim. But his words are lost on Sandy, as he knew they would be.

'Soon as he gets word that the Great White King might be – shock, horror – the Great Black King, he whips the bones and replaces them with some other skeleton he's got handy. It all fits.'

'And that's not all,' says Tim. 'Guess which forensics company investigated the fire in Dan Golding's house.'

But Sandy is there before him. 'CNN.'

Tim nods. 'So Durkin could easily have taken the computer. It was a sealed site but he had access.'

'We'd better go and talk to him,' says Sandy. 'Turn up at his house in a marked car. Put the pressure on.'

Tim sighs, foreseeing an afternoon of reminding his boss of the concept of *habeas corpus*. 'There's another thing,' he says.

Tim has also been looking at Pendragon's computer. His emails are mainly to other wizards and subscriptions to homeopathic health sites. His photos are almost all of a white bull terrier. Except one. It is this picture, printed and enlarged, that Tim puts on the desk in front of Sandy.

'What's this?'

It's a photograph of two men wearing white robes. One is large, white-bearded, with a certain presence. The other man is smaller and plumper and seems to be having trouble with his long skirts. His face is partly turned away from the camera.

'The taller man's Norman Smith, alias Pendragon,' says Tim. 'But do you recognise the other one?'

Sandy peers closer. 'Couple o' nutters. Bloody hell!'

'Do you recognise him?'

'It's the bloke in the windmill. Clayton Henry.'

CHAPTER 25

Ruth meets Cathbad and Kate on the beach. They show her their henge, which is certainly the only such structure on the sands.

'Henge,' says Kate, jumping up and down, her Hello Kitty hat askew. 'Henge, henge.'

'It's positively Bronze Age,' says Ruth.

The circle of sand megaliths is attracting attention. People are crowding round and taking photographs. For once Ruth has her camera with her and she kneels down to take a shot. Cathbad and Kate pose proudly by their construction, and seeing them there with the sea in the background reminds her of a similar photograph showing her with Peter and Erik on the Saltmarsh beach. They had just found the henge and Ruth vividly remembers the feeling of excitement and triumph as they stood by the ancient timbers, Erik waving his hat in the air. This would have been what Dan felt when he raised the stone and saw King Arthur's face looking at him.

'Take it home,' says Kate.

'No, Hecate,' says Cathbad. 'Let the sea take it. That's what it's for, an offering to the gods of the sea.'

Amazingly, this seems to satisfy Kate. Of course, this is what Cathbad had wanted for the original henge, to let the sea come for it rather than preserving the wood in a soulless museum.

'Erik would be proud of you,' says Ruth.

Cathbad shoots her a quick look. 'I still feel his presence, don't you?'

'No,' lies Ruth. 'Let's go back to the house and get some lunch. Thing will be missing us.'

Ruth feels rather nervous about having left Thing alone in the cottage but dogs aren't allowed on the beach in summer. Cathbad agrees that they need to get back and, with one last photograph, they leave the henge to the incoming tide. Kate makes a routine fuss as they pass the posters for the Pleasure Beach.

'Want Dora! Want Dora!'

'We really must take her to Nickelodeon World before we go home,' says Cathbad.

'I'd rather die,' says Ruth.

'I'll take her then.'

In the car, Ruth tells Cathbad about Clayton and his money troubles.

'We should have guessed,' says Cathbad. 'I mean, when you think about his house. And that party. Champagne flowing like water.'

Well, you drank most of it, thinks Ruth. Aloud, she says, 'Do you think Clayton knew about the DNA results?'

'Didn't Dan imply that he'd told someone?'

'Yes. In his diary, he wrote, *I won't tell anyone except . . .*'

'Except Clayton?'

'Well, maybe. He was his head of department. It would make sense to tell him.'

'But if Arthur was black it would make even more of a story and make Clayton even more money. If he knew, why didn't he mention it to you?'

'I don't know,' says Ruth. 'Maybe he was just terrified of the White Hand. Dan thought they had been threatening Clayton.'

'But he also thought Clayton was shielding someone.' Ruth has told Cathbad what was in Dan's diaries but she hasn't let him see the files. It's one thing for her to read them but Cathbad didn't know Dan.

'You ought to tell Nelson,' says Cathbad. 'About Clayton and the money. It could be something for the police to investigate.'

'I will.'

'Do you really think that Clayton was involved in Dan's death?'

'I don't know,' says Ruth. She is thinking of the cafe next to the derelict amusement park, of Clayton boasting, 'I'm a real gadget boy.' Could Gadget Boy have stolen the computer and fixed it so that it would leave a trail, like a thread running through a labyrinth?

Nelson lies back in his chair and heaves a sigh of contentment. He is in the garden of Michelle's mother's house in Newton. The sun is out and he has a cold beer within reach. In the distance he can hear Michelle and her mum laughing as they prepare food in the kitchen. Best of all, he can't hear, anywhere, Maureen's loud Irish voice asking him what on earth he thinks he's doing lying round when there's work to be done, his father never lazed around like that, God rest his soul, honestly how Michelle puts up with such a husband . . . A bird sings in the tree and Michelle's mum's cat stretches out in a patch of sunlight. Nelson closes his eyes.

Michelle's mother, Louise, is sixty, but she could be a generation younger than Maureen. She's an attractive woman with ash-blonde hair and a teenager's figure. She works in the local building society and drives a pink Fiat 500. Like Maureen, she's a widow, but there the resemblance ends. Louise seems to live the life of a happy singleton, going on cruises with friends and belonging to several choirs and bridge clubs. Her home is always immaculate, and when she knows her son-in-law is coming to stay she fills her fridge with his favourite food and drink. Nelson wonders if he's unique in thinking that his mother-in-law is perfect.

He knows that Michelle, too, is happy to have embarked on the second half of their holiday, traditionally the more relaxing week. She gets on well with Maureen but the atmosphere in her house is not exactly soothing. Now Michelle can have a real break at last, and he can look forward to some quiet evenings when Michelle and Louise go to the cinema or out to meet friends. He'll even enjoy taking the two of them out; he likes being seen with two such attractive, well-dressed women. Louise helped a lot when the girls were young and Nelson knows Michelle missed her when they moved to Norfolk. Nice for them to catch up now.

'Harry,' Michelle is standing in front of him. Nelson wonders if lunch is ready. Enticing smells are wafting from the open window.

But Michelle does not look like a woman announcing a delicious light lunch. She is holding his phone at arm's length.

'Call for you,' she says. 'It's Ruth.'

As Michelle walks back inside, a cloud moves slowly across the sun.

Clayton Henry, cornered in his office at the university, denies everything.

'It was just a laugh. We were dressing up for Halloween.'

'There are crocuses on the grass,' says Tim.

'What?'

'In the picture.' Tim points at the photo which lies on Clayton's desk. 'There are crocuses on the grass so it's not October.'

'Another of those pagan feast days then. Pendragon knew them all. There's one in February. Imbolc, I think it's called.'

'How well did you know Norman Smith?' asks Sandy, stretching back in his chair. He looks like a man who is making himself at home.

'Who?'

'Pendragon,' says Tim. 'When did you meet him?'

'I don't know,' says Clayton, twisting his hands together. 'He was always around. He came to lots of history department events, always in his robes and everything. Everyone knew him. He was a character. An eccentric.'

'Do you know he's dead?' asks Sandy chattily.

'I had heard.'

'Who from?' asks Tim. 'It only happened two days ago.'

'One of my students told me. I can't remember who.'

'It's the holidays. How come you're in touch with your students?'

Clayton laughs. 'These days you can't get away from them. They've got my email address, my mobile phone number. They're on at me all the time.'

'So Professor Henry,' says Sandy, 'are you a member of the White Hand?'

'No!' Clayton stands up and attempts to look masterful. Unfortunately, he's only the same height as Sandy is sitting down.

'We've got Norman Smith's computer,' says Tim. 'There's a lot of interesting stuff on it.'

There is a silence. Clayton fiddles with a silver paper-knife. One of Sandy's first rules – never trust a man with executive toys or archaic stationery on his desk. Clayton has an inkwell too.

Clayton sits down again. 'All right. I may have dressed

up in white robes a few times but I'm no white suprema-cist. I'm just interested in druids and the old religion. That's not a crime, is it?'

Sandy looks as if it may well be. Tim says, 'We'll need to look at your computer hard drive.'

'I've got lots of confidential papers on there.'

'I can come back with a warrant.'

Sandy is looking at his mobile phone. Then he raises his head and smiles at Clayton. The professor seems to find this an unpleasant experience. He recoils.

'Sorry not to have a chance to visit your house again,' says Sandy. 'It was quite some place.'

'Thank you.'

'Great idea, converting a windmill like that.'

Clayton says nothing. He looks from one policeman to the other, as if trying to work out what is going on.

'Must have taken a fair bit of brass,' says Sandy.

Clayton stiffens. 'My wife has some money of her own.'

'That's handy.'

'What are you getting at?'

Sandy glances at Tim, who is also looking mystified. 'So, if my sergeant examines your computer records, he'll find all your financial affairs in order?'

'Why? What do you . . . yes, of course.'

'So you haven't been dipping into departmental funds?'

'Of course not. How dare you!'

Sandy smiles again. 'Must have been a shock for you

when those bones vanished. I expect you thought you were on to a nice little earner.'

'It was an important archaeological discovery,' says Clayton stiffly.

'Think it was King Arthur?'

'We can't be sure but, historically, it's possible.'

'Professor Henry,' says Tim. 'Before he died, did Dan Golding discuss the results of the DNA analysis with you?'

'The DNA analysis? What do you mean?'

'It's a simple question,' growls Sandy. 'Did he mention any results to you?'

'No,' says Clayton. 'I hadn't seen him for a few weeks when he . . . when he died. Not to speak to anyway. It was a busy time, end of term and all that.'

'Where were you on the night of Dan Golding's death?' asks Sandy. They already have this information from Pippa, thinks Tim. Sandy must want to give Clayton Henry a shock.

And, it seems, he has succeeded. Clayton Henry stands up. He is shaking all over.

'I had nothing to do with Dan's death. Nothing. I was at home with my wife all evening. And I've got nothing to say about financial irregularities either. I've worked myself into the ground for that department. If I have to abdicate, the whole place will collapse.'

Sandy leans back in his chair, looking delighted, but Tim says, quietly, 'That's an odd choice of word.'

'What?'

'Abdicate. Kings abdicate, not university lecturers. Is that how you see yourself?'

Clayton says nothing. Sandy is still grinning.

'Do I need a lawyer?' Clayton asks at last.

Thing is delighted to see them again. He runs up and down the stairs whimpering ecstatically.

'He obviously thought we'd abandoned him too,' says Cathbad, sitting down to make a fuss of the dog.

'Well, he hasn't chewed the place up,' says Ruth. 'Good boy, Thing.'

Thing thumps his tail and looks smug.

Ruth puts together a hasty lunch of French bread and cheese. Thing makes it clear that he likes both these foods. Kate sits in her high chair dropping mini Babybel wrappers on his head.

'What do you want to do this afternoon?' asks Ruth. 'Go for a walk? Go to the beach?'

'I know what I'd like to do,' says Cathbad, spreading butter thickly on his bread. 'I'd like to go to Ribchester. See where this whole thing started. Be a nice run for Thing as well.'

Before they leave the university, Sandy asks if they can look in Dan Golding's office.

'Of course,' says Clayton, who is clearly dying to get rid of them. 'He shared it with another lecturer, Sam Elliot, and it's his now but I'm sure he wouldn't mind ...'

'Why do you want to look in here?' asks Tim. 'I searched the place after the fire. Didn't find anything of interest.'

Sandy thinks that Tim sounds put out. He resents the idea that he could have missed anything. Sandy makes a noncommittal noise. He's not sure himself why he wanted to come in here except that it might put the wind up Clayton Henry. But there's no harm in Tim thinking that his boss might know something he doesn't. He's a good cop, Tim, but he doesn't know everything yet.

The office is small with two desks very close together, almost touching. You'd have to get on very well with someone, thinks Sandy, to work in such close proximity. He couldn't stand it himself. He likes to have room to spread out. One desk is clear. Sandy presumes this was Golding's and that someone (who?) has cleared his belongings. The other desk has a closed laptop, a book about tanks and a pile of essays.

Sandy opens the laptop and tries to turn it on. After a few seconds, Tim helps him find the switch. A message flashes across the screen: 'Enter password'.

'Want to try and guess it?' says Sandy.

'I wouldn't know where to start,' says Tim. 'And, strictly speaking, we'd need a warrant.'

Sandy grunts and closes the laptop.

One wall is full of bookshelves. Tim goes closer to examine the titles. Sandy starts to open drawers in Dan Golding's desk.

'What are you looking for?' asks Tim over his shoulder. He still sounds disapproving.

'Don't know,' says Sandy. 'But Dan Golding was shagging Henry's wife. That might be motive enough to kill him.'

It was Tim who had alerted his boss to the references to Pippa Henry in Dan's diaries but now he seems disposed to argue.

'Do you really see Clayton Henry as a killer?'

'Not really,' admits Sandy. 'It's one thing to be ripping off the university. He's a shyster, that's obvious, swanking around in that big house like Lord Muck. But torch someone's house, put petrol-soaked rags through their letterbox, burn them alive? I can't see it.'

'How did you know about the money?' asks Tim.

Sandy laughs. 'Got a text from Harry Nelson. And he got it from Ruth Galloway. The archaeologist woman.'

'She seems to get everywhere.'

'She does indeed.'

The drawers yield nothing except dust and a few paper clips. Someone has cleared away very effectively.

Tim is looking out of the window. 'We're very high up,' he says. Sandy doesn't join him. Though he would never admit it to Tim, he's afraid of heights.

'Come on,' he says. 'There's nothing here.'

'No sign of Pippa Henry then?'

'Oh I wouldn't say that,' says Sandy. 'What can you smell, lad?'

Tim sniffs the air. 'Perfume?'

'Exactly. *Ma Griffe*, I think.'

Now Tim really does look at his boss in awe. 'How do you know?'

'It's Bev's favourite. Question is, who else wears it?'

Ribchester is much busier today. It's a sunny Saturday afternoon and that has brought the tourists. They fill the narrow streets and wander into the churchyard where they peer myopically at the Roman remains before heading for a cream tea. Families sit outside cafes eating ice creams, and in the playground near the car park children play on a miniature Roman fort.

'I didn't realise gladiators had ray guns,' says Cathbad, watching them.

'Those Romans were ahead of their time,' says Ruth.

They take the path behind the church and walk along the river bank. Thing pants excitedly at the sight of the water meadows, but with so many children about they daren't let him off the lead. Kate, too, is excited by the landscape.

'Wet,' she says. 'Grass, sky, ducks.'

'A perfect summary,' says Cathbad. 'This is like the Saltmarsh, isn't it?'

Ruth, who has been thinking the same thing, says, 'Too many people about.'

'I bet it was even busy in Roman times,' says Cathbad. 'This was a fort, right?'

'The Roman name was Bremetennacum Veteranorum,' says Ruth. 'Max says that the "veteranorum" might mean that it was a place where veterans retired. They may even have helped with rearing and training horses for the cavalry.'

'Want horse,' says Kate.

'A retirement home for old legionnaires,' says Cathbad. 'I like that. But what about in King Arthur's day ... you reckon that was after the Romans left?'

'Dan thought the Ribchester temple, the Raven God temple where the body was found, was late 400s, which would place it at about fifty to eighty years after the withdrawal of Roman troops. We don't know so much about the post-Roman years. There are fewer written records. But I think Ribchester would still have been important. It's on the river, not far from the sea, and there was a major road running through here.'

They are approaching Dan's excavations. As they get nearer they see that a couple in hiking gear are already there, bending down to examine a section of mosaic. The woman looks up and smiles at Ruth.

'Not much to see here,' she says.

Only the tomb of the Raven King, Ruth tells her silently. But she is only too happy to see the hikers hiking off in search of more interesting ruins.

Cathbad, in contrast, seems enchanted with the place.

'This is sacred ground,' he says. 'I feel it.'

Ruth looks at him with mingled irritation and affection. Cathbad is apt to declare any isolated spot sacred ground, and if you add a pagan temple a psychic experience is more or less guaranteed. But, on the other hand, he has just lost his friend in horrible circumstances. Surely he is allowed some kind of spiritual leeway? And it can't be denied that the site is looking its best in the afternoon light. The hills are dark against the sky. The tourists seem to have vanished and the river runs wide and lonely across the marshes. In the distance, Pendle Hill rises up out of the flat landscape like the hull of a vast ship. As Cathbad stands, head up, eyes shut, absorbing the psychic energies, a flock of geese flies overhead, calling plaintively.

'That's a sign,' he says.

'Of what?' asks Ruth. She is trying to stop Kate digging in the mud. The child's a born archaeologist.

'Geese were sacred to the Romans,' says Cathbad evasively. 'It's a sign of something.'

'Everything's a sign of something.'

'Too true, Ruthie.' He looks sideways at her, wondering if she's noticed the nickname. 'Is this where the body was found?'

'Over here. Clayton thought it would have been below the altar.'

Cathbad lifts a corner of tarpaulin. 'There's a really strong presence here.'

'You reckon?'

'Yes.' Cathbad straightens up. 'You know, I understand some of what Pendragon must have felt. The druids were a real focus of resistance to the Romans. To know that King Arthur was buried here, in such a Roman spot . . .'

'After the Romans had left, though.'

'Yes, but it's a Roman place. It still feels like a Roman place today. A Roman cavalry fort. To Pendragon, Arthur was a mystical British figure, a pagan, a shaman. To find him here, in a Roman grave, to think that he might just have been another Roman cavalryman. It must have been like discovering that Merlin was in the SS.'

Ruth smiles, but the mention of the SS reminds her that Pendragon, for all his harmless mysticism, had some very strange bedfellows, people who, presumably, believed in the master race and the subjection of others. She remembers Dan's diaries and the letters calling him an 'upstart Jew'. Somewhere along the line the shamans have got mixed up with the bad guys.

She turns to check that Kate isn't trying to eat the soil and finds that the little girl is standing stock still, staring at something across the river.

'Funny lady,' says Kate.

Ruth follows her gaze and sees a figure moving steadily along the riverbank. Contrary to Kate's description, it's impossible to tell if it's a man or woman because the person is dressed in a long white robe and hood. As Ruth, Cathbad and Kate watch, the robed figure turns to look at them. There is a black void where the face should be.

CHAPTER 26

'A mask,' says Cathbad. 'It was obviously a black mask.'

It is evening and Kate is in bed. Ruth and Cathbad are eating a Chinese takeaway in the kitchen. Neither of them had wanted to alarm Kate so it's the first time that they have discussed the sinister figure on the riverbank. Not that Kate had seemed frightened. Both Ruth and Cathbad had found her silent acceptance of the apparition rather chilling. She had simply put her hand in Ruth's and said 'Home now'. And they had all, the two adults, the child and the dog, turned for home. Even Thing had seemed subdued. Now Kate is asleep and Thing is happily eating prawn crackers under the table. Cathbad refills their glasses.

'It gave me a bit of a shock,' he admits.

'Me too,' says Ruth, taking a gulp of wine. 'The cloak, the hood, the mask. The way it appeared so suddenly. It was terrifying.'

'Do you think the show was for our benefit?'

'How could it be? No one knew we were going to Ribchester this afternoon.'

'Do you think it was – what do they call him – the Arch Wizard?'

This is exactly what Ruth has been thinking but she feels the need to squash this idea. The idea that the leader of the White Hand should materialise like that, right by the grave of King Arthur, it's too spooky to contemplate.

'Of course not,' she says. 'It was just some random druid. Someone like you. After all, you must give people shocks sometimes, wandering around in your cloak. It probably wasn't anything to do with the site or King Arthur.'

'I don't know,' says Cathbad. 'It felt staged to me. The way it turned and stared at us.'

Ruth shivers. 'Do you know what, Cathbad? I think we should go home.'

Cathbad is silent for a moment, medatively chewing sweet and sour pork. Ruth says, almost apologetically, 'It's just getting too scary for me. The text messages. Pendragon dying. Now the bloody Ghost of Christmas Yet to Come following us around. I don't want Kate to stay here any longer. I want to take her home.'

'I thought you wanted to look at the relics from the site.'

Ruth has made an appointment with Clayton Henry to see the tombstone and the raven inscription.

'That's on Tuesday morning. We could go home straight afterwards.'

Cathbad sighs. 'OK. I've got to go to Clitheroe on Monday to see Pendragon's solicitor. Then we might as well go home.'

Cathbad had been surprised to hear from Pendragon's sister that his friend had made a will and that he had been named as the executor. Ruth is planning to spend the day with Caz.

'Good,' says Ruth. She feels relieved but also rather sad. She can't rid herself of the thought that by running away like this, she'll be abandoning Dan and his great discovery. But the police are investigating Dan's death, and while she doesn't much like Sandy she imagines that he doesn't give up easily. Sandy and Tim will infiltrate the White Hand and will discover who stole the bones and set Dan's house on fire. Then Dan and King Arthur will both be able to rest in peace.

'I can't wait to see Flint again,' she says.

Sunday may be a day of rest but, for DCI Sandy Macleod, it's business as usual. He decides that Terry Durkin needs a shock so he pays him a visit, causing quite a stir in the quiet street of lawn-mowers and car-washers by drawing up outside the house in a marked police car, driven by Tim.

Terry appears on the doorstep in his slippers.

'What the hell's all this about?'

'Few questions we'd like to ask you,' says Sandy, smiling pleasantly at Terry's next-door neighbour, who is blatantly peering over the fence.

'Can't it wait until Monday?'

'Not really. We've had an interesting bit of information about you.'

Terry backs away slightly, which gives Sandy the chance to barrel over the threshold. Tim follows, looking apologetic.

'I didn't say you could come in!'

'I'm sorry.' Sandy pauses. 'Do you want to do this down at the station?'

Terry looks at the large man who seems to be taking up most of the hall. He is clearly weighing up whether to order them to leave, or to co-operate and complain later. After a moment, he says, 'Come through to the front room.' Adding, 'Mr Greengrass will hear about this.'

'Always glad to hear from my old mate Pete,' says Sandy genially. He leads the way through the hall, which smells strongly of roasting meat, and into a room dominated by a flat-screen TV and flowery sofa and chairs.

Sandy lowers himself into an armchair with a sigh. 'Sit down, lad.'

'What's all this about?' asks Terry, remaining standing.

'Live with your mum, do you?' asks Sandy.

'What's it got to do with you?' says Terry, adding in a slightly awed voice, 'How did you know?'

Even Tim has to admire the speed of his boss's deductions, while deploring his methods. OK, the *Inside Soap* and *Chat* magazines on the table are a bit of a give-away, as is the knitting on the arm of the chair. Tim noticed the stairlift as soon as they got in and there are also headphones for the TV and one of those grabbing arms for picking objects off the floor. The whole room is old-ladyish really – white lace covers on the chairs, framed Bible tracts on the walls, a gas fire with fake coals, china horses, and a complete set of Catherine Cooksons. The interesting thing is how little of Terry's personality seems to be reflected in the house. The only signs that a young man lives here are a set of dumbbells in the corridor and a copy of *Cycling Today* lying open on the sofa. Of course, Tim reflects, one doesn't want to be sexist or ageist: both these items could belong to old Mrs Durkin.

'Where's Mum now?' asks Sandy.

'At church.'

'Is she a Catholic?'

'C of E,' says Terry, sounding shocked. 'What do you want anyhow?'

Tim leans forward. They agreed in the car that he would be the one to take the lead. As Sandy so charmingly put it, 'Being questioned by a black copper is sure to piss him off big time.'

'Terry, are you a member of the English Defence League?'

Terry looks from one to the other, then into the hall as if planning his escape (or listening for his mother's return).

'It's not a crime, is it?' he says at last.

'No,' says Tim gently. 'It's not a crime in itself.'

'Well then.'

'Are you involved with any other far-right groups? At the university, for example.'

'I know a few people up at the university. I'm not stupid, you know.'

'Do you talk politics with them?'

'Sometimes. Lots of people think this country's going downhill. Too many immigrants taking our jobs, destroying our culture. You can walk down the street in Preston and not see a white face.'

'Is that a bad thing?' asks Tim politely.

Terry looks away. 'No offence.'

'None taken. So, when you're talking politics with your friends at the university, have you ever heard anyone mention an organisation called the White Hand?'

'No. I don't think so. Who are they?'

'They're a Neo-pagan group who revere the Norse gods.'

'Never heard of 'em.'

'They also revere King Arthur. Have you heard anyone talking about King Arthur recently?'

'Nah.' Terry is regaining his confidence. He attempts a grin. 'Fella's dead as far as I remember.'

He may be dead, thinks Tim, but he's still capable of causing trouble. But now, while Terry is relaxing, it's time to ask the important questions.

'Did you know Dan Golding?'

'Who?'

'The man who excavated the bones that subsequently went missing. The man who died in a house fire.'

For the first time, Terry seems to falter. 'I may have met him. Quite a few people from the university came to look at the bones.'

'You investigated the fire, didn't you? Your firm, CNN Forensics.'

'What? Oh, the fire in Fleetwood. On Mount Street.'

'That's the one. Were you one of the investigators?'

Terry looks sulky. 'Looks like you know I was.'

Tim smiles. 'Yes, we do know. And we also know that some property went missing. Did you take anything from the house, Terry?'

'No!'

'A computer? A mobile phone?'

Terry is shaking now. 'You've got no proof.'

Sandy speaks from the armchair, where he has been examining the knitting with interest.

'Terry, where were you on the night of June the second?'

Terry looks at Tim almost with entreaty. 'What are you accusing me of?'

'Nothing,' says Tim.

'Yet,' adds Sandy.

'You can't just come in here, accusing me of things.'

'No one's accusing you,' says Tim. 'It's a simple question. Where were you on the night of June the second?'

'Here, I suppose. I'd have to check.'

'With your mum?'

'Yes. She doesn't go out much.'

'Except to church.'

'A neighbour takes her.' Terry looks round again. 'They'll be back soon.'

Sandy stands up. 'Well ta-ra for now, Terry lad. Don't forget to give my regards to old Grassy Arse.'

Terry looks as if he can hardly believe it.

'Are you going?'

'Can't hang round here all day. Unless you want to invite us for Sunday lunch. What are you having?'

'Roast beef,' says Terry with a swagger. 'Classic English food.'

'Keen cook, are you?' asks Sandy.

'Nah. My mum cooks. I just keep an eye when she's out. Put the potatoes on and suchlike.'

'My mum doesn't let anyone in the kitchen when she's cooking,' says Tim.

'What does she cook?' asks Terry.

'Oh roast beef, Yorkshire pudding. The usual things. Classic English food. Good day to you, Mr Durkin.'

Ruth is also eating a traditional meal. Chinese traditional. Susan Chow explains, almost apologetically, that the older she gets the more she craves the food of her childhood. Her parents emigrated from Hong Kong after the war and Susan was born in Lancashire.

'But I'm still a bloody immigrant to some,' she says with a grin. 'Despite having a broad Blackpool accent. Might as well live up to the stereotype.'

Ruth thinks of the black soldiers on Hadrian's Wall. Did they too feel like 'bloody immigrants'? And what about their mixed-race children growing up in post-Roman Cumbria ... Did they feel British? Did they hear rumours about a black warrior called Arthur?

'I love Chinese food,' says Ruth. 'Well, I love most food.'

Susan, who is the size of a sparrow, smiles without

comprehension and tucks into a spring roll. When Susan rang and suggested this meal, saying that she could show Ruth the photos of the dig at the same time, Ruth had been pleased. She had liked Susan when she met her (despite the embarrassment of Kate and the papier-mâché model) and here was a chance to find out more about the history department and about Dan as an archaeologist. But since then Ruth has read Dan's diaries and sees Susan in a different light. Was this neat, precise woman really Dan's lover? She remembers something Susan said when she first talked about Dan and the excavation. He was a man possessed, she said. She had sounded sad. Perhaps Susan felt that King Arthur had taken Dan away from her.

'I don't cook much for myself,' Susan is saying. 'Well, there's no need. Mostly it's just me and Trixie. My dog,' she explains, seeing Ruth's quizzical expression.

'It used to just be me and my cat,' says Ruth. 'But now I've got Kate so I try to cook proper meals.'

'Oh yes,' says Susan. 'I remember Kate.'

The photos are spread out on the table, with difficulty as the table is also laden with food. Susan has ordered dishes that Ruth has never encountered before (they don't even appear on the menu) but they are all, without exception, delicious. Ruth tries not to eat too greedily, taking frequent sips of jasmine tea and remembering to wipe her mouth on her napkin.

The pictures show a meticulously organised dig, a perfectly symmetrical trench, everything numbered and measured and recorded. One photo shows the skeleton in situ, arms crossed on the chest. Then the bones are being sorted and bagged. The site looks pretty crowded, volunteers working in the trench, other people just watching and taking photos. Ruth identifies a few faces. She thinks that's Guy kneeling by the trench and surely that's Elaine, swigging from a flask, her blonde hair shining in the sun. Dan seems to be everywhere, kneeling to examine the bones, standing in the trench, hand shielding his eyes, talking into his mobile phone, laughing with the volunteers. Ruth finds herself looking at one picture in particular. Dan is examining the skull, which is lying on a tarpaulin by the trench. There is something Hamlet-like about the pose and certainly, in retrospect, something almost tragic about Dan's bowed head. Did he suspect then that the skull was African? Did he know the danger he was in? In the background of the picture she can see Guy looking intently at his friend. Ruth feels that she would give a great deal to know what was in his mind at that moment.

'Were you close to Dan?' she asks Susan.

She expects the other woman to evade the question but Susan looks at her calmly over the crowded table.

'Yes. We had a brief affair about a year back. Nothing too serious. It ended by mutual consent and we stayed friends. I was fond of him. He was very charismatic.'

'Yes,' Ruth agrees. 'He was.' She can't help thinking that Susan's account of the affair sounds a little too civilised. Nothing's ever that straightforward, surely?

'Dan went out with Elaine too, didn't he?'

Now there is fire in Susan's eyes. She breathes in sharply, nostrils flaring.

'That woman. She trapped Dan into sleeping with her and then threatened to kill herself when he tried to end it. She's a complete nut job.'

Ruth is always sceptical when men say they've been trapped into sex by women and she's not more convinced by Susan's claim. But she's never heard the bit about suicide before.

'Elaine threatened to kill herself?'

'Oh she didn't go through with it,' says Susan dismissively and unnecessarily. 'She's just an attention seeker.'

How far would Elaine go in search of attention, thinks Ruth. Dressing up in a mask and robe? Burning down a house?

'Do you know anything about a group called the White Hand?' she asks.

'No,' says Susan. 'Who are they?' Her gaze is clear and almost child-like. But Susan is a highly intelligent woman.

Ruth smiles back. 'It's not important. Do you want some more egg-fried rice?'

CHAPTER 27

On Monday morning, Cathbad leaves promptly at nine. He feels rather guilty at abandoning Ruth, but as he turns out of Beach Row he sees a huge gas-guzzling monster car pulling up at Number One. That must be Ruth's university friend. He's glad that she's got some company but he can't really see what Ruth would have in common with a woman who drives a car like that. They are spending the day at a water park, something else that Cathbad finds quite inexplicable. Why go indoors with artificial rapids and fake waterfalls when you have the sea on your doorstep? Kate will like it, Ruth had said, but Kate had liked playing on the beach with him, building a henge, collecting shells and driftwood, watching the tide retreat so quickly that the sand had glistened like a mirage. She's not your child, he tells himself, something he finds himself having to do several times a day. She's Ruth's daughter, and if Ruth wants to take her to a water park, that's up to her. After all, isn't he the one who has said he will take her to Nickelodeon World, that vast plastic pleasure ground? Is he only doing it to be popular with Kate? Of course he is.

He drives carefully along the dual carriageway, Thing at his side. The solicitor may be surprised at his turning up with a dog in tow but he could hardly leave the animal alone for the day. Besides, he likes Thing's company. He can see why Pendragon called him his familiar, there is something accepting about a dog that's very comforting when your thoughts are in turmoil. Cathbad likes cats but they are more judgemental somehow. He imagines that Flint would just tell him to pull himself together and break open the Go-Cat.

And his thoughts are in turmoil. Pendragon's face and his ghastly swinging body haunt his dreams (despite the soothing ballet wallpaper). Why did he do it? Why hadn't he confided in Cathbad? Again and again, Cathbad wonders if he could have been more understanding that day when he visited Pendragon. He'd known his friend was worried about something, why hadn't he tried harder to find out what it was? Was Pendragon so terrified of the White Hand that he'd killed himself rather than face their vengeance? Cathbad had been shocked at the evidence of Pendragon's involvement with the Neo-pagan group. He still can't accept that his gentle friend believed in all that rubbish about the supremacy of the white Norseman. After all, Pendragon had lived in Ireland. He must, surely, have had some sympathy with the Celtic gods too. Cathbad has always believed that one of the good things about being a pagan was that you didn't have to settle for one narrow set of beliefs but could choose from a cornucopia of mysteries. But it seems that Pendragon had chosen the narrowest path of all.

They reach Clitheroe at ten. It's a bustling market town, built on steep cobbled streets, overlooked by a magnificent castle. On any other occasion Cathbad would have enjoyed strolling around, absorbing the energies of the place. But today he feels that he is on business. He is even wearing what is almost a jacket. He puts the lead on Thing and walks sedately along the high street. It's almost like working in a *bank*.

The solicitors, J. Arthur Wagstaff, are housed in a reassuringly uncorporate building, a quaint little house with a bow window like a Victorian sweetshop. Cathbad feels his spirits beginning to rise. The receptionist doesn't even blanch at Thing (or Cathbad's jacket). She ushers them into an office and tells them that Stephanie will be with them shortly. For the first time Cathbad realises that the S. Evans mentioned by Pen's sister is actually a woman. He chastises himself for such sexist assumptions. Ruth would be horrified.

To complicate matters further, Stephanie Evans is extremely attractive. She has red hair, which gleams seductively against her black dress. She reminds Cathbad of Ruth's friend Shona. Her accent is pure Lancashire. Cathbad leans forward so as not to miss a word. What she tells him is almost as interesting as the glimpse of cleavage with which he is rewarded. Dame Alice's cottage was rented but Pendragon has left its contents in their entirety to Cathbad. He has also left him his savings, a surprisingly healthy sum. Pendragon also asked his friend to care take of his dog.

'I see you're already doing that,' says Stephanie warmly.

'It seemed the right thing to do,' says Cathbad.

There are a couple of legacies to Pendragon's sister, Margot, and to local charities. Most interesting of all is a donation to a local neurological centre.

'I understand they were treating him,' says Stephanie.

'Treating him?'

Stephanie looks at him in surprise and concern.

'Didn't you know? Pendragon had a brain tumour. Inoperable apparently. He thought that he only had a few months left to live.'

Cathbad leaves the solicitors' office in a daze. This revelation sheds a new light on Pendragon's suicide. And, in retrospect, the headaches and the herbal infusions are also explained. Did the tumour contribute to Pendragon's feelings of persecution and isolation? Or was he, simply, afraid of dying? Did he ask Dame Alice for help, wonders Cathbad, remembering the garden and the raven in the apple tree. It's possible that Pendragon acted not out of fear but out of a desire to be master of his own fate. But then Cathbad remembers his friend's contorted face as he cut him down from the beam. If he'd wanted an easy death he would have taken a gentle poison handpicked from the hedgerows. He would have lain down in Dame Alice's herb garden and waited for nightfall. No, that's not the way it happened.

He is so preoccupied that he gets tangled in Thing's lead and has to stop to extricate himself. As he does so he sees, above a shop, a name that looks vaguely familiar. R. Wade and Sons, Estate Agents.

'Come on, Thing,' he says. 'We've got another call to make.'

Halfway through the morning Sandy Macleod gets an unexpected visitor.

'Lady to see you, boss,' says the duty sergeant.

'Lady?' says Sandy, heaving himself up from his chair. 'I don't know any ladies.'

'This is definitely a lady,' says the sergeant.

And the sergeant is right. Pippa Henry, sitting in the reception area wearing a black dress, white cardigan and pearls, looks every inch a lady. In fact, Sandy muses, ushering her through the swing doors with a low iron-ical bow, it's almost *too* good a performance. Who wears a black dress and pearls on an August morning in Blackpool? She looks like that woman in that film, what was it called? Something about Tiffany's. Bev would know.

Anyway, it's distinctly interesting, her coming to call like this, all dressed up. It means she wants to impress him, maybe even influence him. Why?

'Coffee?' he asks, showing her into his office.

'That would be lovely.'

That's what you think, Sandy tells her silently. He dispatches a WPC for coffee and Kit Kats.

'So,' he says, sitting opposite and pushing some papers onto the floor. 'You wanted to see me.'

'Yes.'

Pippa Henry looks straight at him. She's really a very good-looking woman, thinks Sandy. Mid-forties probably, there are fine lines around her mouth and eyes but the overall impression is shiny and expensive. Her dark gold hair is in a bun and she sits up very straight, without fidgeting, a rare thing in a woman. Poise, thinks Sandy, that's what she has. Poise. He leans forward and sniffs. Chanel number 5. He might have guessed. Pippa recoils slightly.

Sandy smiles encouragingly. 'What did you want to see me about, Mrs Henry?'

Pippa smooths her skirt over her knees. 'I wanted to tell you about Dan Golding,' she says.

'What about him?'

Pippa smiles, revealing small white teeth. 'I think you already know, Detective Chief Inspector. I was having an affair with Dan.'

'Why would I know that?'

'You've found his computer with all his emails and everything. Everyone knows that.'

'Do they?'

Sandy wonders how everyone knows. Could Ruth Galloway have been talking? Nelson seems to trust her with all his secrets but Sandy wonders whether they were wise to give her free rein to look through Golding's files. She could easily have blabbed to one of the Pendle academics. Apparently she met that Guy chap the other day. Anyway, nothing on a computer stays private for long. Tim is actually with the forensic-data recovery people now, probing the mysteries of the hard drive.

Sandy arranges his expression to one of polite interest and smiles encouragingly at Pippa. The coffee is brought in and Pippa sips hers with a grimace.

'Great stuff,' says Sandy, taking a slurp. 'Kit Kat?'

'No thank you. Anyway, I thought I should come and see you. My husband doesn't know about . . . about Dan.'

I wouldn't be too sure about that, thinks Sandy. In his experience, husbands always know, though they might not want to admit it, even to themselves. He thinks of the nervous figure bouncing around the deluxe wind-mill. Clayton Henry seems to have so many problems that maybe infidelity isn't high on his list. Didn't he say that his wife had money of her own? Maybe he can't afford for her to walk out.

'Don't judge me too harshly,' Pippa is saying, throatily. 'My first husband was handsome and charming but he should never have married. He left me for another man.' She looks at Sandy as if daring him to say something but Sandy keeps his face blank.

'I was on my own with a young child. It was very difficult. I decided to go back to university – my father had left me some money – so I went to Pendle and studied history.'

'And that's where you met Clayton Henry.'

'That's right. He was my tutor. He was kind and he

offered security, and although he's been a very good step-father to Chloe, it's not a passionate relationship. But when I met Dan it was different. It was the real thing. He was so good-looking and charming. It was inevitable really.'

'Was it?'

Pippa flushes. 'Well, I suppose I could have resisted but . . .'

'Bit of a ladies' man, was he?' says Sandy sympatheti-cally. 'Very persuasive?'

'No,' says Pippa. 'It wasn't like that. He wasn't some loathsome charmer, oiling around women. He was quiet and rather aloof. It was just . . . well, we started talking at our Christmas party and there was this instant connec-tion. It was more mental than physical.'

I'll take your word for it, thinks Sandy. Beautiful people always claim not to be interested in looks. He has seen a photo of Dan Golding and the man looked like a bloody movie star. (He also saw his dead body when it was brought in for autopsy but then, to be fair, he wasn't looking his best.)

'I'd heard he was seeing his next-door neighbour,' he says now.

'Elaine?' Pippa's lip curls. 'She was mad about him but he was embarrassed by her. She was always turning up drunk, offering him her body.'

Nice, thinks Sandy. The only people who turn up on his doorstep are Jehovah's Witnesses. Perhaps he should move to Fleetwood.

'So there was nothing between Dan and Elaine?' he asks.

'Oh they may have had a fling before I came on the scene, but when I . . . knew him, Dan despised Elaine. She was so out of control. I think he was almost afraid of her.'

'Really?' This was interesting.

'Yes, when she was drunk she'd threaten to kill herself and him.'

In that order? wonders Sandy.

'She threatened to kill him?'

'Only when she was drunk.'

Could a drunk Elaine have set Dan's house on fire in a fit of jealous rage? Sandy wonders. It's possible. Her only alibi is Guy; just as Pippa's only alibi is Clayton.

'What about Guy,' he asks. 'Where does he fit in?'

'He's devoted to Elaine. He's the only one who can handle her. But I don't think they're lovers. In fact I always wondered whether he was gay. He certainly seemed a bit in love with Dan.'

'Popular chap.'

Pippa's eyes fill with tears. Sandy thinks they're genuine because they make her mascara run. 'Dan was a lovely, lovely man. Everyone adored him.'

So it would seem, thinks Sandy.

'It's a real shame,' says Gary, the estate agent. 'I don't expect we'll get another tenant now.'

Cathbad is tempted to say that the real shame is that a man who was alive a few days ago is lying dead in the mortuary. But he decides not to bother. There is a grey materialistic aura over Gary and, indeed, over the whole office, so he contents himself with stroking Thing and asking why Dame Alice's cottage is unlettable. It seems a highly desirable residence to him.

'It's got a reputation,' says Gary darkly. 'I don't know if you've heard of the Pendle Witches? Well, this house used to belong to one of them. An old lady lived there for years and people round here used to say she was a witch too. Then she died and it came on our books. We couldn't get a tenant to stay there. People said there were strange noises, things kept moving about, odd lights appeared in the garden at night. One man said he woke up in the night to see an old woman sitting at the foot of his bed, just staring at him. Someone else said they'd seen Dame Alice sitting in her rocking chair, knitting. The place was empty for years until your friend moved in.'

'And he didn't care about the ghosts?'

'No.' Gary looks dubiously at Cathbad, who smiles blandly back. 'I understood he was into that sort of thing. He said that he'd make peace with Dame Alice's spirit. And now this happens!'

'You think his death had something to do with Dame Alice?'

Gary laughs uneasily. 'No. I don't think it. I don't believe in any of that stuff. But folk round here will believe it. They'll think the old lady got him in the end.'

Cathbad doesn't quite buy the agent's protestations. He thinks that Gary is the type that believes everything and nothing. But he's not concerned with Gary right now. He's seeing himself living in Dame Alice's cottage with Thing, tending the herb garden and walking on the high hills at dawn. He likes the north; there's something clear and honest about it that appeals to him. And, if Judy doesn't want him in her life, he can't keep hanging on in Norfolk hoping for a glimpse of her and the baby. Far better to make a clean break. He can always find work as a lab assistant and, if he's careful, Pendragon's legacy will last for some time.

'If you did find a tenant,' he says, 'I suppose the rent would be quite low.'

Tim comes back from the forensic data recovery company full of news. This is another private company, much used by the police and much resented by Sandy. After his last visit (when Sandy asked one of the analysts, 'Do you do this because you can't get a girlfriend?') it has been tacitly agreed that Tim should handle communication with the outfit. Today's visit seems to have been a success. Tim is not a demonstrative person but he is positively beaming as he looks round the door of his boss's office.

'Glad someone's got something to smile about,' says Sandy.

'They've tracked down the University Pals website,' says Tim. 'You know, the emails that were sent to Ruth Galloway and Dan Golding.'

'Well? Don't keep us in suspense. Who sent them?'

'Clayton Henry.'

Sandy whistles. 'Did he now? Why, I wonder?'

'Could just have been fishing in the dark,' says Tim. 'Pardon the pun.' Sandy looks blank and Tim wonders if he has forgotten the whole phishing/fishing conversation. He hasn't; he just thinks that Tim is being a tosser.

'What I mean,' says Tim hastily, 'is that Clayton might have known that he would need Ruth Galloway's identity at some later point, to find information about the bones. He could just have been trying to see what he could pick up.'

'But how did he know that Golding had contacted Galloway in the first place?'

Tim shrugs. 'He must known that they were at university together. It wouldn't be difficult to work out if he knew where and when Golding was at university. And he would have known all that from the University Pals information.'

'He must have known there was something unusual about the bones,' says Sandy, 'something Golding hadn't told him.'

'Do you think that Henry switched the bones?' asks Tim. 'With Terry Durkin's help?'

'Doesn't make sense,' muses Sandy. 'Why get Dr Galloway up here if he'd removed the original bones? He must have known that she'd spot the switch. She's the expert, after all. And without the bones he wouldn't have his big story. No chance of making megabucks and getting himself out of shit creek.'

'Then who did switch them?' says Tim. 'And where are they now?'

'Don't know,' says Sandy. 'But Clayton Henry's afraid of someone, and if we find out who my guess is we've got our killer.'

'You don't think it's Henry himself then?'

'I had his wife in just now.'

'Pippa? Really? What did she want?'

'To tell me about her affair with Golding. How it wasn't really her fault because she's had a hard life.'

'And has she had a hard life?'

'Well her first husband turned out to be gay.'

Tim often wonders if Sandy thinks he's gay because he wears aftershave and plays tennis. But his boss's face is inscrutable.

'That surprises me,' he says.

'Does it?' says Sandy. 'It doesn't me. Do you remember when we looked at the ex-Pendle students arrested for racist or homophobic behaviour?'

'Yes,' says Tim, though he clearly doesn't remember them as well as Sandy.

'Do you remember the woman? Philippa Moore? Arrested for using offensive language at a gay rights march.'

'Philippa ... Pippa ... do you think that was her?'

'Oh, it was her, all right. I've been looking her up. She's written a few letters to papers complaining about gay men who marry innocent young girls and then desert them.'

Tim doesn't know what surprises him more. That Sandy has actually been using the internet to research the activities of Pippa Henry or that the stylish woman he remembers from the windmill obviously still holds a grudge about something that must have happened ten or fifteen years ago. And if she holds a grudge about that, what might she think about a lover who abandoned her, for example?

'Was it serious between her and Golding?' he asks. 'She's hardly mentioned in the diaries.'

'She says she was in love with him. It was more mental than physical apparently.'

Tim, like Sandy before him, looks sceptical. 'Do you think she could have killed Golding? Maybe he'd tried to finish the affair. We know she doesn't take rejection well.'

'It's possible,' says Sandy. 'Her only alibi is her husband and there are all sorts of reasons why he might back her up. Maybe they were even in it together. I've seen stranger things. They could have planned it together to teach him a lesson. And there's the next-door neighbour too.'

'Elaine Morgan?'

'According to Pippa, she was wild about Golding. Used to turn up on his doorstep offering him her body.'

'Makes a change from double glazing.'

'My thoughts exactly. We know that Elaine Morgan has a drink problem. She's not exactly a stable personality.'

'And her only alibi's her housemate.'

'Yes, and God knows what *their* relationship is. The whole lot of them seem to be at it like rabbits.'

There is a silence, during which Tim's stomach gives a thunderous rumble. He looks at the clock over Sandy's desk. It's one o'clock. He was up at six to go to the gym and he's starving.

'Fancy some lunch, boss?' he says. 'They've got chips in the canteen.'

'No, you're all right,' says Sandy. 'I'm meeting someone.'

Nelson had been surprised when Sandy had suggested that they meet for lunch. The very word 'lunch' has a soft, southern sound that he doesn't associate with Sandy. A pint, yes. Tea, perhaps. But lunch? No. Lunch is for city types in striped shirts or women with too much time on their hands, not for jaded policemen with murder cases to solve. But his surprise doesn't stop him accepting Sandy's invitation. He's getting slightly bored with visiting garden centres and he's keen to know more about the case. As far as he's concerned, someone is threatening his child, which makes it his business.

Sandy named a pub near the station. 'It's about the only place these days where they don't do bloody karaoke,' he said on the phone. When Nelson arrives, Sandy is already there, nursing a pint. He can see why the boozer appeals to Sandy. It's a dour little place, dedicated to drinking, with very few concessions to modern life. There's a TV showing the racing, that's it. No karaoke, no cappuccino, no gastro menu. Food choice consists of a butty or a pie. Nelson chooses a pie.

'This your local?' he asks.

Sandy grunts. 'Don't have locals any more. Pubs used

to be places where men could escape. Now they're full of children and hen parties.'

The clientele of this pub consists of three old men and a greyhound. The dog, who wags his tail at Nelson, might well be the only one who is still alive. Nelson sympathises with Sandy over the karaoke but he's never really wanted to escape from women. He gets on well with men, he couldn't survive in the force otherwise, but he likes the company of women. Maybe it comes from having two older sisters. Maybe it's because, for the last nineteen years, he's been outnumbered three-to-one in his own household.

'When are you going back to Norfolk?' asks Sandy.

'Next week.'

'Sorry to leave?'

Nelson pauses, looking into his pint. Will he be sorry to leave Blackpool? He'll be glad to put some distance between himself and Maureen, much as he loves her. It'll be grand to see the girls again. They're both coming home for a few weeks before term starts in September. It's not that he's longing for Norfolk exactly. It's just that, like it or not, it's home. Jesus. How did that happen?

'I'm always sorry to leave,' he says at last. 'But I'm not much cop at holidays.'

'Me neither,' says Sandy. 'Went to Disneyland once. Shortened my life. I'm not a fan of heights. Dangling upside down in mid air isn't my idea of fun.'

'Reminds me of Madame Cindy's House of Pain,' says Nelson. 'Remember Madame Cindy?'

They reminisce for a few minutes and Nelson starts to wonder if, incredibly enough, Sandy has actually asked him here for a *chat*, when his old friend leans back in his chair and says, 'She's a lovely woman, your Michelle.'

Nelson looks up in surprise. What's all this about? Are they actually going to talk about their *wives*? And in all the time he's known him he's never heard Sandy offer such an enthusiastic tribute to anyone. Of course, Michelle *is* a lovely woman but Sandy can't have seen her for years. He agrees that Michelle is far too good for him and asks politely after Bev. Sandy ignores this overture. More pint-staring and then Sandy says, 'Can I ask you a question, Harry?'

'Of course.'

'Is there anything going on between you and the archae-ologist girl?'

'Ruth? Why do you ask?'

'So there is then.'

Nelson curses himself for falling into the oldest policeman's trap in the book. He says, carefully, 'There was something a few years ago. We're just friends now.'

'And the wee lassie. Is she yours?'

Nelson remembers that when Sandy lapses into the idiom of his Scottish mother, it's always a sign of deep emotion.

'Yes,' he says. 'It's all a right mess.'

He thinks that Sandy will leave it there, go back to talking about the past or discussing Blackpool's prospects in the Premier League. Instead, his friend leans forward and says, almost urgently, 'Be careful, Harry. What you've got with Michelle, that's worth keeping. I've seen the way that Ruth looks at you. She's in love with you. Just don't do anything stupid. I know what you're like when you think you're doing the right thing.'

Nelson can think of nothing to say to this. His pie arrives but he doesn't feel hungry somehow.

CHAPTER 28

Caz delivers Ruth and Kate back to Beach Row, happy and exhausted. It has been a brilliant day, thinks Ruth, as she dumps wet towels in the washing machine and starts to prepare supper. The Water Park had been heaven. Kate had adored playing on the desert island and the pirate ship, splashing in the Blue Lagoon paddling pool and negotiating Ratty's Rapids. Caz's children, when not flinging themselves down death-defying slides, had played sweetly with Kate, leaving Ruth free to enjoy some actual swimming (though it was hard to do lengths in a trapezoid-shaped pool crammed with over-excited toddlers).

Cathbad was wrong to say that it was naff and over-priced, decides Ruth. Well, not entirely wrong, but sometimes, with children, naff is good. It had been expensive, though. Ruth shudders at the memory of the cappuccinos drunk at the 'poolside reef'. But Cathbad has no right to be so judgemental. He keeps going on about how much Kate had loved playing on the beach with him. 'Just the sand and the sea. No commercial rubbish. Just good natural energies.' Well *of course* Kate had liked playing on the beach. She's two, for God's sake. That doesn't mean that she can only enjoy herself in Cathbad's wholesome company. He should try looking after her on a rainy afternoon when she's got toothache and the DVD player's broken. That would test his powers as a godfather.

Where is Cathbad anyway? She had expected him to be back when she got home. He is probably wandering somewhere in the Pendle Forest, Thing at his side. Well, she doesn't begrudge him that, exactly. He's had a tough few days – a tough year – and she knows that he finds walking therapeutic. Still, she hopes he's back before dark. She doesn't want to be alone with Kate in the cottage. She is so pleased that they are going home tomorrow. Even in the water park, surrounded by grinning plastic dolphins and mermaid friezes, she kept thinking about that figure on the riverbank. The hooded man, the monster without a face. So many stories involve the appearance of an unknown 'other', the stranger whom nobody recognises. Who is the third who walks beside you? Christ on the road to Emmaus. Poor Tom on the blasted heath. Countless fairy tales about the mysterious traveller who arrives by night. Guess my name or I will take your soul.

After a desultory supper, Ruth takes Kate upstairs for her bath. One of the best things about spending the day at a vile commercial theme park is that, by half past six, Kate is so tired that she can hardly keep her eyes open. Ruth is barely two pages into Dora the Explorer when her daughter's steady breathing informs her that she is asleep and the rest of the evening is, miraculously, her own. She goes downstairs wondering if it's decadent to drink wine when it's still light outside. Oh sod it, she'll just have a small glass.

She pours herself a small glass but it looks so lonely that she tops it up. She's sure it still only counts as one unit. Then, carrying the wine, she goes into the sitting room, sits on the sofa and opens her laptop. She wants to have another look at Dan's diaries before Cathbad gets back.

The best thing about electronic diaries is that you can use 'Find'. Feeling rather guilty, Ruth searches for mentions of herself. There are just two. The one about asking for her help with the bones and one dated 2nd April, in the very early days of the dig, before the skeleton had been discovered:

For some reason, found myself thinking about the old days at UCL. About Finn, Kamal, Ruth and Caz. In those days I always thought I'd be a big success as an archaeologist – write a best-selling book, make a devastating discovery. Well, it hasn't quite worked out like that. I've been a jobbing archaeologist, nothing more. Teaching bored students and doing a bit of desultory digging at weekends. Coming up to Pendle felt like defeat. I was only here because of Karen and I have to admit it hurt that she had a better job than me. Her career was going places whereas mine seemed to have stalled. I knew, as soon as I met Clayton, that the department was in bad shape. They don't attract enough students or enough funding. The Dean, I think, would like to get rid of history altogether and replace it with something more lucrative and trendy. In the interview, Clayton told me that I'd have a free hand to run the archaeology courses but, in reality, there are so few students that we struggle to maintain anything like a proper programme. Clayton has no feel for or interest in archaeology. It's too dry and labour-intensive for him. Sam's really only interested in the modern stuff. Guy is keen and has a good mind. Elaine is just too weird ever to amount to anything as an academic – though she's bright too. Pendle really seemed like a dead end, the graveyard of my hopes. But this find – this could change everything. A Romano-British temple dedicated to the Raven God. This could be worth an article, even a book. If only I could get the funding, we could do some really good digging here. Who knows what lies buried here?

Who indeed, thinks Ruth, draining her glass without noticing. Dan was right that greater treasures lay beneath the earth but was it this discovery that led to his death? Was Pendle – 'the graveyard of my hopes' – literally the death of him?

There are other things here that are interesting too. She remembers Finn and Kamal from their archaeology class. She wonders what they are doing now. She thinks that they, like Caz, got out of archaeology as soon as they could. Didn't she hear somewhere that Kamal had become a solicitor? Dan's feelings about his career strike a chord too. Ruth has also been feeling that her professional life has somehow stalled, despite her work with the police (which has proved interesting, if unexpectedly dangerous). She sympathises with Dan, coming to Pendle and finding a failing department full of warring individuals. He does say that Guy has a good mind and, of course, it's Guy who wants to carry on his work, making a name for himself in the process. Elaine is 'weird', which chimes with what Guy has told her. There is little here to suggest that Dan was ever in love with Elaine. Karen must have been his wife. What's she doing now?

Some of these questions are easily answered. A google search for Kamal Singh comes up with hundreds of entries but Ruth tracks him down via Friends Reunited. Yes, he's a solicitor, married with three children. What about Finn? Here she has a horrible shock. Finn is dead. He died three years ago of prostate cancer. She tracks him down via a tribute page at the school where he was clearly a much-loved history teacher. Poor Finn. Irish, rugby-loving Finn. Dead at forty. Finn and Dan both dead. Ruth shivers, as if the Grim Reaper is reading over her shoulder. The moving finger writes and, having writ, moves on.

A search for Karen Golding reveals her to be a professor of theoretical physics at Manchester University. Still a high-flyer then. Ruth wonders how she feels about Dan now. Caz said that she seemed very upset at his funeral and it was apparently Karen, the career woman, who wanted to settle down and have children. Why didn't Dan want children? Ruth remembers his bitter observation that she was probably married with ten children 'like everyone else'. Maybe Dan just didn't want to be like everyone else. Maybe he was happy living on his own, having a succession of affairs. But in his diaries he doesn't sound like a happy man exactly.

She searches the diaries for Pippa and comes up with a couple of mentions. There's the reference to her presence at the excavation and, a few days later:

Pippa came round. We both know it has to stop but I think neither of us wants to say the word. Pippa talked about leaving Clayton but I don't think she ever will. She loves the lifestyle – the windmill, the parties, the adoring husband. She couldn't survive on her own. Does she mean to throw in her lot with me? I've never encouraged her to think that we have a future together. I told her that after Karen left I vowed never to marry again. She accepted this at the time but she may think that she can get me to change my mind. I asked (again) if Clayton suspected. She said he didn't, that he trusts me and would never think that I would betray him. Afterwards, I felt bad about this. Clayton has been good to me, according to his lights, and, whichever way you look at it, I am betraying him. Then I thought that it was odd that she had said that he trusted me, he didn't think I would betray him. What about Pippa? What about his wife? Didn't he trust her?

Ruth reads this with, once again, mixed feelings. She finds Dan's tone a little hard – 'I've never encouraged her to think that we have a future together' – but at least he had felt some remorse about deceiving Clayton. The part about Pippa is interesting though. Did Clayton trust his wife? Did he know about the affair? And if he had found out, what would he think about the man who had betrayed him, the man he had welcomed into his department, into his life? Would Clayton have been angry? Angry enough to kill?

Did Dan end his relationship with Pippa? Ruth scans the rest of the diary but can find only one other reference to Pippa Henry. Dan is writing about the possibility of organising another dig to explore the area around the temple. He says that Guy and Elaine are keen to help but 'Pippa thinks that Elaine is dangerous'. That's all. Was Pippa just prejudiced against Elaine because she knew that she was Dan's ex-lover or did she know something else about her? Ruth suspects that there are many words that could describe Elaine Morgan but *dangerous*? It's an uncomfortable choice. Was Elaine dangerous? To herself? To Dan?

She looks at the time displayed on the side of the screen. Eight o'clock. Where is Cathbad? At least she hasn't got Thing pacing around, driving her mad. She gets up and pours herself another glass of wine. They're very small glasses, more like sherry glasses really. She checks her phone. No messages from the wandering warlock. She's not worried about Cathbad – he's a grown man and he's got a bull terrier to protect him – but she does hope he hasn't decided to stay the night at the cottage. She doesn't want to be on her own, that's all. Not with the texter still on the loose and the memory of the hooded figure on the riverbank so clear in her mind. She goes to the front door and looks out. It's nearly dark outside and the street is deserted. No sign of Sandy's mythical patrol car. The holiday-making crowds have all gone home. Ruth puts the chain on the front door and goes back into the sitting room.

There is nothing else in the diaries about Pippa or Elaine – or Ruth. The last entry is the one where Dan received a letter from the White Hand containing the names and addresses of his family. The last lines are: *I rang Clayton and once again said that we should call the police. He refused. He's shielding someone. But whom?*

Who was Clayton Henry shielding? His wife? Himself? He was scared enough of the White Hand to sanction the removal of the bones to a private laboratory but why won't he call the police when a member of his department is being threatened? It's as if the White Hand are moving closer and closer. They write letters, they leave dead birds on Dan's doorstep, a few days after this last diary entry his house was set on fire. Did they come closer still? Did Dan ever see the cloaked figure standing in the shadows outside his house? Did he ever look into the blackness where the face should be? If so, the diaries aren't telling.

Ruth is really spooked now. *Ladybird, ladybird. Fly away home.* Well, she'll be home tomorrow and she'll never again go further north than the Wash. Should she check on Kate again? Calm down, she tells herself, it only half-past eight on a summer night. What's going to happen to you? But, all the same, she thinks she'll just draw the curtains.

She has just got to the window when the doorbell rings. Ruth smiles with relief. Typical of Cathbad to have forgotten his key. She approaches the door rehearsing her reproaches, just as if she really is his wife. What time do you call this? Why didn't you ring? Don't you know we've got an early start in the morning?

But it's not Cathbad standing outside.

It's the last of the triumvirate. It's Elaine.

CHAPTER 29

'I hope you don't mind me calling round like this,' says Elaine.

Ruth does mind but Elaine doesn't actually seem dangerous or deranged. In fact, she looks rather forlorn, standing there in the twilight. In contrast to her glamour at Clayton's party, she looks distinctly scruffy in faded jeans and an oversized jumper. She also looks very young.

'Come in,' says Ruth.

'I've been driving round all day,' says Elaine. 'Trying to get up the courage to come and see you.'

Ruth takes Elaine into the sitting room; it seems more formal somehow than the kitchen. It is only when they are sitting on the sofa that Ruth notices her laptop on the coffee table, open at Dan's diaries. Will Elaine look at the screen? Surely not, but even so Ruth wishes that she could move it. But how can she do this without drawing attention to it?

Elaine, though, seems hardly to notice anything. She sits, huddled in her big jumper, her knees pulled up to her chest.

'I'm so frightened,' she says. 'I don't know what to do.'

'I'll make you a nice cup of tea,' says Ruth, aware how ridiculous this sounds. She hurries out, casually sweeping up the laptop on the way. In the kitchen, she hides the computer in the larder and crashes about with mugs and biscuit tins. She wonders about offering Elaine a drink (she could certainly do with another herself), but, remembering Dan's diary, thinks it's safer to stick to tea. It looks as if their conversation is going to be sticky enough without alcohol.

When she goes back into the sitting room, Elaine is still in the same hunched position. Ruth puts a mug in front of her.

'Here's some tea. There are biscuits in the tin.'

'Thank you,' says Elaine tonelessly. 'You're very kind.'

Ruth waits, wrapping her hands round her mug and listening for noises from upstairs. But the only sound in the room is Elaine's ragged breathing. Ruth wonders if she's ill.

'I'm so scared,' says Elaine, again.

'Why?' asks Ruth.

Elaine looks at her. She has very pale blue eyes and blonde eyelashes. It gives her an exotic albino appearance.

'Guy says you've found Daniel's laptop.'

Ruth thought at the time that her story about the police

having the laptop hadn't convinced Guy. He must have guessed that she would have taken copies of the files. If so, he knows exactly how much she knows. She thinks of her computer, at this moment crammed into the larder next to the cornflakes and teething rusks. Luckily, Elaine doesn't wait for an answer.

'If you've read his diary, you'll know all sorts of things about me. I thought I ought to come and set the record straight.'

'You don't owe me any explanations,' says Ruth. She is dreading a heart-to-heart with Dan's ex-girlfriend. Oh God, why doesn't Cathbad come back?

Elaine ignores her. She is crying now but makes no attempt to stem the tears; they run, unchecked, down her pale cheeks.

'I loved Daniel,' she says. 'I thought he loved me but he didn't. I was convenient, I was next door. But when I started to get heavy he dumped me. He could be a cold-blooded bastard, you know.'

Funnily enough, Ruth can believe this. Hadn't she felt a faint chill, reading his diary just now? Against her will, she feels sorry for Elaine.

Now Elaine reaches forward and grabs Ruth's hand. 'But I would never do anything to hurt him. You must believe that!'

Gently Ruth extracts her hand. 'No one thinks you did,' she says.

'The police do,' says Elaine. 'That awful detective, the fat one, he came round asking all these questions. I know he suspects me, he kept giving me these horrible looks. And the other one, the good-looking one, he kept asking about the White Hand.'

'Well, they think the White Hand might be involved,' says Ruth. 'After all, they're Neo-Nazis, they're capable of anything.'

Elaine stares at her. Wet with tears, her eyes look almost white.

'Don't you understand? We were in the White Hand, all of us.'

Cathbad hadn't realised how late it was until he went into the garden and saw that the hills were in darkness. Thing, clearly delighted to be back in his old home, is running around, barking at the gathering birds. Cathbad doesn't wear a watch as they tend not to work on him (too much natural electricity, he suspects) and there don't seem to be any clocks in the house. Pendragon didn't have a TV or a radio or any electrical gadget – if you ignore the high-tech office upstairs, which Cathbad is trying to. He fumbles in his pocket for his mobile phone and looks at the display. It's eight-thirty. He'd better get back to Ruth.

It had been easy to extract the cottage keys from Gary. Once he'd had a sniff that Cathbad might want to take over the rent, he had fallen over himself to be helpful. Yes, take the keys. Drop them back tomorrow. Take as much time as you want. So Cathbad had spent a peaceful afternoon at Dame Alice's cottage, praying for Pendragon's soul and offering libations to the good spirits. Anxious to cover all spiritual bases, he said a decade of the rosary (his grandmother would be proud of him) and made a symbolic sacrifice of one of Pendragon's old robes, which he burnt in the sun-dial. He even forced himself to make a trip to the woodshed where he scattered herbs and said the Catholic prayer for the dead. 'Eternal rest give unto him, O Lord. And let perpetual light shine upon him.' Despite this cleansing, Thing had flatly refused to enter the shed.

Sometime during the afternoon, Cathbad realised that all the contents of the house belonged to him. Really, he could just move in tomorrow. Now, as he is locking up, he wonders whether he should take the crucifix from Pendragon's bedroom. It might transfer some of its protection to Ruth and Kate. But when he stands by the bed, as smooth as a shroud, he feels curiously reluctant to touch the heavy wooden cross. After all, it didn't bring Pendragon much luck. He is about to leave the room when his eye falls on the book beside the bed. *Old English Ballads*, it's called. He opens the book and sees that a page has been kept by a bay leaf. A verse has been annotated in pencil. Cathbad reads, Thing panting at his side.

> *The wind doth blow today, my love*
> *And a few drops of rain*
> *I never had but one true love*
> *In cold grave she was lain.*

The word 'she' has been changed to 'he'. The ballad is called 'The Unquiet Grave'. Cathbad stands still, listening to the silence of the house. There is no wind today and no rain. Why did Pendragon mark this poem? Was he thinking of his own mortality? Of the fact that he was planning to take his own life? The will gave no instructions about a funeral or interment but Cathbad has an idea of what his friend would have wanted. Is this bleak little verse referring to an unmarked grave on Pendle Hill? Is that where Pendragon wanted to lie at rest? And who was Pendragon's 'one true love'? Cathbad never heard him mention a woman but he supposes that everyone has one true love in their lives. Not wanting to think about this, he takes the book and makes his way downstairs. It's cold now so he borrows a cloak that's hanging on a hook by the back door. He also liberates a large packet of dog biscuits. Everything else can stay where it is.

He sends Ruth a quick text and, with one last farewell to Dame Alice, sets out for the car.

'What do you mean "all of you?"' whispers Ruth.

Elaine seems to understand what she means. 'Oh, not Daniel. He couldn't join, could he, being Jewish and everything. No, me, Guy and Clayton.'

The casual anti-Semitism shocks Ruth almost more than anything. But Elaine had loved Dan. Ruth notices again how, alone of all his acquaintance, Elaine always refers to him by his full name.

She still can't quite believe it. 'You belong to a Neo-Nazi group?'

'You don't understand,' says Elaine, sounding quite impatient. 'The Neo-Nazis on campus, stomping around protesting about Chinese cockle-pickers in Fleetwood, they weren't anything to do with us. The White Hand was different. It was about going back to the old days. The days of the High King.'

'King Arthur?'

'Yes, even before we joined the White Hand, we used to talk about recreating Camelot, the four of us. Clayton was King Arthur, I was Guinevere, Guy was Lancelot. Pendragon was Merlin.'

'So why did you join the White Hand?'

'Pendragon told us about it. He said there were magical powers associated with belonging to the group. Strong psychic energies. And he was right. We had an initiation ceremony on Pendle Hill. It was wonderful. There were lights in the sky, voices from the heavens, a great black bird appeared above us with wings of fire.' She smiles reminiscently.

There is a lot that Ruth could say to this. You can admire the Arthurian legends without belonging to a sinister secret society associated (whatever Elaine says) with racist and homophobic groups. As for the heavenly voices and the fiery blackbird, she suspects the presence of hard drugs. But there are other things she needs to know.

'Who else was in the White Hand?' she asks. 'Who was in charge? Who was the Arch Wizard?'

Elaine's eyes flicker from side to side. 'I don't know. You only know your chapter and our chapter was the four of us.'

'Someone must have known.'

'Clayton, Guy and Pendragon were knights. They had messages from the Arch Wizard sometimes but I don't think they ever met him.'

'And you weren't a knight?'

'Oh no. Women weren't allowed to be knights.'

Sexist as well as racist and homophobic, thinks Ruth. But surely someone must know who the Arch Wizard is. Somebody prancing round in robes, setting people's houses on fire, that can't stay a secret for long. She thinks of the masked figure on the riverbank and shivers.

'Who was Dan?' she asks. 'Did he have a role in all this?'

'Oh, he didn't know about the White Hand. We couldn't tell him. But he was Percival, wasn't he? The one who found the grail.'

So when Dan wrote about the White Hand, he had no way of knowing that two of his closest friends and his boss were actually members. But, even so, both Guy and Clayton had clearly been scared of someone or something. Guy had insisted that the bones be stored in a safe place and Clayton had received threatening letters (or so he said). Did they know the identity of the Arch Wizard? Did they know that he was capable of murder?

'Elaine,' she says. 'Do you know who killed Dan?'

Elaine seems to sag in her chair, becoming young and

vulnerable again. When she speaks, it is in almost a baby voice.

'I didn't have anything to do with the fire. Guy and I had been to the pub. When we got back, there were flames everywhere. I thought it was our house at first. Guy called the fire brigade. It was awful. I was screaming. We saw them bring Daniel's body out. The paramedics were giving him mouth-to-mouth but Guy wouldn't let me go to him. I was hysterical. I had to take a tranquiliser.'

Ruth declines the invitation to pity Elaine. Instead she says, 'You know something, don't you? That's why you're so scared.'

Elaine looks at her. Her face is not so much pale as drained of life. Her lips are almost white and Ruth can see the veins beneath her skin. She looks around the room, hands clenching and unclenching.

'Elaine,' says Ruth, more gently. 'Why did you come to see me?'

'I think the White Hand killed Daniel,' says Elaine in a whisper.

She sounds so scared that, despite herself, Ruth looks over her shoulder. The French windows are dark now and the night is quiet. She would give anything to hear Sandy's patrol car driving past. She turns back to Elaine, who is still clenching and unclenching.

'Do you know why they killed him?'

'Guy thought that Daniel had discovered something about the High King,' she says at last. 'Daniel didn't tell Guy what it was but Guy suspected.'

So much for it being a joint project, thinks Ruth. She is unreasonably pleased that Dan hadn't shared his suspicions with Guy, even though he had planned to take her into his confidence. Despite his protestations in his diaries, Dan obviously hadn't completely trusted Guy.

'What did Guy suspect?' she asks.

'He didn't say,' says Elaine. 'But he thought it could be something that could dishonour the High King. Daniel didn't understand, you see. He liked the idea of King Arthur but all he cared about was making a great discovery. He wanted to be famous.'

Don't we all, thinks Ruth. Once again, she feels a terrible sadness for her friend, who was, indeed, on the verge of great distinction in his field. And Elaine will never know how much Dan too was under the spell of King Arthur. It's just that he didn't care if the Raven King was black or white. All that mattered to him was the truth.

'Does Guy know who killed Dan?' she asks.

'No,' says Elaine. 'But I know he suspects it was on the Arch Wizard's orders.'

Ruth leans forward. 'Elaine, is Clayton Henry the Arch Wizard?'

'I don't think so. He was so fond of Daniel.'

'Was it Clayton who switched the skeletons?' She doesn't think it's worth pretending that she doesn't know about this. Everyone will know by now that Ruth has spotted the switch. Only yesterday she had the C14 results on the two sets of bones that she examined at CNN Forensics. They are a few hundred years old, no more.

Ruth wonders where they came from. But, at the time, Clayton had seemed genuinely surprised.

'No,' says Elaine. 'I don't know who did that. It wouldn't have been Clayton. He wanted to carry on with the investigations. He thought that he could make a lot of money out of the tomb of King Arthur. He's terribly in debt, you know.'

'Where are King Arthur's bones now?'

'I don't know. Guy thinks they've probably been burnt on a funeral pyre somewhere. That would be the respectful thing to do.'

Despite everything, Ruth feels a pang for those precious, irreplaceable bones. If they are gone, there is no way that Dan's discovery can ever be tested. All that will remain will be the DNA and isotope findings, Susan's photos and Dan's diary. Not enough.

She looks at Elaine, now calmly sipping tea. 'Why are you telling me all this?' she asks again.

Elaine looks back, wide-eyed. Her expression is utterly transparent and candid and Ruth does not trust her an inch.

'Well, you know anyway. You've got the memory stick.'

'You said you were scared. What are you scared of?'

Elaine's gaze does not falter. 'I'm afraid they'll kill me too. They know I'm emotional. Occasionally I drink too much. I'm a liability.'

Ruth remembers what Guy said about Elaine, the woman he claims to love like a sister. *Mental health issues ... sometimes, the slightest little thing ...* She thinks of Dan's diary and the description of Elaine, drunk, in the hotel bar. She can imagine that Elaine – sensitive, highly-strung, bruised from an unhappy love affair – would be a threat to any secret society. But does Elaine really think that her fellow White Hand members would kill her? Ruth looks at Elaine, huddled on the flowery sofa, and believes that she does. There is fear everywhere at Pendle University. There was fear in that first letter from Dan, fear in Clayton Henry's eyes when he realised that the bones had been switched, fear in Guy's face when he sat on the pier telling Ruth how he wanted to continue Dan's work. And Pendragon, of course, was scared enough to kill himself.

She is about to speak when Elaine stiffens and looks round. She has heard something. A wheezing, snuffling sound just outside the back door. Ruth gets to her feet, just as a tall cloaked figure appears at the window. For a moment, Ruth is frozen in terror. Is this it? The Grim Reaper? The Arch Wizard come to exact his revenge? But then the door opens, and a white dog rockets into the room.

Elaine screams.

'Hi, Cathbad,' says Ruth, struggling to contain Thing's welcome. 'What time do you call this?'

CHAPTER 30

One way or another, Ruth is not looking forward to her meeting with Clayton Henry. But it's their last day in Lytham, the bags are packed, the house is clean and the car full of petrol. Cathbad is going to take Kate to Nickelodeon World (to her great delight) so, hopefully, she will sleep the whole way home. Ruth is meeting Clayton at his office at eleven. They will see the relics, which are being held at the university, and she should be finished by midday. Ruth will pick Cathbad and Kate up at the Pleasure Beach, they can call in at Beach Row to collect Thing, and then they'll be on their way. She never has to think about Elaine, Guy, Clayton or the White Hand, ever again.

Ruth has rung Tim to tell him about Elaine's revelations but is currently getting no reply. In the light of day, Elaine's story seems stranger than ever. Is there really an Arch Wizard whose command has to be obeyed on pain of death? And is it possible that no one knows the name of this demonic figure? Did Elaine really not know who killed Dan? Does Clayton not know who moved the bones? Elaine doesn't trust Guy, Guy doesn't trust Elaine and neither of them trusts Clayton. Ruth doesn't understand any of it. All she knows is that the sooner she and Kate (and Cathbad and Thing) are out of this place the better. Sandy still doesn't know who is sending the texts but Ruth is pretty sure that her every move is being watched. It's a horrible, frightening thought. Kate will have some happy memories of this holiday – the donkeys, the sand henge, the water park – but for Ruth, Lancashire will always be the place where the courtly Arthurian legend dissolved into the darker realm of the Raven King.

When she had told Cathbad about Elaine and the recreation of Camelot, he had quoted dreamily, 'Elaine the fair, Elaine the loveable, Elaine, the lily maid of Astolat.' Except that this Elaine is not loveable or even (in good light) particularly fair. But maybe it was her Arthurian name which started this dangerous obsession. Ruth thanks God that she resisted the temptation to name her daughter after a tragic character in legend or literature.

She tries ringing Tim again but his phone goes straight through to voicemail. She hesitates for a moment and then rings Nelson.

'Hello, Ruth.' He sounds wary. She wonders who is listening.

She tells him about Elaine's visit and about the revelation that she, Guy and Clayton were members of the White Hand.

'I've been trying to get hold of Tim all morning.'

'They've gone to Lancaster. They've got a lead about the White Hand.'

Ruth laughs, she sounds slightly hysterical. 'They should talk to Elaine. She knows all about the White Hand. Apparently they all dressed up in Arthurian clothes and had a ceremony on Pendle Hill. Does Sandy know about that?'

'Sandy knows that Clayton Henry was involved in some way. Tim found a picture of him on Pendragon's computer.'

'Does he think Clayton was behind Dan's death?'

'I'm not sure.' Nelson sounds rather put out. 'He doesn't confide in me.'

'I'm seeing Clayton Henry today,' says Ruth. 'He's going to show me some artefacts found at the site.'

'Jesus, Ruth.' Nelson's voice is sharp. 'Be careful. Man sounds like a nutter. Katie's not going with you, is she?'

Kate's the one he's worried about, thinks Ruth. *She* can have a breakfast meeting with Jack the Ripper as long as Kate is safe.

'Cathbad's taking her to Nickelodeon World.'

'Well, she can't come to any harm there.'

Nelson puts down the phone feeling frustrated. He wishes he could ask Ruth not to go to her meeting, he wishes he could haul Elaine Morgan in for questioning. But he's not Ruth's husband and he's not the officer in charge of this enquiry. And even if he was her husband, he reflects gloomily, he doubts if she'd listen to him. Over the last few days Michelle has been pleasant but detached. She and her mother are always whisking off to places, ostensibly leaving him free to relax, in reality to fret about the case and wish that he could do more than just attend interviews 'as an observer'. Sandy's warning had disconcerted him too. On the one hand, the idea of old Sandy as a marriage counsellor is laughable. On the other, if *Sandy* has noticed something between him and Ruth, who else might become suspicious? His sisters? His mother? Michelle's mother?

He doesn't like all this stuff about Arch Wizards and King Arthur. In his experience, when people start dressing up they lose track of what is real and what is make-believe. Maybe whoever killed Dan Golding thought that they were preparing a sacrificial victim, atoning for some ancient wrong. In reality, a man was burnt to death in his own home. He can't bear the thought of Katie (or Ruth) mixing with these people. At least they're going home this afternoon. Katie can have a nice morning at the Pleasure Beach with Cathbad, then back to Norfolk and safety. Jesus, it's come to something when he thinks of Cathbad as the perfect babysitter.

He knows that Sandy and Tim have gone to Lancaster on the trail of some suspected White Hand members. Nevertheless, he leaves a message for Sandy, saying that he has some new information and asking him to ring as soon as possible. Then, on impulse, he dials a more familiar number.

'Detective Sergeant Dave Clough.'

'Hi, Cloughie.'

'Boss! How are you? Is it grim up north?'

'You don't know the half of it, Cloughie. What's it like being in charge?'

Clough is nominally in charge of the department, but with Nelson and Judy away his team consists of only three people: a frighteningly simple PC called Rocky Taylor, a grizzled old hand called Tom Henty and an extremely keen WPC, Tanya Fuller.

Nevertheless Nelson can almost hear Clough expanding his chest. 'Not too bad. Think I'm running a pretty tight ship. Everything's under control.'

'That's good to hear. Listen, I need a favour. Could you check the files for anything on a woman called Elaine Morgan.' He spells it out.

'What's this about? Thought you were on holiday.'

'It's a long story. I'm almost looking forward to coming back to Norfolk.'

Clough laughs. 'As bad as that? Leave it to me, boss.'

Nelson switches off his phone feeling slightly better. He trusts Clough to find the information, and though he hates to admit it, it feels good to be called 'boss' again and to have someone jump to do his bidding. He paces Louise's spotless front room, wishing there was some more action that he could take, the more forceful the better. One of his abrupt turns brings him into collision with a small table bearing a bowl full of pot-pourri. Nelson scoops up the mess, cursing under his breath. Louise's house is full of such things. Normally, he gets some pleasure from staying in such a pretty, well-ordered home but now, somehow, it gets on his nerves. How many fragrant leaves and sea shells does one house need, for God's sake?

'What are you doing, Harry?' Michelle is standing in the doorway. He can see her feet, which are clad in unusually low-heeled shoes. She must be going out for a walk.

'Knocked something over.'

'Do try and be careful. Mum keeps the house so nice.'

Nelson ignores this. 'Where are you going?'

'Pendleton. For a walk and a pub lunch. Are you coming?'

Pendleton. That must be near Pendle Hill and that awful, spooky witch's house. Nelson never wants to see the place again. He thinks of searching the house with Cathbad, neither of them knowing that its owner was hanging, lifeless, in one of the outhouses. He thinks of the garden and the raven in the tree, of the twinkling dream-catchers and the herbs brewing on the range.

'I'd better stay here,' he says. 'Sandy might call.'

'Honestly, Harry.' Michelle tosses her blonde pony tail. 'This isn't your case, you know.'

'I know.'

'You've been so funny this holiday. Even mum has noticed it.'

'I'm useless at holidays. You know that.'

'You might try, Harry.' Michelle gives him a significant look, eyelashes lowered. 'For my sake.'

'All right,' says Nelson. 'I'll get my hiking boots.'

*

Ruth parks outside the cigarette factory. As it is now August, there will be no one at reception and Clayton has told her to come straight up to his office. Standing outside the building, looking up at its grim grey industrial walls, she feels an odd disinclination to go inside. Come on, Ruth, she tells herself, best foot forward. Jesus, even the voice in her head is sounding like her mother now. She squares her shoulders and climbs the steps to the main entrance.

As she passes through the atrium full of pictures of scientists, Ruth thinks about Dan, who must have walked past these dusty display cases every day. She feels that she hasn't really justified Dan's faith in her. True, she spotted the trick with the switched skeletons but she hasn't managed to track down the original bones and now fears that they have been burnt on some pseudo-Arthurian funeral pyre. She hasn't made any archaeological breakthroughs herself though she now understands the nature of Dan's great discovery. The trouble is, without evidence, she might well be the only person who ever knows the truth about the Raven King. Still, it will be interesting to see the artefacts today, and the tomb itself may be worth a paper or two. She dismisses this ignoble thought as she starts to climb the metal stairs.

She doesn't really feel any closer to Dan, even though she is in his university, working with his colleagues. In some ways he seems further away than ever. He was sleeping with several women but didn't love any of them. He had friends but didn't seem to take any of them into his confidence. He felt an outsider, as indeed he was. The only emotions with which Ruth can completely empathise are the professional feelings – the sense that his career has stalled and then the incredible excitement of a new discovery. She can imagine the febrile, intense atmosphere of the days surrounding the excavation. It must have been something like the henge dig all those years ago when she was falling in love with Peter. Although she hadn't known it at the time, Erik, Cathbad and Shona had also all been conducting clandestine business of their own. Strange how a dry academic exercise like an archaeological dig can arouse such violent human emotions. Both excavations, in their way, led to murder.

She is out of breath by the time she reaches the fourth floor. She should have started going to the gym again after Kate was born. Oh well, plenty of time for that when the new term starts. She takes a deep breath and heads for the door marked Prof. C. Henry.

Clayton Henry is sitting at his desk. It is some moments before Ruth notices the silver paper knife protruding from his chest.

CHAPTER 31

Ruth stands in the doorway, frozen with shock. She thinks of the occasion, last year, when she went into a deserted museum and discovered a dead body. For some reason, she is reminded, not of the corpse, but of a waxwork figure in one of the galleries, a man seated at his desk, quill raised, dusty eyes unseeing. Perhaps it's the absence of blood, perhaps it's the almost comical expression of shock on Clayton Henry's face, but the scene does not seem quite real somehow. It's like a tableau: posed, unconvincing. She steps closer. The knife's hilt is embedded in Clayton's smart pink shirt. A darker pink stain is slowly spreading but that is all the blood she can see. She touches Clayton's hand, still – like the waxwork – holding a pen. It's warm. She feels for a pulse but can't detect anything. She reaches for her phone.

Nelson is sitting outside The Swan With Two Necks when he gets the call. At first he can't take in what Ruth is saying. It seems so at odds with the idyllic village scene, the perfect country pub, the stream running the length of the street, the tables and umbrellas, the two pretty women in front of him.

'Clayton Henry? Murdered?'

Michelle looks up, almost crossly, as if it's bad taste to mention *that* word in this setting. Two elderly women at the next table lean forward avidly.

'Are you sure he's dead? Have you called an ambulance? OK, love. Listen. Don't stay there. Get into your car and lock the door. Don't get out until the police get there. I'll ring Sandy and the local boys. Yes, I'm on my way.'

He looks up at his spellbound audience and spreads his hands apologetically.

It is not until Nelson tells her to get into her car that Ruth realises she might be in danger. Clayton Henry's killer might still be in the building. In fact, probably is, given the warm body and the still spreading blood. She stands still, listening, thinking of all the hundreds of rooms in this huge old industrial building. The killer could be anywhere, in an office, in one of the labs, hiding in the students' Common Room, lurking behind one of the scientific displays in the atrium. She listens. Silence except for the traffic outside and the dim mechanical whirr of computers and plumbing and alarm systems. Then she hears something. A very faint tap like the hooves of a tiny horse. Someone is running about on the floor above. Someone in high heels.

She turns and runs, down the stairs, skidding on each landing, through the atrium, bumping off the display cases. She flings herself through the double doors and doesn't stop running until she reaches her car. Then she locks all the doors and sits slumped in her seat until the ambulance and police cars arrive.

'For Christ's sake, put your bloody foot down!'

Tim, who is already driving at ninety miles an hour with sirens blaring, grits his teeth and presses the accelerator even harder. They got the call about Clayton Henry when they were already on their way back from Lancaster, but now all thoughts of a leisurely pub lunch have vanished and Sandy is in full Sweeney mode. He knows that the local boys will be on their way and there is nothing that Sandy hates more than letting uniforms in on a murder case.

'Who's your money on?' he asks as they take the turn for Preston.

Tim hates being asked this sort of question, especially when he is cutting across three lanes of traffic.

'The Arch Wizard,' he says, half-joking.

But Sandy replies seriously, 'My thoughts exactly. And we know who the Arch Wizard is, don't we?'

Tim, who doesn't, says nothing.

Nelson is pulling into the university car-park when he gets the call from Clough. He listens as he takes the steps at a run.

'Elaine Morgan, boss. There's something on her, all right. Conviction as a minor for grievous bodily harm.'

'What did she do?'

'Stabbed her mother.'

Nelson finds Ruth in the atrium, sitting below a poster of chemical engineering in Chile. She looks pale but manages a rather shaky smile.

'Are you OK, love?'

'Yes. I took them up to the room. The police are in there now. They're sealing it off.'

Sandy will go mad if the forensics boys get there before him, thinks Nelson.

'He's definitely dead then?' he says.

'Yes. Paramedics pronounced him dead at the scene. It was weird, Nelson.' She shivers. 'He looked just like a statue or a waxwork, sitting propped up at his desk with a knife sticking into him.'

Nelson reaches out a hand to her but doesn't quite make contact.

'Sandy here yet?'

Ruth shakes her head. 'Someone called Peter Greengrass seems to be in charge.'

'Have you seen anyone else? Anyone leaving the building?'

'No.' She tells him about the footsteps.

'You say they sounded like a woman's steps?'

'Yes. Someone wearing high heels.'

Nelson looks around the deserted atrium. He wants

to go up to the crime scene but he knows that he'll be given short shrift by the forensics team and by Sandy's nemesis Peter Greengrass. Also, he doesn't want to leave Ruth on her own. But he hates doing nothing. Comforting witnesses is not one of his strengths; that's Judy's job. Not for the first time, he wishes she and Clough were there.

As he hesitates, the doors crash open and Sandy and Tim erupt onto the scene.

'Where is he?' barks Sandy.

'Fourth floor,' says Nelson. 'The forensics boys are up there.'

With a furious expletive Sandy charges for the stairs. Tim stays to confer with Ruth.

'Are you all right? Shall I get someone to drive you home?'

'It's OK. Nelson's looking after me.'

Tim gives Nelson a rather doubtful look.

'Has anyone taken a statement?'

'Yes. A policewoman. She was very nice.'

'Can I have a word?' says Nelson.

He tells Tim what he has learnt about Elaine Morgan. He can't help adding, 'I'd get her and that Guy chap in for questioning.'

Tim doesn't betray any annoyance at being told how to do his job. 'I'll tell the boss,' he says. Then he turns and takes the stairs at a run. He must be very fit, thinks Nelson enviously.

'I'll run you home,' says Nelson.

'I'm meeting Cathbad in Blackpool,' says Ruth. Her phone rings. 'That'll be him now. He'll be wondering where I've got to.'

The caller ID says Cathbad but Ruth hardly recognises his voice. 'Ruth, I'm so sorry. I've lost Kate.'

CHAPTER 32

The world spins. Nelson and the engineering posters blur into one dizzying, whirring kaleidoscope of shape and colour. It's Kansas, and Dorothy's house is disappearing into the vortex of the tornado. But Ruth herself sits quite still in the centre of it all.

'What do you mean, you've lost her?'

Cathbad's voice is high and strained. She thinks dumbly that she hardly knows this person. 'It was just for a second. We were in Nickelodeon Land and I'd just bought her an ice cream. I turned round for a second to put my wallet back in the backpack and she was gone.'

The backpack. Ruth had made him take the backpack. 'There's more to taking a child out than you know,' she'd told him bossily. 'You need drinks, snacks, wet-wipes, spare clothes in case she goes on the log flume.' If she had let Cathbad look after Kate in his own way – conjuring drinks and snacks from the air – maybe she would still be at his side.

'I'm sure she's just wandered away,' Cathbad is saying. 'I've told the Pleasure Beach people. They're being very good. Apparently kids get lost all the time.'

But Kate isn't a 'kid'. She's Ruth's baby and now she's . . . nowhere. Lost. In Limbo. In the liminal zone between life and death so beloved of Erik. The floor tilts and she has to grip onto the sides of her chair to stop herself from falling. She looks up, trying to remember where she is, and, as she does she so, she becomes dimly aware that one of the spinning shapes has materialised into Nelson.

'Give me the phone.'

She can hear Nelson barking into her mobile, telling Cathbad to stay where he is, to contact the police, to retrace his steps. At the same time Nelson is pulling her to her feet and propelling her across the atrium and through the double doors. All this happens without her once being aware of her feet moving. She has left her body and is hovering somewhere among the cast-iron rafters and industrial lifting devices.

She is in Nelson's car and hurtling towards Blackpool at the speed of light before she manages to take a proper breath. Her ribs ache and she feels as if she's about to pass out.

'It'll be OK,' Nelson is saying. 'I've seen this hundreds of times. Kids wander away, parents panic, ten minutes later they're back together again. Lots of tears and wasted police time. No harm done.'

Ruth glances at his set profile and wonders why she

isn't more reassured. Because there's a muscle going in Nelson's cheek and his knuckles are white on the steering wheel? Because Cathbad hasn't rung back to say it's all a terrible mistake and he and Kate are enjoying complimentary Krabby Patties in Sponge Bob's Snack Shop? Because deep down she has always known that they will get her – the shadowy figures who killed Dan and goaded Pendragon to his death. And how better to get her than to attack the most precious thing in her life? *Ladybird, ladybird, fly away home.* Oh why hadn't she flown back home as soon as she received those texts? Why is she still here, in this nightmare world where people are thrown into the air for pleasure and cartoon animals guard a land where children can disappear forever? She starts to cry.

'It'll be OK,' says Nelson again. 'We'll find her. She'll have just wandered off to see Dora.'

'She loves Dora.'

'I know. I saw the book by your bed.'

Will she ever read to Kate again? She would give everything – *everything* – to be lying beside her sleepy child, ploughing through Dora's interminable adventures. Please God, she prays fiercely, I've never believed in you but, please, prove me wrong. Please find my darling daughter.

Nelson screeches to a halt on double yellow lines outside the Pleasure Beach. They run through a hall full of people queuing for tickets, and out again to more queues and a row of turnstiles.

'Have you got day passes sir?' asks a polite doorman. Nelson waves his police badge and pushes Ruth past the outraged pleasure seekers. Ruth rings Cathbad as she runs. He says he's waiting for them outside Nickelodeon Land.

'Have you found Kate?' asks Ruth though she knows that, if he had, it would have been the first thing he'd said.

'No.'

They run past ghost trains and carousels and people hanging upside down in the air. A vast skull in a Viking helmet guards the entrance to something called Valhalla. The giant raven of the Raven Falls spreads his baleful wings, as black as night. For Ruth, the place could not seem more hellish if there were actual devils manning the rides. The visitors to the Pleasure Beach resemble not happy families in search of an innocent thrill, but sinister misshapen creatures, their features smeared with face paints, ghastly smiles enhanced by comedy hats and T-shirts saying 'I'm with Stupid'. Some of these monsters are clutching the furry corpses of stuffed animals won in arcades, others are swilling lurid drinks from oversized plastic glasses. Many of them are wearing the Simon Cowell masks Ruth first saw on the pier. The effect is of hundreds of dark-haired, icy-toothed showbiz supremos on the rampage. It's as if Cowell has been cloned by some evil pharmaceutical lab intent on taking over the world. Ruth rushes past these abominations, head down, phone clasped to her heart. She hates everyone for not being Kate.

A white-faced middle-aged man is standing by a ride featuring demonic cartoon children with oversized teeth and knowing leers. Screams and splashes fill the air. A giant sign exhorts riders to 'Hold on to your nappies'. 'By the Rug Rats log flume,' Cathbad had said, otherwise Ruth might genuinely not have recognised him. He seems to have aged twenty years since this morning.

'Ruth,' he takes a step forward.

Ruth backs away. 'You lost Kate.'

Nelson takes hold of Ruth's arm. 'OK, OK. Let's all be calm. Cathbad, who's in charge here?'

A young woman in a high visibility vest steps out from behind one of the cartoon children.

'Hi, I'm Holly. I'm the Duty Manager. Are you Kate's mum and dad?'

Ruth is about to deny this when she realises that actually – yes – they are Kate's mum and dad. She nods mutely.

'Try not to worry too much,' says Holly. 'I'm sure we'll find her. I've taken a full description of Kate and I've radioed it to all our staff. We've got a specialised lost child unit and I'm checking in with them every few minutes. I've also sent out messages on the tannoy. Would she recognise her name if she heard it on the tannoy?'

'Yes,' says Ruth. 'No. I don't know.' Kate is a bright little girl – a wonderful, clever, adorable little girl – but would she pick out her name from the cacophony of fairground music, screaming children and current pop hits? Ruth doubts it.

'Have you got CCTV?' asks Nelson brusquely.

'Yes,' says Holly. 'We've got cameras at every exit. It's impossible for her to leave without our staff knowing.'

'Why is it impossible?' asks Nelson. 'There must be thousands of people here. Your staff can't check everyone.'

'She'll have her bracelet on. The staff at the gates all have Kate's details. If anyone . . . if anyone tried to take her out of the park, the staff would check her bracelet.'

Bracelet? Kate wasn't wearing a bracelet. But then Ruth sees that Cathbad has a white paper band round his wrist, stamped with an orange 'Pleasure Beach' exclamation mark.

'The bracelet will record the time Kate entered the park, which rides she went on and so on,' says Holly. 'And it would show the time she leaves. I mean . . . it's impossible for her to leave.'

Holly is being kind, Ruth knows, but her words have conjured a new spectre. A sinister figure leading Kate out of the park to . . . Where?

She knows that Nelson is thinking the same thing because he cuts in, saying, 'Have you called the police?'

Holly looks slightly defensive. 'We've got a community officer on the beat and she's looking at the CCTV now. As I say, though, the child usually turns up within ten minutes.'

'Meanwhile a pervert's halfway to London with my child in the boot of his car,' says Nelson brutally. Ruth gasps and Cathbad makes a choking noise. Holly looks shocked, 'I know you're upset but . . .'

Nelson thrusts his warrant card in her face. 'I am the police,' he says. 'And I want all units here now.'

He has hardly finished speaking when the wail of sirens

is heard in the distance. Ruth knows that Nelson called Sandy on the way to the Pleasure Beach, but to Holly this must seem proof of immense, almost supernatural, influence. She stares at Nelson in awe.

'I want police at every exit,' he says. 'And I want to see the CCTV footage now.'

Holly is about to speak when her walkie-talkie crackles. Ruth's heart contracts. Please, please let them have found Kate. She wishes it so hard that she can almost hear Holly's soft Lancastrian voice saying, 'She's been found and she's fine. She just wants her mum.' She even feels her face relaxing into a relieved smile. But Holly's actual words are very different.

'There's been a development,' she says.

The CCTV cameras are in a room above the booking hall. From the window they can see the startled faces of punters on the Ice Blast, an infernal machine that shoots its occupants two hundred feet in the air and then back down again. But the shock and horror on the faces of the Ice Blastees are nothing to the expression on Ruth's face as she enters the room. She knows that the news cannot be good.

A young man is sitting at a frozen TV screen. The picture is blurred and indistinct but Ruth can just make out a tiny figure in a Hello Kitty hat.

'That's her!' she screams.

Nelson and Cathbad surge forward. Over Nelson's shoulder Ruth sees that the tiny figure is holding someone's hand, a woman with blonde hair, wearing a long coat. It's such an everyday image, a child holding a woman's hand, that Ruth can hardly take in the horrific implications of what she is seeing.

'Zoom in on the woman's face,' barks Nelson. The young man does so but the grainy pixels give nothing away. The woman has shoulder-length blonde hair, that's all that is visible.

'Who is it?' asks Nelson. 'Ruth, do you know who it is? Cathbad, do you?'

'No,' says Ruth. 'But I think ... I think ... it's Elaine Morgan.'

'Elaine Morgan's here,' says a voice behind them.

Sandy and Tim stand framed in the doorway. Between them is a smartly dressed woman in a black suit. Ruth finds her eyes drawn immediately to Elaine's shoes. High heels.

'She's under arrest,' says Sandy. 'Found her at the university, trying to get out by the fire escape.'

'I didn't kill him,' says Elaine tearfully. She looks round the room in search of a sympathetic face and finds Ruth. 'Please believe me. I didn't kill Clayton. He was like a father to me.'

Ruth stares blankly back at her. She no longer cares who killed Clayton Henry. She no longer cares about the White Hand, about Pendragon, Guy, Elaine, even about Dan. She only cares about Kate.

'Thought she might be able to throw some light on

this business,' says Sandy, bending over to look at the CCTV screen. 'If it's the same mob involved.'

He hasn't said one word to Ruth but Tim presses her arm sympathetically. 'We'll find your little girl. I promise.'

Ruth turns to him desperately. 'They've got a picture of her holding some woman's hand. Who is she? What does she want with Kate?'

'She can't have left the park,' says Holly again but Ruth thinks she is sounding less certain. 'We've been watching all the exits.'

But a woman who introduces herself as the community police officer confirms this. 'I'm certain she hasn't left.'

'Then, what are we waiting for?' Nelson turns for the door. 'Sandy, have you got reinforcements coming?'

'I've got back-up from three forces.'

'Then let's turn this place upside down.'

Ruth allows herself a slight breath of hope. The police-woman says that Kate hasn't left the park. If she's here, Nelson will find her. Ruth is sure of that. She sees his dark, intense face across the room and, in that instant, knows something else. That she loves him.

Then her phone buzzes.

It's a text message, caller unknown:

She is young to fall from such a height. Perhaps she will fly? Who knows?

Ruth turns to the window and sees the roller-coaster, that nightmare railway track across the sky.

*

Judy puts Michael into his Moses basket. If she's careful, he might stay asleep and she might just get an hour to herself. She could have a cup of coffee, do the Sudoku, maybe even have a sleep. She looks at the clock on the mantelpiece. Two o'clock. It'll be at least four hours until Darren is home. Four hours until she can speak to another adult. She looks at Michael, sternly asleep, eyelashes fanned out on his cheek. She loves him more than anything in the world but, right at this moment, she wants him to sleep all day, all week, all year, until he leaves home for university. She hardly dares breathe as she leaves the room and goes into the kitchen to put the kettle on. Please, Michael, stay asleep.

Judy stares dreamily out of the window. Usually their garden is a riot of colour by now, but this year Darren has been too exhausted by co-parenting to do more than mow the lawn. Their hanging baskets are empty, the bulbs have all sprouted unseen in the garage. She can hear the laughter of next door's children in the paddling pool, a radio playing, the far-off call of the ice-cream van. Summer sounds.

And then, suddenly, she is hit by a spasm of anxiety, as sharp and unexpected as the first onset of labour pain. It's like the time, during police self-defence classes, when Clough hit her before she'd put on her body armour (he's always claimed it was a mistake but Judy's never been convinced). She doubles over, clutching her stomach. Someone she loves is in danger. She runs back into the sitting room but Michael is still sleeping peacefully.

Darren? But he's at work, surely nothing dangerous can happen to a computer programmer on a Tuesday afternoon. Her parents? She'd better ring them. She staggers across the room to get her phone but by the time she reaches it she knows.

Cathbad.

The Pleasure Beach is swarming with policemen. Nelson and Sandy run ahead. Tim follows and Ruth realises that he's handcuffed to Elaine. She runs to catch up with them.

'You know who it is, don't you?' she pants to Elaine. 'You know who's got Kate.'

Elaine looks at her. Ruth sees fear and – worse – pity in her pale eyes.

'The woman. Who is she?' As she asks the question, a picture appears in Ruth's head. A suburban street and a blonde woman with a dog. The woman she has seen several times outside the cottage on Beach Row, innocent because she was a woman.

'I've seen her before. She's been watching me.'

Elaine still says nothing. Ruth is about to yell at her, or strangle her, when Sandy calls over his shoulder, 'What did the text message say again?'

Ruth tells him.

'And what's the tallest ride? The Big One?'

'Yes.'

Sandy looks up at the track looping across the sky. Ruth sees that he has gone quite green. Perhaps he cares more than he is letting on.

'Bloody hell,' he mutters.

They run past the Ice Blast and the flying machines and the people eating hamburgers and ice creams. Ruth finds herself elbowing past small children who are staring at the policemen as if they're part of the day's entertainment. Giant skulls, leering witches and grinning Cheshire cats seem to lurk on every corner. Above the sound of police sirens the rides still blare out their advertising jingles offering adventure, excitement, thrills to make your blood run cold. Ruth looks up at the towering structure of the Big One and thinks that her blood is already as cold as ice. Is Kate really up there, on the highest roller-coaster in the country? Is she scared? Is she calling for Ruth? And what will happen when she reaches the top?

She is young to fall from such a height. Perhaps she will fly? Who knows?

But Kate won't fly. She will fall like a stone, like Icarus, onto the unforgiving concrete below. And then Ruth will kill herself.

They reach the ticket booth. 'It's impossible,' the attendant is saying. 'No one could take a child onto the ride. You have to be over the height barrier.'

'What if he smuggled her on in a bag?' asks Nelson.

'You're not allowed to take bags on,' says the attendant.

'I don't care what you're allowed to do. Stop the bloody ride.'

'I can't,' says the attendant. 'Not in the middle of a circuit.'

'What if my daughter's on there?'

'I keep telling you, she can't be.'

'Nelson,' says Ruth. 'Look.' As the carriages go past them, preparing for their vertiginous journey upwards, they see a woman with shoulder-length blonde hair. She is wearing a Simon Cowell mask. As she passes the knot of policemen, she waves.

'It's her,' says Ruth.

'Is Kate with her?' asks Tim.

'I don't know. I can't see.'

Nelson grabs the attendant by his lapels. 'Stop the ride!'

The attendant grabs at a switch. The carriages stop. But it's too late. The woman is already high. She's not at the top of the track but she's above the Pleasure Beach and the surrounding houses. Ruth looks up and sees her silhouetted against the sky, blonde hair like a helmet. She waves again and seems to search for something inside the car. The other riders, realising that something is wrong, start to scream.

Suddenly Sandy's voice rises above all the rest. 'What the fucking hell is he doing?'

Ruth turns to look. Cathbad has sprinted past the police and the park attendants and is climbing the steel structure of the ride, hand over hand, his long grey hair flying out in the breeze.

'Cathbad!' Nelson calls. 'Come back, you lunatic.'

They all watch, frozen in horror. Cathbad climbs, higher and higher. A policeman starts to climb after him but Sandy, who has found a megaphone, yells at him to come down. He yells at Cathbad too but Ruth isn't surprised when her friend pays no attention. Since when has Cathbad done what he's told? He's a druid, a shaman, Ruth's protector, Kate's godfather. He climbs up and up, leaving the earth far below.

Nelson turns on his old friend in a fury. 'Do something!'

'I've got a chopper on the way,' says Sandy. 'They should be able to see into the carriage, find out if your daughter is in there.'

Nelson grabs the megaphone. 'Cathbad!' he bellows. 'Come down, you bloody lunatic! They've got a helicopter coming.'

But Cathbad is way beyond hearing. He is a black speck against the blue sky, an agile, almost unearthly figure, like Anansi the Spider in the stories that he likes to read to Kate.

'How tall is this thing?' asks Tim.

'Over two hundred feet,' says the attendant. 'They had to put lights on it to warn passing aeroplanes.'

As he says this, the air is filled with the sound of rotors. A helicopter moves steadily across the horizon. The woman in the carriage stands up. It seems as if she is shouting, gesticulating. Ruth screams and, at that moment, Cathbad falls.

CHAPTER 33

Ruth carries on screaming even as the police converge on Cathbad. She can hear Sandy yelling for an ambulance and Nelson just yelling. Tim seems to be in contact with the helicopter because she hears him asking, 'Is there anyone else there? In the carriage?' And, above it all, she hears something very small and soft, which, all the same, soars above the mayhem around her.

'Mum?'

She whirls round. A motherly attendant is standing a few feet away, holding Kate by the hand.

'Found her in Dora's World. Fast asleep, poor little mite.'

'Kate!' Ruth scoops her daughter into her arms, oblivious of anything but the sight, smell and sound of her. She buries her face in Kate's dark hair.

'Mum,' says Kate sleepily.

'Oh, my baby.'

She hasn't called him but Nelson is beside her. She thinks he's crying but she can't be sure. She hears Tim telling the attendant to start the ride moving again. 'As quick as you can, don't go through the whole circuit.' Screams as the carriages start to move backwards. An ambulance is driving past them through the goggling crowds, but Ruth, holding Kate, can think of nothing else. She is aware that Elaine, too, is crying. The ride screeches to a halt in front of them. Sandy rushes forward and pulls the woman out of her seat. The mask and the wig come off together.

Leaving Ruth staring at the open, friendly face of Sam Elliot.

And, in Norfolk, Judy cries out, loudly enough to wake the baby.

CHAPTER 34

It is the perfect day for a druid's funeral. The sun has just risen over Pendle Hill and the four robed figures stand, arms raised, as if to lift it higher into the pale blue sky. The main celebrant, a woman named Olga, calls out in a thin but carrying voice:

'Oh great spirit, Mother and Father of us all, we ask for your blessings on this our ceremony of thanksgiving, and honouring and blessing. We stand at a gateway now. A gateway that each of us must step through at some time in our lives.'

Ruth, standing shivering with Kate in her arms, thinks of the people she knows who have passed through the gateway. Erik, Dan, little Scarlett – the girl whose death really started everything. Are they really just out there, beyond the sunrise, waiting? Cathbad once said something like this to her, that he had travelled to the land between life and death to save Nelson and had seen Erik, guarding the portal to the afterlife. Nelson had dismissed it, of course, but Ruth had thought at the time that he looked rather uncomfortable. She suspects Nelson of having had a near-death experience when he was ill last year. Not that he would ever admit it.

The four druids, Olga explained earlier, represent the four elements: earth, fire, water and air. The ceremony relieves the elements of the responsibility of supporting the dead soul. The druids now chant:

'Earth my body,
Water my blood,
Air my breath,
Fire my spirit.'

The sun rises higher and a flock of geese flies westwards, towards the sea. Sacred birds, Cathbad had called them, sacred to the Romans and maybe also to the ancient Britons who had worshipped the Raven God.

Olga turns and raises the clay urn. 'May his soul be immersed in the shining light of the unity that is the Mother and Father of us all.'

She takes a handful of dust and flings it into the air where an obliging gust of wind takes it and sends it spiralling upwards, a second's transitory glitter before dispersing to the four corners of the earth. One by one, the other druids place their hands into the urn.

'Earth my body,
Water my blood,
Air my breath,
Fire my spirit.'

Olga offers Ruth the receptacle, but she shakes her head. 'Want,' says Kate, but quietly. Ruth is surprised to see not only Nelson, but Tim take a handful of ashes and throw them into the air. She is surprised how much there is but, eventually, Olga turns the urn upside down to show there is nothing left. The four druids come together and bow.

'Go in peace, our beloved,' says Olga. 'From his spirit a pure flame shall rise. Hail and farewell.'

'Hail and farewell,' answer the others.

Ruth raises her eyes to the sky, surprised by the sudden sting of tears. The druids are walking down the hill now, Tim, Nelson and the other mourners following behind.

One of the robed figures stops beside Ruth. 'A beautiful service.'

'Yes.'

'Did you see the birds flying across the sun?'

Ruth looks sceptical. 'I suppose you're going to tell me that it was a sign of something.'

'Everything's a sign of something,' says Cathbad.

Cathbad's fall to earth had been cushioned by a stall selling giant slush puppies. Tim, racing to the scene, described his horror at seeing Cathbad's face covered by a virulent crimson liquid that seemed mysteriously to be full of ice.

'Poor soul,' said a voice in the crowd. 'His blood's frozen from being so high.'

'Bollocks,' said Sandy, pushing his way through the throng. 'It's one of those bloody silly kids' drinks.'

Cathbad had opened his eyes, blinking back chunks of strawberry-flavoured ice. 'Kate?'

'She's been found,' says Tim. 'Safe and sound.'

'Thank the gods,' said Cathbad, closing his eyes again.

The police think that Sam drugged Kate, leading to a heavy sleep behind a giant statue of Dora in Latin America. His threat to throw her from the Big One was an attempt to scare Ruth into dropping her investigation into King Arthur's bones, but as the police rushed to the Pleasure Beach he must have known that the game was up. Maybe he just wanted one more laugh, waving to Ruth as the roller-coaster began its journey into the sky, grinning behind his Simon Cowell mask. Maybe he was planning to jump himself. Police found a suicide note at his house, alongside instructions on how to look after his dog. Like Pendragon, Sam hadn't forgotten his faithful familiar. But, unlike Pendragon, Sam hadn't taken the fateful plunge but had allowed himself to be taken away by the police, where he is currently in the process of convincing them that he's insane.

'Perhaps he always was mad,' said Elaine. 'It's hard to tell, isn't it?'

Sam's fingerprints were on the paper knife, and that same evening he confessed to the murders of Clayton Henry and Dan Golding. Elaine was in the clear and appeared desperate to talk to Ruth. That first night, Nelson had whisked Ruth and Kate to his mother's house, where Maureen looked after them, sure that Ruth was frantic with worry about her 'lovely boyfriend Cuthbert'. Ruth *was* frantic with worry, but once she knew that Cathbad was in no danger (the fall had left him with nothing worse than concussion and two cracked ribs), she felt a kind of mad exultation. Kate was safe. She hadn't been kidnapped or killed or thrown from the highest roller-coaster in Britain. She was safe with her mother – and her father. That night, Ruth had sat watching Kate as she slept, feeling guilty happiness at the thought that Nelson was sleeping under the same roof. He hadn't been able to make too much of a fuss of Kate under his mother's eagle eye (besides, he was on the phone to Sandy for most of the evening), but that didn't matter. For that one short night, they were all together.

When Ruth drove back to Beach Row the next day, Elaine was waiting for her. Ruth remembered the other time that Elaine had turned up at her door, full of tales of King Arthur. Except that she had left out the most important fact: the identity of Mordred.

'I didn't know,' she said to Ruth, who was trying to contain Thing's frantic welcome. Nelson had been over the night before to feed the dog and take him for a walk but Thing clearly seemed to feel that he had narrowly escaped abandonment yet again. In fact, it took Ruth several minutes to feed Thing and get Kate settled with juice and her toy cars. By that time, Elaine was already ensconced on the sofa.

'You must have had some idea,' said Ruth.

'I didn't. Honestly. I thought Guy was the Arch Wizard. I really did. That's why I was so scared. I didn't even know that Sam was in the White Hand. I thought he was quite boring actually, always going on about the war and all that. I thought he was just an anorak, quite sweet but dull, you know.'

But what better indication of fascist sympathies, thinks Ruth, than an obsession with the Second World War? After all, hadn't Sam's first words to her been about Adolf Hitler? And, when she met him at the library, he had been going to give a talk about the war. It seems, though, that Sam's interest had gone beyond mere local history. Police had found his house stuffed with Nazi memorabilia, as well as hundreds of books about King Arthur and a rather worried Jack Russell. This, of course, was the dog that Ruth had seen being walked along Beach Row by the blonde woman.

Surprisingly, it seems that Elaine knew, or suspected, about the cross-dressing. 'Dan said that he'd caught him at it once. He called round unexpectedly and found Sam all tarted up in a dress and high heels. To be honest, I didn't think too much about it. I mean, each to their own.' She looked at Ruth earnestly, her face naked and vulnerable, like an actress without make-up. 'We've all got something to hide. I'm sure you've heard all about my past.'

Nelson had told Ruth the night before. The young Elaine Morgan had a history of schizophrenia and, at fifteen, had stabbed her mother after a row about homework. A spell in a secure institution had followed, beginning a cycle of mental illness and hospitalisation interspersed with impressive academic achievements. Meeting Guy had proved to be a turning point. He had proved a remarkably stabilising influence, and for the last five years Elaine had lived with him in relative tranquillity – apart from dressing up as Arthurian characters and getting involved with white supremacist groups, of course.

'We didn't care about the politics,' said Elaine. 'We only cared about Arthur.'

But what about Guy, the man who loved Elaine but was forced to watch her have an affair with his friend and next-door neighbour? Guy was clearly involved with the White Hand, he knew Pendragon well, and he knew that Cathbad had been to Dame Alice's cottage and found the laptop. Did Sam tell him? Did Guy know that Sam was the Arch Wizard? Ruth thinks not; she thinks that Sam stayed hidden behind the persona of a geeky war enthusiast, always on the outskirts of the group, always in the shadows. She remembers Terry Durkin mentioning Guy that day at CNN Forensics. That was the link, she thinks. Terry must have told Guy about the computer. Terry was probably the only person who knew about Sam and that was because Sam needed him, his man on the inside. The police are charging Terry Durkin with the theft of the computer. As a member of the forensics team, he would have had ample opportunity to remove evidence. Sandy is in ecstasy at the thought of the possible embarrassment to Peter Greengrass. And Terry also helped Sam to switch the bones. Didn't he say that nothing entered or left CNN Forensics without his knowledge?

How much did Dan know? His diaries showed that he trusted both Guy and Sam. He thought that Clayton was shielding someone but had no idea who. His main concern was that Clayton would find out that he was sleeping with his wife. Not for the first time, Ruth wondered what it was that her old university friend really cared about. Not Elaine certainly. Not Pippa, who hardly merited a few words in his diary. In fact the only person mentioned with any passion was the Raven King himself. King Arthur.

Dan had loved the legend of King Arthur. The discovery of his tomb was the thrill of his life, professionally and personally. But Dan had made a fatal mistake. He must have told his friend Sam, his office mate, about the amazing test results that proved that Arthur, King of the Britons, though born in the north of England, had African DNA and was almost certainly black. This had sealed his fate. Sam says that he had pushed the burning rags through Dan's doorway himself but the police think that he must have had accomplices, other members of the White Hand. Terry? Other members of the group? Sandy and Tim have still got a lot of work to do, tracking down all the neo-fascists at Pendle.

But Sam must have still had his doubts about Clayton, the man who was in so much financial trouble and who, in the tomb of King Arthur, saw his potential salvation. Didn't Elaine say, that evening when she turned up at the cottage, that Clayton wanted to carry on with the investigation? And it was Clayton who had summoned Ruth, the so-called bones expert. From the moment that she arrived in Lytham, Ruth realises, she must have been in danger. And Clayton . . . Clayton signed his own death warrant.

It was Sam who sent the text messages: the phone was found in his possession. He must also have been the cloaked figure on the riverbank. Well, his attempts to scare Ruth away almost worked. If it hadn't been for that last visit to the university and the discovery of Clayton Henry's body . . .

Elaine told Ruth that she had received a phone call that morning asking her to come to the university for an interview. 'I'd been applying for jobs as an assistant lecturer but no one seemed to want to employ me.' She looked at Ruth out of mad blue eyes. 'I don't know why.' So Elaine had dressed in her black interview suit and high heels and arrived at the university to find Clayton dead at his desk. 'I panicked. I didn't know what to do. I ran around trying to find a place to hide.' Ruth remembered the ghastly figure at the desk and the footsteps skittering about on the floor above and found herself feeling sorry for Elaine. She might be mad and seriously lacking in judgement, but she didn't deserve to be framed for murder. Because that must have been what Sam was trying to do, surely? Elaine, with her history, would have been the perfect suspect. If Sandy hadn't been distracted by Nelson's frantic phone call, he would probably have charged Elaine on the spot. And she, in her fragile emotional state, might even have confessed. And, if Ruth happened to recall a mysterious blonde woman hanging around her house, wouldn't that also have pointed to Elaine?

Ruth remembers looking at Elaine as she sat curled up on the sofa. Elaine had thought she was Guinevere and Ruth had once figured her, as her name suggested, as Morgan-le-Fay, but, in reality Elaine was a peripheral figure in the drama. Dan had not loved her and Clayton had not trusted her. Sam had seen her as the perfect scapegoat. Only Guy had stayed loyal, Sir Lancelot to the last. Ruth only hoped that Elaine appreciated him.

Ruth and Cathbad walk through the gate leading to Dame Alice's cottage. Cathbad has prepared a post-funeral breakfast for all participants. When Ruth agreed to stay a few more days in Lancashire so that she could attend Pendragon's funeral, she was surprised when Cathbad had announced that he was moving into the cottage. 'I think it's what he would have wanted,' he said. 'Thing will like it too.'

'Why can't you stay in Lytham with us?' Ruth grumbled. The events at the Pleasure Beach had proved to her that, however unsatisfactory he was as a babysitter, Cathbad really loved Kate. After all, he was prepared to risk his life to save her. Nelson might call him a bloody fool but Ruth feels rather in awe of her friend. Would she have climbed nearly two hundred feet to save her baby? Well, yes, she would have tried, but the amazing thing is that Cathbad had nearly succeeded. 'He looked like sodding Spider-Man up there,' Sandy had said, and

Cathbad's feat had even made the later editions of the local papers. 'Spider-Man's Climb To Save Tot,' said one, ignoring the fact that the tot was several hundred yards away and fast asleep at the time. 'Superman to the rescue,' read another. Cathbad claimed not to have seen any of the headlines but Ruth suspected that he was rather enjoying his fifteen minutes of fame. So why was he proposing to abandon them in favour of a deserted (probably haunted) cottage?

'I can't explain,' he had said. 'I've got a lot of thinking to do.'

Ruth understands this. After all, she had been the one to take Judy's hysterical phone call, received as Ruth and Kate accompanied Cathbad to the hospital.

'He's dead, isn't he?' Judy had shrieked. 'Cathbad's dead.'

It was several minutes before Ruth could convince her that Cathbad, though injured, was still alive. Judy had only calmed down when Ruth had held the phone to Cathbad's ear and he had croaked a feeble, 'Not dead yet, sweetheart.' Sweetheart. For some reason that had brought tears to Ruth's eyes. But how had Judy known? 'We have a strong psychic connection,' said Cathbad, when they discussed it later. Despite everything, he looked rather pleased with himself.

'I think she really loves you,' Ruth had said.

'I love her,' said Cathbad. 'But that's not enough, is it?'

Is it enough, thought Ruth, looking at Cathbad as he lay in his hospital bed with Kate at his feet, playing happily with a 'Nil by Mouth' sign. Is it?

Two days later, Ruth received a late-night phone call.

'What is it?' she asked, seeing the name on her phone. She was exhausted, having spent another action-packed day with Caz at the water park. It had been great to get away from everything for a few hours, and if Ruth had been afraid to let Kate out of her sight even for a minute that will surely pass. Will Ruth keep in touch with Caz? She's not sure. It's been great spending time with her but she's not sure how much they have in common, apart from the past. Caz is married with three teenage children, she lives in a designer house and drives a four-by-four. Ruth is a single parent who drives a clapped-out Renault. They're not equals any more.

Cathbad, who is almost certainly her friend for life, sounded wide awake and certifiably insane.

'I've found him,' he was saying.

'What are you talking about?'

'King Arthur. I've found him.'

When Ruth arrived at the cottage the next morning, Cathbad had led her out into the garden. 'I always knew there was something about this garden,' he said. 'There was always a raven in that tree. I knew he was trying to tell me something. And then there was the poem.'

'What poem?' said Ruth, feeling bemused.

'There was a poem in an old book by Pendragon's bed. A ballad. It said something about 'in cold grave she was lain'. Pen had changed the 'she' to 'he'. I thought he was talking about his own grave but I think he was pointing us to King Arthur.'

'Telling us that he was buried in the back garden?'

'Yes,' says Cathbad seriously. 'Then, when I let Thing out for his run last night he wouldn't come back in, just kept running round and round barking at the moon.'

'Maybe he was turning into a werewolf.'

'So I went out and the moon was shining really brightly, right on the herb garden. And I heard Dame Alice's voice. She said, "He's here. The Raven King is here."'

'In the herb garden?'

'I think so, don't you? I always wondered why that was the only place where Pendragon had dug. It all makes sense, doesn't it?'

The weird thing was, it did make sense. Sam had brought Dan's computer to Pendragon for safekeeping: it stood to reason that he would have brought Arthur's bones to the same place for sanctuary. Ruth looked at Cathbad, who was smiling.

'Have you brought your excavating kit, Ruthie?'

'Yes.'

'Well, there's a spade in the shed. Let's go for it.'

And that was how Ruth came to supervise the excavation after all. Of course, strictly speaking it wasn't an excavation, just uncovering recently buried bones, but that's what it felt like. And when, after only a few feet of digging, she saw her first glimpse of the skeleton, she experienced the self-same thrill described by Dan in his diaries: *Oh my God, my first sight of the exposed skeleton! He looked so kingly and peaceful, lying on his back, hands crossed over his chest.* And Arthur was still lying supine and peaceful; he had clearly been buried with great reverence. Slowly, almost as if she was sleepwalking, Ruth photographed and then removed the bones, cleaning and numbering each one and placing them in individual bags (Pendragon had a surprising amount of freezer bags in his cupboard). Cathbad was the perfect assistant, double-checking the numbers and marking each one on Ruth's bone chart. They worked in silence while a bird sang high above them and Thing and Kate played happily in the long grass. When they had finished, Ruth rang Guy, almost the sole survivor of Pendle's history department.

'I can't believe it,' he said. 'I thought the bones must have been burnt.'

'I'm taking the skeletal matter back to Norfolk with me,' said Ruth. 'Is that OK?'

As Cathbad remarked, in some amusement, Guy wasn't really in a position to argue. So Dan's great discovery came into Ruth's possession, as perhaps he would have wanted. Even so, Ruth is pretty sure that Guy will get a book out of it. And so, with any luck, will she.

Tim walks back down the hill, keeping a respectful distance from the druids. He is representing Blackpool CID, Sandy having flatly refused to attend the funeral ('Lot of bloody weirdos capering about on a hill? No thanks'). Tim was quite willing, though. He likes new experiences and he enjoyed the dawn start (something else Sandy viewed with extreme suspicion). Tim gets up at six every day, anyway, to go to the gym but he has to admit there is something about actually being outside, feeling the cold air on your face and hearing the birds singing high above you. Perhaps he should go jogging instead. The trouble is, he lives in a rather insalubrious area of the city. He would probably lose his iPod in five minutes and his kneecaps in ten.

The pagan ritual fascinated him too. Tim was brought up in a highly religious household and, in his mind, church-going is associated with a kind of hysterical fervour that always made him uncomfortable. Even as a child, he had preferred science, which could be proved, to anything arty, which couldn't. This is probably what led him into the police force. He doesn't, for one second, go along with all this 'mystical gateway' business but at least fire, water, earth and air are tangible physical realities, unlike the Big Daddy in the sky, a personage his mother always refers to as Father God. Well, for Tim, one father was enough. His dad left the family home when he was ten and Tim has never been inclined to search for him.

Courteously holding open a five-bar gate for the other mourners, Tim thinks about Pendragon and about Dan Golding and Clayton Henry. None of these men were fathers, unless you count Henry's stepdaughter. Tim met her when he interviewed Pippa Henry about her husband's death. By that time, Sam had confessed to the murder and so the visit was a mere formality. Sam had, in fact, admitted everything within ten minutes of entering Bonny Street Station. 'He's going to play the nutter card,' predicted Sandy, 'but he's as sane as you or I.' Sandy had appeared not to notice that Sam had still been dressed in a skirt and high heels and Tim admired his boss for realising that cross-dressing was not, in itself, a sign of insanity. He couldn't help noticing that Sam also smelt strongly of *Ma Griffe*.

The WPC who had broken the news of Henry's death described Pippa as a 'cold fish', reporting disapprovingly that the bereaved wife failed to shed one tear. Tim was more forgiving. Pippa was calm, certainly, but grief takes people in different ways. The stepdaughter, Chloe, had certainly been upset, wiping away tears when she described how Clayton had been looking forward to their planned summer holiday in Tuscany. Had it been paid for, wondered Tim. Sandy said that Clayton had been up to his eyes in debt, the windmill mortgaged up to the sails. Pippa apparently had some money of her own, but if that had been enough to support the Henrys' lifestyle, Clayton would surely not have resorted to stealing from the department.

Pippa gave nothing away as she sat stroking her little dog, occasionally extending a soothing hand to her daughter. It was only when she was showing Tim out that Pippa had said, 'I warned him. I knew that all this King Arthur business would lead to trouble. There are some very strange people out there.' This was the first indication that Pippa had known anything about her husband's membership of the White Hand.

Tim had agreed that there were, indeed, some strange

people out there but inwardly he doesn't feel that the pagans are any stranger than his mother's fellow worshippers in Basildon. People everywhere need ritual and make-believe to get them through their lives. Tim firmly believes that he is different, that he can exist in a purely rational world. But he is young; he knows he has a lot to learn.

Nelson too found himself rather enjoying the lunatic pagan service. Well, enjoy wasn't exactly the word. *Appreciate*, maybe. Certainly it seemed to make more sense than some Christian funerals he has sat though; dreary events in anonymous crematoriums where the minister struggled to remember the name of the deceased and the mourners looked bored rather than heartbroken. A full-blown Catholic funeral is something else, such as the service that Maureen has planned for herself, in exhaustive detail. 'You'll outlive me, Mum,' said Nelson that morning, as he ploughed through the list of music (most of which would need the Berlin Philharmonic for maximum effect). 'Don't say that,' said Maureen, crossing herself. 'It's a terrible thing for a parent to outlive their child.' Well, for a few terrible hours last week, Nelson had thought that this would be his fate, that he would lose the daughter he still can't fully acknowledge and would be doomed forever to grieve in silence. The thought of this made him feel unusually tolerant towards his mother and he had given Maureen a quick, unexpected hug. 'You're good for a few years yet,' he had said. 'Oh I know that,' Maureen had replied. 'Cuthbert read the tea leaves and said I'd live to be ninety.'

But today's ceremony was different. There was something fitting about the early morning, the clear sky and the chanting figures. Nelson hadn't known Pendragon but he is sure that the air and the earth meant more to him than some half-imagined deity. He remembers the day that he came to Dame Alice's cottage with Cathbad, the day when, unbeknown to both of them, Pendragon's body had been hanging in the wood store. Why had he done it? No one will ever know, though Cathbad said that he was terminally ill, which might explain some of it. Guilt at Dan Golding's death might also have contributed, plus a realisation of the sort of organisation that lurked behind the Arthurian posturing of the White Hand. Nelson doesn't understand any of it, he is only here today at Cathbad's request. 'I think it's important that you come,' he had said and Nelson was hardly in a position to argue, given Cathbad's recent heroics. He hasn't brought Michelle; capering about on hills isn't exactly her scene and, besides, he's hoping for a few words with Ruth later. 'Rest in peace, Pendragon,' he says now to himself, looking up at the white house on the hill. 'Wherever you are.'

As he begins the trek up the path, he finds that Tim is walking beside him. The two policemen smile at each other although Tim carefully maintains his expression of respectful neutrality. Tim, Nelson thinks, will go far.

'A pagan funeral,' he says now, taking the slope with a long, easy stride. 'One to tick off the list.'

'What else is on the list?' asks Nelson, panting slightly. The only thing he dislikes about Tim is that he makes him feel old and unfit.

'Swim with dolphins,' says Tim. 'Read *Ulysses*. Learn Italian. See the Taj Mahal. Leave Blackpool.'

Nelson turns to look at the young policeman. They are almost at the house; he can hear Thing barking inside and the sound of quavery Celtic voices singing. Jesus, please don't let Cathbad have brought his Enya CDs.

'Are you serious?' he asks.

'Yes,' says Tim, 'I'd like to move back down south. I'm an Essex boy really. Just ended up in the north because of university. I'd like to try somewhere new.'

'What about Norfolk?' says Nelson, only half joking.

Tim turns to him. 'Would you give me a job?'

'I can't promise anything,' says Nelson. 'My boss is a stickler for procedure. But I'd certainly put in a good word for you.' He smiles to himself, thinking how much Tim would stir things up at King's Lynn. Cloughie would hate him, he's sure of that, and the sight of a bright, ambitious young sergeant wouldn't exactly fill Judy and Tanya's hearts with joy either. But new blood is always good. Tanya isn't ready to be a sergeant yet and he sometimes doubts whether Judy will ever return from maternity leave. He had a very strange phone call from her the other day, almost accusing him of covering up Cathbad's accident. 'If he had died,' she had said, 'would you have let me know?' 'Listen, Johnson,' said Nelson, 'It'd take more than a two-hundred-foot fall to kill Cathbad.'

Cathbad now greets them at the door of the cottage, offering them coffee or a rather dubious-looking 'Loving Cup'. Nelson chooses coffee: the Loving Cup looks potent and he has a feeling that the local police won't extend the same leniency to him as they do Sandy if they catch him driving under the influence. All in all, he's not sorry to be leaving Lancashire tomorrow. It has been great to catch up with Sandy and to ride the mean streets again but it's not his home any more. For years he's been labouring under the delusion that one day – when the girls have finally left home, perhaps – he and Michelle will go back to Blackpool. Now he knows that this will never happen. He has lost his accent and, according to Sandy, his edge. It's time to admit that he could never go back to those hard-drinking, fast-driving, politically incorrect days. It's not just that Norfolk has softened him up, either. It's more that the Blackpool Nelson was a product of his upbringing, a reflection of what Archie Nelson would expect in his son. The middle-aged Nelson is a product of his marriage to Michelle and, if he's honest, his affair with Ruth. He's now a husband and father first and a policeman second. Jesus, what an admission. Next thing, he'll be looking forward to retirement in a Cromer seaside chalet. No, that's going too far. When he retires it'll be to a place with decent rail links.

Inside, a long trestle table is filled with food and drink. Nelson moves forward, remembering what Ruth told him about Cathbad's cooking. To his disappointment, though, breakfast is light on bacon and heavy on things like kedgeree and grapefruit compote. Across the room he can see two of the druids tucking in with a vengeance. He takes a roll and some cheese and then, on second thoughts, goes back for a Danish pastry. Might as well make the most of the last days before his traditional post-Blackpool diet.

'Detective Inspector Nelson.'

It's the blonde woman, Elaine Something, who was mixed up in the Clayton Henry murder. She is rather inappropriately dressed in a flowing dress and shawl and has a look in her eyes which Nelson privately characterises as 'bonkers'. Nothing that Sandy has told him about the history department makes him revise this judgement. Sam Elliot seemed to spend most of his time dressing in women's clothes, Elaine and the others were all members of some loony sect that danced on the hills at night pretending to be King Arthur and the Knights of the Round Table. He remembers Clayton Henry bouncing around his converted windmill on a giant rubber ball. It's not exactly a good advertisement for higher education.

'Hello,' he says now, warily.

'I'm so pleased to meet you,' says Elaine. 'Ruth has told me *all* about you.'

Nelson glances at Ruth who is standing by the door to the garden talking to Cathbad. Cathbad is holding Kate, looking for all the world as if he is her father. Nelson suppresses his irritation, knowing that he's not in a position to object. He doesn't believe Elaine's statement anyway. Ruth never tells anyone *all* about anything.

'I love Ruth,' Elaine is saying. 'She's such a warm, caring person.'

At that moment, Ruth looks over and catches Nelson's eye. She sees Elaine and raises her eyebrows. Warm and caring are not the words that spring to mind.

'She has her moments,' says Nelson.

'You know she's found King Arthur's bones? She's going to do a full investigation. King Arthur will live again!'

She raises her glass of orange juice and looks more unhinged than ever.

'And you don't mind what colour he turns out to be?' asks Nelson drily.

'Oh no,' says Elaine. 'That was Sam, not the rest of us. We never got involved with that side of the White Hand.'

Nelson, remembering some of the things that Sandy told him about the group's activities, is not convinced by this airy disassociation. From what Ruth says, Elaine suspected that the White Hand were behind Dan Golding's death. This must mean that she knew exactly what kind of organisation it was. All the same, the arrest of Sam Elliot has meant that Sandy and Tim were at last able to infiltrate the group. With any luck, that will be the last of the Neo-pagans at Pendle University. Maybe, without their baleful influence, Elaine will be able to live a normal(ish) life.

'And I'm in AA,' she is saying, waving the orange juice. 'Guy and I are thinking about getting married.'

Nelson hasn't met Guy but he knows what his advice to him would be.

'Congratulations,' he says. 'Excuse me. I must go and talk to a friend.'

Ruth and Cathbad are looking out into the garden. There is still a neat trench where Arthur's skeleton was excavated. Ruth looks at it with pride. Tomorrow, she'll be back in Norfolk and she can start preparing for a new term. She'll have a lot to do, writing up the case of the Raven King, but she's determined to do more real archaeology. Maybe she can bring a team up to Ribchester.

'Looking forward to going back?' asks Cathbad, displaying a flash of his old sixth sense.

Ruth smiles. 'Well I can't wait to see Flint again. And I'd like to see something of Shona before the end of the holidays.'

'Give her my love.'

Ruth looks at him. 'You're not coming back, are you?'

Cathbad shakes his head. 'I'm sorry, Ruth.'

'Are you going to live here? In Dame Alice's cottage?'

'Yes. I like this house. It has good energies.'

'Despite . . . despite what happened here?'

Cathbad pats Thing, who has come galloping through the hedge to his side. He is trailing mud and hawthorn branches but Cathbad doesn't seem to mind.

'Yes. I feel Pendragon is at peace. We set his soul free this morning. I think that he wants me to live here.'

'Won't you be lonely?'

Cathbad smiles. 'No. I'll have Thing, and Guy thinks he'll be able to find me a job at the university. Besides, I like solitude, as you know.'

'What about Judy?'

Cathbad is silent for a moment, stroking Thing, who has his eyes shut in ecstasy. 'I've got to give her a chance to make it work with Darren. It would be impossible, with me being in Norfolk. I wouldn't be able to keep away.'

'Even if Michael is yours?'

Cathbad smiles again, but sadly. 'Children don't belong to us but to the universe.'

Ruth looks at Kate, who is now sitting on the grass pulling up daisies. She may belong to the universe, she thinks, but she's mine for now and I'm going to keep her close for as long as possible. To her embarrassment, she feels tears coming to her eyes.

'I'll miss you,' she says.

'I'll miss you too,' says Cathbad, 'but you can come and visit. And there's always our psychic connection.'

'And Skype.'

'Skype too has its place in the universe.'

'What has its place in the universe?' Nelson looms behind them. 'Should Katie be sitting on the ground, Ruth? It might be wet.'

Ruth ignores him. 'Cathbad's staying in Lancashire,' she says.

Nelson nods and Ruth realises that he already knew. 'You're a lucky man,' he says. 'Ruth and I have got to go back to God-forsaken Norfolk.'

'Oh, I don't think God has forsaken you yet,' says Cathbad.

'You sound like my mother.'

Cathbad brightens. 'I hope to see a lot of Maureen while I'm living here. It'll make me feel closer to you, Nelson.'

Nelson and Ruth go into the garden. Kate comes running up to them and Nelson lifts her onto his shoulders. Max does that, thinks Ruth. She realises that she hasn't thought about Max for days.

'It's been a funny sort of holiday for you,' says Nelson.

Ruth thinks about finding Clayton's dead body, about seeing the cloaked figure on the riverbank, about the terrible moment when she thought that Kate was going to die. Then she thinks about the sand on Blackpool beach, about the donkeys, about sailing artificial rapids in a pink plastic boat.

'We've had some good times,' she says.

'And you've made a big archaeological discovery. It could make you rich.'

Ruth grins. 'Archaeologists never get rich but it could be good for my career, that's true.'

'And what about us?' asks Nelson.

Ruth looks away. 'There is no us, you know that.'

'You don't believe that.'

Ruth turns back to him. Since she has known Nelson, his hair has grown greyer and the lines about his mouth more deeply etched. Knowing that she loves him makes it somehow easier to say what she has to say.

'You would never leave Michelle,' she says. 'And I wouldn't want you to.'

'Really?'

'Really,' she lies. 'I've got my life, you've got yours.'

'Your life, does it involve that Max fellow?'

'No,' says Ruth, thinking that this decision must really have been made long ago. 'My life is just me and Kate and Flint.'

Nelson looks as if he is about to speak, but in the end he just smiles and, with a flourish, takes Kate from his shoulders and hands her back to Ruth.

ACKNOWLEDGEMENTS

Most of the places in this book actually exist. The Pendle Forest and the Pendle witches are real enough, though Dame Alice and her cottage are imaginary. Pendle University is also fictional. Blackpool and the Pleasure Beach certainly exist in all their glory. Thanks to Katie Stainsby for the information about Blackpool Pleasure Beach. All the rides mentioned in book, with the exception of the Raven Falls, can be found at the Pleasure Beach, although the events described are entirely fictional.

This book is set in 2010, when Blackpool had just been promoted to the Premier League. The statue of Jimmy Armfield at Bloomfield Road was not actually unveiled until May 2011 but I hope Blackpool fans will forgive this slight distortion of the facts. I just wanted Nelson to be able to talk to his hero.

Thanks to Matt Pope for telling me about the world of the Neo-pagans, though the White Hand are (thankfully) fictional. Thanks to Andrew Maxted for the archaeological information, though I have only followed his advice as far as it suits the plot and any subsequent mistakes are mine alone.

Special thanks to Michael Whitehead for the Blackpool back-ground. This book is for him and Sarah and for my father-in-law, John Maxted.

Thanks, as ever, to my editor, Jane Wood, and my agent, Tim Glister. Heartfelt thanks to everyone at Quercus and at Janklow and Nesbit for working so hard on my behalf.

Love and thanks always to my husband Andrew and to our children, Alex and Juliet.

EG
January 2013

WHO'S WHO
IN THE DR RUTH GALLOWAY
MYSTERIES

Dr Ruth Galloway

Profession: forensic archaeologist

Likes: cats, Bruce Springsteen, bones, books

Dislikes: gyms, organized religion, shopping

Ruth Galloway was born in south London and educated at University College and Southampton University, where she met her mentor Professor Erik Andersen. In 1997 she participated in Professor Andersen's dig on the north Norfolk coast which resulted in the excavation of a Bronze Age henge. Ruth subsequently moved to the area and became Head of Forensic Archaeology at the University of North Norfolk. She lives an isolated cottage on the edge of the Saltmarsh. In 2007 she was approached by DCI Harry Nelson who wanted her help in identifying bones found buried on the marshes, and her life suddenly got a whole lot more complicated.

Surprising fact about Ruth: she is fascinated by the London Underground and once attended a fancy dress party as The Angel Islington.

Harry Nelson

Profession: Detective Chief Inspector

Likes: driving fast, solving crimes, his family

Dislikes: Norfolk, the countryside, management speak, his boss

Harry Nelson was born in Blackpool. He came to Norfolk in his thirties to lead the Serious Crimes Unit, bringing with him his wife Michelle and their daughters, Laura and Rebecca. Nelson has a loyal team and enjoys his work. He still hankers after the North though and has not come to love his adopted county. Nelson thinks of himself as an old-fashioned policeman and so often clashes with Super-intendent Whitcliffe, who is trying to drag the force into the twenty-first century. Nelson is impatient and quick-tempered but he is capable of being both imaginative and sensitive. He's also cleverer than he lets on.

Surprising fact about Nelson: he's a huge Frank Sinatra fan.

Michelle Nelson

Profession: hairdresser

Likes: her family, exercising, socializing with friends

Dislikes: dowdiness, confrontation, talking about murder

Michelle married Nelson when she was twenty-one and he was twenty-three. She was happy with her life in Blackpool – two children, part-time work, her mother nearby – but encouraged Nelson to move to Norfolk for the sake of promotion. Now that her daughters are older she works as a manager for a hair salon. Michelle is beautiful, stylish, hard-working and a dedicated wife and mother. When people see her and Nelson together, their first reaction is usually, 'What *does* she see in him?'

Surprising fact about Michelle: she once played hockey for Blackpool Girls.

Michael Malone (aka Cathbad)

Profession: laboratory assistant and druid

Likes: nature, mythology, walking, following his instincts

Dislikes: rules, injustice, conventions

Cathbad was born in Ireland and came to England to study first chemistry then archaeology. He also came under the influence of Erik Andersen though they found themselves on opposite sides during the henge dig. Cathbad was brought up as a Catholic but he now thinks of himself as a druid and shaman.

Surprising fact about Cathbad: he can play the accordion.

Shona Maclean

Profession: lecturer in English Literature

Likes: books, wine, parties

Dislikes: being ignored

Shona is a lecturer at the University of North Norfolk and one of Ruth's closest friends. They met when they both participated in the henge dig in 1997. On the face of it Shona seems an unlikely friend for Ruth – she's outgoing and stunningly beautiful for a start – but the two women share a sense of humour and an interest in books, films and travel. They also have a lot of history together.

Surprising fact about Shona: as a child she won several Irish dancing competitions.

David Clough

Profession: Detective Sergeant

Likes: food, football, beer, his job

Dislikes: political correctness, graduate police officers

David Clough ('Cloughie' to Nelson) was born in Norfolk and joined the force at eighteen. As a youngster he almost followed his elder brother into petty crime but a chance meeting with a sympathetic policeman led him into a surprisingly successful police career. Clough is a tough, dedicated officer but not without imagination. He admires Nelson, his boss, but has a rather competitive relationship with Sergeant Judy Johnson.

Surprising fact about Clough: He can quote the 'you come to me on my daughter's wedding day' scene from The Godfather off by heart.

Judy Johnson

Profession: Detective Sergeant

Likes: horses, driving, her job

Dislikes: girls' nights out, sexism, being patronised

Judy Johnson was born in Norfolk to Irish Catholic parents. She was academic at school but opted to join the police force at eighteen rather than go to university. Judy can seem cautious and steady – she has been going out with the same boyfriend since school, for example – but she is actually fiercely ambitious. She resents any hint of condescension or sexism which can lead to some fiery exchanges with Clough.

Surprising fact about Judy: she's a keen card player and once won an inter-force poker competition.

Phil Trent

Profession: professor of Archaeology

Likes: money, being on television, technology

Dislikes: new age archaeologists, anonymity, being out of the loop

Phil is Ruth's head of department at the University of North Norfolk. He's ambitious and outwardly charming, determined to put the university (and himself) on the map. He thinks of Ruth as plodding and old-fashioned so is slightly put out when she begins to make a name for herself as an advisor to the police. On one hand, it's good for the image of UNN; on the other, it should have been him.

Surprising fact about Phil: at his all boys school, he once played Juliet in *Romeo and Juliet*.